P...

OA...

Philip Shelb... selling novels THIS FAR FROM PARADISE and DREAMWEAVERS, which have been translated into ten languages. He is currently writing his next book which is set in Bali and Southeast Asia.

OASIS OF DREAMS

PHILIP SHELBY

Penguin Books

PENGUIN BOOKS
Published by the Penguin Group
Penguin Books Canada Ltd,
10 Alcorn Avenue, Toronto, Ontario, Canada M4V 3B2
Penguin Books Ltd, 27 Wrights Lane, London W8 5TZ, England
Viking Penguin, a division of Penguin Books USA Inc.,
375 Hudson Street, New York, New York 10014, USA
Penguin Books Australia Ltd, Ringwood, Victoria, Australia
Penguin Books (NZ) Ltd,
182-190 Wairau Road, Auckland 10, New Zealand

Penguin Books Ltd, Registered Offices:
Harmondsworth, Middlesex, England

First published 1992

1 3 5 7 9 10 8 6 4 2

Printed and bound in Canada

Canadian Cataloguing in Publication Data

Shelby, Philip, 1950–
Oasis of dreams

ISBN 0-14-015237-7

I. Title.

PS8587.H4503 1992   C813'.54   C92-093935-X
PR9199.3.S5403 1992

British Library Cataloguing in Publication Data Available
American Library of Congress Cataloguing in Publication Data Available

*This novel is dedicated to
the memory of Hugh MacLennan,
a friend and teacher
who helped lay bridges to dreams.*

Philip Shelby

OASIS OF DREAMS

PART ONE

*Where Kings of Tyre and Kings of Tyre
did rule
In ancient days in endless dynasty.
And all around the snowy mountains
swim
Like mighty swans in heaven's pool*

—Flecker

1

Switzerland, 1965

Armand Fremont was sitting alone in the darkness in the smaller of the two offices of St. Gallen's police station. A harsh April wind blew off the surrounding mountains and caromed through the streets of the little village thirty kilometers north of Geneva. Whenever gusts forced their way through the cracks in the walls and floorboards of the building, they rattled the metal cage of a space heater sitting on the floor near the desk.

The heater provided the only sound in the room, and the only light. The glow from its orange coils enhanced the elegance of Armand's patrician features, diminished the deep creases on his tanned face, but couldn't soften the expression on it. Fierce, almost cruel, his expression mirrored a mind impatient for explanations, furious that he could not change the events that had brought him here, fearful that death had been cheated for only a few hours or days.

He knew what had happened. Possibly even how. But he didn't know why. And no matter how earnest and detailed the explanations of police officials, he was not satisfied.

"The caprice of the gods, monsieur. The car was traveling at an excessive speed. The macadam is treacherous this time of year, you understand? As soon as the sun goes down, the water collected during the day's thaw freezes. It may be only a very thin film, but that is enough. And of course we cannot discount the tractor. It lurched onto the road out of nowhere. The farmer was careless, even negligent, and we shall prosecute him vigorously. Perhaps if it hadn't been there, Monsieur Maser would have regained control of his vehicle coming out of the turn. As it happened. . ."

Armand had argued. It was true, he'd conceded, that the
car had been moving fast, there were patches of ice, the
farmer had turned onto the road without warning. But
Alexander Maser was an expert driver. His superb physical
condition, his quick reflexes should have proved more than
equal to the sudden appearance of a tractor on an icy road.
The lack of skid marks in the turn proved that Alexander
had had the car under control.

The officials were deaf to his words. Polite, patronizingly
so, they had shaken their heads, shrugged, denied there was
anything more to investigate. When he persisted then, they
had done nothing to disguise their exasperation and resentment. Behind his back they had called him difficult, rude.

He would not yield and demanded to see their reports, the
car. He *would* know why.

The shadows lapped at his strapping, powerful body as
he waited. He saw first the woman's silhouette cast on the
frosted glass of the door, then heard her tentative knock.

"Monsieur Fremont?" The question was rapidly followed
by the click of the latch and the overhead light coming on.
"Ah, so you *are* here."

He did not reply. The policewoman walked farther into
the room. She suddenly felt uneasy. Perhaps it was the
man's absolute stillness or the expression of savage intensity on his face that chilled her . . . or something else not immediately identifiable about him that unsettled her. His dark
gaze seemed riveted to a far-off spot beyond her that lay
still in deep shadow though light now flooded the room.

Emilie Weinmeister was a no-nonsense woman, her uni-
form as severely tailored as her hair was tightly drawn back
into a bun. She wasn't given to fanciful thoughts, and yet
she couldn't shake off the odd sensations that the brooding
man was inspiring. She cleared her throat.

"They are ready for you, monsieur."

Armand rose, buttoned his alpaca overcoat, slipped on his
gloves, and picked up a bag before following the policewoman. She led him across the road to an enormous shed.
Bright orange snowplows and blowers lined the walls; the

concrete floor, painted white, was immaculate. In the center the red Ferrari looked like some crushed, exotic flower. He walked slowly around the car, flinching at the shattered windshield with its bloodstained shards, the hideously twisted metal of what had been the passenger and driver's seats, the crumpled front fenders and skewered chassis. It was unbelievable that Alexander had lived through such a smashup.

A man detached himself from the threesome standing to the side of a card table and walked briskly over to Armand. Introducing himself as the chief forensic inspector, he held out a neatly typed report in French. "If monsieur requires a translation—"

Armand abruptly took the report. "Not necessary," he said, beginning again to pace around the car, this time with his head bowed as he read. There were no surprises in the report. The examination of the wreckage by police automotive experts had revealed the car was free of any mechanical defects. The investigation at the scene and interrogation of the tractor driver yielded nothing suspicious. Therefore, an anonymous official had written, there was only one conclusion, sad but inescapable: driver error.

Placing the report on the card table, Armand thanked the men for their help. "Now," he said authoritatively, "if you don't mind, I'd like to examine the car myself." He took off his overcoat, folded it neatly, and put it next to the report.

The chief inspector angrily took a step forward, but was restrained by a senior colleague. "Let the fool waste his time," his expression seemed to say. "You know he won't find anything."

The ranking officer didn't mention the bulletin he'd received from the Swiss Federal Police in Bern. Armand Fremont was *very* well connected. The chief federal prosecutor, who had signed the telex, had stated in no uncertain terms that Fremont, the Lebanese multimillionaire and owner of Beirut's legendary Casino de Paradis, was to be extended every courtesy and given complete cooperation.

"Is there anything you require, monsieur?" the senior

official asked smoothly.

"No, thank you."

"Officer Weinmeister will look after you then," he said, glancing at the policewoman.

They both looked at Freemont and realized he hadn't heard any of it.

By the clock it was dawn but the darkness refused to budge. Fräulein Weinmeister was sitting at the card table, an electric coffeepot at her feet. For hours she had been watching Armand Fremont, mechanic's overalls pulled over his hand-tailored suit, as he examined the wreckage with the care of a physiotherapist working on an injured body. Except here there was nothing to mend. Nor anything, from what she could see, to learn.

Still he had gone over the car meticulously, starting at the engine compartment in the rear and working his way forward along first one flank, then the other. He had spent a great deal of time on his back, underneath the chassis, a penlight between his teeth so that he could use both hands, one of which held an oily rag. He had given even more time to the well beneath the steering column. He'd painstakingly examined pedals, rods, wires. Now he was at the very front of the car, concentrating his formidable attention on the brakes and suspension.

Emilie Weinmeister shifted on the uncomfortable metal chair. This Armand Fremont seemed to be a man of character with a temperament as remarkable as his physical appearance. She wasn't one to be impressed by broad shoulders or a mane of silvery hair, but she was impressed by tenacity and perseverance. One would be lucky, she thought, to have this man as a friend.

Armand focused the penlight on the left wheel strut and wiped it with the last clean edge of the cloth. The strut was perfectly smooth to the touch, just as it should be, as it was in the Ferrari he drove, a model identical to this one. He grunted and, still on his back, pulled himself forward to the right wheel well.

Perhaps the Swiss police were right. Perhaps it had been an accident. Twilight was deceptive, creating false distances and margins for error that didn't exist. Even professional drivers could be fooled. He had seen it happen at the Le Mans Twenty-four Hour Race. It could have happened to Alexander—

But it hadn't.

Armand took a deep breath and lay rock still. His eyes were closed as his fingertips caressed the edge of the tie-rod. It whispered to him what must have happened. His blood raced in hot fury, while a chill seeped through his gut.

He lay very still under the car until he was certain he had control of his emotions and they would not show on his face. Then he pushed himself from underneath the chassis.

"Are you finished, monsieur?"

"Yes."

The fräulein was tempted to ask if he'd found anything. But of course he hadn't. His expression remained as stony as ever. If he had discovered something, he would have to report it to her superiors. Regulations. The policewoman wouldn't have been able to fathom Armand Fremont's attitude toward regulations.

"I want to have the car shipped to Monsieur Maser's address in Paris. Will you help me with the paperwork?"

She certainly would. Her superiors had made it clear that their investigation was done, and besides, the car, even if wreckage, was personal property.

Armand watched Fräulein Weinmeister start to fill out a form, her eyebrows furrowed in concentration. It could have been worse. She could have asked questions about whether or not he'd found anything. And then he would have had to lie, something he loathed to do, because there was no way he was going to explain to the obliging Officer Weinmeister that this was not an accident but attempted murder.

The surgeon hadn't bothered to remove his bloodstained gown. Lighting a cigarette and drawing deeply, he sat down behind his desk.

Armand was intensely aware of being in a hospital. His senses were overwhelmed by the smell of disinfectant and alcohol, the sounds of soft chimes summoning nurses who hurried along, padded heels tapping on the tiled floor.

"I am very, very sorry," the surgeon said at last. "There was little we could do. His injuries are massive, the trauma much too severe. The most I can promise you is that Monsieur Maser will feel no pain."

Armand stood motionless.

"How much time?"

The surgeon shook his head and rolled the ash off his cigarette. "Frankly, I'm amazed he's made it this far. He is dying but he refuses to succumb."

"Is he able to talk?"

"I very much doubt he'll regain consciousness."

He's going to die. He really is going to die.

"Take me to him, please," he said urgently.

Preceded by the surgeon, Armand stepped into Alexander's room and closed the door behind him. When he had first reached the hospital, he'd harbored some hope for his friend. How the surgeon's words and what he had learned in the course of the long night at St. Gallen's had stripped him of his strength and resolve. The broken body on the bed, so frail, shook Armand to the core. Alexander, always ready with a smile and a kind word, lay wrapped in bandages, hoses, and tubes linked to machines doing the living for him. Armand's hand curled around Alexander's fingers, so cold to the touch.

Why did you want to see me? What did you have to tell me that was so vital, that couldn't be said over the telephone . . . ?

Armand recalled their last conversation, the pitch of Alexander's voice, the urgency—and a terrible sadness, as though he had suffered an incalculable loss. . . . He had insisted that Armand come to Geneva immediately, refusing to divulge any details over the telephone.

Why? Was someone threatening him? Did he even know who?

Armand's fingers tightened over his friend's hand.

Reach for me, Alex! I'm here. Don't have come so far only to falter now. I need to know. You need to tell me . . .

Armand felt a tentative touch and started, twisting around sharply.

"He is gone," the surgeon said, reaching down to pry loose Armand's fingers. Then he passed his thumbs over the dead man's eyes.

"Leave us," Armand said hoarsely.

The surgeon hesitated. He believed that once death had come, the living should humbly step back and allow it to tidy up the ends of a life. But the face of Armand Fremont reflected anger and portents of violence, not grief. Perhaps here, the surgeon thought, not even death had the power to put matters to rest.

The Maaser-el-Chouf was an ancient clan in an ancient land. In the mountains above their lands were the largest cedar groves in Lebanon. It was said that these groves had supplied Solomon with the wood for his temple. Tyrian woodsmen cut the forest on the east side of the peaks and rolled the cedars down into the Litani River, floating them to sea a few miles north of Tyre, the beginning of the long journey to Jerusalem.

The Fremont family had a summer home on the Litani and, though newcomers with a mere hundred years in the country, they became friendly with their neighbors, the Maaser-el-Chouf, whose sixty-room palace was called Mouchtara, "The Chosen Place." The two families became even closer after the births of sons, three years apart.

Along the banks of the Litani and the forests above and on the grounds of Mouchtara with its statues of lions, gardens of roses, and stands of kingly cypress trees, Armand Fremont and Alexander Maaser-el-Chouf passed the summers of their childhood and adolescence. Closer than most brothers, they forged the bonds there that would link them for life. And though younger, Armand was the leader.

Beiruti born, Armand had traveled widely with his family

and seemed very worldly to Alexander. It was Armand's tales of life in Beirut and the great European cities that gave Alexander a vision of what lay beyond the sleepy, protective indolence of Mouchtara and ultimately inspired him to leave his ancestral home and abandon its traditional occupations. The Maaser-el-Chouf were aristocracy, land rich, but politically weak. Traders, businessmen, entrepreneurs were gaining more power in Lebanon with each passing year. While there was never any question that Armand would assume control one day of the casino his grandfather had founded, Alexander's future was not so clear. After long discussion and some dispute with his father and uncles, he was allowed to accompany Armand to Paris to study at the university. Alexander was twenty-one, Armand eighteen when they set off for France.

They spent more time in cafés than in classes and made a wide circle of friends. Philosophers and artists and political theorists mingled at La Coupole and Deux Magots, at Le Dome and Le Flore. And Armand and Alexander were in the thick of their conversations and debates, many of which had at their heart the causes of and remedies for the economic depression that gripped the world. It was a heady time.

Alone, Armand and Alexander immersed themselves in discussion of the future of their country. The French governed Lebanon and Syria under a 1923 League of Nations mandate, a mandate they agreed could not last forever. Indeed, they believed it would end quite soon.

As much as they desired independence for their country, they feared it, for undercurrent social tensions and political unrest threatened hopes for stability. The greatest dangers seemed to them to emanate from the political and monetary fixers of Beirut, whose actions compared frighteningly to their counterparts in the Ottoman Empire who had brought it down with their graft and corruption. Armand and Alexander vowed to oppose such forces. But how could they create a counterweight to those who would destroy the country?

The power of money held the answer. Armand had come to the conclusion that the United States, pulling and pushing its way out of economic disaster faster and more forcefully than European governments, would become the next seat of power, its money the world's currency. When Alexander was persuaded to share that opinion, he determined the course of his life.

Leaving Armand in Paris after one year at the university, he returned to Mouchtara and persuaded his family to allow him to buy gold with the last of their hard currency. He transferred the gold to the United States, turned Alexander Maaser-el-Chouf into Alexander Maser, and opened a modest bank. During the waning years of the depression, his bank succeeded when others were ruined because he turned his back on speculators and forged solid alliances with progressive businessmen and government leaders. By the time Europe was plunging into war, Alexander's Maritime Continental Bank was thriving, its assets, both paper and property, worth tens of millions of dollars.

He built himself a grand house and married a beautiful American girl from a prominent New England family. In the summer of 1941 he and his bride were blessed with the birth of a daughter whom they named Katherine.

Armand studied the face of his dead friend. Miles and time had separated them for long periods, but neither had betrayed the vows they had made in Paris to work for the best interests of their homeland. While Armand stayed in Beirut, carving out a position of great authority, Alexander had worked in the shadows. Over the years his worldwide banking contacts had become legion. After the end of the Mandate the greedy, voracious *zuama*, those fixers Armand and Alexander had feared would take over from the French, did so.

The *zuama* was an entity unique to the Middle East, particularly to Lebanon. It was composed of political bosses whose power rested on the idea of fidelity and a man's obligation to his superior. It was a medieval concept that had persisted and flourished in Lebanon, keeping alive a feudal link between a *zaim*, an overlord, and the rest of the society, whose members were, for all intents and purposes, his subjects.

A *zaim* arose either because a man was the eldest son of a *zaim*, or of a newly powerful family, or because he had become successful in business and held great sway over other businessmen. A *zaim*'s power over his people was based as much on personality and charisma as on his ability to take care of his subjects' interests, further their fortunes, and look out for them in time of need.

Alexander supplied Armand with information vital to keeping the power of the members of the *zuama* in check. He set up blind trusts for the *zuama*'s political opponents, men who refused to be bribed or coerced. He made sure that money for the cause he and Armand shared was delivered in such a way that its origins could never be traced. Later, as their work had become more complex, demanding even greater subterfuge, Alexander and Armand had created Interarmco, their private security organization that functioned as their eyes and ears—and, when necessary, as their hands—in the Middle East.

Armand reached out and ran his fingers over his friend's face. And he almost wept. Only fifty-one . . . only fifty-one . . . with so many good, productive years of life snuffed out. And a diabolically effective weapon against the men of the *zuama*. They were like bull elephants maddened by a single wasp, never sure where or when it would settle and sting next—only that it would.

"If the *zuama* had known you were their wasp," Armand whispered to the lifeless Alex, "they would be dancing in the streets of Lebanon. But I will carry on what we began. Sleep peacefully, old friend, for that is my promise to you . . ."

David Cabot paced the hospital corridor outside the hospital room. He stopped to stretch his muscles, tense from waiting for Armand and news on Alexander's condition. He'd seen the grim-faced surgeon leave, but hadn't approached him for information. It wasn't only the natural reticence of an Englishman that made him hold back, but also the caution he had developed during the ten years he'd headed Interarmco, doing much of the most dangerous work himself. His greatest loyalty was to Armand Fremont. And he carried the scars of bullets that on two occasions he'd taken to save his mentor's life.

The door opened with a crack, causing David to wheel around. Armand stepped into the corridor, which suddenly seemed to David too narrow, its air growing thinner. He knew in that instant that Alexander was dead.

He rushed over, putting a consoling arm around Armand's shoulders. Less than fifteen years separated them in age, but even a stranger looking at them then would have been convinced they were father and son. Which, in a way only the two understood, they were.

"He's gone," David murmured.

With a nod of sad acknowledgment, Armand pulled away and led David to an alcove that would allow them some privacy to talk. He took two short rods from his coat pocket, pushed the ends together, and held them out to David.

"The Ferrari's right tie-rod," he said in a hollow voice. "At first I thought it had snapped during impact. Then I found this."

David leaned down to get a closer look at the rod. He ran his finger along its edge.

"It's serrated, as though—"

"Someone had taken a hacksaw to it." Armand finished coldly. "Cut in part of the way, enough to compromise the metal's tolerance, enough for steering weight and road vibrations to do the rest." He thrust the pieces back into his pocket.

"Someone *murdered* him?"

Armand's silence was all the answer he needed.

"Don't let the Swiss police know anything's wrong," David said at last. "If you do, they'll take over the investigation, and in the end we won't learn anything at all."

Armand gripped David's arms. *"I want to know who did this!"*

"What we can learn from this rod isn't nearly enough to tell us that."

"It must tell you something!"

"That whoever tampered with Alex's car was a professional who knew exactly what he was doing. An amateur would have tried a bomb or gun. This one made sure that the kill would take place well away from Paris, where the work must have been done, that it would appear to be an accident, raising no suspicion and allowing nothing to come back to the killer."

"There can't be many professionals capable of doing this!" Armand whispered.

"No," David agreed. "Nor do their talents come cheap. And they don't advertise. You have to know how and where to look for them and, when you've found them, what to say, how much to pay."

"You're telling me someone was hired to kill Alex!"

"Alex was a banker. He never would have had occasion to come across such people much less cross them in a way that would make them come after him. No, this was a paid killing."

"And who is the paymaster?" Armand demanded fiercely.

"If anyone knows that, it would be you," David replied. "Did Alex say anything to you in that room? A word, a phrase, a name?"

"He never regained consciousness. . . ."

"Think!" David said urgently. "Alex called from Paris insisting that you meet him in Geneva. You told me he wouldn't give you a reason. But did he say anything else?"

Armand closed his eyes and replayed the brief conversation in his mind. He could still hear the anger, the tremor of fear in Alex's voice. *Why? Why did I let that pass?*

"Let's try another tack," David said quickly. "Was Alex in some kind of trouble—financial, political, sexual? Was he being blackmailed?"

"Don't be absurd!"

"It's possible, Armand!" David retorted. "Men aren't killed like this because of some petty argument. Someone either wanted to settle a score, or he had to remove Alex because he had become a threat—"

"A threat?"

"I know, it doesn't wash, because as far as both of us know, Alex had no enemies in financial circles—"

"But he may have had them elsewhere," Armand said, cutting him off.

It took David a moment to grasp the implications of Armand's words.

"You think this has to do with *Beirut*?"

"Perhaps," Armand said measuring his words. "But that too would be fitting. Think, David. Our esteemed prime minister, a doddering geriatric, has announced that he will not run again. The *zuama*, led by Nabil Tufaili, are already squabbling among themselves about which candidate to back. You would think they would have settled on one by now except that they are too busy, each promoting his favorite son. But one thing is certain: they loathe and fear the man I intend to support, Eduard Zayedi. If somehow they got wind that this was the case, if they also discovered that Maritime Continental was the conduit for Zayedi's funds, they would have a motive for getting Alex out of the way!"

"I don't know," David said. "It's an enormous risk on their part!"

"Tufaili and the others have made their runs at me before," Armand reminded him.

David was all too aware of that. The past ten years had provided him a firsthand education in how cruel and vicious Levantine politics could be. Men such as Armand Fremont, few and far between that they were, represented the best of Lebanon. They loved their country passionately and were ready to risk everything rather than see it fall prey to jackals like Tufaili and the powerful merchants, brokers, and middlemen to whom life was percentage of profit. The *zuama*'s code was founded on bribery and corruption and reinforced with violence. They had rigged elections, intimidated those who dared to voice dissent, financially ruined their opponents. Only Armand Fremont, with his vast wealth and international stature, seemed invulnerable, but perhaps he was not.

"Do you really believe it was the *zuama*?" he asked. "Would they really dare do something like this?"

"You yourself said that whoever hired this professional had to have a great deal of money and the wherewithal to find him," Armand replied. "The *zuama* have both. And quite possibly they had the motive as well."

"One question," said David. "Why not you? Why target Alex when you are by far the greater threat? *You're* the one who's been fighting them in their own backyard for all these years!"

"Perhaps it was Alex who found out something he shouldn't have. Perhaps this is Tufaili's way of sending a message."

"He'd be a fool even to try such a thing!"

"This is the Middle East, David. You should know by now that matters are never what they appear to be." He paused. "Now let's go to the office and get through the hospital paperwork fast and get the hell out of here. There is a great deal of work to do."

David stopped Armand. "What about Katherine?"

At the mention of Alex's daughter, Armand's anger melted to sorrow. "Leave her to me. She has to hear this from me."

Suddenly Armand realized the enormity of what he had to do in managing the news of Alexander's death. It would turn New York's financial world upside down. Maritime Continental's clients would be burning up the transcontinental phone lines and telex wires. Emil Bartoli, Alexander's second in command, had to be contacted immediately after Kate. He could be counted on to hold the bank together, to prevent a crisis of confidence and reassure Wall Street watchers.

Others had to be notified too. He frowned. His relatives who held shares in the Société des Bains Mediterranien, the holding company for the casino in which Alexander had an interest had to get telegrams. One by one Armand called up their faces: the beautiful but alabaster-cold Jasmine, his cousin; Louis, her husband, whose political ambitions far exceeded his abilities; Pierre, his nephew, a financial wizard who masterminded Lebanon's economy from his director's office at the Central Bank of Lebanon. But first there was Katherine . . . precious Katherine.

2

"Hey, hey, LBJ, how many kids did you kill today?"

Demonstrators moved along Telegraph Hill toward the Berkeley campus, their numbers swelling at every side street.

Kate Maser stood on a rise just below Boalt Hall, the law-school building. The early-afternoon sunshine was exceptionally brilliant for San Francisco, and she whipped out a pair of sunglasses to shield her eyes. Tall as she was, she had to stretch to see all the way to the end of the long line of blue-helmeted policemen along the sidewalk. They were watching the marchers, slapping nightsticks into open palms. Farther up Bancroft Way cruisers and paddywagons waited, along with two busloads of specially trained riot troops.

Oh, lord, Kate thought, don't let this get violent! The fate of all the people she could see for blocks around rested on the police and on the leaders of the demonstration, foremost among them Ted Bannerman. Her Ted. The man who'd changed her life. She could feel his magnetism even at this distance. He was leading the crowd, his arms raised in revolutionary salute.

Tall, his dark brown hair pulled back in a ponytail, Ted was a dervish of energy, building the tempo of the crowd as skillfully as a great conductor would pull a magnificent performance from an orchestra. He was a silver-tongued conjurer who made others believe what he believed, made them want to follow, to serve . . .

Hey, hey, LBJ, how many kids did you kill today?

Kate's long russet-colored hair blew across her face, strains stinging her large green eyes. She scraped her hair back and knotted it loosely at her nape. Maybe, she thought wryly, she should let it blindfold her. Maybe she was about to witness a disaster. She closed her eyes briefly. She was no longer in awe of Ted, the firebrand revolutionary who was a Massachusetts Institute of Technology graduate, the man a university president had called Ted the Trotskyite, a sobriquet that had stuck. Kate respected Ted's genius at having seen the tragedy of American involvement in Vietnam, the growing quagmire into which President Johnson was leading the country, and she was as impressed as hundreds of thousands of others by his unerring predictions about American involvement and its consequences. But Kate was troubled by the consequences of Ted's fame, of his being hero-worshiped. Being catapulted onto the front pages of national newspapers and magazines and lionized by so many was heady stuff. And lately she had felt her attraction to him wearing thin, like a surface that, rubbed too long and hard, was revealing its flaws. Where was the shy veterinarian's son from the Midwest she'd fallen in love with? Gone forever? Or merely submerged in his new, somehow threatening identity?

Kate couldn't be sure, not sure at all, that Ted was going to lead prudently today. As she watched him now, chanting with and exhorting the marchers, she saw a man who had made himself into a leader, overcoming his natural reticence and indecision, his look confident, his voice clear and determined. And when she looked beyond him, at the faces of the demonstrators, she saw in them the same adoration for and trust in Ted that she had once given without reserve. Once. Now she suspected that she saw a fledgling demagogue, a man in love with the image he had created and others had polished. It was a man who could lead the crowds to do his bidding and all the while allow them to be convinced it was their own. Ted had the fire and the rhetoric but no police record. He appeared in court in support of others, the darling angry young man the press coddled and courted, but who had never seen the inside of a holding cell.

Kate had been living with Ted for about four years now, working with him on desegregation projects that were springing up in predominantly black Oakland, and on

Vietnam War protests. She'd been determined to finish law
school in two years and had succeeded, but not without paying a high price in stress. Ted took all her time but what she
had spent in law school and now as a junior associate in a
law firm. Ever since passing the bar exams a few days after
her twenty-fourth birthday, she had been doing legal work
for Ted. She'd become a familiar face at the local precinct,
charging in at all hours of the night to see yet one more "po-
litical-action prisoner." It wasn't exactly that Ted had been
using her, for she was certainly committed heart, soul, and
mind to human and civil rights, but . . .

"*Hey, hey, LBJ, how many kids did you kill today?*"

The three hundred or more protesters had reached the
foot of Telegraph Avenue, where it dead-ended at Bancroft
Way. Coffee cups and beer glasses, metal chairs and
wooden chessmen were knocked to the ground as people
pushed across the sidewalk tables of coffeehouses and tav-
erns. The human mass flowed across Bancroft Way, and
drivers hit their brakes and horns. In less than a minute the
demonstrators had seized control of the street, their front
ranks only a few feet away from the police.

"*Attention! Attention!*"

The metallic twang of the bullhorn reverberated over the
shouts and confusion.

"*This is the police. This is an illegal demonstration. You
have no permit—*"

"Fuck your permit!"

"*—to assemble here. You are disrupting traffic and are
subject to arrest!*"

As boos showered the police announcement, Kate saw
Ted, a bullhorn in his hand, step between the demonstrators
and the police.

"We have *every* right to assemble here. Here or anywhere
we want to!"

The crowd roared its approval.

"We have *every* right to demand that this university sever
its ties to the fascist warmongers who send our children to
murder Vietnamese children! We have *every* right and *every*

duty to bring the administration to its *knees, close it down,* until our demands are met!"

Oh, no, Ted, Kate cried to herself, what are you doing?

The crowd, which had been seething, now seemed to gather a will of its own, surging toward the police ranks.

"Cool Sproul! Cool Sproul! Cool Sproul!"

Kate couldn't believe it. In demonstration jargon "cool" meant to shut down and occupy. "Sproul" referred to Sproul Hall, the main administration building on the Berkeley campus. Ted was inciting his followers to take over the nerve center of the university!

As well as a few other things, Kate thought, like trespassing, illegal occupation, damage to private property, and, because a confrontation was inevitable, assault and resisting arrest.

The police lieutenant with the megaphone voiced Kate's points.

"Attention! If you do not disperse immediately, you will be arrested. If you attempt to cross the police line, you will be arrested. If you attempt to prevent an officer from carrying out his duty, you will be arrested!"

All at once the crowd quieted. Its collective conscience warned that the moment of truth had come. There was still a chance to step back, avert bloodshed and disaster. Kate held her breath. The only sounds she heard were faint clicks, from the cameras of photographers from the Berkeley *Barb,* *Village Voice,* as well as the national papers.

Kate saw Ted hesitate, as though mesmerized by the cameras. He knew his choices: pull his people back and risk his confrontational, revolutionary image or lead them on with a dramatic gesture that would make headlines across the nation. The cameras were waiting.

Ted's clenched fist shot into the air. He flung his head back and roared, *"Cool Sproul!"*

The demonstrators charged. Instinctively Kate retreated, backpedaling up the knoll. She slipped on the grass but continued to scramble on her hands and knees. When she turned, she saw the fight was on. The demonstrators tried to break through the police line, and in turn the officers waded into the melee, nightsticks swinging. Cries of pain and screams of rage filled the air as the police wildly clubbed anyone around them. The few protestors who had managed to get through the line were being chased in hot pursuit.

Shakily, Kate rose to her feet. Clearly the police were outnumbered, even with the additional force of riot troops that had joined the fray. She tried to find Ted in the crowd, but it was impossible. Shaking with fear, she edged toward the sidewalk where a dozen protesters, the first wave of the assault to be hacked down, lay bleeding. She went from one to the other, looking at pain-twisted faces.

The crowd roared when it heard the distinctive pops of tear-gas canisters being fired. A few seconds later thick, acrid smoke poured across the streets. Now the police, having donned masks, had the advantage. The demonstrators were choking, running blindly in every direction trying to escape the gas. They were easy prey and one by one were clubbed to the ground.

Kate turned just in time to see several protesters staggering through the clouds of gas, pursued by two policemen. When the officers caught up with them, blood erupted from their heads.

"No!"

Without thinking, Kate jumped up, placing herself squarely between the pursuers and the quarry.

"I'm a lawyer—"

"Fuck you, bitch!"

The policeman's riot baton struck her on the elbow, paralyzing her arm. A second blow caught her just above the knees, taking her feet out from under her. Kate heard herself scream, then curled up in a tight ball and tried to shield her body as army-style boots lashed out at her. Gasping and coughing, she managed to roll away and lay very still, her cheek scraping the grit of the asphalt, her pain and anger and humiliation trickling out with her tears.

"Hold on a minute. Let me see her."

Her hands cuffed behind her, shoulders pressed against the side of a paddy wagon, Kate felt herself pulled around. She recognized the lieutenant with the bullhorn who had tried to convince the protesters to disperse. His skin was grimy except for a patch of white dotted with freckles where the gas mask had covered his face.

"Kate Maser, right?"

"Right."

Kate's reply came out as a croak. Her throat was raw from the tear gas.

"I remember you from the precinct. My name is Crandall. Maybe you've seen me around." The lieutenant turned to his sergeant. "Cut her loose. I want to talk to her."

As soon as her hands were free, Kate used the sleeves of her blouse to wipe her eyes.

"Sting pretty bad, don't they?" he asked as he guided her past ambulance attendants who were tending to the beaten and wounded, some lying on stretchers, others sitting up, staring off into space, oblivious to their blood and pain.

"Here, put this over your eyes," Crandall said, handing her a cool, wet compress. "It didn't have to turn out this way, you know. Your boyfriend could have stopped them."

Kate pressed the cloth to her eyes, feeling relief immediately.

"Where is he?"

"Bannerman? Who knows. He never stays around to see the result of his handiwork."

There was no mistaking the contempt in the officer's voice.

"You weren't with him, were you?"

Kate shook her head.

"Didn't think so. In fact I saw you *behind* our lines. So how come you ended up like this?"

Kate told him about trying to reach the fallen protesters after the tear gas had been fired. Crandall shook his head.

"Dumb. Admirable, but dumb." He led Kate to a police cruiser, opened the back door, and motioned for her to sit.

"Did you know what was going to happen?"

"No."

"This little number goes well beyond what Bannerman's pulled before. Look around you."

Kate followed his arm, catching her breath when she saw shattered windows and broken-up storefronts along Bancroft Way.

"This wasn't a demonstration," the lieutenant told her. "We're going to come down on him for inciting a riot. And that's a felony."

He let the legal term hang in the air for a moment, then leaned on the open door.

"Tell me one thing: how come a bright, good-looking girl like you ties herself to a bozo like him? I mean, what's the attraction? He goes out and gets everybody—*except himself*—in deep shit, then you come along and bail them out. What's the point?"

"The point is, Lieutenant, that I believe in what Ted is trying to do, the principles he's standing up for. And as for the charge of inciting a riot, you might want to rethink that one. From what I saw, it was *your* men who went berserk."

Crandall's face hardened. "Listen up, Miss Maser. My people were outnumbered five, maybe six to one. I've got a dozen injured, two seriously. Everyone held his ground until those assholes came at us. At first it was self-defense. Then we attempted to prevent a full-scale riot. What happened here is on your boyfriend's head, no one else's."

The lieutenant paused. "In two hours I'm going to have a warrant for Bannerman's arrest. You know the charges. By that time I expect him to turn himself in at the station. My men are truly pissed off by what happened here. They want a little payback for their injured buddies. So if I have to send them to your place, they'll take it apart, and maybe Bannerman too. Do everybody a favor: get his ass down to me. Knowing you, you'll make his bail, and he'll be out in time to soak up a little glory on the eleven o'clock news."

Crandall stepped back, offering Kate his hand. "If you still feel shaky, I'll have someone drive you home."

Kate winced at the pain shooting through her leg but held

her chin up.

"No, thanks. I'll walk."

"Remember to give him the message. Two hours."

Usually Kate enjoyed the hike across campus to her Highland Avenue apartment, nestled in the hills below the Lawrence Berkeley Labs. Now, as she limped along, drawing curious glances from students and frowns from passing faculty, she was thinking hard about what Crandall had said. This time it seemed that Ted *had* stepped over the line. The police, smarting from what had occurred on Bancroft Way, were going to make him pay.

First she had to convince Ted to turn himself in, not a sure thing by any means. Bail would have to be arranged. Undoubtedly he'd want her to look after some of his friends who'd been arrested, call up the American Civil Liberties lawyers . . .

Here she went again, Kate thought, stopping to catch her breath. She was the one who had been beaten and gassed, and she was worrying about how to keep Ted from spending a night in jail?

After the long hike the interior of the house was deliciously cool. Kate leaned against the door, eyes closed. In familiar surroundings she suddenly realized how dirty she was. Her nose wrinkled at the sour smell of tear gas clinging to her clothes.

"Katie, is that you?"

Kate went around the corner into the L-shaped living room–dining room and saw Ted sprawled along the sofa. He was not alone. He was with a young girl with the soulful face of a madonna and the figure of a Playboy playmate. Judging by the array of ointments and bandages on the coffee table, Kate figured this angel of mercy had emptied the entire medicine cabinet.

"Hi, I'm Rosemary," the girl said, then went back to her ministrations, swabbing what looked like a superficial cut on Ted's cheek.

"Hey, Katie, you all right?"

Anger boiled up in Kate. "No, I'm not! Do you realize what your little stunt cost? Did you see what happened to those people?"

Kate hobbled closer and sank into a chair.

"Jesus, Katie, I'm sorry. I never saw that you were hurt. What happened?"

"I got beaten up is what happened! And I was one of the lucky ones. What happened to *you*?"

Ted pulled himself up, touching Rosemary lightly. "Why don't you make us some tea."

"Katie, I'm so sorry," he continued, staring earnestly at her. "When the cops started pounding on us, I tried to get our people out of there—"

"As I recall, *you* let that mob loose on the police."

"That's not true! We had every right to be there. Freedom of assembly. If the administration had sent someone to talk to us, maybe there wouldn't have been any reason to march on Sproul."

Ted leaned forward and touched her cheek, causing Kate to flinch and pull back.

"Katie, I'm really sorry about what happened to you. But you saw what the cops did. That's the reason I asked you to come. I knew there'd be a confrontation. I wanted you to be a witness."

Kate despaired at the sincerity in Ted's voice, at his utter conviction that his was the only true version of events. She was too tired to argue. Somewhere behind her Kate heard the kettle whistle.

"I talked to one of the officers, a Lieutenant Crandall," she said wearily. "He's getting a warrant for your arrest. If you don't turn yourself in, he'll send some cops here to pick you up. He promised me they wouldn't be gentle about it either."

"What the hell are you talking about?" Ted leapt off the couch, his injuries obviously forgotten. "What are the charges?"

"For starters, inciting a riot."

"Bullshit! You saw what happened!"

Kate looked at him steadily. "Yes, I did."

"Meaning *what*?"

"Meaning that the police have photographic proof of you stirring up mob violence."

"Jesus, Katie! Listen to what you're saying! They busted you up too!"

"Ted, they're coming for you. I have to wash and clean up. You better do the same."

"Is that your legal advice, to shuffle along like a sheep to slaughter?"

Furious, Kate pushed herself out of the chair. "Do what you want! I'll be ready in half an hour if you want me to come with you."

The hot bath soothed her, taking away some of the aches and pain. Drying herself off, Kate noticed the blue-and-yellow bruises on her arms and legs. Remembering the carnage, she considered herself lucky. She went into the bedroom and began to dress.

"Yeah, they want me to turn myself in, but it's not going to be that easy. When I get down there, I'll tell them to stuff their warrant . . ."

Through the partially opened door Kate listened to Ted map out his confrontation on the steps of the police station. Just before the conversation ended, she heard a name and realized he had been talking to a sympathetic reporter at the *San Francisco Chronicle*. The news that Ted Bannerman was going to make a stand against the police would spread like wildfire among the media. A simple appearance would be turned into a "happening."

When Kate came out, he was on the phone again. What she heard of the conversation stunned her.

"Is that who I think it was?" Kate demanded.

Ted looked around, like a little boy caught with his hand in the cookie jar.

"Jake Hirsh," he mumbled.

"Really? Are you changing counsel?"

"Listen, Katie, I can see that this thing has really shaken you up. You're in no condition to hassle the court scene."

"And you happened to get Hirsh on the phone, just like that?"

Jake Hirsh was a prominent San Francisco criminal lawyer who specialized in representing high-profile clients. He was a master manipulator of the press and loved to grandstand. Kate recalled meeting Hirsh at a rally Ted had organized at Berkeley's Greek amphitheater. She remembered that the two men had gone off and spent a good deal of time together. Later, when she had asked about that, Ted had been evasive. Kate warned him about Hirsh, mentioning the low opinion most judges—and prosecutors—had of him.

Now, seeing Ted flustered, Kate pieced together what had happened.

"You called Hirsh as soon as you got here, didn't you? You figured that this time the police would come after you. You wanted to be ready."

"Katie—"

"While the people who looked up to you and followed you were having their heads beaten in, you were getting ready for act two of your command performance!"

"Come on, Katie! I had to cover myself—"

"Which you do so well!"

Ted looked at her and smiled sadly. "You don't understand, do you? This thing is bigger than just one protest. It goes to the very heart of what's happening in this country. To the rights of people who are willing to make a stand—"

"Please, spare me the platitudes."

The silence between them threatened to suffocate Kate.

"Look, this isn't the time to talk. Rosemary will drive me to the station. I'll call you after it's over."

Dumbfounded, Kate watched them go, Rosemary placing a proprietary hand on Ted's shoulder. She was still looking after them when the door closed. Then she turned to the coffee table and began to snatch up the array of bottles, tubes, and bandages. Her arms full, she deposited everything in the bathroom and came out for the rest. That was when she saw the distinctive yellow-and-black Western Union envelope, with her name on it, that Ted had never bothered to tell her about.

The hour was very late, three o'clock in the morning according to the luminous hands on the alarm clock. Kate reached out and lit another candle, adding it to the ones she had lined up in a row in front of the empty fireplace. The fresh wick sputtered and flared, then the flame steadied, pushing back the darkness of the living room.

She sat crosslegged before the marble frontpiece, staring at the yellow telegram, the typed words swaying in the candlelight.

I didn't even know he'd gone to Paris, or would be traveling in Switzerland. Jesus Christ, I didn't really know him at all!

The telegram came from Armand Fremont. The name took her back a dozen years. She was twelve years old, it was spring, and she and her father were in Beirut. She recalled a grand hotel, the Hotel St. Georges it was called, and a nice man who had come up to her father as they came through the doors, greeted him, then smiled at her.

"You must be the charming Mademoiselle Katherine," he said, bowing and kissing her hand.

To this day Kate could remember how her name, with a distinct French pronunciation, had rolled off his lips, how wonderful and ladylike she'd felt at his courtesy. From that moment on Kate had a crush on Armand Fremont, her father's best friend.

Later, at teatime, her father brought her to the Salon Orientale, a spectacular room done in red and black lacquer, partitioned with ornate Chinese screens depicting mist-laden mountains and dragons and tiny birds hidden in lush trees. The waiters wore padded silk gowns, and the cookies were nothing like she'd ever had before. Kate was so enthralled, she was startled when someone said her name.

"Hello, Katherine."

There he was again, tall, devastatingly handsome, his black eyes making her blush and tremble.

Kate panicked when her father excused himself to take a phone call. Armand Fremont's voice seemed very far away even though he was sitting opposite her.

"Will you tell me something about yourself, Kate?" he asked her. "The things you like to do, what you want to see while you are here?"

Kate crimsoned and mumbled something under her breath.

"Now that won't do," Armand said firmly. "Beautiful young ladies such as yourself must tell a gentleman exactly what it is they want to do."

Fine for you to say! Kate had thought. She was all knobby knees and elbows, taller than most of the boys who never asked her to dance when they came over from St. Matthias for "socials." And one of the reasons she mumbled was because she was mortified by her braces.

"Well, then," Armand had said. "Perhaps I can make a suggestion. I would very much like you to be my guest at the casino tonight. Will you do me the honor, Kate?"

And just as she saw her father coming toward them, Kate whispered, "Yes!"

Bathed in pink, blue, and purple lights, the Casino de Paradis seemed to rise from the sea. When Kate passed through its doors for the first time, it was like stepping into an Arabian Nights fantasy. Women in evening gowns trailed exquisite perfume, their jewels blazing as they swept by beneath enormous crystal chandeliers. Laughter and delicious whispers cascaded across a hand-painted cavernous ceiling, followed by music from an invisible orchestra. The thing Kate remembered most clearly was how, in the middle of the grand antechamber, she had suddenly stopped walking and stood dead still. She had craned her head back and looked up at the ornate artwork, enthralled as an early astronomer would have been by the constellations. The whole world seemed to be spinning around her . . .

As she passed through her teens, Kate went through a phase when she read every fashion magazine she could get her hands on. Most of them had gossip and society sections, and in this vicarious fashion she kept track of Armand Fremont. He was always dressed in black tie or a dinner jacket, photographed either inside or in the grounds of the Casino de Paradis, always with a beautiful young woman whose perfection made Kate jealous. In her daydreams Kate wondered what it would be like to reenter the fairy tale, to see Armand once more and recapture the moment when he had made a gawky adolescent feel like a princess. But the passing years did not take her in that direction. There was never again the occasion to visit Beirut, and Armand's cards, sent at Christmas and on her birthday, took on the aura of notes from a considerate but dimly remembered stranger.

Kate poured herself the last of the hot chocolate and drew her knees up to her chin, her cheek against the fuzzy cotton of her comfy old bathrobe. Next to the telegram she had placed the last photograph taken of her father and herself. It had been four years ago, when he had come out on a business trip to San Diego and she had taken the train down to meet him in La Jolla. The backdrop was breathtaking, the horseshoe cove with its blue waters and white surge, and in the distance, the cliffs studded with caves and arches where the sea had worn through the stone. But judging by her set expression in the photo, Kate recalled that the beauty of the surroundings had done nothing for her. She could feel the anger leaping off the face in the photo.

Her mother had died when she was ten. As a child Kate spent her summers in New Hampshire and Cape Cod, and winters in Vail or Aspen. Although her father was seldom present during the holidays, so surrounded was she by cousins and nieces and nephews that she didn't realize how much she missed him.

Although Kate was grief stricken when an aneurysm abruptly stole her mother away, deep down she never believed that anything would change. For the first few months her father picked her up every day in front of the Lowry School on Madison and together they drove to their home, a town house on Park Avenue. But then her father's handyman and chauffeur began to appear at the school, and dinners became a strained affair as a childless housekeeper did her best to talk to a puzzled, frightened, and increasingly lonely girl who only picked at her food.

The postcards came from Paris, Geneva, Rome, and Athens. Through them Kate followed her father and the growing fortunes of the Maritime Continental Bank. By the time she entered Wellesley College, the loneliness had abated. The relationship between father and daughter was changing, with the daughter venturing forth to explore the world by herself, eager but a little afraid, impulsive but still hesitant.

Like most women of her day, Kate followed a liberal-arts curriculum. But living in New York had made her different from her less cosmopolitan sisters. She knew the Village like the back of her hand and on weekends frequented the bohemian cafés where the Beat Generation gathered to listen to the readings of Jack Kerouac and Ginsberg. Over endless cups of coffee she debated the merits of Colin Wilson's *The Outsider* and arrived at the conclusion that her generation, skinny, pale, and favoring black turtlenecks and pants, were destined for greater, far more important things than their parents, trapped in the smug righteousness of the fifties, could ever imagine. The tougher part of the question was what that glorious destiny might be.

There were times when Kate longed to pick up the telephone and talk to her father. But by now she was on better terms with his secretary, who was the one to tell her he was away and then, out of guilt or pity, chatted with her for a few minutes. On the rare occasion she and her father met, what little conversation they had was forced. He knew next to nothing about her life, where she had been, the seemingly limitless choices before her, the terrible lack of any critical way to choose. Sometimes Kate sensed he was reaching out to her, trying to get her to explain what it was she felt and why. She saw the pain and disappointment in his eyes when the evening drew to a close and they still remained on opposite sides of a chasm that was deepening with every passing year. What she feared and was angry with him for was that there seemed nothing either one of them could do to make that distance shrink.

"I love you, Kate. You must never forget that."

Deep in her heart she believed him, but over the years the words had become devalued.

"If you love me, why can't you make the time for me?"

"I try, Kate. Believe me, I do. It's not that I don't care—"

"Just that you care more about that rotten bank."

Kate looked at the La Jolla photograph again. She could read his pain, hear the echo of her harsh words, telling him that she was in Berkeley for good now . . . and she would never be coming home.

The photograph had frozen a moment in time she had had to live with all these years. Years of regret and recrimination, of ignoring her father's offers to come to New York, of reducing her words to him to scribbles on Christmas and birthday cards. Years that would never be given back to her . . .

Goddamn it, I can't even remember the last time I told him I loved him!

And now he was gone forever. . . .

The flames began to sputter as the wax ran out into puddles along the marble. Kate rose and pulled back the curtains. The sky was growing light, the stars and crescent moon fading. Kate looked down at the two open suitcases filled with clothing. She had packed mechanically, needing to do something with her hands, and now she couldn't for the life of her remember what she'd put into them.

"Katie? Katie, are you still up?"

Ted closed the door behind him and padded into the living room. He saw the suitcases and glanced sharply at her.

"What the hell's going on?"

Kate picked up the telegram and handed it to him.

"You didn't even bother to tell me it had come."

He shook his head. "Aw, Katie, Jesus, I'm sorry. This is awful." He reached for her, but Kate brushed past him.

"The funeral is in New York. I don't know how long I'll be gone."

"Are you okay? I mean, has this guy called you or

anything?"

"This *guy's* name is Armand Fremont. And no, he hasn't called me."

"Is there anything I can do?"

Kate managed a faint smile. "No. I'll be all right."

"Look, Katie, I don't know what to say. It's not like you and your old man were all that close, right?"

"Ted, don't say anything. Just don't say a damn thing. I can handle this."

"Yeah, well, it's going to be tough not having you here right now."

"Meaning?"

"Hirsh made bail for me, but the cops are still nailing me with inciting a riot as well as a dozen other bullshit charges. This isn't going to be a trial, Katie. It'll be *theater*. Goddamn drama is what we're going to put on. You want to be a part of that. It's going to be history!"

Maybe because she was exhausted and hypersensitive Kate immediately detected a false note in Ted's voice.

"I'm afraid you and Hirsh will have to make history without me."

"But it's not just me. Hirsh is going to arrange to have Mario, Jerry, Tim, and a bunch of others tried together. The papers are already calling us the Berkeley Ten."

Kate wondered who had thought that up and fed it to the media.

"I still don't see why you need me."

"Well, Hirsh can't handle so many defendants at the same time. And even though he's going to use people from his office, there's a lot of important stuff that he can't get to. So I told him that you'd be willing to help out."

Kate couldn't believe what she was hearing.

"You had no right to commit me like that!" she said.

"Hirsh said he needed someone to research the law and check records," Ted replied hastily. "I thought it would be a great opportunity for you, Katie. You know Hirsh's reputation. Someone starting out would *kill* for the chance to be on his team."

"With *his* reputation? Besides, all Hirsh wants is an errand boy—or in my case, girl. He needs someone in the library and registrar's office when she isn't busy photocopying or answering the phone."

Ted averted his eyes, and Kate realized he already knew this. He had gone along with whatever Hirsh had wanted and promised to deliver the warm body of one Kate Maser, donkey.

"Look, Katie, I'm sorry about your old man, okay?" Ted said, fighting to control his temper. "I'm also sorry that I didn't give you the telegram. I forgot. I mean, after the confrontation with the cops . . . And I know you have to go to New York. But I don't understand what is there to keep you after the funeral. And I need you *here!*"

"I don't know *what's* waiting for me in New York," Kate said. "So I can't promise when I'll be back. For that reason alone, I wouldn't commit myself to being a part of your defense. Nor should you have presumed otherwise."

Ted sighed and began peeling off his dirty clothes that reeked of sweat, the street, and jail.

"And if you didn't have to go, would you help out?"

Kate bit her lip. "I told you, I'm nobody's errand girl, especially not Jake Hirsh's."

Ted trailed his fingertips along her cheek.

"I always thought you'd be there, Katie. I really did. I still believe you will be. So go and do what you have to in New York, then come home."

Kate's heart twisted as he walked away, so beautiful and desirable and pure in his unashamed nakedness. A part of her cried out for him, a part detested her weakness because he was always able to pierce her soul like that while destroying a little bit of her.

Kate almost cried out to him. Almost. She took the first step, then froze. She knew the smell of the jail cell. There was something else she knew about that clings to a man's clothes, to his body: the scent of a woman sated by a lover.

Oh, Ted had been to jail, all right, and he had huddled with Jake Hirsh. But then, before coming home, he had gone somewhere else. To the adoring Rosemary, who, Kate reminded herself, had walked out of this apartment with her hand on his shoulder.

Had clever Rosemary, who had been smiling then, known what was to come? Had Ted?

Kate heard the shower going. *A little too late.* She wrote a note to Ted. It was a single word, good-bye. Then she snapped the locks on the suitcases, slipped on her trench coat, and let herself out into the damp mist that flowed down the open-air hallway.

The stupid, insulting thing was that Ted had been right: she would have been there for him. She knew it in her heart. But not anymore. Because here, like New York and her father, there was no longer any home to return to.

3

The day after the tragedy at St. Gallen, April 16, marked the debut of the powerboat racing season with the Monaco-Nice 32. Manufacturers provided their hand-hewn, exotic boats costing hundreds of thousands of dollars, and spent millions in advertising and promotion. From the air the vessels looked like magnificent birds of prey—red, green, black, and yellow glittering off azure blue, silky white plumes trailing in their wake. They bore predators' names: *Mako*, *Scarab*, *Panther*, and *Lupo*. But their hunting ground was not the sky but the sea, where they were piloted by the fearless who knew how to coax the last ounce of speed from their supercharged engines to achieve the ultimate goal: victory.

Aficionados cleared their calendars and flocked in from around the globe. There were races whose courses were longer, held in trickier waters, and ones with more substantial purses, but for sheer, hell-bent speed, which magnified the danger tenfold, nothing matched the Monaco-Nice 32, so-called because of the thirty-two kilometers that separated the principality from France.

The festivities had begun in Monte Carlo at a champagne breakfast where the racers had been introduced to the press. The names were legends in the sport: Marcello of Italy, de Dion of France, Manitas de Plata of Argentina, Baker-Howard from London. But out of a field of twelve it was a relative newcomer, the driver of a Brazilian boat, the *Panther*, who had received the most attention. The manufacturer knew he was gambling heavily. His driver had been in the field for only three years, and despite numerous victories, had never attempted a major competition like the Monaco-Nice 32.

Nonetheless the Brazilian had been more than satisfied

with the trial runs conducted off Salvador in Brazil's Bahia Province. Others would have thought this driver reckless, taking far too many risks, sacrificing safety for speed and position. The Brazilian did not. He'd been looking for a driver with guts. Now, after thousands of hours of tests, he knew he had one. But statistics and pretty pictures would never convince potential buyers. Offshore racers would accept the boat—and buy it—only if it was a proved winner. Watching the photographers snap away, the Brazilian heard his little voice telling him he had two: the boat *and* the driver.

Over breakfast the drivers and patrons were polite to each other, but no one tarried. After a final cup of coffee and the obligatory exchanges of good luck, the groups dispersed to their respective boat houses, where mechanics were already fine-tuning the engines. Except in the *Panther*'s lair. Its driver had insisted that no one, not even the engineers, be allowed near the *Panther* twenty-four hours before the race. When the Brazilian had queried, with mild sarcasm, who would do the work, the reply was succinct:

"I will. You know I'm qualified."

The Brazilian agreed, then asked why.

"Possible sabotage. You know how much the other manufacturers stand to lose if we win. A bribe, even one that would set a mechanic up for life, would be a pittance in comparison. Besides, it may be your boat, but it's my life."

The Brazilian couldn't argue with that.

The day was pristine, almost windless, the swells negligible. The manufacturers and drivers exchanged smug smiles: these were just the kind of conditions their vessels had been built for. The *Panther*, designed to smooth out the Atlantic chops found off Brazil's coast, seemed ungainly, even clumsy, next to its sleek cousins.

The driver was unperturbed. "Don't worry."

The Brazilian shrugged. "Luck," he murmured, and climbed into his rented helicopter to follow the race from the air.

The Brazilian watched as the *Panther* was guided out of

Monte Carlo Harbor to a point three hundred yards off shore. As his helicopter gained altitude, he saw the course laid out in the water, the lanes clearly marked by red buoys. There were referee boats every two kilometers to make sure the drivers didn't stray beyond the markers. Overshooting the foul lines, even by a half-boat length, meant automatic disqualification. The jostling for position, the strategy and pursuit, would all take place in a corridor less than one hundred yards wide. It was a frighteningly small combat arena for twelve boats with the combined thrust of over seven thousand horsepower.

As the boats drew up to the starting position, thousands of spectators who lined up along the shore or perched on the balconies of the grand hotels and private villas held their breath. Then a red flare shot up, and the still of the morning was lost to thunder.

As expected, the Frenchman, de Dion, and Baker-Howard of England sprang into an early lead. But the rest of the pack was charging hard—all except for the *Panther*, which, to the Brazilian's dismay, was running dead last. Unconsciously the Brazilian crossed himself and, without knowing it, offended his pilot, who thought the foreigner was afraid to ride with him.

On the sea below, the driver of the *Panther* was exultant. The boat was performing exactly as it had been designed to do. The engines were spooling up to a banshee wail, and the fact that the *Panther* was last in the field was of no concern.

The first mishap occurred at the ten-mile marker when the Italian, Marcello, swerved viciously to his right and cut off a less-seasoned competitor. The other boat, which had been threatening to pass, caromed off Marcello's wake, the bow clawing at the sky. The audience along the Bas Corniche gasped in horror as the boat, no longer able to defy gravity, fell back on itself and its driver. Within seconds rescue vessels were speeding toward it.

The *Panther*'s driver immediately took advantage of Marcello's lapse in concentration and neatly pulled past the Italian, who gaped in astonishment. The accident seemed to

create a chain reaction of misfortune. Within minutes one
boat engine blew, and another, belonging to the Spaniard,
coughed, sputtered, and ignominiously died, leaving the
driver smashing his fists on the wheel.

A mile later another vessel was disqualified when, in order to avoid a collision with the Frenchman, its driver
swerved beyond the foul lines. A referee fired a yellow flare
and radioed in the disqualification. The field was reduced to
eight, but as far as the spectators were concerned, the race
was between de Dion and Baker-Howard.

How wrong they were. The *Panther*'s driver positioned
the boat where it was, by design most effective, in the
swells created by the vessels ahead of it. Other craft would
have slowed under such conditions, but the *Panther* surged
forward, its engine screws biting hard. Effortlessly it out-
distanced three competitors, creating a wake so powerful
that the others were obliged to cut speed or risk being cap-
sized.

At the three-quarter marker the *Panther* was firmly in
third place. The leaders had taken note and moved closer
together, running flat-out but changing course just a fraction whenever the *Panther* attempted to come abreast. The
driver had anticipated their strategy: block out the *Panther*
while making a headlong dash for the finish line. There was
a solution for that too.

The spectators along the Nice harbor front were amazed
at the sight: three boats, running in a perfect inverted trian-
gle, bearing down on the finish line a scant three-quarters of
a mile ahead. Aloft in the helicopter the Brazilian mentally
saluted his driver: victory was impossible, given how his
vessel was being blocked out. Nor was there enough time or
sea left for it to overtake the leaders. But the driver had
shown mettle, and because the boat would certainly place,
the publicity would be extensive.

What happened next stunned everyone. Instead of pulling
back and being satisfied with third place, the *Panther* increased speed. Those with high-power binoculars couldn't
believe how close the driver was bringing the craft to the

sterns of the lead boats.

Bloody insane! thought the Englishman.

Not only an idiot but a suicide! thought the Italian.

Suddenly both were jolted forward as the *Panther*'s bow first kissed, then nudged the sides of their craft. Baker-Howard and Marcello reacted from experience and a very strong sense of selfpreservation. They veered off to right and left respectively. The *Panther* never stopped. Its throttles wide open, it roared through the gap, flying toward the finish line and the welcoming flotilla.

Baker-Howard knew he'd been had, but it was too late. His turn had been so sharp that there was no way he could get back on course fast enough to reclaim a share of the lead. Although disappointed, he had to admire the *Panther*'s driver. Had the bump been too hard, all three of them could have been sent catapulting to their deaths. There was no loss of face losing to someone who had the balls to succeed with that kind of maneuver.

Marcello was not so generous. He too had been obliged to veer off-course and saw certain victory slipping away. But he'd be damned if he let this novice make a fool of him. Engines screaming, Marcello twisted his craft around and set it on a diagonal course straight for the *Panther*.

The savage pleasure of having gambled and won was greater than any aphrodisiac to the driver of the *Panther*. As though sharing its driver's lust, the boat flew on, breaking its own speed records and engineers' estimates.

Marcello's *Scarab*, a black sea beast intent on killing its prey, bore down on the right-hand side of the *Panther*. Any other driver would have veered off. It was the only possible move. The spectators, screaming in horror, thought so. Marcello was convinced of it.

They were equally wrong. Instead of surrendering to the threat and abandoning the lead, the *Panther* slowed. Amazement, then panic, showed in Marcello's face as the *Scarab* thundered past the bow. At precisely the right second the *Panther*'s driver pushed the throttles down all the way, just in time to nick the onrushing *Scarab* amidships.

Given the speed at which Marcello was traveling, the move was fatal. Later the race officials would privately agree it could even be called homicidal. Completely out of control, the *Scarab* climbed on its side, then suddenly collapsed, the engines causing it to twirl round and round while it skimmed the water like a skipping stone. Marcello was a dead man.

The *Panther* roared across the line, then did a victory loop. Passing by the referee boat, the driver plucked the white flag and paraded it before the flotilla and the Bas Corniche with its cheering spectators. After the obligatory salute, the *Panther* turned and docked in front of the Nice Maritime Club. The judges, ashen-faced, waited behind the magnificent four-foot-high sterling silver trophy.

After the *Panther* was safely docked the driver jumped out and took off helmet and gloves, revealing a mass of raven hair and long, elegant hands.

Jasmine Fremont-Jabar held her arms high in victory. Her face, already familiar to the paparazzi who fed off her, caused hundreds of flashbulbs to explode. Caught up in the euphoria of the moment, no one noticed Jasmine's slight turn to look directly at the patch of water where the *Scarab* was still burning. And no one saw her smile of satisfaction.

Jasmine was in her suite at the Negresco Hotel on Nice's oceanfront boulevard, the Promenade des Anglais. The adrenaline from her win at the helm of the *Panther* was still pouring through her. It gave her anger an ugly edge.

She was a magnificent creature with long, muscular legs, small waist, and generous breasts that bore no hint of the surgeon's scalpel. She appeared to be at least ten years younger than the forty she had lived. Only the anger in her face, dominated by high cheekbones and lips that tended to curl at the corners, gave away her years, wrinkling the pampered skin around her flashing blue eyes.

"Where the hell is it?" she demanded, pacing, the jade cigarette holder in hand swinging like a walking stick.

Anthony, her dapper, sloe-eyed Lebanese assistant and

factotum, moved languidly around the dressing room, picking up pieces of her racing suit and gear, which littered the carpet.

"What did you say, *cherie*?"

"You heard me!"

Anthony threw up his hands. "I don't know *what* to tell you, *cheri*. The front desk said they were sending it right up."

At that instant both the chimes and the telephone sounded. Jasmine flung open the door and snatched a telegram off the silver tray held by an elderly porter. She dug deep into the pockets of her white mechanic's coveralls and dropped some crumpled notes on the tray.

"It's Pierre, calling from Paris," Anthony informed her in a bored tone. "He sounds quite distressed, *cherie*."

"Go make yourself useful elsewhere," Jasmine said, taking the receiver. "Pierre?"

"Jasmine, have you heard?"

The hysteria in Pierre Fremont's voice made Jasmine smile.

"Oh, yes, Pierre. I've heard." With a blood-red thumbnail she slit open the telegram.

4

The eighteen-year-old delivery boy was from the country and considered himself fortunate to get a job with a prestigious Parisian jeweler. And especially fortunate at this moment. Standing in front of him was a beautiful and totally naked woman, golden hair streaming over her shoulders, blue eyes reflecting the tease in her full sensuous smile.

"P . . . p . . . package, madame?" he stuttered.

Unperturbed, the girl took a half step forward, her upthrust breasts swinging lightly. Languidly she held out her hand and took the package. The boy, who was trying to focus his stare on some invisible point over her shoulder, promptly let go of the invoice, which fluttered to the floor. Instinctively, he dropped to his knees, which turned out to be a big mistake, because on the way down he saw the kinds of treasures that fantasies were made of. And he had to go up the same way, which he did, slowly . . . The girl, perhaps only two or three years older than he, smiled saucily at his predicament.

"When I reach the middle of the room, you may close the door," she murmured.

Slowly, with her arms by her sides, the long, slim jewelry box swinging lightly in her hand, she walked across the foyer. As she passed the ornate, gilt-edged mirror that divided the room, she heard the door lock. She grinned and continued through to the bedroom, where her lover was dressing for dinner.

"*Cher*?"

Pierre Fremont looked up, startled. "What?"

"This just came."

Pierre stared past her at the front door.

"Cleo, is that how . . ." He fumbled, waving his hand at her nakedness.

She tossed back her head and laughed, then sat, drawing her legs up until her heels rested on the seat cushion. At the sight of the golden down between her legs, Pierre's mouth went dry.

"Don't be silly!" she said, trying to sound cross. "Would I show myself to a complete stranger?"

"No, of course not," Pierre replied hastily.

No, his Cleo wouldn't do a thing like that. Oh, she enjoyed parading around in the nude, and he loved her all the more for it—especially when she wore black stockings with elastic tops and high heels and had applied a thick, wet-looking coat of wicked red lipstick. The Babylonian harlot, the child madonna, the monster who at once allowed him to consume her, yet by so doing left him insatiable.

How he loved his precious Cleo! Looking at her, he drank in her beauty and swore that nothing would ever cause him to lose her, nothing. . . .

I have kept my word, and she doesn't even know it.

Watching Pierre, Cleo knew exactly what was going through his mind. She always did. Her mother had been like that, gifted with second sight. She had also been a drunk and a whore who had made ends meet by swindling unsuspecting tourists fresh off the cruise ships and eager for a taste of exotic Araby. Fortune-telling, palmistry, tarot, Ouija, the money poured in from middle-aged and elderly passengers who had read in the shipboard magazine about Madame Trubetskoi's mysterious connections to the worlds beyond. It was an expensive way to advertise, and the Beirut waterfront hole in the wall, decorated like Valentino's tent in *The Sheik*, cost a king's ransom. But the suckers kept on coming.

If it hadn't been for the liquor and drugs, the money from the scams would have been enough. But during the tourist season Madame Trubetskoi's tastes shifted from cheap *arak* to vintage champagne and gray opium. During the winter she used her body to pay off the landlord. When Cleo turned ten, the rent was raised to include her as well . . .

Cleo fought the temptation to snatch another strawberry.

Instead she reached for it, as though she had millions to choose from, any time she wanted to. It had taken her a long time to discipline herself like this. Even now, when she had a life her mother could never have conceived of, somewhere deep inside her was the sad, silent, quivering child who still feared everything would be snatched away from her.

"Is it for me?"

"What?"

"Pierre, really! You're not paying attention to me!"

Her pout shamed and engorged him at the same time. He stared at the package.

"If I wasn't sure you weren't married, I'd think it was a present from your wife!" Cleo stood up in a feigned huff. "Or perhaps to another woman?"

"Cleo, no!"

Frantically Pierre tore at the wrapping paper and opened the jewelry case. Nestled in black velvet was a galaxy of diamonds and sapphires, intertwined like serpents to create a unique bracelet.

"Come here!" he whispered hoarsely.

He fumbled with the clasp because he could not tear his gaze away from her perfect breasts. Finally the bracelet closed around her wrist. Cleo stepped back and extended her arm, like a dancer reaching for the sky.

"You remembered!" she whispered over and over again.

Of course he had. Cleo had only to mention something— such as how much she liked the bracelet in the display window at Bulgari—and Pierre took it as subtle command to get it. He wanted only to please her and make her look the way she looked now. As Cleo paraded around the room, Pierre thought, "Mine . . . She is mine!"

Without warning, that thought jolted Pierre, reminding him of the telegram he'd received from Armand Fremont only an hour earlier. He remembered how fear had squeezed his heart when he read the words. Yet at the same time he had felt an exhilaration the likes of which he had never before experienced. The threat to him, *to Cleo*, had been destroyed with Alexander Maser's accident on the road outside Geneva. Yet with elation and relief came foreboding. A hundred things could still go wrong. Which was why, when he at last collected himself, he had called Jasmine, Jasmine who had anticipated all his questions and given him all the answers he needed to hear.

"Pierre, darling, I asked if you really want to go out to celebrate." Cleo rolled her wrist, the stones igniting before Pierre's eyes. Then she ran the tip of her tongue across her lip. "Or do you want to stay in?"

"Let's stay in, just the two of us."

"Whatever you prefer, my love," Cleo whispered, settling in his lap.

As taken as she was by his gift, Cleo knew that Pierre was keeping something from her. He was nervous, a poor liar. She was glad she had coaxed him to stay in. In private she could get him to overindulge in wine. Pierre might be an oenophile, but he had little tolerance for alcohol. When he grew sleepy, she would put him to bed and rummage through the place he thought she knew nothing about where he kept his deepest secrets.

Until two months before, Pierre Fremont had considered his world perfect. As a Fremont, he had been raised in an atmosphere of power and privilege. Cautious and meticulous by nature, he discovered he could interpret the arcane world of banking as easily as some scholars read the dead languages. To him, banking was order, and without order nothing else mattered.

As a doctoral student at the Sorbonne, he had worked for the Rothschilds, then moved on to several other European institutions, not only picking up experience but cultivating valuable contacts. By his midthirties Pierre had earned the respect of international bankers and finance ministers and had recently reached the pinnacle of his career by being appointed the youngest governor in the history of the Banque de Liban. Given his position, he could, of course, have nothing to do with either the Casino de Paradis or its holding company, SBM. To avoid even the hint of impropriety his shares were held in a blind trust.

The arrangement suited Pierre perfectly. He had always been overwhelmed by Armand's powerful personality. Preferring the shadows to the limelight, Pierre was content to let Armand run the Casino de Paradis, which, Pierre agreed, he did magnificently. Beyond the cost of maintaining the Paris and Beirut residences, which came out of the trust, Pierre had few expenses. His travel, entertainment, and incidentals were taken care of by the bank, and his monthly allowance was more than adequate to cover his sole indulgence: his love of gourmet food. Pierre felt he had enough money to spend over two lifetimes. He was soon to learn how mistaken even his expert calculations could be.

For all of Pierre's wealth and worldly ways, the sleek and polished women of Beirut seldom gave him a second glance. He was only five feet six inches tall, with a plain face, dominated by an overly long nose and washed-out gray eyes, which would never become even remotely distinguished. Over the years his indifference to exercise had endowed him with a generous potbelly. His hairline was receding faster than ice left out on a summer afternoon and at only thirty-six he already had the pallor and mannerisms of an old man.

Had Pierre been more fortunate, nature might have compensated by giving him a sparkling, magnetic personality. But while his family name and bank account were undeniably impressive, so was his stupefying boredom. Pierre was neither a raconteur, nor could he tell jokes. At dinner parties he tended to ramble on endlessly about the cuisine and the wines. Beiruti women might love to eat, but they didn't want to talk about food. What about gambling and parties? The yachting weekends and shopping sprees to Rome and Athens? The delicious gossip about adultery in high places and the slumming into the city's dangerous *souqs* to arouse even the most jaded senses? Pierre had no liking for any of this.

Resigned to eternal bachelorhood, twice a year Pierre visited what was considered Beirut's most staid bordello. He accepted that the lust he heard whispered about at the Jockey Club was something that would never come his way.

Pierre's one passion was food. He was the founder and president of an intimate club whose members dedicated themselves to cuisine, meeting twice a month at each other's homes. It was a point of honor that the host, no matter how wealthy, chose the dishes, did the shopping, and cooked every course.

Being the host one particular night, Pierre had chosen venison for his main dish, and he was fretting that the juniper berries he'd ordered from Goodies Supermarket, Beirut's purveyor of gourmet ingredients, hadn't yet arrived. So when the antique bells over the kitchen entrance tinkled merrily, he threw open the door, expecting to find an Arab delivery boy.

Instead he beheld a vision. She was tall, her height accented by legs that seemed, as the miniskirt revealed, to go on forever. The thick cotton sweater molded itself to her bosom, and her hair was pulled back in a ponytail, making her look very young. In her arms were the flowers for the dining-table centerpiece.

"Delivery for Fremont," the girl said, looking around at the professionally laid-out and equipped kitchen.

"I'm . . . I'm Fremont."

Cleo regarded him skeptically. This twerp with the chef's apron almost dragging on the floor was *the* Fremont that the flower shop owner had made such a fuss about?

"Then these are for you. You want them here or in the dining room?"

"The . . . the dining room."

"I'll need a vase."

"Yes, of course, right away . . ."

Nervous, embarrassed, and shy all at once, Pierre almost demolished the Sevres vase he had chosen for the occasion.

"Why don't you let me do that?" the girl suggested. "No charge."

Before Pierre could say a word, she settled herself at the dining table and began to create a beautiful centerpiece.

Pierre sat down opposite her and watched. It took him five agonizing minutes to screw up his courage.

"If you don't mind my asking, what is your name?"

Her cornflower-blue eyes teased him. "Why do you want to know?"

"Well, it's just that . . ."

Pierre scrambled for some smooth, witty repartee but found nothing of the kind in his inventory. He began to blush.

"That's all right," the girl said. "At least you didn't put the make on me. My name's Cleo."

Cleo! How wonderful that sounded to his ear. Pierre couldn't stop now.

"Perhaps I can offer you a glass of wine?"

Cleo regarded him quizzically. She knew exactly what was going on. Her only choice was how far along to string this imbecile. If she was nice to him, at the very least she'd get a large tip. As it was, she ended up with much more.

Cleo stayed for two hours, and Pierre was close to tears when she left. Dinner that evening was an unqualified success, but he really didn't care. He couldn't get Cleo out of his mind, but he also didn't have the courage to call her at the flower shop. He skirted that problem by ordering more flowers and praying that Cleo would be the one to deliver them. She was. After a dozen bouquets he finally got up the nerve to ask her out and was ecstatic when she accepted. That evening Pierre was the proudest man in Beirut as he escorted Cleo to the Oiseau Bleu restaurant at the Casino de Paradis, followed by a cabaret show.

Their relationship soon became the talk of *tout* Beirut. Pierre was embarrassed until he realized he was being lionized. Not only was he considered the eternal bachelor, but his friends knew how careful he was with money. They couldn't believe he was paying this girl to be with him. That left only two other alternatives: either Pierre Fremont was hung like a horse, or else he had a butterfly's tongue.

Pierre felt more alive with Cleo than at any other time in his life. Her youth invigorated him. Whenever they went out

dancing, he felt her energy pour into him. He knew he was
becoming the object of ridicule. He noticed the smirks on
the faces of young men lounging in Beirut's clubs and overheard their sarcastic remarks. But for the first time in his
life he didn't care who said what. When he was with Cleo,
nothing else mattered because they made their own world,
one that Pierre had never believed he'd find, much less sa-
vor and share. He swore that come what may, he would
never, never give it up.

After six months of courtship Cleo moved in with him. It
could have happened sooner, but Pierre was cautious. His
second greatest fear was that Cleo would leave him; the
greatest was that she had boyfriends on the side and was
playing him for a fool. So Pierre hired a very discreet, very
expensive private detective, who shadowed her for three
months.

Pierre was overjoyed by the reports. She had not lied to
him. She lived in a small apartment in the touristy part of
Beirut harbor. Her mother, now deceased, had earned a living as a psychic. Cleo's formal education had ended during
her senior year at a parochial school when she had gotten
her job at the flower shop. There had been several legitimate modeling jobs, but a career hadn't taken off.
According to the detective, Cleo lived quietly, dated occasionally, but had no romantic involvements. Pierre couldn't
believe that such a priceless gem had been overlooked by
the rest of the world. But he wasn't about to question his
luck. Nor did he ever suspect that for all he was paying his
detective, the man might have been found out by his subject
and offered something money couldn't buy to omit certain
details, to polish the tarnished ones.

With Cleo installed in his home Pierre was puzzled to
discover that two could not live as cheaply—or in his case,
equally well—as one. The allowance he provided for Cleo,
and which he thought to be a generous one, soon proved
woefully inadequate. Monthly invoices began to appear
from Beirut's most fashionable and expensive clothing
stores. Never having priced women's apparel, Pierre was

mortified until Cleo gently explained the facts of designer-creation life.

Bills continued to pour in. Clothes needed accessories, which in turn demanded jewelry. A stunningly turned-out woman required nothing less than a Bentley to get her to the hairdresser, manicurist, and masseur, as well as a Maserati for those get-away-from-it-all drives up and down the coast. New friends had to be entertained in appropriately lavish fashion, which included a spanking-new sixty-foot yacht.

Pierre, who could summon government ministers in the middle of the night to justify their expenditures, didn't raise a whisper of protest at Cleo's profligacy. Yet every time he had promised himself to put Cleo on a budget, she carried him away to ecstasies that left him limp. All was forgiven and forgotten, and secretly Pierre was relieved. He couldn't bear the thought that if he raised objections to Cleo's spending habits, she would regard him as cheap.

Since Beirut considered Pierre fabulously wealthy, no eyebrows were raised at his largesse. His own books told a different story. By the end of his first year with Cleo, Pierre had to face up to the fact that he was broke. All of his million-dollar yearly income, all of his cash and stock reserves, were gone. By the end of the second he was in hock to three London-based banks whose patience for repayment was wearing thin.

Cornered, Pierre confronted his dilemma. If he reined in Cleo's spending, he ran the risk of her leaving him. Totally unacceptable. If he did not repay the English banks, sooner or later word of his financial difficulties would leak out. Equally unacceptable. Therefore, a new source of revenue had to be found.

Pierre considered his options; they were threadbare. He could not go to anyone for money, including family, because as a director of the national bank, he could not risk even a semblance of impropriety. He could not sell his stock in the casino holding company, Société des Bains Mediterranien, because the shares all held by family members could be sold only to other family members. That was Armand, who might have caused grave difficulties if he discovered Pierre's desperate need, and Jasmine, who was hoarding any money she had to further her schemes.

All of this left him one alternative—an alternative he could act on all by himself. No one would be the wiser, not even his powerful uncle Armand, who had eyes everywhere. Everything would be fine as long as he moved carefully . . . as carefully as a lamb around a lion.

In his wildest dreams Pierre never suspected it would not be Armand, but a man six thousand miles away—Alexander Maser—who would break open his secrets.

"Darling, are you all right?" Cleo swept out of the dressing room, the red sequins of her Saint Laurent miniskirt sparkling and shimmering.

Pierre smiled at Cleo's concern.

"My stomach is a little sour. Would you bring me a Fernet-Branca?"

Cleo poured him a pony of the bitter purple Italian liqueur and watched him drink it down.

"Now you must tell me what's wrong. I know it has to do with that telegram you got today."

"Alexander Maser died in a car accident," Pierre said.

Cleo frowned, and Pierre could spot the fleeting recognition in her eyes when she heard the name.

"Maser?"

"He was a banker, from New York. I knew him quite well. He was also Armand's best friend. They grew up together."

"How terrible for Armand!"

"Jasmine insists that Louis and I must go with her to New York for the funeral."

Cleo was quick to notice that Pierre did not include her, but did not press the point.

"Then we are going to bed early tonight," Cleo said firmly. "You've been working much too hard, and now with this awful news . . . I want you rested before you travel to the funeral."

Before the evening was out, Cleo watched Pierre consume a full bottle of wine and three ponies of liqueur. Nothing short of à war would wake him this night. She could count on it.

Cleo lay naked between the cool Egyptian cotton sheets. The ceiling was an abstract collage of black streaks, shadows of tree branches, against a background of pale blue new moon. Soundlessly she slipped from the bed and padded over to Pierre's side, facing the painting mounted on the wall. It was a Modigliani, a doe-eyed Madonna executed in grays and blues, her features elongated as though her face had been stretched like saltwater taffy. Cleo knew the artist was famous and that the painting was worth a great deal of money, but she had never liked it, only what lay behind it.

She had been living with Pierre for less than two weeks when she discovered the secret of the wall safe behind the painting. It had been so funny to watch Pierre working the combination. She'd seen it all because the mirrors of her dressing-room vanity, if adjusted just so, gave her an unobstructed view into the bedroom. The first time she opened the safe herself, so many things had become clear.

Cleo caressed the diamond-and-sapphire bracelet she had worn to bed. She was glad there were things about her that her lover would never know. The scales over Pierre's eyes were so heavy that he would never see her love for him was a mirage. Love was something of which she was incapable. To Cleo, it was just another deception, no greater than the fact that this gift of the bracelet would, like so many others Pierre had lavished on her be replaced by paste, the original disappearing into the safety-deposit box of a Rome bank. He hadn't been able to tell the difference about that either.

Cleo would never take Pierre or his love for granted. With a street child's cynicism she believed that someday, one way or another, for a reason that didn't matter, both would be snatched from her. Unlike her mother, Cleo had made provisions for that day. The jewels she had cached would set her up for life. But knowledge of Pierre's little secret had changed her plans. Why should she have to be satisfied with selling the jewels to get that million or so dollars? Why couldn't she keep them and still get that much money—even more?

Cleo looked back at Pierre, curled up against a pillow like an overgrown child. It pleased her enormously that she could open the safe right now and rifle through what he held most secret. And she would have, had he not told her about Armand's telegram, which explained why Pierre, who couldn't stand the sight of a bleeding finger, had been so ill at ease. Cleo decided to let the matter rest. Pierre would be gone in a day or two. There was all the time in the world to do what she slyly thought of as inventory.

5

The offices of Interarmco, taking up the entire top floor of a nondescript building in the lakefront business district, were chilly. The temperature was set to accommodate machines rather than their human tenders. There were a dozen cubicles for staff and only three executive offices on the entire floor. The rest of the space was devoted to computers, the fastest, most powerful machines IBM and Univac had to offer. They were the heart and mind of the security organization David Cabot had set up. Ingesting, processing, collating, storing, and, when called upon, retrieving hundreds of thousands of pieces of information from worldwide sources, the computers made Interarmco a formidable private security organization. It was the computers' ability to bring together seemingly disparate facts on thousands of individuals as well as an ever-changing world situation that often had put Armand Fremont ahead of his competition.

The rosy fingertips of dawn crept toward the sleeping form on the couch. A part of David Cabot's mind registered the light shining on his face, the rest did not. He was caught in the coils of a nightmare that made him groan in agony and left his skin bathed in sweat. The dream was always the same, its intensity undiminished even after twenty years.

David is at the helm of a fifty-four foot sloop, *Celeste's Dream*, named for his mother. The breeze sweeping across the eastern Mediterranean, thirty miles off the Turkish coast, fills the sails and sends the vessel gliding across the waves. A spray breaks over the side, drenches David, but he only laughs. He is a tough, skinny boy of thirteen, brown as a coffee bean from the sun. His mother, sitting on the deck over the cabin, turns back to him, wags her finger. His father, working a sail near the bow, smiles but tells him to be careful.

The family has been at sea for two weeks, having put out from Cyprus and meandered their way through the Greek isles. Now they are on the last leg of their journey which will take them down the Turkish coast, past Syria, toward Lebanon. The trip is both the family's reunion and gift to itself. David's father had been away in the war for four years. His mother worked as a Red Cross nurse in London during the Blitz while David stayed with friends in the country. Each in his own way had endured and survived. This is their celebration of life.

That evening the boat rocks gently in the swells, and the family watches the lights of Tripoli sparkle along the Lebanese coastline. It is the time of day David loves most, his belly full from supper, his muscles, hard as knots, relaxing, his thoughts, though heavy with sleep, still crackling with anticipation. His father, who served in Africa, has told him so many wonderful stories about Beirut. He cannot wait to see it.

David nods off to sleep on deck. He is dimly aware of movement and whispers around him, but he does not stir. He knows he is safe, that the sounds are only his parents—

Then comes the first explosion. David leaps to his feet and is blinded by the flare arcing high above the vessel. He hears guttural words in a language he does not understand and his father shouting. David stumbles toward the stern, then backs away in terror as dark men swarm over the gunwales like an invasion of rats. Suddenly his father is at his side, holding a shotgun. He grabs David by the scruff of the neck and pulls him back. The shotgun roars, but it is his father who is thrown back. When David looks down, he sees only a bloody mass where his father's torso used to be.

Celeste Cabot doesn't stop to think. She has tended to soldiers with wounds more hideous than the imagination could conceive. David sees his mother pick up the gun and fire into the onrushing men. Two go down, but a third throws himself at her, his arm held high, the blade glittering red in the last sparks of the dying flare.

David hears himself screaming. He lashes out at anything

around him, taking savage satisfaction in the grunts of pain. But there are too many. Something very hard strikes him behind the ear . . .

When David wakes up he is cold and wet. His hands are tightly tied, and there is a foul-smelling cloth in his mouth. But he can still see. In the distance a boat is burning, the orange flame reflected across the waters. Tears swell in David's eyes, and he shivers violently as he watches the mast of *Celeste's Dream* crack, then pitch into the sea. He hears laughter beside him, a hoarse whisper, and then feels himself being fondled . . .

When David regains consciousness, he finds himself in a large, high-ceilinged room with a tiny barred window set near the top of the thick wall. A hawk-nosed man with large gold loops through his ears and a golden tooth hauls him to his feet. Somewhere in the darkness David hears the soft shuffle of bare feet on the earthen floor, punctuated by sniffles and whimpers.

The man pushes David toward the light. Suddenly the room is filled with children, holding each other's hands. There are dark Africans and tawny Arabs, children with olive complexions of the northern shores of the Mediterranean and some who are as blue-eyed as Nordics harkening back to the Vikings. David sees the terror in their eyes, unaware that they see exactly the same in his. For all their differences in age and hue of skin, the fear and the manacles that bind their ankles make them brothers and sisters.

The man with the gold loops claps his hands. The door opens and several well-dressed men enter. Without a word they pass in front of the children, running their hands over their hair and skin, lifting up the dirty cotton shifts to look at their private parts.

David's hands clench into fists. His heart is pounding as much from anger as from fear. All he can see is the burning mast toppling into the sea, his parents' watery grave. He realizes what is happening even though he cannot believe it is happening to him. He knows that he must fight back.

One of the men lifts David's robe and squeezes his penis.

His nose and eyes are very close to David's fingers, which spring forward. The man screams and rears back. David drops to his haunches, prepared to defend himself however he can, as the man with the golden loops charges, whip in hand.

But the slave trader never reaches him. He freezes in midstride, his rabid expression replaced by one of incredulity. As he topples forward, David sees a knife embedded in his back.

One by one the buyers fall, their bodies riddled by bullets from silenced guns. Through the smoke and stink of cordite David sees a man step forward, tall, powerfully built, with eyes that glitter like ebony. He gestures and others join him, kneeling at the children's feet, working on their chains with bulldog cutters.

"Who are you, boy?" asks the man.

David staggers to his feet. There is something in his expression that makes the man smile.

"You are safe now, boy," he says. "Soon you will go home."

David's lips tremble, but somehow he forces the words out. "Who are you?"

"My name is Armand Fremont. You don't have to be afraid—"

"My name is David . and my home is dead!"

David Cabot stood under the hot shower for a long time, but even so he couldn't scrub away the residue of the nightmare. This wasn't the first time nor would it be the last. The nightmare always left something behind, another thin layer of pain fused against those that had come before it.

Nor were the rest of the memories far behind, although these were a balm. As he dressed, David remembered how years later, when he knew so much more about Armand, he had asked him,

"Why didn't you give me up?"

Armand had looked at him, and David realized that even after all this time Armand was not sure if he had found the real answer.

"Because when I looked into your background, I understood that your home was truly dead. No one had ever said such a thing to me before. No one had made me feel it."

"But there must have been hundreds of other orphans!"

Armand nodded sadly. "But we chose each other, did we not?"

It was true. For David, there was nothing to go back to in England. His only relatives were a distant elderly aunt and uncle. When the British Red Cross had come to the hospital where the children were being looked after before returning home, he had refused to budge. Armand had noticed his fierce determination, underlined by fear and grief. Most of the other children had loved ones waiting for them, who would make their lives whole again. But not this bewildered adolescent whose stormy eyes challenged Armand.

The arrangements to keep David in Beirut were finalized with a minimum of fuss. The British ambassador was a close friend, and his opinion that David Cabot would be well looked after as a ward of Armand Fremont carried great weight. David came to live in Armand's house. He was enrolled in the best private schools and in less than two years spoke fluent French and Arabic. Later he attended the American University in Beirut, followed by graduate studies in economics and business at Harvard.

When he felt that the classroom had few things left to teach him, David returned to Beirut and announced to Armand that he wanted to work with him.

"You are not under any obligation," Armand had told him. He was very proud of David and had watched his progress carefully, wondering what he would decide to do in his adult life.

"I know that," David had replied. "It is something I want to do. You saved me, gave me a second chance. I don't want to waste it."

And Armand asked himself if the time for the idea he'd had in the back of his mind had at last come. . . .

David spent the next few years studying and training with

some of the most prestigious police forces in the world: Europe's Interpol, Britain's Scotland Yard, and the American FBI. He became a first-rate criminologist, skilled in self-defense, and an expert marksman. Once again Armand monitored his progress carefully. When David returned to Beirut, Armand felt he was ready.

"Information is power," Armand had told David. "Nowhere is this more true than in the Middle East. Without it I would not survive, much less prosper."

Armand had gone on to explain the concept he and Alexander Maser had been working on and which was almost ready to be translated into reality: a private security agency that would pick and choose its clientele from a worldwide roster of wealthy individuals and globe-straddling conglomerates, people and entities that needed protection against industrial espionage, kidnapping, extortion, blackmail . . .

Armand had suggested that Interarmco be headquartered in Beirut, but David had immediately vetoed the idea. Beirut was an open city where secrets, no matter how closely guarded, fell victim to bribes and intrigue. Sooner or later the connection between the casino and Interarmco would be made, security compromised, and the trust—even lives—of those who had put their faith in the company ruined.

Instead David had suggested Geneva, and that Interarmco have no link to the casino other than carrying it as a client on its books. The distance from Beirut worked in their favor as did the neutral Swiss location.

"There's something you're not telling me," David had said to Armand when it seemed their discussion was finished. "Yes, Interarmco will double or triple the amount of information flowing in to you now. But that's not all of it. You have a hidden agenda, having to do with the slave trade. Armand, I wasn't the first child you rescued. I wasn't the last either."

At that moment Armand knew he had chosen well.

"How much do you know about the trade?" he had asked David.

The reply astonished Armand. Obviously David had studied the subject thoroughly. He went over its history, dating back to the pharaohs, and traced the routes that had carried human chattel through the time of Christ, through the Crusades, and into the present.

"It has never stopped," David had said in a low voice. "Not during war, famine, or plague. Nor has any race been spared. At some points, Africans were highly prized, then Asians. Now it is Europeans. But the common denominator throughout is that children have always been the targets of choice, fetching the greatest amount of money. Ironic, isn't it? The most defenseless are the most valuable, snatched off streets, lured into alleys, or, like me, kidnapped by pirates, then drugged, trussed up and shipped into whorehouses or private torture chambers. . . ."

"I have been fighting this scourge all my life," Armand had told David. "I have broken slave rings only to hear that others have sprung up in their place. I work with the few honest police officials that exist in the Middle East, with Interpol and even certain members of the United Nations, at the UNICEF offices. It is an ongoing battle, David. It is mine and Alexander's—and now Interarmco's—hidden agenda."

David's eyes had burned fiercely. "Mine too."

After David finished dressing, he walked from his bathroom into his office. A bundle of telexes that had arrived overnight awaited him on the coffee table. None had to do with the project he and Armand had been working on for the past five years.

In late 1960 Interarmco had helped break up a dozen small slave-trade rings operating out of Syria, Jordan, and Egypt. But the satisfaction had been short-lived. The next year rumors of a new ring filtered through the Middle East. Police agencies and UNICEF reported that the abduction of children and teenagers in Western Europe had increased dramatically. Given their past successes, Armand Fremont had thought he could swiftly quash this new threat. It was one of the few times he'd been wrong. Whoever was operating this ring was a master, so well hidden that not even the best-paid informants could get close to him. Those who ventured too far into the pipeline were found dead, their bodies horribly mutilated.

Over the years the number of children abducted and never seen again grew inexorably. Police in Europe redoubled their efforts, but to no avail. International pressure was brought to bear on certain Middle Eastern countries whose ministers merely threw up their hands in innocence and demanded proof. Armand Fremont had vowed to give it to them. He had targeted this ring, made it his own personal crusade, and told David Cabot that he wanted nothing less than the identity of the mastermind.

David filed the telexes. In his years with Armand and as director of Interarmco, he had never come across such an impenetrable maze. Whoever had set up this ring had had the devil's own cunning, ruled it by fear as well as money. It was a combination hard to crack. But that only made David even more determined to succeed. The boy had grown into a man, but his eyes still saw, still remembered the moments when his world had been corrupted and destroyed that moonlit night on board *Celeste's Dream*.

The minute David slipped behind his desk, he turned his attention to the matter at hand. His secretary brought in coffee and croissants along with overnight messages from Paris.

The word had been sent forth, discreetly. Interarmco was making inquiries about Alexander Maser—whom he had met, where, for how long. Interarmco would pay handsomely for an eyewitness who had seen or overheard something. Those versed in the ways of the street or whose stock-in-trade was information had glided out into the night. Interarmco had a well-deserved reputation for paying generously, promptly, and in the currency of one's choice. But it had an even better name as an organization that always remembered those who had assisted it, even in the smallest way.

The pickings were disappointing. Neither personal contacts

in the metropolitan police forces, nor specialists in private security firms, nor a host of informants from cabinet offices, nor madames at exclusive bordellos had any idea what Alexander Maser had been doing in Paris. But each message ended on the same note: the search would continue.

David knew that Armand had been hoping to have information before he went to New York. But it hadn't come to light. A routine call to Alexander Maser's tearful secretary had only deepened the mystery: Alexander had made his own travel arrangements. The secretary hadn't been aware of his going until the very last minute.

Why didn't Alexander want her—or anyone—to know?

He forced himself to look over the notes his secretary had left for him. A memo stated that Jasmine and Pierre Fremont had been notified of Alexander's death and the subsequent funeral arrangements in telegrams from Armand. The telegrams had not, as David would have expected, been sent to Beirut. The one to Jasmine had gone to Nice. David remembered she was racing in the Monaco-Nice 32. And the one to Pierre had been delivered in Paris . . .

David stared at the memo; then, as if on their own accord, his fingers marched forward and picked it up. Holding up the pink slip of paper, he tried to recall if there was any connection between Pierre and Alexander Maser. They had attended two or three of the same banking conferences, but that was the extent of it. Alexander traveled frequently to Paris on business; Pierre Fremont had maintained a residence there for years. That they happened to be in the same city at the same time was . . .

Coincidence. Don't grasp at straws.

David tossed the memo aside and drew out the photograph in Katherine Maser's file. There was something different about the girl, though David couldn't quite pinpoint it. Maybe her cheeks were a shade too full or the lips too ripe. And the eyes, so intense and concerned. Even if he hadn't read the press clippings about her, David would have guessed that Katherine Maser was the kind who believed in the power of causes and the triumph of truth and justice.

She could be trouble.

David hoped that Armand's famous charm would weave its magic, and that after the funeral Katherine Maser would return to California to march on behalf of a better world. David knew that sooner or later he would solve the mystery of Alexander's death. In doing so, he didn't want amateurs in his way.

6

Emil Bartoli was executive vice president of Maritime
Continental and had been Alexander Maser's right-hand
man. He was a Venetian, a thin, ascetic man whose face
clearly revealed the lineage of Doges ancestors. At twenty
he had known more about finance than bankers four times
his age. It was in the blood, he said. Although he'd had his
choice of employers, he had gone with Maritime Continental—or more accurately with Alexander Maser. It was the
sort of closed shop he was comfortable with and knew best.
In New York over a hundred people answered to him, but
he also had faithful contacts in every marketplace around
the world. If there was a flutter on the Tokyo, Hong Kong,
Zurich, or London exchanges, Bartoli was the first to hear
about it. And, more important, the reasons for it.

As most perennial bachelors tend to do, Emil Bartoli had
adopted the child of someone close. Kate was the daughter
of his heart. He supervised her trust fund, and when Kate
had moved out to California to go to school, Bartoli had
made it a point to write and telephone her once a month.
But what he had wanted to be his greatest accomplish-
ment—the reconciliation of father and daughter—had
eluded him. Now the opportunity was gone forever.

"I'm so very sorry, Kate," he said. "Everyone at the bank
offers you their condolences. If there's anything you need,
you have only to ask."

"Thank you, Emil."

Kate was having this meeting in her father's office. She
felt distinctly uncomfortable. She was wearing a long multi-
color peasant skirt, Russian-style embroidered blouse, and
her well-worn but carefully maintained Lucchese boots.
Around her forehead was a green scarf, its ends trailing
along her back. This morning at the hotel, as she was dress-

ing, she knew she'd be out of place. Her father's office was a real American stage, cherrywood furniture from the Pacific Northwest, soft pine paneling from New England, credenzas and armoires of Carolina's burled walnut. All the men would be wearing Brooks Brothers.

When Kate had pictured this, her defiance moved up a notch. She'd be damned if she'd change her style. Now it was she who felt awkward, and her gesture seemed to her trivial and mean spirited.

"Have they brought him back, Emil?" she asked, looking down on the Park Avenue traffic.

Unlike most financial institutions, Maritime Continental had eschewed Wall Street. Alexander had felt more comfortable with the Park and Forty-eighth Street address, a minor architectural masterpiece whose ground floor was rented out to carriage-trade boutiques. Most passersby never even suspected there was a bank there, which had suited Alexander perfectly.

"Yes, he's back, Kate," Bartoli replied. "Everything has been arranged. My secretary has the details. If there's anything you want to add or change, just tell her."

Kate turned to him. "Then I guess there's only one thing left to take care of." She swept her arm around the room. "What happens to all this."

"That's pretty much straightforward," said Bartoli. "The terms of the will stipulate that you and the Société des Bains Mediterranien each have forty-nine percent of the shares. The remaining two percent are in my custody. Should there ever be any diverging views as to the policy or direction of the bank, I would cast the swing vote. But I do not see that as being likely," he continued. "Your father and I have had a long-standing arrangement, whereby in the event of his demise, I would take his place as president. The policies and objectives of the bank would remain the same. Selling or merging is out of the question. We have a fine client list, and over time, with due care, we shall add to it. But it will be done to the criteria Alex laid down, none other."

"And me?"

"Well, Kate, in fiscal terms, you receive a substantial dividend payment every quarter. Naturally, the money is yours to do with as you will."

"What about active participation in the bank?"

Bartoli was surprised by her question, but betrayed nothing.

"It is, of course, your choice. I hadn't made provisions for that, given that you seem to be cutting your own path as an attorney."

"You mean you've been reading the newspaper," Kate replied, eyebrows arched.

"That too," Bartoli agreed. He paused, then added, "*Would* you be interested in coming to us?"

"I don't know," Kate murmured.

Would she? Maritime Continental, or any bank for that matter, was the epitome of the Establishment. Their resources fueled the machines of war; the faceless men who ran them siphoned funds designated for the President's Great Society program, putting it into the pockets of cronies and hacks while blacks and poor whites were left holding out their hands. Banks moved silently and in mysterious ways. They were the custodians of secrets.

"I don't know," Kate repeated.

"No need to decide right away."

Kate was startled by the voice. She hadn't heard it in so long, yet it rang true and sweet in her memory. Taking a deep breath, she turned around.

"Armand?"

He was almost exactly as she pictured he would be, older to be sure, but the lines across his forehead and slanting across the cheeks gave his face more character. His hair was swept back in a mane all silver now, but the eyes, deep and hypnotic, and the rich timbre in his voice were precisely as she remembered them.

"Kate, I'm so very sorry."

She was in his powerful embrace, her hair against his chin, the scent of his cologne emanating from the soft cashmere of his suit. Kate felt his strength and reassurance pour into her, and for the first time since she had read the telegram did she honestly believe that somehow she would come to terms with what had happened, that one day she would be able to put it behind her.

Armand smiled at Kate. He knew that his expression betrayed nothing except genuine caring and concern. But there was more going on behind his eyes where conflicting emotions puzzled him. He had been fond of Kate the child, had been drawn inexplicably to her. Now he was reacting far too strongly to her as a woman.

Armand's presence so dominated the room that Kate felt unsure of herself, and oddly a little afraid of him.

"Are you satisfied with the arrangement Emil has made?" she asked at last.

He shrugged. "I can't tell you how many bribes from other banks Emil has turned down. Outrageous. I even wanted him to come to work for me. He wouldn't dream of it. So hang on to him. He's the best."

Emil Bartoli inclined his head at the compliment.

"Did you . . . and my father have any business that I should know about?" Kate asked Armand.

"Not really," Armand replied easily. "Maritime Continental made and monitored the casino's American investments. But these are long-term instruments—bonds, treasury bills, some real estate. Emil can track those with one eye closed—or both."

"Fine," Kate said slowly. "I guess things can stand the way they are." She paused. "But there is one thing I do want to see now: the police accident report."

"Really, Kate—" Bartoli started to protest.

"No, Emil. It's all right. I have it right here. I believe your father told me you were quite an accomplished linguist. Do you read French?" She nodded, yet Armand hesitated before handing her the report. "I must warn you, Kate. The Swiss were thorough. The details are graphic."

"I just want to know how he died," Kate said in a low voice. "I need to know."

"Of course," Armand said gently, casting a warning

glance at Bartoli. "We'll leave you now. When you're ready, we can have lunch. There is ample time for you to freshen up."

Kate winced at Armand's reference to her clothes. Wherever lunch was to be, she obviously couldn't go dressed as she was.

"Kate . . ." Armand squeezed her shoulder, then followed Bartoli out.

Kate thought the gesture had been for courage. It was really a wordless apology.

As Armand Fremont passed through the vestibule into Bartoli's office, he mentally calculated that it was already six o'clock in the evening in Maranello, where Ferrari had its headquarters. By now the wreckage of Alexander's car, taken not to Paris as he had informed the Swiss police it would be, but in the opposite direction, to Italy, would have been examined by factory engineers and mechanics. Armand had no reason to think that their findings would be any different from his own. But for all his experience, he was not a professionally recognized expert. He needed depositions from men whose qualifications and reputations would go unquestioned in any court of law in the world. If it came to that . . .

He hoped Kate would forgive him. The Maranello report, along with others, would never reach her hands. She might never learn that her father had been murdered.

When Armand reached the elevators, he turned to Bartoli.

"Delmonico's in an hour?"

Bartoli nodded.

"I'm worried about her, Emil," Armand said suddenly. "She's putting up a brave front, but—"

"She will come through, Armand. Believe me."

"I hope so," Armand replied, but without conviction.

Uncertainty was a feeling he seldom encountered, and it was disconcerting. Even more disconcerting was the attraction he felt to Kate. Inappropriate, he warned himself. But still the feelings would not go away.

Instead of returning to his hotel, as he had led Bartoli to believe he would do, Armand Fremont walked the few blocks to the First Manhattan Bank at Madison and Fiftieth. He smiled at the young female trainee behind the customer-service desk and presented her with a safety deposit box key.

"I need to take something out."

The girl grinned and held Armand's gaze a shade longer than politeness dictated. She would be back in a minute, she said, with the signature card and the master key. Armand's smile faded as he watched her walk away. His heart began to beat faster. God knows how long he and Alexander Maser had had this box. They had rented it as a precaution, to store sensitive documents having to do with each other's current projects. In case something happened to one of them, the survivor would always have access to the material and so be able to finish the work. But Armand was hoping for more. There was a chance Alexander might have committed something to paper that would produce a clue as to why he had had to die on that lonely road outside Geneva.

"Mr. Fremont?"

Armand took stock of the earnest young man who had materialized behind the counter, reading Fremont's name off the signature card.

"I'm Nelson, the assistant manager."

"Yes?" Armand replied pleasantly.

"I'm terribly sorry," Nelson said, tripping over his words. "But there is a slight problem." He lowered his voice. "You *have* heard about Mr. Maser?"

"Heard what?"

Nelson looked around nervously. "That he died in a car accident in Switzerland."

Armand's feigned shock was so convincing that Nelson guided him into his office and insisted he have a cup of coffee.

"All the more necessary for me to open the box," Armand sighed. "We did business together, you see, and well, you understand these things . . ."

"Of course I do," Nelson sympathized. "However, there are obstacles."

"Really?"

"By law we're required to seal the box until probate has been conducted, then it is up to the executor to dispose of the estate according to the deceased's instructions."

"I see," Armand murmured. "And this is the case even though I have a legitimate claim to the box and its contents."

"I'm afraid so."

Armand masked his disappointment and impatience behind a smile of resignation. He had acted too late. Had he been thinking, he would have flown to New York even as Alex lay in that Geneva hospital.

No, you could never have abandoned him. This will keep. There are other ways . . .

Armand thanked Nelson with the proper gravity and left the bank. He still had a few minutes before lunch with Kate and Bartoli. He would use them to call Alex's lawyer, who knew him very well. In the past the attorney had needed some very special, very sensitive favors, which Armand had been able to grant. He could be counted on to appreciate what had to be done.

The rank-and-file employees of Maritime Continental were a close-knit group of people. Their loyalty to Alexander Maser, whom they'd seen often in the course of everyday business, was unquestioned. His sudden death shocked everyone.

"Isn't it awful about poor Mr. Maser? He was such a good, decent man."

Prudence Templeton dabbed her eyes with a balled-up handkerchief. She was the kind of woman fashion magazines referred to as "handsome," her looks veiled behind pouches of soft flesh that no amount of dieting seemed able to dissolve. But nature had compensated, giving her thick, lustrous hair, sparkling blue eyes, and skin that was like satin to the touch. Unfortunately, few men appreciated such qualities. It wasn't until just this past year that Prudence

Templeton, just turned thirty-eight, had found one who did.

"Yes, it is," Michael Samson murmured, his fingertips grazing her arm. He felt the woman shiver and could scarcely keep himself from smiling. He so enjoyed his power over her that it almost made up for the disgust he felt when he made love to her.

"I suppose Mr. Bartoli will tell us about the funeral arrangements," Prudence said, sniffing. "Maybe we should take up a collection for a wreath."

"Mr. Maser might have wanted us to give something to a charity instead," Michael Samson said gently. "He was that kind of man."

"Oh, Michael, of course! How perceptive of you!"

It was the end of the working day, and banks across the eastern United States had closed. The six clerks in the wire-transfer room of Maritime Continental were tallying the day's business, which, Michael reckoned, had been mediocre. Only a hundred million dollars had been run through, some of it leaving Maritime Continental for banks across the world, some pouring in from those same institutions. When he'd first started with the bank, Michael had been staggered by the sums bandied about—seven million to Hijai Bank, Tokyo; twelve million to Bauhaus in Frankfurt; ten million to China Commercial in Hong Kong. What had further impressed him was the fact that so very few people even within the organization were aware of what transpired in the wire-transfer room, buried beneath the bank in a large, rectangular room carved out of Park Avenue bedrock. It was serviced by a single elevator, operated by a key which the room's nine employees were handed in the morning and which they turned in every night. In the center was a long, wide table with a four-foot-high divider. On both sides were telephones with dozens of lines that connected the wire-transfer room to similar warrens in banks around the world. Beside each chair was a telex to receive and send confirmations and instructions, and along the far wall there was a bank of computers that processed and tabulated the transactions. Yes, Michael Samson had been impressed. But that had been a year ago. Now he found the work tedious and the room stifling, even claustrophobic. Nonetheless, he hid his boredom and impatience well. He had come a long way to get into this hidden heart of Maritime Continental. He had forced himself to do things that repelled him. He had learned to lead a double life and dreamed of that wonderful day when he would betray those he had charmed into trusting him and set himself free.

"Michael? Michael, are you all right?"

"Yes . . . yes, of course. Forgive me. It's only that with everything that's happened . . ."

Prudence Templeton patted his arm, something she would never have done under normal circumstances. She was the head of the wire-transfer department, and Michael Samson was supposed to be just one of her seven clerks. She was careful not to show him any more or less attention than the others. She thought no one suspected that two or three times a week Michael visited her and did things to her she could not believe possible. These precious secrets were like candles, burning hot and bright, bringing light and color and warmth to the drab existence that she had once resigned herself to.

"Michael, will you be coming by?" Prudence asked in a low voice.

He shook his head. "I can't. It's Wednesday."

Prudence sighed. Wednesday Michael practiced with a jazz combo that played in the Greenwich Village clubs. Prudence didn't care for jazz nor for blacks, whose company Michael enjoyed. She had never been to his apartment in the Village and, if the truth be told, had no desire to see it. Christopher Street was full of the kind of people whom she, as a North Carolina lady, had been raised to avoid and ignore.

"Perhaps later, when you're done?" she asked hopefully.

"It'll be too late by then. But on Sunday we can go to Central Park."

Prudence caught the promise in his voice and drank in his rugged beauty. Michael Samson was the Mediterranean lover she'd fantasized about as a girl. He wasn't tall, but his body was sculpted muscle, his features highlighted by thick black eyebrows and lashes and exotic dark eyes, both sensuous and cruel. Prudence, who loved the classics, imagined that this was how Odysseus or Jason had looked.

"Sunday," she whispered.

Later Michael made small talk with his co-workers as they walked through the bank and past the guard at the front door. He said his good-byes and watched as the others headed toward Lexington Avenue and the noisy, crowded bars that catered to the five o'clock white-collar crowd. When he'd first joined the bank, he had been invited to come along for a martini or two. He had always politely declined, and the offers had stopped, as he intended. He didn't want people getting to know him well. That, like the seduction of Prudence Templeton, was part of the plan.

Michael emerged from the subway at Sheridan Square and walked the rest of the way to his apartment on West Fourth Street. The Village reminded him of Beirut. A dozen races and ethnic groups filled its streets, making them come alive with their languages and songs. There were hole-in-the-wall restaurants that served every kind of food imaginable. Unlike Beirut, however, the bars and coffeehouses were full of female NYU students who loved to think they were avant-garde by sleeping with dusky-skinned poets and musicians. To Michael, they were naive waifs who all but fell into his bed. It was one of the many things he missed about Beirut—the challenge of its women, the chase, the clash of wits, the struggle that made the inevitable surrender so sweet.

Michael picked up his mail and impatiently shuffled through it as he walked up to the third floor. A year ago, when he'd first arrived in New York, he'd had fire in his belly. He had come for a reason, a purpose, to achieve certain things. Now he found himself chafing, marking time, pacing the cage that was his job at Maritime Continental. He wanted to take the next steps toward the promise that had brought him here. But for months there had been only silence from Beirut. The promise had begun to tarnish.

Michael pushed open the door and immediately, like a veteran New Yorker, relocked it. He sensed something was out of place. The smell—it was foreign but so familiar . . .

"Hello, Michael."

She was framed by the entrance to the bedroom, eyes glittering in anticipation and hunger, bidding him to come closer.

"Jasmine . . . ," Michael said hoarsely.

"Come to me, my beautiful one," she whispered. "It is time."

He had first met Jasmine Fremont five years ago, in his native Beirut. Michael Samson hadn't even existed then. His name had been Michael Saidi, the only son of a widowed senior croupier at the Casino de Paradis.

His father was a man "born into the trade" who, when his wife died, leaving him a six-year-old son, had been a senior usher. By the time Michael was ten, his father had fulfilled his lifelong ambition of becoming a full-fledged croupier, a position he was immensely proud of. It was also a position that Michael despised.

As an adolescent Michael was tormented by many things. If his father went to work each night dressed in a flawless black tie, why was it Michael wore secondhand clothes that came from rich women's charities? Whenever he walked his father to the casino, why did he never go up the broad front steps, past the uniformed porters, and through the grand doors? Why did they have to use the little mouse hole around the back? Why was it that all the splendid people who gathered at the casino came in beautiful automobiles with drivers in livery, and his father always walked the three miles from their house, even when he was too old to do so?

When Michael asked him about this, his father laughed.

"Alas, my son, I do not have their money."

And from that moment on Michael Saidi understood that his father was, and would be forever, a servant. The realization changed his life. He would *not* be like his father. He wanted more, *demanded* more, and would have more! He loved the shiny cars and the gorgeous, bejeweled women, but he *coveted* the self-satisfied expressions, the easy masculine banter, that indefinable but undeniable quality that singled one out as *belonging* among the privileged of this world. A son of a servant, he dreamed the dream of royals.

His father died when Michael was twenty, a student subsisting on a partial scholarship at the American University of Beirut. A few days after the funeral Michael was summoned by the casino manager. The casino had an employee's insurance plan that provided a generous death benefit. There would be enough money to finish his studies and perhaps take a year abroad. Michael would have dearly loved to turn down the benefit. The manager's shocked expression alone would have been worth it. Or would it? Michael knew he didn't have the guts to find out. In the end he took the money and condolences and hurried away before his humiliation became too much to stomach.

"Drowning our sorrows, are we?" a melodious voice at his shoulder had asked.

Michael had been sitting at the poolside bar of the Phoenicia Hotel, one of Beirut's most elegant watering holes. He was so intent on savoring his amber whiskey that he never noticed the woman slide into the stool beside him. She was dark and stunning and reminded him of a sleek and dangerous cat.

The Phoenicia always had been good to Michael, providing a cornucopia of rich British, French, and German girls who bought him drinks and took him to their rooms. But this woman was different. There was a depth to her beauty, an inbred sophistication in the way she moved, how she spoke. He had no doubt she was filthy rich.

"If you are going to get drunk at lunch, then you must do so on champagne."

The woman looked at him expectantly. On impulse Michael ordered a bottle of the hotel's best wine, which cost more than a month's rent. The bartender brought two glasses, and without waiting for an invitation, the woman raised hers.

"To you."

Michael returned the salute and asked, "Who are you?"

"Someone who is going to make you feel much, much better."

Three hours and two more bottles later Michael was drunk. The wine and the woman's sweet voice had coaxed every last ounce of poison out of him. He had told her all his secrets, the resentments he harbored, the dreams he fed on.

"You never told me your name," he said, his words thick.

The woman laughed. "Given your low opinion of the Fremonts, among others, perhaps I shouldn't tell you."

Michael gaped.

"My name is Jasmine Fremont," the woman told him sweetly. "And don't worry, pet, I didn't take offense. You see, I'm not too fond of some of them either. But no matter. You see, my sweet, I'm going to give you a new life."

First, however, she gave him raw, impassioned sex of a kind he'd never had before. Exhausted and sated Michael listened to Jasmine's soft promises of everything that would come to pass for him. He drifted off to sleep in her arms not believing a word.

His cynicism proved wrong. The next day Jasmine began reorganizing his life. She found him a small but chic apartment in Ra's Beirut, one of the few neighborhoods where both Muslims and Christians lived side by side. She had the apartment furnished by a professional decorator. Accounts were opened for him at the best tailors and haberdashers as well as at the finest restaurants and clubs. Jasmine drilled him mercilessly on proper attire, manners, and etiquette. She never hesitated to correct him, often sarcastically, when he made mistakes. She made him quit the American University, replacing his professors with tutors. Out of class Jasmine had him read all the major newspapers, especially their financial sections that referenced the dealings of multi-millionaires.

"These are some of the most powerful men in Beirut, in

the world. Memorize their names, follow their lives, watch what they do and learn!"

It was all a heady experience for Michael, but he absorbed everything. Proof of his success was an acceptance letter from a school Jasmine wanted him to attend, the prestigious Centre Polytechnique in Paris, one of Europe's foremost business schools. Over a celebration dinner, Michael suggested that it might be time for Jasmine to introduce him to Beirut's business community, which had strong ties to the French capital.

"No, no, my pet. You're going in a different direction."

Instead of having drinks in the gilded splendor of the Jockey Club, Michael found himself on a dusty road that trailed over the Shouf Mountains deep into the reaches of the Bekaa Valley. It was wild country, beautiful but dangerous, populated by tribes who seldom ventured beyond the mountains. This was the hidden face of Lebanon, where hemp and poppy flowers were cultivated by silent, suspicious men carrying guns rather than hoes.

Michael tried to hide his fear, but Jasmine saw through him.

"Don't worry," she told him. "These people know me well enough to trust me."

Michael was skeptical. In Beirut, which prided itself as a Western window on the East, women were treated courteously and, if they were clever enough, with respect. But in backwaters they remained little more than chattel, beasts of burden and bearers of children, to be given away in marriage or, if it proved more profitable, sold into slavery.

Michael was taken aback by the warm greetings the tribesmen offered Jasmine. After taking the traditional tea, they were led into the fields where the flowering tops of Indian hemp covered the valley as far as the eye could see. Soon, Michael knew, the tops would be harvested and drained of their resin, which after careful cooking, would become paste and finally bricks of brown-black hashish. Four months later, he was told, the opium crop would be ready, and the cycle would continue.

"What the hell are we doing here?" he demanded.

"This is where we will build your future," Jasmine said coldly. "What did you think, Michael? That pretty clothes and knowing how to use a dessert spoon would get you your dreams? Make you a *zaim*? The sons of servants do not become *zuama*. If they have no family, no connections, no money, then they have nothing! So I am going to make you very rich, Michael. And very powerful. You will make people very, very afraid of you. Enough so that they will do your bidding and never dare to ask where you came from or what you were. That, Michael, is what will make you a *zaim*—fear."

Michael had been dazzled by what Jasmine had shown him, but as he soon learned his education was far from over. During the next few months he and Jasmine traveled to Cairo, Amman, Damascus, and Baghdad, staying at palatial hotels and opulent private homes as well as run-down apartments in some of the worst slums Michael had ever seen. He quickly learned that those who lived in luxury were the buyers; those who moved through the shadows were the purveyors. In both cases the commodity was the same: human beings.

Michael paid close attention as Jasmine explained how the slave trade worked and the enormous profits to be had from it.

"But the risks are equally great," she warned him, and went on to say how a number of established rings had recently been exposed and overturned.

"That is our opportunity," Jasmine continued. "A vacuum has been created, and you must step into it."

Michael hesitated, not because he was averse to trafficking in human lives, but because he had no idea where he would begin. Jasmine heard him out and laughed.

"In Europe, where you'll be going in a little while. The greatest profit is to be made out of European children, ten, eleven, twelve years old. Older girls are also highly prized. What we have now is a situation with many buyers but no one to service them. The authorities have picked up the traders' ringleaders and broken the chain. However, many of the lower echelon remain in place. They can move the traffic along, from Rome's seaport, Civitavecchia, or Piraeus in Greece. But they have no cargo."

"And that's where I come in," Michael murmured.

"Yes, my pet. With your looks and charm you shall pluck those lovely European girls as if they were rose petals and earn a bit of your way now. Bring our buyers the best, and they will remain loyal."

"What if someone tries to interfere?" asked Michael.

"Then you will have to do what you must to protect our investment, won't you?"

Michael, who had never shrunk from violence as a child, had one last question.

"You said that the old rings had been broken. By whom? And how can you be sure it won't happen to us?"

Jasmine smiled. "Because, dear one, I know the man who did that. I talk to him every week. He doesn't tell me much, but it will always be enough to warn us if he is getting too close."

"And he is . . . ?"

"Why, Armand Fremont, of course."

Michael Saidi's education continued in Europe. Before he left, Jasmine took him into the teeming *souqs* of East Beirut where the poor Arabs, servants, and day laborers lived. There they met a cadaverous old man who wore glasses with lenses as thick as bottles.

"Don't be deceived." Jasmine laughed. "He is the best forger in Lebanon."

Michael had his picture taken, wads of money changed hands, and in short order he became Michael Samson, a Maltese citizen of Valetta with the birth certificate, passport, driver's license, and work permit to prove it.

Michael looked to Jasmine for an explanation.

"One day you will come back," she told him. "When you do, no one must be able to make the connection between the man you were then and who you are now."

"What about my past here—the records at the American

University?" he demanded.

"They will cease to exist," Jasmine replied, as though it were the most simple thing in the world.

When Michael asked why, Jasmine only replied, "Trust me. I have far more planned for you than the slave trade. That is only a beginning."

Michael Samson, as he was now known, spent two years at the Polytechnique and graduated with honors. At Jasmine's direction he took his first job in a large commercial French bank, where he learned about the mysteries of foreign exchange and how billions of dollars in various currencies were moved around the globe every hour.

At the same time Michael gained quite the reputation as a *boulevardier*, a sophisticated man about town on whose arm hung the most beautiful women. Although Michael's few male acquaintances noticed that the same girls seldom showed up twice, they never inquired about them.

After his apprenticeship in France, Michael accepted a position with a smaller but much more distinguished Swiss bank in Zurich. Michael thought he was closing in fast on the inner circle.

"That's precisely where you *don't* want to be," Jasmine admonished him. "You keep forgetting that these are just stepping stones and that you are the invisible man. Try to get into the Sauer Bank, their wire-transfer division if you can."

Michael bridled. Zurich was a wealthy city, and he could almost touch the glitter of the good life that swirled around him. But Jasmine kept him on a short leash. The Sauer Bank might be an august institution, but it paid its clerical and low-level staff niggardly wages. Only a tiny allowance from Jasmine permitted him the occasional luxury.

Following Jasmine's instructions, Michael avoided making close friends, an easy task among the aloof Swiss. He saw the reason for this soon enough. Four or five times a year, Jasmine directed him to take vacation or sick leave and discreetly fly back to Lebanon. On each trip he spent the night in Beirut and at first light was headed into the Bekaa Valley. By now he was welcomed among the farmers who grew the hemp and poppy and the tribesmen who prepared the drugs for shipment and saw to it that they safely reached the ports of Tyre and Sidon. Michael spent long hours with them, squatting around braziers, the smell of mint and oranges heavy in the air. Together they spoke of the great things that were to come. . . .

On one such occasion, before he was to fly out of Beirut, Jasmine said to him, "It's time to broaden your horizons. You're going to America."

Michael was no longer surprised by Jasmine's sudden announcements. He waited for her to continue.

"Sauer does a lot of business with a private bank called Maritime Continental. I want you to get a job in their wire-transfer department."

"Maritime Continental . . . that's Alexander Maser's bank." Michael looked at her pointedly.

"Yes, it is," Jasmine replied softly. "And that's where you want to be."

"How long?"

"A year, perhaps eighteen months."

"Buried in the electronic transfer department like some cretin?"

"Oh no, my pet. There will be many interesting things for you to do." Jasmine smiled. "Trust me."

Even though Michael Samson's employment record was sterling, landing a job at Maritime Continental took almost four months. Michael touched down in New York on a blustery, freezing February day and thought he'd arrived in hell. The noise of the city drove him crazy, the steel and concrete wore down his soul, his job turned out to be stultifying. But just as in Zurich, Michael had a hidden agenda, drawn up by Jasmine.

Having gained a reputation as a slightly eccentric recluse, Michael stepped into a different world when the working day was done. Since New York was a giant melting pot, there was no problem meeting Cypriots, Maltese, Lebanese, and Arabs who worked in most of the city's service industries. Michael was quickly accepted into their communities.

He broke bread, drank tea, and after he had gained their trust, was treated to the hashish pipe. In less than six months Michael knew the names of the major importers, distributors, and street dealers. He met with cold-eyed Sicilians who ran the heroin trade and beefy Neapolitans who controlled the longshoremen's union. He listened to the drivel of university students in Greenwich Village and made mental notes of their constant references to marijuana and hashish. Clearly a new age was dawning, and experimentation with drugs was a big part of it. Equally true was that the best hashish and poppy came from the Middle East, and the finest of that from the Bekaa Valley. But, as Michael learned, no one had access to this rich source. Buyers sent into the Bekaa were never seen again, and the place had gained a fearsome reputation. No one, it was said, could do business there. Jasmine told Michael to go ahead and prove them wrong.

It took months to organize and bring in the first shipment, but the Sicilians and Italians disposed of it in three days and came begging for more. Michael obliged, but the price went up. He kept on pushing it up until he was making four hundred percent profit on every pound of hashish that he was smuggling into the port of New York. The profit on raw opium delivered in Marseilles was even greater.

Michael was very careful to keep his two worlds apart. To the Sicilians he was known only as Michel, a Levantine Maltese with impeccable taste in clothes, who held the key to the fortunes of the Bekaa. To Maritime Continental, he was a faceless clerk who was diligent, competent, and unimaginative. To Prudence Templeton, he was a dream come true.

As his drug business expanded, Michael began to chafe under the constraints of the bank. He loved the feeling of power his money and connections gave him. He dreamed of shaking off the dusty Michael Samson, saddled with his frumpy, middle-aged lover, and preen before the world. Sometimes when the temptation became overpowering, he even dreamed of ways of getting rid of Jasmine. She had given him much and brought him far, but now he had enough, knew enough, to fly alone. Such dreams came more and more frequently as the months passed. When Michael heard about Alexander Maser's death, he wondered if this wasn't a sign that it was time to change his life.

It was, only he mistook its meaning completely.

Jasmine stretched luxuriously. She straightened up and swung out of bed, reaching for a cigarette. Tangled among damp sheets, Michael watched her.

"I'd almost forgotten what it was like," he murmured.

Jasmine laughed softly. "Oh, but I haven't." She looked at him. "You're dying to know why I'm here."

Michael shrugged. "Alexander's funeral."

"Yes, partly because of that." Jasmine drew deeply on her cigarette. "And partly because it's time for you to come home."

Michael sat up quickly. "Go back? But who'll look after everything here?"

"You mean your drug business? Why, you'll be taking that with you. Your people here can handle ten times the volume they're getting now. And that's what you'll be sending them, as master of the Bekaa, the new *zaim* of Beirut."

Michael closed his eyes. It was all coming to pass, just as he imagined it would.

"However, there are a few loose ends that have to be taken care of," Jasmine said.

Michael recognized the cold edge to her voice.

"Such as?"

"Are you still on intimate terms with that cow?"

"Prudence? Yes, unfortunately."

"Be especially nice to her for the next few days. You'll want her deaf, dumb, and blind around the office."

"Why?"

Jasmine crushed her lips to his, reaching for his groin.

"I'll tell you later."

7

Like most Lebanese Christians, Alexander Maser had been a Maronite, whose adherents were part of the Roman Catholic Church. But Kate had believed that religion had never played much of a role in her father's life, so she was quite surprised to learn the instructions he had left for his funeral and burial. He'd directed that a service be held in a small Maronite church in Pawtucket, Rhode Island, his body to be interred in the church's cemetery.

Kate asked Emil about all this.

"The Lebanese who came to America," he explained, "chose to live in small towns rather than the large cities. Alexander was a generous supporter of their churches and the work they did."

All these things I'm learning about him, Kate thought sadly. *How much more will I discover?*

True to his word, Emil had arranged for everything. A chartered helicopter brought him and Kate to the small airport in Pawtucket, where limousines waited to take them to the church.

Kate was relieved to be away from New York. The day had that fresh, crisp April tingle to it, and the air smelled of salt. In the middle of the morning on a week day Pawtucket was the perfect image of a sleepy New England town, with white rambling clapboard homes, graced by towering maples and elms, overlooking the harbor.

The funeral was a private affair, limited to family and Pawtucket's small Lebanese community, which regarded Alexander Maser as kin. A memorial service, to be attended by Alexander's business friends and associates, would be held at St. Patrick's Cathedral later in the week. An old priest, with a black, bushy beard, and eyebrows like angels' wings, greeted Kate when she stepped out of the car and ushered her into the church. Along the way he introduced her to the heads of the Lebanese families, who bowed to Kate and kissed her hand.

"Your father was very much loved here," the priest murmured. "He was a generous man who took great joy in sharing his bounty."

Kate accepted the condolences as gracefully as she could. These people were treating her as though her father had been some feudal lord, and she their princess.

Armand Fremont stepped beside Kate as the priest disappeared into the sacristy. "Don't be ashamed on their account. Remember, a Lebanese is first a member of his family, then his village, then his religious group. After all that, he's a Lebanese. When you moved to California, Alexander spent a great deal of time here. He loved these people and they loved him, and so they are showing you the respect they feel you deserve as his daughter."

Before Kate could reply, Armand took her arm and was leading her toward the last row of pews.

"There are some people you should meet," he said. "I don't know if you will remember them."

Kate looked at the two men and a woman standing together. She vaguely recognized them from old photographs, but their names eluded her.

"Ah, Katherine! You remember me, do you not? Pierre Fremont? I know, it's been so long since Beirut, and to meet again under such tragic circumstances, well . . . I'm truly sorry."

"Thank you," Kate replied, trying to place his face.

"You probably don't remember me, Katherine," Jasmine said, introducing herself. "You were just a child when we met."

But Jasmine was not the kind of woman anyone could forget. Even on this somber occasion her elegantly cut black dress, tightly drawn-back hair, and perfect makeup served notice that she was someone to be reckoned with. Kate felt uneasy beneath the older woman's coolly critical, slightly amused gaze. Suddenly Kate recalled the first time she had ever been introduced to Jasmine and how awed and embarrassed she'd been because she felt this woman could see right through her . . . just the way she was doing now.

"And this is my husband," Jasmine said.

Kate had only seen pictures of Louis Jabar and remembered thinking that *no one* could be that handsome. But he was.

"We're all very sorry for your loss," Louis was saying. "If there's anything we can do, anything at all to help you . . . Perhaps you could come to Beirut, for a short vacation, I mean."

"That's very kind of you," Kate said.

"I'm sure Kate will be returning to San Francisco and her law practice, won't you dear?" Jasmine asked.

"Of course," Louis added hastily. "Armand mentioned to us how successful you've become."

"Plus the fact that the bank is in good hands," Pierre said. "I understand that Bartoli will be assuming your father's responsibilities."

Kate was nodding but the words that came out took her by complete surprise. "I haven't yet decided whether or not to stay on."

Pierre blinked. "In New York?"

"With the bank," Kate said quietly. "Maritime Continental was my father's creation. Now it is my legacy and, to some degree, my responsibility. I can't simply walk away from it."

Although she was addressing the three of them Kate was facing Pierre, who seemed to have grown even more pale.

"That is a very noble sentiment, Katherine, and perfectly understandable under the circumstances," Pierre was saying. "But Maritime Continental's dealings are so . . . so complex. Don't you think your lack of experience might hinder rather than help it?"

"Pierre is absolutely right," Louis chimed in. "Maritime Continental is an international bank, with worldwide obligations. You can't possibly be expected to appreciate all its workings—"

"But I can learn!" Kate said sharply. She resented the condescension of these two urbane men.

"No need to take offense, *cherie*," Jasmine said. "Pierre and Louis are only saying what all women already know— business is terribly humdrum. The only fun is spending the money it brings. Right now you have plenty of that. You are young and free, so go ahead and enjoy it."

"Perhaps we find enjoyment in different things," Kate replied.

Jasmine smiled. "Touché, my dear. I understand you have quite the reputation as a litigator. I'm beginning to see why. You know I meant no offense."

"None taken," Kate replied. "It's just . . . well, it's a surprise to see you all. It means a lot to me that you're here."

Armand, who had been standing off to the side with Prudence Templeton, had picked up most of the four-way conversation. The more he'd heard, the more puzzled he'd become. The telegrams about Alexander's death had been sent out of family duty. But Alexander had not been kin. And, as far as he knew, none of them, except Pierre on occasion, had ever had any dealings with Alex. Armand had expected condolences, but never that all three of them would interrupt their lives to come to a quiet funeral held in a place they undoubtedly hadn't heard of.

And they were treating Kate as though she were a long-lost relative. Why? What could she mean to them?

Armand dismissed Kate's inheritance immediately. Both Jasmine and Pierre had more money than they knew what to do with. And if it wasn't the money . . .

The service was about to begin, and Armand shrugged off his curiosity. But not soon enough for it to have gone unnoticed.

The bank's founder had passed away, and its senior officials were at the funeral, but on this day the machinery of Maritime Continental continued to turn over as smoothly as ever. There was, however, one difference, and it was crucial to Michael Samson's plans: Prudence Templeton was absent from the wire-transfer room.

Not that this affected the department's activities. The clerks didn't need Prudence Templeton in order to carry out their duties, and if something came in that required an executive decision, an upstairs supervisor would handle the matter. The critical thing to Michael was that Prudence was not around to look over his shoulder, checking and tallying transactions.

Michael had kept himself busy all morning, making it appear he was swamped with work. If anyone had any intention of asking him to join them for lunch, one look at the piles of paper would have dissuaded them. Everyone knew Michael Samson wasn't the kind to leave until every last order had been processed.

The rules of the wire-transfer room stipulated that the clerks took their lunches in two shifts, so that there were at least four people to handle the incoming business. But because Prudence wasn't there and traffic was slow, five of the clerks left at the same time. It was the chance Michael had been waiting for.

Prudence Templeton's desk was at the head of the counter. Michael sat to her immediate right; the remaining clerks were grouped around the other end. Michael slid a long, thin key from his pocket. It was a duplicate of the one Prudence Templeton used to unlock the top drawer to her desk. One of the times he'd spent the night at her apartment, he had managed to slip the original off her key chain and make a wax impression. For two hundred dollars an obliging locksmith had produced what he claimed was a perfect replica.

It had better be. . . .

Michael swung around so that he could reach the drawer. The key went in smoothly, followed by a telltale click.

"Hey, Mike, can you help me out with this?"

The key clattered to the floor, the drawer rolled back an inch. Michael swung around just in time to block the view of Prudence Templeton's desk from the clerk coming toward him.

Don't look at it! It's not open!

"Put that stuff down here." Michael grabbed the computer printouts from the clerk's hands and dropped them on his desk. "What seems to be the problem?"

"Geez, Mike, it's nothing earth-shattering. Just a couple of glitches on the transfer."

Michael's eyes darted between the clerk and the printout and he spoke very quickly, trying to hold the clerk's attention. But now two others had wandered over, passing right in front of Prudence's desk, with its open drawer and the key lying behind a chair leg.

After what seemed like an eternity Michael found the problem and a solution. He despaired when the clerks stood around nodding, chewing the eraser tips of their pencils like goats.

He wanted to scream at them to move.

Finally they shuffled back to their desks. Michael glanced at the wall clock, astonished that less than five minutes had passed. He bent over and surreptitiously retrieved the key.

The next part of his plan was the most dangerous. The information he needed could not be removed from the drawer. It was written on a piece of paper taped to the bottom. Getting to it meant rolling the drawer out completely. There was only one way to do that.

Like most people who worked under constant pressure, all the clerks smoked. Michael had a foolproof plan. He watched the end of the table until one of the men emptied an overflowing ashtray into a wastebasket. Casually Michael walked down and threw in some crumpled paper along with a balled-up tissue soaked in lighter fluid. He was barely back at his desk when a wisp of smoke curled up from the wastebasket.

"Hey, what's going on?" he cried.

The others saw the smoke and immediately scrambled for the fire extinguisher. Keeping his eyes on the confusion, Michael slid open the drawer and lifted the files off the bottom. Only then did he glance down. A few seconds were all he needed to memorize the two numbers. The drawer was closed, the lock snapped. In the confusion, no one had seen or heard a thing.

The fire was doused before the alarms sounded. Everyone breathed a sigh of relief and, after a few puzzled exchanges as to how this could have happened, returned to work.

So did Michael. His fingers danced over the telex keys, quickly establishing a link with the Banco de Brasil in Rio de Janeiro. The connection made, he typed in the first of the two security numbers he'd memorized, followed by his request to open an account. Michael knew that no reputable bank in the world would do that unless its officers were certain about the identity of the person with whom they were dealing. The only verification they would accept was the number code corresponding to the name of the person requesting the account and, if it happened to be a different one, the number of the individual in whose name the account would be established. Michael furnished this as well. Now there was nothing to do but wait.

Clerks who had been to lunch began drifting in; those waiting to leave filed out. Michael took out a sandwich and forced himself to eat a few bites. One hour passed, then another. The teletype clattered intermittently, rattling off messages from around the world—everywhere except Brazil. The working day waned.

As the others were getting ready to leave, the telex began spewing out still another message. Michael read the first lines intently. It was the Rio confirmation. Followed by the designated account number. Followed by a word of thanks and how nice it was to do business.

You don't know how nice!

Michael folded the telex and slipped it into his pocket. Then he glided over to the computer terminal, the casters on his chair whirling soundlessly. The numbers of the accounts he was about to pillage rolled up before his eyes. They belonged to some of the largest charities, museums, and nonprofit organizations in the country. From each Michael looted hundreds of thousands of dollars, instructing the computer to transfer the funds, over a period of three days, to the account he had set up at the Banco de Brasil. In each case he authorized the transaction with one of the two numbers he had stolen off Prudence Templeton's list.

Michael sat back and took a deep breath. It was done. There could be no second thoughts, no going back. Everything he had done over the last five years, the self-effacing half of the double life he'd led, had all been for this moment.

But his work wasn't quite over. Michael joined the lines of employees streaming out of the bank. He turned up his collar against the unexpectedly cold April wind twisting and turning in the stone canyons and made for the subway station. A half hour later he was on Christopher Street in the Village, looking for a particular bar that chose not to advertise. He found it, appropriately enough, beneath a sex shop.

Even though it was early, the long, low-ceilinged room was smoky and jammed with men. Leather and denim was the favorite garb of the young crowd, while the older men, cruising for an evening's companionship, preferred vicuña and cashmere. Michael drew admiring looks from both as he passed through. He squeezed into a space at the bar and began his hunt.

In the next two hours Michael turned down better than fifteen offers for drinks, dinner, a show. One old roué even went so far as to offer him a weekend in St. Thomas. Michael continued to sip his beer and scan the room. He'd know his mark as soon as he saw him. And if it wasn't here, he could always try the S and M bars in the meat-packing district below Hudson.

The man was an angel—swept-back golden hair, perfect cheekbones, eyes as moist as a doe's. Much more important, he was exactly Michael's build and height. Michael caught his attention and made room beside him.

"Savage weather, isn't it?" the angel murmured.

"Terrible," Michael agreed. "Whiskey?"

"You're so kind."

The angel's name was Hector, and as Michael had suspected, he was a model who did a lot of work for Brooks

Brothers. They made small talk over drinks, and Hector was delighted by Michael's suggestion about dinner at a Spanish restaurant a few streets away.

"I hear it's *divine!*" Hector whispered.

"But I want to change first," Michael told him. "Come keep me company. I'm just around the corner."

Usually Hector never went to a man's apartment on the first date. He'd had some bad experiences with older men who turned out to be too rough-and-tumble for him. But he so liked Michael . . .

"It's not much to look at," Michael said apologetically, opening the front door and motioning Hector inside.

"Nonsense. I think its cozy—"

That was all the angel managed to say before Michael's fist crashed down behind his ear. Hector staggered from the blow, then crumpled to the floor as Michael hit him again.

Quickly Michael dragged him into the studio apartment and closed the door. He stripped Hector and put him on the Murphy bed, which reached across the room almost to the fireplace. Michael stuffed Hector's clothes into a cheap flight bag, then slipped a chain with a Roman coin on it around Hector's neck. He checked the apartment to make sure he had taken everything he needed and left only what he wanted to be found.

At the mantel he lighted two long candles, which he set on either side of the fireplace. Then he reached into the hearth and turned on the gas.

"Good night, angel!"

He climbed out the window onto the fire escape. The clamor of the traffic drowned out any noise he made, and the pouring rain made people bow their beads as they hurried along, so no one was looking up.

Michael crossed the street and took shelter in the doorway of a bakery already closed for the evening. He didn't have long to wait. The explosion was spectacular, blowing out the windows of the apartment. Within seconds flames shot out, casting a reddish-orange glow over the street. Just as he expected, the building was in such bad condition that the roof collapsed before the fire trucks arrived.

Michael turned his back on the shouts and sirens and walked down to Hudson Street, where he flagged a cab. A twenty-dollar bill silenced the driver's protest about going all the way out to Kennedy Airport. He didn't worry about the driver remembering his face. Eighteen hours from now he would step off the plane in Rio de Janeiro. Two days later he would go under the knife held by one of the best plastic surgeons in the world. The changes to his face would be subtle, just enough so that if he was confronted by someone from his past, that person might remark on a likeness but nothing more than that. For an additional fee the doctor had also agreed to alter his fingerprints.

Michael smiled as the ungainly Checker cab bounced and jolted its way out of Manhattan. As far as the world was concerned, Michael Samson was dead, burned beyond all recognition in a tragic fire. He thought of Prudence Templeton and smiled. He hoped she wouldn't mourn him too long.

They returned to New York just as the sun was setting along the Hudson. Armand insisted that Kate and Emil join him for one last drink before he had to leave for his evening flight to Paris.

"Do you have to go so soon?" asked Kate. She regretted the words even as they left her lips. She realized that during her ordeal she had inadvertently come to rely on Armand, had counted on his presence to calm and reassure her. Now she saw this for what it was becoming: a dependency born of and nourished by the romantic fantasy she'd had of him as a girl. She tried to shake the feeling. She had to guard against illusions. Ted had taught her that much.

"Yes," Armand replied, "I'm afraid I do have to go." He gestured at Bartoli. "But I know you will be well taken care of." He paused. "What will *you* do, Kate?"

"I'm going to stay on, at least for a while. I don't know yet if I want to sell the town house. And the lawyer said there were other things he wanted to go over with me."

Armand took a thin pen of rolled gold from his breast pocket and scribbled a number on the back of a card on which only his name was engraved.

"My private line. You can get through to me on it anytime, day or night. If there's anything I can do for you, Kate, or help you with, you must call."

Armand rose and embraced her, touching her cheek with his three times in the continental fashion. He shook Emil's hand.

"Look after her," he said.

Bartoli noticed how intently Kate stared after Armand as he headed for the elevators. He knew the look well—and exactly what it meant. He was glad, for Kate's sake, that Armand was leaving.

When Armand returned to the suite he called the bell captain to send a porter for his bags. He used the time to make one last call to Alexander's lawyer. The arrangements the attorney had promised to make were in place. Armand would be notified when the window of opportunity opened. The rest would be up to him. Armand expressed his thanks, making it clear to the lawyer that his debt had been repaid. One chance was all Armand ever needed.

Prudence Templeton shivered and drew her coat tightly around her, as much out of fear as from the chill. She had never believed she would have occasion to go to the city morgue. Yet here she was, flanked by two detectives, walking down a dingy tiled corridor, barely able to keep her composure.

She had returned from Pawtucket tired and dispirited. Funerals always depressed her, and she was looking forward to calling Michael and asking him to come over. She needed the feel of his body against hers to drive away her awful loneliness. The thought had made her smile. Michael was so sensitive about such things.

Then she had heard the doorbell. *It couldn't be him, could it?*

Her fantasy had been cruelly dashed by the appearance of the two grim-faced men at her door. They told her about a fire in the Village on the top floor of a tenement and asked if she knew someone by the name of Michael Samson. Yes, she had answered. Then would she mind coming with them? Why? Was Michael hurt? *No, ma'am, I hate to tell you this, but your friend died in the fire. . . . We need you to make a positive identification.*

Prudence recoiled now at the sharp smell of embalming fluid and decaying flesh that hung over the autopsy room. She lowered her eyes so as not to see what lay on the stainless-steel cutting tables and allowed herself to be guided to the built-in wall refrigerator.

"There's been a lot of damage," one of the detectives said. "I know it won't be easy, but please take you time. We have to be sure."

When the coroner's assistant pulled back the sheet, Prudence gasped. The room began to spin, and she steadied herself on the detective's arm. Then she forced herself to look at the charred remains of the face. The image of Michael swam before her eyes, placing itself over the horror so that she could stand it. It was a natural defense mechanism, but it inevitably led to the wrong conclusion. Prudence had been told this was Michael Samson. She had no reason to disbelieve the detectives. Nor to think that by imagining Michael as he had been she was putting his face on a body that did not belong to him.

Prudence nodded. "That's him."

The detective handed her a blackened piece of metal. Prudence looked at it closely, then covered it with her fingers.

"I gave it to him for his birthday," she whispered. "It's a Roman coin, from the time of Julius Caesar."

The detective didn't know about the Caesar part, but the piece had been identified already as an old coin. As far as he was concerned, this was proof positive. The case was closed.

"There are a few more questions," the detective said,

leading her away. He held out his hand. "I'm sorry, but I need the coin back. Maybe you can talk to his next of kin about it."

"He didn't have anyone in the world," Prudence murmured.

She told them the rest in a cramped office that smelled of cold coffee and stale tobacco. Michael Samson was Maltese. He had come to Maritime Continental from Europe the year before. Prudence could relate very quickly the personal details in his employment file because there were so few. During his tenure at the Sauer Bank in Switzerland, he had listed the Red Cross as the beneficiary on his insurance. When he arrived in the States, he had changed that to the United Way. His parents were deceased. There were no brothers or sisters. And no, Michael Samson had never married.

Prudence assured the detectives that the bank's insurance policy on its employees was more than sufficient to give Michael a dignified burial. Of course she would see to all the arrangements.

The two detectives taking her statement looked at each other and shrugged. One of them placed the coin in front of Prudence.

"Look, it's against department regulations, but since Mr. Samson didn't have anybody, why don't you take it? If we hand it over to the probate people, they'll probably lose it. At least this way . . ."

Prudence's fingers trembled as she reached for the coin. First Alexander Maser, now Michael. Oh God, how she had loved them both! And how was she to go on without Michael, without anyone in the world for her to touch?

8

The first alarm went off the following Monday. At ten forty-five, the treasurer of the New York Historical Preservation Society, which purchased and maintained historical properties around the city, received a call from First Hudson Bank informing him that a check for six hundred thousand dollars had not been cleared by Maritime Continental. Puzzled, the treasurer ran down his figures and determined that there should have been more than enough funds to cover the check. He promptly telephoned the Maritime Continental vice president who handled the account and explained the anomaly.

Thirty minutes later the vice president ascertained that the account was indeed short because four hundred thousand dollars had been taken out the previous week. He did not bother to check the nature of the withdrawal, thinking that the Society treasurer, once reminded, would remember it. The treasurer indignantly replied that his figures were accurate and up-to-date and that he had never authorized any such payment.

The apologetic vice president returned to the hunt. In short order he traced the withdrawal as a wire-transfer payment. When he examined the actual documentation, he came to the brink of his second heart attack.

Emil Bartoli agreed to see the vice president immediately. As he reviewed the paperwork, his expression hardened.

"Clear the Society check through discretionary funds," he ordered. "And get me Prudence Templeton!"

No sooner had the vice president, much relieved, departed than a second call came in, this one from a major national charity. Its chairman was incensed because a 1.2 million check had bounced. Bartoli calmed him down and promised to look into the matter immediately. But he couldn't get to it that moment because a third crisis erupted, involving a national political figure whose reelection war chest had just been lightened by two million dollars.

"Miss Templeton, *what* is going on?" Bartoli demanded icily.

Bewildered as much by Bartoli's uncharacteristic display of anger as by the summons itself, Prudence Templeton was completely lost. To make matters worse, she was distracted by her grief over Michael. She had spent the last four days mourning and had used every bit of willpower she possessed to get herself out of bed this morning to come to work. She tried to concentrate on the printouts Bartoli had handed her, but what she saw made no sense at all.

"Excuse me, Mr. Bartoli, are you certain you didn't authorize these transactions?"

"Of course not!"

"The reason I ask is that your code number is listed here."

"I know that! The question is, how did it get there?" Bartoli paused. "And look at the second one."

Prudence Templeton gasped. The second authorization number belonged to Alexander Maser.

"But how?"

"That's what we have to find out—and quickly!"

"Do you think someone . . ." Prudence couldn't bear to finish her question.

Bartoli's silence answered for him.

"I'll get on this right away," she said.

"As quickly as you can, Miss Templeton. We don't know how far the rot has spread."

By the middle of the afternoon Bartoli knew. Three more accounts had been pillaged, and the losses had exceeded six million dollars.

Where is it going to end?

But the worst, which Bartoli prayed wouldn't come to pass, was still to come. No one knows how or where rumors start in the banking world. It might be an overheard conversation, a careless slip of the tongue, a disgruntled employee gloating over some inhouse difficulty. Whatever the case, at three o'clock Bartoli took a call from the chief of the Federal Banking Regulatory Commission. Washington had heard there was a burgeoning scandal at Maritime Continental. The poisonous word *embezzlement* was being whispered in many quarters.

Holding back the details, Bartoli acknowledged that certain irregularities had been discovered. The bank was investigating.

"Not good enough, I'm afraid," the commission chief told him. "Formal charges have been pressed."

Bartoli was aghast. "By whom?"

"Your fair-weather friend with presidential ambitions. He's worried enough about his two million, but he's having a fit because he might be connected to a major scandal."

"That's preposterous!"

"I agree. But he has the clout to get things done. Under the circumstances, I have no choice but to act."

"What do you mean?" Bartoli demanded.

An hour later he had his answer. Three FBI agents along with a team of banking regulators arrived at Maritime Continental, and within minutes they were into the files, digging for the paper trail. They were confident they'd find the proof they needed and they did. "Mr. Bartoli," the senior FBI agent said, "you are under arrest for embezzlement, fraud, and attempting to remove monies in excess of ten thousand dollars from the United States without prior notification to the Treasury Department."

Emil Bartoli was marched out in full view of the office staff.

The moonlight, pouring through the floor-to-ceiling windows of the Park Avenue town house, mesmerized Kate. Kate had left her hotel and moved into a home she hadn't set foot in for five years. She had felt awkward at first, walking tentatively through the rooms and around the elegant furnishings her father had collected over a lifetime. The room Kate entered only once was her father's study.

She was not ready to deal with his sanctuary. She didn't leaf through the photo albums she found in what had once been her bedroom, left exactly as she had remembered it. There wasn't enough strength for that yet.

The house made Kate think of how far she'd gone—gone away, really—and unbidden images of Berkeley drifted into her thoughts. By working in the Berkeley legal clinics, she had made a commitment of sorts—helping those who were struggling to change society. There were enough civil liberties cases to keep her busy for years. And she thought of Ted. She had seen him on television the other night, accompanied by his attorney, Jake Hirsh, giving an interview on the steps of the San Francisco courthouse. Kate had listened closely to what he was saying. The passion and conviction were familiar enough, but something was different. There was an anger and intransigence in Ted's words that she had never heard before.

Or maybe I never wanted to hear it. . . .

Kate couldn't help but wonder if he really wanted to find solutions for the problems he spoke against. Or did he live for the rhetoric, the rallies, the theater?

What kind of man would he be if he didn't have his causes?

Kate knew the answer: not much. *To hell with his posturing and to hell with Rosemary too!*

Kate was wondering about Armand, letting her imagination run free, when the door chimes sounded and the world she was only beginning to come to grips with spun out of control.

"These two gentlemen—" the servant who'd tended the door started to say, walking into the study followed by two men.

"Are you Katherine Maser?" one of them interrupted.

"Yes, I am. What's this all about?"

"I'm Detective Young, ma'am. This gentleman is a federal marshal. We have a warrant for your arrest."

Kate had witnessed dozens of arrests. She knew that

those first few moments, when a suspect felt the police-man's grip and the cold steel of the handcuffs, were the worst. Fear, desperation, panic, even terror—she had seen them all in suspects' eyes.

She couldn't believe it was happening to her. She tried to stay calm. After the detectives had finished reading her her rights, she asked him where they were going and what the charges were.

"The district attorney's waiting for you downtown, Miss Maser," Young told her. "He'll be the one to tell you."

"At this hour?"

"We have our orders, ma'am."

The Manhattan DA's office never closed. The corridors were jammed with prostitutes, thieves, drunks, arresting officers sipping coffee, harried public defenders holding whispered plea bargains with overworked assistant district attorneys. Kate was escorted through the mayhem to the tranquillity of the third floor, the offices of the district attorney's senior associates.

"Your lawyer's waiting," Young said as he opened the door for her.

Behind the brilliantly polished desk, with its inlaid leather blotter, sat a tall, athletic man in his early forties. The creases of his three-piece suit were immaculate, the notes he was making meticulous.

"Saul Muskat, Miss Maser, from Charlie Treloar's office."

Charles Treloar was a familiar name to Kate. He had been her father's lawyer for as long as she could remember. Charles Treloar had also been her mentor, her ideal of what a lawyer should be.

"Where is Mr. Treloar?" Kate demanded.

"Home sleeping. Look, Miss Maser, you don't need corporate commercial advice. The charges against you are criminal. You need a gunslinger. And I'm it."

Unsteadily Kate sat down. "*What* criminal charges?"

Saul Muskat came around and leaned against the front of the desk. His eyes bored into Kate.

"You want to tell me about account forty-seven-eighty?"

Kate shook her head. "I don't know what you're talking about."

"How about the New York Historical Preservation Society?"

"No!"

"The Banco de Brasil in Rio?"

"I never heard of it! Listen, I want to know what's going on!"

"So do a lot of people," Muskat said harshly. "Don't you watch the news?"

"I didn't today."

"So you have no idea what's happened?"

"No. And if I need a lawyer, suppose *you* tell me!"

Saul Muskat looked at her thoughtfully. "Okay. You're charged with embezzling over six million dollars from Maritime Continental. At least that's the figure so far."

"That's crazy!" Kate whispered.

The criminal lawyer had been studying Kate's every move, the pitch of her voice, looking for that tiny discrepancy that would indicate guilt. He hadn't seen it.

"Yeah, well, it's a crazy world. Listen up, Miss Maser, and I'll tell you what happened. Then you can tell me how it was possible."

Without leaving out a single detail, Muskat explained what had happened, from the moment the funds had been discovered missing to the arrest of Kate and Emil Bartoli.

"Emil?" cried Kate. "How is he involved?"

"The wire transfers needed two authentication codes. One belonged to you and your father, the second to Bartoli."

"What codes?"

The lawyer picked up a sheet of paper. "This is a sworn deposition from a Miss Prudence Templeton, who runs the wire-transfer room. According to her records—and we have those too—your father's number and yours were both forty-seven-eighty. Does that ring a bell?"

Kate was thinking furiously. The numbers were familiar.

"Yes, I know!" she said. "That's the access code my father gave so that I could transfer money from here to Berkeley without bothering him."

The lawyer sighed. "Did you know it was *his* personal code as well?"

"No!"

"Well, it was. Sure as hell your father didn't authorize the transfer. So that leaves—"

"Me."

Muskat nodded. "That's the way it looks to the DA."

"How does it look to you?" Kate challenged him.

The attorney smiled. "I think you're innocent. I don't know how all this got started, but I don't believe you played a part in it."

"Thank you, I think," Kate replied. "I would have thought the district attorney would have wanted a few other things before he had a judge cut the warrant. Like a motive."

"As far as he's concerned, he has one," Muskat told her. "You've been affiliated with some weird people out in Berkeley. Most folks call them radicals. And then there's your boyfriend, who keeps making the news when he's not out trying to burn down campus ROTC offices. Word is you embezzled because you support the revolution, whatever that may be."

"That's insane!" Kate whispered.

Muskat shrugged. "It plays for the powers that be. You're going to have to convince them otherwise."

"What about Emil? Is *he* a radical too? Why is he involved?"

"His code is on the transfer papers," Muskat reminded her. "The story is that after your father's passing, his status at the bank was uncertain. You came to him with an offer he couldn't refuse: help me burn the bank, and I'll see to it you're set up for life. Three million dollars, just half of what they've discovered missing so far, can take a man a long way."

"You can't really believe that!" Kate said, dumfounded.

"I don't. But as I said, it plays." Muskat paused. "Look, the DA will want to go over all this with you. Answer him as you answered me. I don't give a damn if he decides right now whether you're innocent or not. I just want him to have doubts. If he's not sure, then I'll get you out of here on bail tonight. Do you have your passport handy?"

"It's at home, my father's house, I mean."

"Good. I'll call and have one of the servants bring it down."

"Why?"

"Tit for tat, counselor. I want you to walk, but I have to give the judge something. If the court has your passport, there's no way you're going to run away to Rio and spend all that money, right?"

"Right," Kate said weakly. She was angry with herself for not seeing the obvious. "I want to see Emil," she said.

Muskat shook his head. "Not allowed until after the DA gets through with you—and him. Cross your fingers, Miss Mascr, and maybe in a while you two will be comparing notes over breakfast at the Plaza."

It wasn't the Plaza but a luncheonette around the corner from the federal courthouse. It was still dark at six o'clock in the morning, and the place was filled with patrolmen, secretaries, clerks, young attorneys, the day shift of the court system. The stained leatherette seats clung to Kate's skirt, and the smell of doughnuts and bacon made her feel queasy.

"I can't tell you how sorry I am, Kate," Emil said, hands around a coffee cup.

Kate thought he looked so out of place in his beautifully tailored Italian suit. She herself felt dirty and exhausted, her throat raw. The assistant district attorney's inquisition had been relentless, his questions, after the fourth time around, frustrating. Kate had been ready to scream.

Then, as if by magic, it was all over. She was standing in front of the judge with Saul Muskat, who was handing over her passport. Bail was set at one million each for her and Emil. The usual ten percent cash requirement was immediately met in the form of a check drawn on Charles Treloar's firm. A hearing date was fixed, the investigation would continue, and she and Emil agreed not to leave the New York metropolitan area without first notifying the court. Failure to do so would result in an immediate warrant for their arrest.

"Emil, what's happened to us?" asked Kate.

"I wish I had an answer, but I don't."

"You have to tell me what you know. Are they sure it's not a clerical error?" she asked, clutching at straws.

"Our own people, not to mention the regulators, would have found that kind of mistake by now," Ernie replied. "No, Kate, some very clever fox went in and looted the henhouse."

"Any idea who?"

He shook his head. "None. Our hiring policies are the most stringent in the business. We demand a complete professional curriculum vitae and character references. We run police and background checks. Believe me, no matter how good the prospect or how much we'd like to have him or her, we don't make an offer until we know all there is to know."

He ground out a cigarette. "Which makes it so hard for me to believe some bastard slipped by us. Someone who not only knew the wire-transfer procedures but was able to obtain the security codes."

"How many people had access to that information?"

"As far as I know—or knew—just myself and Prudence. Obviously I was mistaken."

Kate saw how hurt and angry Emil was. More, she could feel his shame.

"Emil, can you pinpoint which department the thief worked in? Was it the wire room?"

"No question," he replied softly. "It had to be one of the eight clerks working there. Or seven, I should say."

Kate frowned. "Why eight?"

"One of the clerks, Michael Samson, was killed in a fire last week. A gas explosion in his apartment."

"How awful!"

The waitress came by to refill their cups, and Kate waited until she was gone.

"I take it the police are talking to everyone in the wire room."

"Oh, yes. If there's something to be found, they'll unearth it."

"Then it's just a matter of time," Kate said, trying to lift Emil's spirits. "Sooner or later the thief will be caught."

He smiled wanly. "I suppose so. But that doesn't change the fact that I've failed you, Kate. You and your father. Such a thing should never have happened, least of all now."

"Emil—"

"No, let me finish. I may not be in jail, but until I'm declared innocent, I am a terrible liability to the bank. Besides, the Federal Reserve has already appointed an interim overseer."

"No!" Kate declared. "Damn it, you're innocent until proven guilty!"

"Kate, you don't understand! Money has been misappropriated. The scandal is in the open now, and by tomorrow depositors will be pulling their funds out. Oh, we'll hear a lot of pious excuses and promises to come back, but that's lip service. Clients like that *never* return. They don't have to take the chance."

He held up his hand to ward off Kate's protest.

"But there are other problems. We still haven't heard from the Rio bank where the funds were transferred. When we do, the bank can start tracing the criminal's steps, perhaps even recover the discretionary account which has been completely wiped out. But until at least that much is cleared up, there is nothing I can do, as much as I would want to."

Kate took a deep breath and forced down her frustration.

"Whom is the Federal Reserve putting in charge?" she asked.

"There, at least, we have a bit of luck," Emil replied. "They are bringing in Matthew Savage. He used to be with Salomon Brothers but over the last few years has been a troubleshooter for and temporary custodian of banks on the skids. He and I go a long way back. I trust his judgment and decisions. He will do everything he can to keep Maritime

Continental afloat."

Kate looked at him keenly. "There's more, Emil."

He allowed himself a modest smile. "Savage will keep me informed of the investigation. We will know what is happening before the government does."

Kate squeezed his hand. "Emil, I promise you everything will work out. The police will find whoever did this. In a few days it will all seem like a bad dream."

Emil Bartoli held his tongue. His Venetian bones were telling him it wouldn't be as easy as all that. Secretly a very superstitious man, he believed that bad dreams never really went away. They just came back as recurrent nightmares.

Wall Street would come to call it Black Tuesday. By noon of the following day sixty of Maritime Continental's biggest depositors had fled. At the end of the business day that figure had quintupled, threatening the bank's liquidity. Only because Maritime Continental had followed such conservative investment policies did the Federal Reserve come out and publicly state that no depositor's assets were at risk.

Far from reassuring anyone, the Federal Reserve's announcement only served to heighten the stampede. The logic of depositors, skewed as it might be, was: Why would the regulatory body have taken over Maritime Continental if there was nothing wrong with it? The account closures and withdrawals continued at an alarming rate, and no amount of behind-the-scenes pleading or reassurance on Emil Bartoli's part could change that. Even more insulting, individuals with whom Bartoli had done business for years refused to accept his calls. The most devastating blow came on Wednesday. After forty-eight hours of silence the Rio bank, where the embezzled funds had been transferred, informed Matthew Savage and the American regulators that the money was no longer in their accounts. It had been moved via automatic forwarding instructions spelled out in the original telex, a detail the Rio people had conveniently overlooked until after they had pocketed their hefty transaction fee.

"The situation is impossible and getting worse by the minute," Emil told Kate over dinner that evening.

She was alarmed as much by his appearance as by the aura of defeat that hung over him. "Money can't just disappear," she insisted. "There must be records. Somewhere someone has to know something!"

"The trail always comes back to us, Kate." He added bitterly, "You can read all about it in the papers."

Kate knew exactly what he was referring to. The financial press had been cautious rather than evenhanded in its reporting, but other papers were far less charitable, splashing the details of the arrest and alleged embezzlement across the front pages. Furthermore, the regulators weren't coming up with any other suspects. So far there wasn't a grain of evidence against a third party.

All of which only served to irritate Kate further and heighten her sense of frustration. As an attorney she had been trained to use the rules of law not only to construct the best possible defense for her clients, but also to ferret out the pivotal facts on which a case could be made or broken. She had never felt as helpless as she did now. Her enemies were phantoms, playing by rules they had set down, working on a game plan completely foreign to her. She saw herself as floundering, unable to get a grip on any of the forces buffeting her. The feeling of helplessness was both unnerving and frightening.

"One thing bothers me," she said aloud.

"What's that?"

"This Michael Samson's death."

Emil frowned. "I don't understand. It was an accident. He was killed by a gas explosion."

"And burned beyond recognition," Kate added.

"But Prudence identified him. He was wearing some kind of medallion she had given him."

"True," Kate agreed. "And a woman doesn't give a man something so personal if there's nothing between them. It's too much to be simply a Christmas or birthday gift for an office co-worker."

"You're saying they may have been involved?"

From his tone Kate gathered Emil hadn't even considered the possibility. After all, since Prudence Templeton had dressed and behaved like a spinster, that's what she had to be.

"I think it's possible," Kate replied. "For the moment let's assume that was the case. If it was, then there's something you didn't know about Michael Samson, and there might be more."

"From what I remember of his personnel file, everything was in order. In fact, he had sterling references from the Sauer Bank."

"Yes, I read the file too. But do you realize, Emil, that no one really knew him? He was a loner who never so much as had an after-work drink with anyone. Doesn't that strike you as a little odd?"

"Perhaps," Emil admitted. "I can go over his file, trace the references."

"It's a start, but I doubt you'll find anything there. Our Mr. Samson seems to have shared his life with only one person—Prudence Templeton."

It was the apartment of a single woman living alone. But the emptiness did not stop at the four walls. On the sideboard and mantelpiece were touristy mementos of Hawaii and Florida, but no pictures of anyone who might have shared the holidays. The small three-legged circular holders, covered with doilies, had porcelain figurines, but no framed portraits of family or loved ones. The walls were bare except for a crucifix and, in one corner, a picture of St. Paul. The pot on the tea tray was covered by a woollen jacket, the stitching and design identical to the ones on a shawl around Prudence Templeton's shoulders. Long hours of patient work by a woman fighting off silence and loneliness. Kate imagined hearing the clicking of the knitting needles and how loud they must have sounded.

"Thank you, Miss Templeton," Kate said, taking the proffered cup. "It really wasn't necessary."

"Of course it was, Miss Maser. It's so cold outside."

Kate sipped her tea. Grief had done its grim work on Prudence Templeton. Her eyes were red and swollen, the lids puffy. Her eyes darted constantly, yet her voice was terribly calm, as though it belonged to someone else. As she served tea, her blue-veined hands shook perceptibly.

"I really don't know what more I can tell you, Miss Maser. The police and the regulators have asked me hundreds of questions about the people who work—" she caught herself—"that is who *worked* for me. I've told them all I could, including everything about Mr. Samson."

"Did you know him well, Miss Templeton?"

Prudence shrugged. "Not really. He kept to himself mostly."

Kate put down her tea. "Miss Templeton, I'm not here to cause you any more hardship than you're already going through. But I must ask you these questions. You know how much is at stake, what's being said in the papers."

Prudence looked away. "You mean those vile rumors about you and Mr. Bartoli? Pure garbage."

"Of course they are. But the press won't stop there, they love a scandal. Sooner or later they will link you to Michael Samson."

Prudence waved her hand dismissively. "There's nothing to link."

"Miss Templeton, when Michael Samson was killed, you identified his body. You were the one who gave him an expensive medallion. You looked after the funeral arrangements. Besides the priest, you were the only one at his grave. Now you mourn him because you loved him and he is gone." Kate leaned across and touched the other woman's forearm. The skin was ice cold. That and her harsh expression told Kate she'd hit on the truth.

"I don't want to intrude on your privacy or pry into your feelings for Michael Samson," Kate carried on, praying the woman would give her *something* to work with. "But we know so little about him. His employment record doesn't really give us any kind of picture of what kind of man he was. Do you know, Miss Templeton? Can you tell me about

Michael Samson?"

Prudence Templeton stared at Kate with such sorrow and disgust that Kate was shocked.

"You are cruel, Miss Maser," she said at last. "Not because you ask your questions. As difficult as they are for me, I understand that you have some right to ask them. You are cruel because you are everything that I am not: young, beautiful, rich. I am sure you draw men easily; I do not merit even a first glance. And what truly pains me, Miss Maser, is that you don't see any of this. You try to make believe we are the same when you know very well we are not. I find that insulting."

"Miss Templeton—"

"No, you have asked your questions and now I will say my piece. Yes, I loved Michael. Yes, we were lovers. He gave me everything I never had, everything that belongs to women like you. I'm not bitter. I'm telling you this only so that you understand how much I appreciated Michael. More than someone like you can ever know.

"But as you say, Michael was a private man. The time we shared was ours. The past didn't intrude, and as for the future, to tell the truth, I was terrified of it because I knew one day Michael would be gone. So I didn't ask him questions about who he was and where he had been. I reveled in him, accepted what he gave me.

"I can see the question in your eyes: but did I give *him* something? Look around you, Miss Maser. What could I possibly have that he'd want? The wire-transfer room is not the quick way to promotion. And while my recommendation would have carried weight, it alone wouldn't have landed Michael in the executive suite. Michael was very bright. Perhaps he could have risen higher and faster, but he enjoyed his work and he was damn good at it. Beyond that, there's nothing I can say."

Prudence Templeton poured out more tea. It was dark and obviously cold. Kate rose.

"I'm very sorry if I offended you, Miss Templeton. If it's any consolation, I want you to know I think you're innocent, and if necessary, you'll have the best counsel to prove that."

Kate paused. "I have one final request. We haven't been able to find a picture of Michael Samson. If you would have one to spare, I would appreciate a copy."

Prudence Templeton opened the door. "No, I don't have one, Miss Maser. And even if I did, do you really think I would give it to you?" She paused. "Why did you come back? Why did you bring us your troubles? I *know* Mr. Bartoli is innocent. But I can't say the same about you."

9

David Cabot was waiting for Armand in a small hotel near the Ferrari factory in Maranello, Italy. The two men spent Saturday afternoon and all day Sunday going over the evidence David and the engineers had found in the wreckage of Alex's car. By Monday morning when they departed for Rome en route to Beirut, Armand had documented proof that Alex's death had been premeditated murder. But the evidence didn't help to determine the killer's identity.

Armand had been expecting only to change planes in Rome. At Fiumicino Airport, he and David fought their way through the crowds to the refuge of Alitalia's private lounge reserved for its first-class passengers. Its amenities included a television, which was tuned to the national news station. That was when Armand first heard about the mushrooming scandal in New York.

They immediately adjusted their itinerary, driving into Rome to an exclusive businessmen's club where Armand was a member. With a dozen telex links to financial centers, the club was a clearinghouse of concise, up-to-date information. For the next two days Armand and David watched helplessly as the pillars of Maritime Continental splintered and crashed.

"I can't believe it!" David exclaimed, pacing the length of their suite at the club. "Bartoli stealing from the bank? Involved with Katherine Maser?" He laughed shortly. "The saving grace is that the press hasn't managed to get hold of *you* for comment."

Armand stood by the French doors that opened onto the balcony. He was brooding, staring down at but not seeing the tourists as they huffed and puffed their way up the Spanish Steps.

"Someone is out to destroy Maritime Continental," he

said, his voice icy soft. "Why? Is it some vendetta that had
to do with Alexander? Or is the bank their *first* target? Do
they know more about its activities, its connections, than we
think?"

He looked at David. "As for Bartoli, he's just trying to
keep me out of his trouble."

He paused. "Don't I sound like a callous old bastard?
Bartoli is a friend of mine. His reputation is being destroyed, yet I don't lift a finger to help him. The irony is
that he's doing exactly the right thing but for reasons he
doesn't know anything about."

"What about Katherine?" David asked.

"I don't understand her involvement at all!" He slapped
the wrought-iron balcony railing with both palms, causing
the metal to vibrate and hum. "In fact, I think it's a gross
mistake on the part of the New York authorities. Whoever
used Alexander's security number wanted the blame to fall
on him, not Kate."

"You're sure?" David asked. "You don't think there's
anything to this alleged link with the radicals?"

Armand snorted. "Kate wants to change the world, not
blow it up. Her involvement with this Ted Bannerman may
have been bad judgment, but that's the extent of it.
Somehow I have to help her."

Arms folded across his chest, Armand turned his back to
the Steps.

"I think—no, I am sure—that what is happening to
Maritime Continental is somehow linked to Alex's death."

David smiled wanly. It was typical of Armand to ask a
question with a statement. "Of course," he replied. "The
problem is the link. What is it? Why was it forged? By
whom?" David continued to fire questions. "Who stands to
gain with Alexander and the bank gone? And what would
they get through that?"

Armand's raised eyebrows, which made him look almost
satanic, spoke eloquently.

"Nothing from Paris yet, I'm sorry," David said.

He pressed his hand to David's shoulder. The younger

man's haggard appearance was testimony to how tirelessly
David had been working to unearth some clue to the identity
of Alexander's killer. Armand knew that David would not
rest until he had found the answer.

"We should be getting back to Beirut," David was saying.
"I told my people in Paris to call me there if anything
broke."

"There's something I must do first. Alex had papers that
detailed our activities—"

"What?"

"I have similar ones," Armand said. "They exist for just
such a contingency: to allow others, in my case, you, to pick
up and carry on in case something happened to either
Alexander or myself." He produced a thin, flat key, then
said, "Alex's safety-deposit box was sealed at the time of
his death. His attorney told me that the order would be re-
scinded by this coming Friday, day after tomorrow. I had
been planning to return then to New York."

David turned the key over in his fingers.

"Who has the other one?"

Armand gave him a pointed look. "Kate. I don't think she
even knows the box exists. I want to be there as soon as the
legal formalities are done with. Who knows? Maybe Alex
left us something we can work with."

Kate had no choice but to barricade herself in her home.
When she returned from her ordeal at the district attorney's
office, she had to fight her way through the reporters parked
on her doorstep. There was no sanctuary inside either. The
phone rang incessantly, and she finally told the servants to
leave it off the hook.

Through sleepless nights Kate searched for answers. She
called Emil several times a day, but his secondhand accounts about the news at Maritime Continental were heart
wrenching. Depositors were bailing out in droves.

"Haven't the police found *anything*?" Kate demanded.

"Nothing that would help us. But at least they absolved
Prudence Templeton of any blame. She has nothing to fall

back on if she should lose her job."

Kate struggled to believe that their luck would change. Calls to Saul Muskat did nothing to lift her spirits.

"Neither the police nor the feds have anything to go on," the lawyer told her. "That Michael Samson character you told me about? Well, Prudence Templeton gave him a gilt-edged reference. As far as the police are concerned, he's clean. They're not even looking in that direction anymore."

That, as much as anything, troubled Kate. She found the coincidence unsettling and refused to believe that she was so overwrought as to be making connections that obviously weren't there.

There had to be an answer, she told herself. Or a place where she could find one.

Kate sat down and thought hard about her father's personal habits. It was a frustrating exercise. So much time had slipped by. What had been his quirks, his little idiosyncrasies? She tried to remember her teenage years, and even earlier when her mother had been alive. She called back her mother's comments, parenthesized by laughter, about her husband's personal habits. Nothing clicked. Then she tried to recall if her father had said or shown something special to her, a secret he had shared only with her. And there it was, a small box, the size of a jewelry case, teak with inlaid ivory, made over a hundred years ago in Thailand. Her father had brought it back from a trip, and when Kate had asked what was inside, he had smiled and said, "That's where I keep my secrets."

Kate opened the door to the study. Slowly she looked around the floor-to-ceiling bookcases, the beautiful desk, the huge mounted globe, and dozens of pictures in sterling-silver frames. She almost wept because her father was still alive here.

And there was the Thai box, the wood glowing from countless polishings, sitting on a shelf next to her picture. Kate brought it down and held it for a very long time. Her father's secrets.

She drew back the lid. There was a long, thin key . . .

Horn-rimmed glasses prominent on his pale face, Nelson was waiting for Armand when the doors of the First Manhattan Bank opened punctually at nine-thirty.

"Ah, Mr. Fremont. I've received instructions from Mr. Maser's attorney—"

"I'm aware of them," Armand said shortly as he swept by Nelson. "I trust I may access the box now?"

"Of . . . of course. I'll show you the way."

"I know the way, Mr. Nelson, thank you."

As he crossed the floor to the steps that descended to the vault, Armand watched the two other revolving doors, keeping track of the people coming into the bank. The chances were slim, perhaps nonexistent, but he couldn't be sure that through some terrible coincidence Kate wouldn't suddenly materialize in the crowds.

The guard downstairs, an older man, was courteous. His master key and Armand's copy unlocked the box. The guard drew out the long, thin box and brought it into a cubicle, closing the door. Armand flipped open the cover and removed a thick manila envelope, folded in half. The clues to Alex's death, if any, were at his fingertips. The temptation to break the seal Alex had affixed to the flap, to be sure one way or the other, was almost overwhelming. At the instant he was about to succumb, he slipped the envelope into his attaché case. A minute later he was headed up the stairs to the lobby, once again carefully checking the traffic in the bank. It was her voice he heard first.

"I don't care what you've been told! I have every right to get that box!"

"Miss Maser, believe me, it's nothing personal," a helpless Nelson was saying. "But we have instructions from the district attorney's office and our lawyers—"

"Fine! Then you follow those, and I'll do what I have a legal right to do!"

With a toss of her head Kate stormed past the beleaguered official into the stairwell, passing less than ten feet from where Armand was standing, partially screened by a massive granite pillar. The thought of going after her entered his mind, but he dismissed it almost in the same instant. Clever girl, thought Armand. How did she find the second key? He knew she hadn't gotten it from Alex's lawyer.

He owed Kate better than this, but he owed Alex even more. If there was truth to be found among these papers, it was not something that Kate needed to know about.

"May I help you, miss?"

Kate took a deep breath. "My name is Katherine Maser, and I'd like you to get box number one twelve A for me, please. The number code is two eight seven five. Here is my key."

She managed a smile, hoping it would help overcome the guard's hesitation. "Is something wrong?" she asked.

"No, miss, not really," the man replied. "Just strange to have two people asking for the same box five minutes apart."

Kate's heart jumped. "Please! I must get into that box!"

"Right away, miss!" the guard declared, twisting his key.

"No, don't bother taking it anywhere," Kate said. "Just hold it."

She pried open the lid and stared at emptiness.

Think, Kate! Don't you dare panic!

"The man who was in here before me? Who was he?"

"Can't say, miss."

"But he must have signed in! Everyone has to."

"Yes," the guard said warily. "But I can't let you see the ledger, if that's what you're getting at."

Kate could have hugged him. "Of course you can. In fact, I should have signed in before I opened this, isn't that right?"

The guard gave her a broad wink. "Those are the rules."

She raced to the ledger and ran her finger down to the last name. Fortunately the handwriting was neat. Armand Fremont—passport number ZN26845—country of issue, Lebanon.

*Lebanon . . . Armand. Why was Armand back? What was go-
ing on? And why had he not told her he was coming back . . . ?*

Kate dashed out of the bank and down Forty-eighth Street
to the Barclay Hotel. She searched for a public telephone
and found one next to the bar. She fumbled in her pocket-
book for change, and seconds later she was talking to a
helpful travel agent at American Express. There was no direct flights to Beirut from New York. Connections had to be
made either through London, Paris, or Rome. According to
the agent the connection through Rome was the most conve-
nient, only a two-hour layover. Would Miss Maser like to
reserve a seat?

"That won't be necessary," Kate replied, and hung up.
She knew where to find Armand—and why he had come to
New York. He hadn't traveled six thousand miles to find an
empty safety-deposit box. He had come to *take* something
. . .

The ice in his vodka martini had melted, but Armand
Fremont hadn't noticed. Nor was he aware of the hum in
Pan Am's busy Clipper Lounge while he waited for the
Rome flight to be called. Beside his chair stood his briefcase, firmly locked. The fine leather was like silk beneath
his fingertips, but he felt as though he were touching a live
bomb.

Beware of your fondest wishes lest they come true . . .

The bitter truth of the Chinese proverb rankled. He had
wanted nothing more than to know who had been responsible for Alex's death. Now he did, and he was sickened. His
imagination had conceived mysterious enemies or powerful
interests as the murderers. But not this. *Never this!*

Armand touched the rim of his glass and looked out the
soundproof plate glass to the runways. The murderer had
been family, someone he never would have suspected.

Pierre.

The notes Alex had left behind detailed how and when
he had gotten wind of Pierre's having embezzled funds
from the national bank of Lebanon.

Pierre covered his tracks very well, Alex had written. *Without an informer coming forward, it would have been almost impossible to trace the money to him. But there had been such a man in one of the London banks who had become suspicious about the sudden deposits, had done some quiet checking, smelled the embezzlement.*

Stapled to this handwritten note were photostats of the bank's statements. The amounts involved were staggering.

Another note detailed Alex's confrontation with Pierre, Pierre's indignant reaction, and how it collapsed before Alex's relentless questioning. Finally the reason was torn loose.

"For God's sake, Pierre, don't tell me you did it for Cleo!"

But he had. No amount of begging or pleading had moved me.

"It's over, Pierre. If this is what it takes to keep her, then I'm afraid you cannot have her. You have sixty days to make restitution. Once I am satisfied that has been done, I will expect to read about your resignation."

Truly I have never seen a more pitiful man than the one facing me at that moment.

"But what will I do? How will I live?"

I could offer him nothing. "I do not know—but not as you have. Not ever again."

And Pierre understood that the alternative was a scandal that would ruin him.

But there was a second alternative, Armand thought, a possibility Alex had never considered: that Pierre, cornered, would strike back. That's what Pierre had decided upon. That was the reason for the second meeting in Paris, one which, according to Alex's notes, Pierre had asked for.

Alex believed Pierre was giving up, Armand realized, that he was coming to tell him how he would repay the money. Instead, he told him nothing of the kind. That was when Alex asked Armand to meet him, when he got into the car to drive to Geneva. Never suspecting Pierre already knew that was exactly what he would do. . . .

Now, without Alex's corroboration, the notes could be contested. Armand had already decided to retrace Alex's steps, but there was no guarantee he would get what he needed: third-party confirmation from Alex's source in the British bank. If Pierre had gone to these lengths to deal with Alexander, then the still-anonymous Englishman was probably dead as well.

Armand tasted his drink and grimaced. The asthmatic, taciturn Pierre a killer? The idea was absurd. Pierre was not a man of action. Moreover, he didn't have the expertise to tamper with the Ferrari. He would have had to hire a professional. But was Pierre the kind of man who would know where to look for a killer much less a way to contact one? Of course not!

Which meant he had an accomplice . . .

Cleo's image once again snapped into Armand's mind. Less than a week after Pierre had started seeing Cleo, Armand knew everything about her. She wasn't in the same league as the beautiful, idle women who prowled Beirut's parties and clubs in search of a rich husband, but on her own scale Cleo was an adventuress. Proof of her skills was that she had snared a prize that had deluded other Beiruti predators. Armand had not begrudged her her trophy. It had been a fair hunt, without intimations of blackmail or other threats. For his part Pierre was very happy.

Could it have been costing him so much to keep her happy?

Armand considered the possibility. Pierre's life-style had certainly become more extravagant since Cleo, but he was a very wealthy man to begin with, and a stickler when it came to living within one's means. He frowned upon others' debts and would have despised them in his own circumstances. Armand couldn't believe that money difficulties had anything to do with Pierre's actions.

As for Cleo being an accomplice, her guile and talents were suited to the bedroom, not to finding and hiring an assassin.

It all came down to *why* Pierre had embezzled the money,

Armand thought. Knowing that would be a starting point to find out who else was involved in the crime, who had helped Pierre or maybe even blackmailed him into committing it. Armand knew he would have to be very careful from this point on. His inclination, driven by the fury of his discovery, was to confront Pierre the moment he landed in Beirut. But that would not do. He had to watch Pierre, listen and learn and hope the governor of the Banque de Liban would play out enough rope with which Armand could then hang him.

The irony was that Armand, who recognized how anger could blind, never suspected he was missing the point completely. Fear that the embezzlement would be discovered, which he was sure was Pierre's motive, was not necessarily the entire motive. Armand never considered that Pierre's accomplice might have had entirely different reasons for wanting Alexander Maser dead.

"I want what you took from me."

As startled as he was by Kate's voice, Armand did not show his surprise.

"Hello, Kate," he said quietly, getting to his feet.

The anger and confusion in her eyes made him flinch.

"You owe me an explanation," she said. "For a lot of things."

"Yes, I do," he agreed. "How did you find me?"

"I just missed you at the bank."

"I see." Armand gestured for her to sit. "Would you like a drink?"

"No. I want you to tell me why you came here without letting me know. I want to see what you took from my father's safety-deposit box."

"Both Alex and I had keys," Armand told her. "I had a right to do what I did."

"Fine. Then I have just as much right to see what was in there."

The first announcement of the gate for boarding the Rome flight came over the loudspeaker. The lies tasted like ashes in Armand's mouth.

"I haven't even looked at those papers," Armand told her. "It may well be that they don't concern you at all."

"For God's sake, Armand! Haven't you heard what's happening to Maritime Continental? And Emil Bartoli?"

"Yes . . . and to you as well. Kate—"

"I've been praying that you would call. Every time the phone range—" she bit her lip. "Now you come to New York without even letting me know. And you wouldn't have done that unless you had a damn good reason."

She gripped his hand. "Help me, Armand, please. If my father left anything I could use . . ."

Armand heard the boarding announcement for his flight. He silently cursed himself for not having seen what, in Kate's anger and anguish, was so clear. What if the destruction of Maritime Continental wasn't complete? What if, in an evil master design he could not yet discern, Alexander's only heir had to be removed as well?

"Come with me," he said urgently. "There's nothing for you here, no one who can help you. Whatever's happening to Maritime Continental, *to you,* you won't find the answer here."

Kate backed away. "Are you crazy?"

Armand held her by the shoulders. "Listen to me! Everyone thinks you looted your father's bank. The evidence may be circumstantial, and a good lawyer might get you off. But that doesn't vindicate you. Suspicions will remain. They will cripple your career and dog you for the rest of your life! I'm giving you a chance to prove your innocence. I want to help you. But you must make the decision. Right now!"

Kate's mind was spinning. What Armand was saying was madness! But deep down she also knew it was the truth. The judicial system might vindicate her in the end, but she would be pilloried in the process. More important, if she stayed she wouldn't have the means or the freedom to find out exactly who it was who had ruined Maritime Continental. Armand was offering her that chance.

"I need your decision, Kate."

She closed her eyes. Did she really have a choice? She had to find the truth behind Maritime Continental's ruin. Her fate as well as Emil Bartoli's and her father's reputation depended on that. Without proof that they were all innocent, there would never be any rest for her.

"I don't have a ticket," she blurted. "I had to give up my passport—"

"I will look after everything."

Kate stared at Armand, knowing she was about to make a life-changing decision. As upset as she was with this man, she believed wholeheartedly that she could trust him, and not just to "look after everything," but to give her good advice with her best interests at heart. She took a deep breath.

"Okay, I'll leave with you . . . no passport, no ticket, no clothes. I just hope you can work miracles with airlines and immigration officials."

He smiled at her, then surprised her mightily by giving her a broad wink. "Merlin off to work wonders," he said jauntily before swiftly walking toward the desk at the entrance to the lounge.

Oddly enough, Kate reflected, she felt calm, reassured, and consoled by Armand's obvious self-confidence in this situation. Feeling peculiarly detached, she watched as he swung into action, first initiating phone calls, then walking off with a young woman who had arrived in the lounge, obviously at his request.

A considerable amount of time passed. Kate was beginning to get edgy when the young woman who'd left with Armand returned, coming directly over to her.

She smiled charmingly. "Miss Maser, I'm a friend of Mr. Fremont's. My name is Elizabeth. We have some business to conduct, you and I, and it is best done in private. Will you follow me?"

Kate nodded, gathered up her handbag and jacket, and followed the attractive Elizabeth along the same path Armand had taken before. They entered a private office, where he was on the telephone.

"Since Mr. Fremont is still busy on the phone and time is of the essence here, let me explain what we are going to do. Mr. Fremont recalled seeing me earlier here at the airport and had me paged. I've just returned from a European run. He thinks that you and I look enough alike to be able to double for each other if someone is doing only a cursory scan." She paused and eyed Kate from head to toe. "We are of about the same height and weight, and our coloring is similar, yes?"

Kate murmured an agreement.

"I am going to provide you with my passport. I think if you wear some glasses, perhaps a hat, too, and if you don't look too directly at any of the immigration men you encounter, you'll have no trouble." Elizabeth went to a chair near the door and pulled a document from her purse there. She strode back to Kate's side and handed her the passport.

Dumbfounded, Kate accepted it, but she couldn't help blurting, "You would do this for a stranger?" The lawyer in her wouldn't let her stop there. "You're breaking the law. You could get into terrible trouble for this, do you understand? And how will you work, what will you do while I have your passport?"

Elizabeth laughed with delight. "Trust Armand Fremont to make it worth my while to be a little under the weather for a few days and have to bow out of my next assignment." She sobered. "I do understand the seriousness of what I'm doing, but I also understand how much Mr. Fremont did for me about a year ago when I was having a very bad time. Loaning you my passport is the very least I can do in return." She smiled again. "Besides, that document will be returned to me within three days, brought back by a very good friend who does the Beirut–Rome–New York run. Not to worry."

Swallowing hard, Kate looked down at the passport. To get out of the country and to Beirut, she would be Elizabeth Bartholomew. She glanced up and started to say how grateful she was.

"Stop," Elizabeth said. "We haven't much time. Mr.

Fremont is arranging your ticket now. I expect it will be delivered to the gate before the final boarding call. Let's get a bit of shopping done for some toiletries and whatever else we can find in the duty-free shop that will help you get through the next seventeen hours."

Before she knew it, Kate was whisked through a shop or two, Elizabeth paying for everything, met Armand at the gate, and was settled next to him in a first-class seat. As the plane taxied to the runway, she was struck with the enormity of what she was doing.

Katherine Maser, an officer of the court, had crossed the line and become a fugitive.

High over the Atlantic, Kate felt herself succumb to panic. She tried hard to steady herself.

No one forced you into this, girl. It was your choice to make, and you made it.

But if Kate was going to suffer the consequences, whatever they might be, she'd damn well get what she had come after, what had gotten her into these impossible circumstances in the first place.

"I want to see what you took from my father's safety-deposit box," she said to Armand after the dinner service had been cleared away.

Armand looked at her coolly.

"I'm sorry, I can't do that."

"Damn you, whatever was in there belonged to my father!" Kate cried softly. "It might help me to figure what's happening to Maritime Continental, why it's being destroyed."

"Kate, I understand how you feel. I am as concerned as you are about the bank. You trusted me—or your instinct—far enough to get on this plane. I am asking you to extend that trust a little further. This is neither the time nor the place to start looking through what your father left. But believe me, if I find something that I feel you should know, which is related to what is happening to the bank, I will tell you immediately.

"Now, it is a long flight to Rome. You have had an exhausting day, so I suggest you get some sleep."

Kate saw that it was no use to argue, but she had to try to make him understand.

"You're right, Armand," she said. "I *have* trusted you, and I'm risking not only my career but a prison term for having done this. Don't hold out on me. Share with me. Give me something I can fight back with!"

Armand was struck by the force of Kate's words. Watching her as she shifted in her seat to find a comfortable sleeping position, he suddenly realized that she was not at all the grieving, wounded woman he had comforted at the funeral, much less the shy teenager he'd had in his mind's eye when he had left Beirut. Her determination and resilience surprised him, made him wonder how much more there was to discover about her.

Alexander would have been proud . . .

The cabin lights were dimmed, and one by one the passengers drifted off to sleep. Bathed in a pool of overhead light, Kate watched Armand's chest rise and fall. Men asleep revealed so much of themselves, their content or vexation, the peace or fury of their hearts, the candor or deception that grew in their souls. If Armand harbored any regrets or misgivings, Kate did not see them. His weathered face was a study of smooth planes and shadows, no nervous tics or twitching muscles. Kate envied him his peace . . . and wondered if this was the time to slip away, ease open the overhead bin, and reach for the briefcase Armand had placed there. It would surely be locked, but she could take it into the rest room, go to work on the clasps with the trusty Swiss Army knife she always carried in her purse.

The instant Kate became convinced she could successfully open the briefcase, she also realized she would never do it. In a way she could not articulate, she felt she would be betraying him. By going to sleep he had declared his trust in her, making himself vulnerable. It was, Kate thought, as though he'd know that such an expression of faith was his most powerful protection.

PART TWO

[Beirut is] a kind of
Las Vegas–Riviera–St. Moritz
flavored with
spices of Araby.

—*Life* Magazine, 1965

10

Kate waited in a small outer office as Armand dealt with Beirut customs and immigration. Her head rested on the back of the chair, her eyes closed over tears. She wasn't afraid now, not even the least apprehensive about leaving the United States as she had. Her emotion was for this place where her father had been born, his home. She felt as if fate had brought her here, perhaps to tell her that the home of her father could be her home too.

It had come rushing at her, so much emotion, as the plane had prepared to land, circling Beirut in wide arcs. The pictures were still vivid beneath her lids. The distant Shouf Mountains, dark green and capped with dollops of snow, gave way to a series of foothills, dusty brown terraces speckled with red bougainvillea, the roofs of villas carved into the slopes. Suddenly the city had risen from the plain, the glass-and-steel skyscrapers gathering all the sunlight, magnifying it a hundredfold, then reflecting it back across a sprawl of white stucco, orange tile, and brick.

"Beautiful, isn't it?" Armand had murmured.

"More than that," she'd said, her voice choked. "It's magical."

Armand had chuckled. A sound so intimate to Kate that she had felt bumps rise on her flesh. "Everybody has your reaction, Kate," he'd said softly. "People who have been to Acapulco, Monte Carlo, Hong Kong, San Francisco, people who think nothing can impress them anymore, they melt when they see Beirut. It's like no other place in the world."

"Even for someone like me who got here in a very . . . well, accidental fashion?"

"Ah, Kate, especially for someone like you."

The mere memory of his voice now made her shiver. Kate forced herself to open her eyes wide and sit up straight. Dear God, were her emotions running wild? Completely out of her control? Her father's homeland. Armand. Oh, yes, Armand was getting to her. They hadn't really been alone together before this flight. The people surrounding them and the rushing events of the past weeks had made it easy for her to repress and deny the feelings he evoked in her. But not now. Not after the last seventeen hours they'd spent together. He was everything he'd been to her as a girl of twelve . . . with promises of much, much more.

"All is taken care of, Kate," Armand said into Kate's ear, startling her so that she jumped. His hands gripped her upper arms lightly to steady her, and he leaned forward, his eyes full of mischief "Did you think," he whispered, "that I was a policeman, here with shackles to take you away?"

She laughed, perhaps a little too loudly, delighted at his touch, his lightheartedness, at being in Beirut, at being alive and free. "*Are* you my special cop?"

"Certainly not. Your tour guide, madam. Come, just outside here in the terminal you can get your first real taste of Beirut. I'm sure you've forgotten everything from your last trip."

"Hmmm, not quite everything," Kate murmured, rising and taking Armand's arm to go into the terminal.

Emerging from the air-conditioned office, they stepped into a pillow of dry, silky heat that was thick with the scent of orange. Armand gestured toward the shops, and Kate's eyes widened. She'd walked into a bazaar. The halls were lined with window displays from Europe's most exclusive designers—Gucci, Chanel, Dior. French and Italian jewelers as well as every major Swiss watch manufacturer were represented, their velvet-lined cases holding a dazzling array of gold, diamonds, and precious stones set in exquisite mountings. Arabs in flowing white robes bordered with black and gold, Western businessmen in hand-tailored three-piece suits, women sporting the latest Mary Quant fashions from London's Carnaby Street, crowded the cool green marble floors.

But it was not all unabashed opulence. Closer to the exits Kate saw the less expensive tourist shops, their wares over-flowing from the shelves onto the floor. There were leather bags, rugs, "genuine" antiquities, and every conceivable shape of narghile, the ubiquitous brass "hubbly-bubbly" pipe, made expressly for American and European tourists so they could prove that they really had been to the Middle East.

Shwarma stands, where black-robed women sliced off strips of meat from a joint revolving on a tall standing skewer, jostled for space with vendors who crushed fresh mint into their vanilla ice cream, and drink carts that offered everything from local *arak* to sixty-year-old cognac. Ancient porters with red fezzes, their backs curved like tuning forks, carried what seemed like impossible burdens, while sharp-eyed, gap-toothed boys scampered through the crowds at waist level, their swift, clever hands dipping into purses and trouser pockets.

"It's one giant carnival!" Kate exclaimed.

"Just the introduction," Armand told her, and cuffed an urchin whose hand was reaching for the watch on Kate's wrist.

Outside the terminal a pearl-white Rolls-Royce was wait-ing for them, the chauffeur holding the door open.

The drive took them along Beirut's major artery, the oceanside Grand Corniche. On the left side Kate could see golden beaches stretching the length of the boomerang curve, the sand speckled with red, blue, and yellow umbrel-las. Sunbathers, stretched out on towels or on loungers, seemed to be one on top another yet somehow tawny girls, their sunglasses bigger than their bikini bottoms, wended their way as easily as you please to the water's edge.

Armand noticed the *O* formed by Kate's lips and chuckled.

"Not *quite* like California, is it? Almost everyone goes topless here."

Kate smiled and looked to her right, where there were grand apartment buildings that reminded her of the fashion-able quarters of Paris. In between them were the famous hotels—the legendary St. Georges, whose restaurant her father had so much enjoyed, and the Phoenicia, the newest one, whose three-tiered swimming pool with connecting waterfalls was, Armand mentioned, already a landmark.

"And this is home," he announced.

The car had swung off the Corniche and climbed effortlessly into the hills, along narrow lanes bordered by olive trees and the pastel-colored stucco walls of private villas. After a dozen twists and turns it entered a gated drive and stopped before a three-story mansion overlooking St. George's Bay.

"Balthazar will look after you," Armand said, indicating the waiting gray-haired gentleman in a white jacket and black trousers, every inch a polished, professional retainer. "Unfortunately, I have to go to the casino. But I'll come by for you around eight. We'll have an early dinner and talk then."

Before Kate could protest, Armand was leaving. When Balthazar guided her inside the cool interior, washed by the sea wind and anointed by the scent of the gardens, Kate realized just how exhausted she was.

"Let me show you to your room, mademoiselle," he suggested. "The maid will draw you a bath, and you can have a massage if you like. Then a nap, perhaps?"

"A bath sounds perfect," Kate said gratefully.

Her room turned out to be picture-perfect Laura Ashley with matching flower-pattern curtains, bedspread, and canopy. The French doors leading to the balcony were ajar just enough for Kate to smell the sea. After Balthazar had excused himself, Kate stripped off her traveling clothes and lay back on the marvelously soft bed.

"Five minutes," she murmured. "Just five minutes, then I'll . . ."

And she was asleep.

The fifteen acres of land at the tip of the horseshoe peninsula jutting out into the Mediterranean were the most prized and valuable in all of Lebanon. Purchased from the sultan of the Ottoman Empire in 1861, they had remained intact in the hands of the Fremont family, surviving all the political turmoil that swirled unabated across the breadth and width of Arabia.

The land had been sold because it was little more than a series of rocky ledges, useless for agriculture or herding. But that was not what Aristide Fremont had in mind when he paid the sultan his one thousand gold napoleons. On the plain and foothills behind him, along the beaches and rocky coastlines to the north and south, he saw in his mind's eye a mighty city, which would one day become the bridge between East and West. For Aristide Fremont was a student of history who knew the stories of the region better than the inhabitants did. A magnificent race of traders called the Phoenicians had made this land their home fourteen centuries before Christ, and this city, the greatest merchant capital the world had ever seen.

Beirut had been the crossroads of trade for Egyptians, Canaanites, Greeks, and Babylonians. In Aristide Fremont's imagination, one day all the world would again come to Beirut. To welcome and embrace it, he built what was considered to be the first modern wonder of the Arab world: the Casino de Paradis, the Paradise Casino.

The building consumed almost all of Aristide's fortune, gleaned from a lifetime of trade in the region. Only materials indigenous to the area were used: granite blocks carved out of quarries in the Shouf Mountains, the precious cedar that had been a favorite of King Solomon, glass and metal created in a hundred different forms and hues by artisans using methods that had remained unchanged for centuries. The construction, supervised by Europe's preeminent architect, Charles Garnier, took over ten years, but when the casino was completed a year after the end of the Franco-Prussian struggle, a war-weary world knew immediately that something extraordinary had been bequeathed it.

The casino was an unqualified success the moment it opened its doors on May 3, 1872. Royalty, aristocracy, merchant princes, and gamblers of every persuasion sailed the length of the Mediterranean or endured week-long train journeys via Istanbul to reach it. When they did, they were convinced they had stepped into an earthly paradise.

Guarded on three sides by jagged coral outcrops and the booming tides of the Mediterranean, and on the fourth by high, spiked wrought-iron gates, the grounds of the casino were an arboreal fantasy. Dozens of varieties of trees and shrubs had been imported to shade and accent the pristine lawns. The flower beds were repositories of the world's most exotic specimens, carefully tended by a small army of gardeners.

But such a setting was merely a hint of the glories of the interiors of the casino. It actually consisted of four separate buildings linked by magnificent galleries. Following the major theme of the Belle Epoque, architect Garnier had chosen the Liberty style, a triumph of sensuality, curves, rotundas, and feminine aesthetic. Although conceived and executed on a grand scale, the entrance, concert and spectacle halls and the gaming salon, which included private rooms, the cabaret, and the famous Bluebird restaurant, radiated warmth and intimacy. Nymphs, melancholy youths dreaming over a leafless rose, peasant girls chased by satyrs, offered a pastel mood with hints of decadence.

For almost a century the masterpieces that Aristide Fremont had chosen so presciently had looked down upon the virtues and follies of a hundred different nationalities, creeds, and races. The figures in the hand-woven Flemish tapestries had eavesdropped on the murmurs of princesses and maharajas. The ebony roulette tables had imprinted upon them the hands of gaming sheiks who, in thoughtless innocence, had brought not only gold but slaves as collateral. The vaulted, stained-glass rotundas still carried faint echoes of the curses and prayers cast upon them by desperate men who had arrived in frayed dinner suits convinced, as only true gamblers can be, that one spin of the wheel or throw of the dice would change their destinies forever.

Perhaps even more than gaming, it was illusion that the casino catered to. In the midst of such substance and opulence, it was impossible not to believe that one was some-how charmed, fated to win. And it was the allure of the illu-sion, with its tantalizing promise of victory, that without pity or mercy drew the prince and the pauper, the Sybarite and the recluse, the virgin and the courtesan.

Three stories above the entrance hall, running the sixty-foot width of the building, was Armand Fremont's office. Referred to as the Crystal, it had windows facing both the exterior entrance, with its wide steps, circular drive, and garden in the background, and the interior, overlooking the vaulted antechamber. The glass on the interior side was one way, allowing Armand to study his arriving guests without their knowledge. At this particular moment he was watching as Jasmine, gowned in a garnet-red creation he correctly identified as a Dior, made her way past Salim, his giant of a chauffeur, and up the carpeted staircase to his retreat.

In contrast to the other rooms in the casino, the Crystal verged on the austere. The far walls were hung with Armand's favorite paintings—old masters and a handful of van Goghs—and the floor was covered with an enormous Shariz rug that his father, Aristide, had accepted as payment from a member of the Saudi royal family. In contrast, the desk and credenza, both custom designed, had clean Scandinavian lines. The telephone system and the audio-video surveillance apparatus were state-of-the-art.

"We are about to have company," Armand said, indicat-ing the television monitor.

David looked up from his reading, saw Jasmine on the screen, and put away the papers Armand had brought back from New York.

"So we know who and why," he said tonelessly.

"We have identified the *principal*," Armand corrected him. "Not the *accomplice*."

"I'm sure I can convince Pierre to remedy that."

The intensity of David's gaze unsettled Armand. Although David had read the words that damned Pierre in silence, Armand could feel the anger churning within him.

He wasn't afraid that David would act rashly; he never did that. "We do not yet know enough to approach Pierre directly," Armand hastened to say. "Given what Alexander left us, can you retrace his steps?"

David shrugged. "Alexander had a contact inside one of the British banks Pierre is using. Finding out who that was won't be a problem. But if Alex paid for the information and the man bolted—" David checked his watch. "London won't be open for another nine hours. I'll call then."

He rose and looked at Armand. "We don't have to wait, you know. There are ways to rattle Pierre's gilded cage— anonymous voices in the middle of the night calling to tell him they know all about his secrets, a photostat of a portion of Alex's notes. Pierre is fragile, Armand. He'll crack or run. Either way it may be the best chance we'll have to pinpoint his partner."

The idea was tempting, and Armand had no doubt David could force Pierre into panicking. But something held him back, the fear that the accomplice was far more slippery, much more dangerous than Pierre.

"Find out what you can in London," Armand said.

"Let me start digging here too," David insisted. "No personal involvement on my part, everything at arm's length. I can nail down his daily routine, habits, and so on. We'll have to know a hell of a lot more about him before we can move in."

Armand understood David's reasoning, but the result was no less distasteful to him.

"Do what you think is best. But be careful."

Armand stopped David as he turned toward the door.

"Kate is among us now. I don't want her becoming involved in this in *any* way."

David smiled briefly. "No one will get to her, Armand. Or you."

David almost bumped into Jasmine as he rounded the turn on the staircase.

"David, how lovely to see you," cooed Jasmine. "What

nefarious plots are you and Armand hatching now?"

"Just trying to turn a dollar," David replied lightly.

"Ah, David, you're too modest. Always have been. I do wish we would see more of you."

David pulled his arm out from under her fingers. "Armand is expecting you. Good night, Jasmine."

David wended his way through the guests milling in the antechamber and slipped into the cool darkness of the Oiseau Bleu bar. He took a stool at the one end, which was permanently cordoned off by velvet rope, reserved for Armand or his guests. Patina, not only an exotic blend of Lebanese, Syrian, and Egyptian womanhood, but one of the best bartenders in the Middle East, served his usual mineral water.

"You look like you could use a drink, partner." Patina was a fan of American westerns.

"Not tonight, thanks."

Patina sighed. David never had a drink when he was working. In fact, Patina had never seen him touch alcohol, and she had gone so far as to spy on him. One night David had jokingly said that the day Patina caught him with a drink in hand, he would marry her. She was still spying.

David nursed his mineral water, oblivious to the traffic in the bar. He was thinking of Jasmine and that she was Pierre's cousin . . . and how cunning she was beneath her shellacked tortoise-shell beauty.

Did you know about Pierre's troubles, Jasmine? Were you the one he ran to after Alexander had spooked him? And if you were, what was it you whispered in his ear, Jasmine?

No, it doesn't play, thought David. Jasmine looks out only for Jasmine. She wouldn't jeopardize a hair on her head to help someone out. Least of all a gray little man like Pierre. There would be nothing in it for her except risk. No money, no glory . . . no sense at all.

David let go of that thread. His thoughts, like iron filings, were drawn back to Pierre. Because of his years in the Middle East, the actions of wealthy men no longer surprised

David. Only when the powerful preyed on the weakest and most helpless did he take action. Pierre had stepped over that line. He had killed a man David had admired and respected, and injured one he loved like a father. It was an act that David, who could find so little to love in his life, could not permit to go unpunished.

"Armand, how well you look!"

Jasmine swept into the room, ruby-and-diamond necklace shooting fire from her neck and bosom. She embraced Armand, cheeks touching three times in the continental manner.

"The season is off to a grand start," she commented, gazing at the throngs of gowned women and tuxedoed men crowding the hall below.

Traditionally, the official opening of the "season" in Beirut was the second Tuesday in May. However, private parties and charity galas started before, with hostesses vying for the most spectacular display of food, drink, and entertainment.

"Is Louis not coming tonight?" Armand asked casually.

"He'll be along later."

So this wasn't a social call, Armand realized.

Jasmine settled herself in one of the two chairs facing the desk. Armand had chosen them because in spite of the fact that they were splendid examples of Second Empire furniture, they were also exceedingly uncomfortable. The ancient springs and clumps of horsehair made a visitor's backside miserable. Which was why no one ever overstayed his or her welcome. If Jasmine felt any discomfort, she hid it well.

"Armand, I've come to tell you how awful I feel about what's happened to Maritime Continental. It's scandalous what the Americans are saying about Alex, especially under the circumstances."

Armand retrieved a Romeo y Julietta cigar from the humidor and circled the end with his clipper.

"I appreciate your sentiments and concern," he said. He raised his eyes to meet hers. There was a sharp crack as the blade bit through the tobacco.

"Do you have any idea what really happened, about the missing money, that is?"

"Unfortunately not. The New York authorities are doing their best to find out."

Jasmine shifted in the chair. "Surely you're not thinking of allowing Maritime Continental to close its doors."

"American bank regulators, not I, will decide that."

"Not if restitution is made."

He struck a kitchen match and held it to cigar. He smiled pleasantly, to remove the sting from the words he would utter. "Jasmine, your attempts at subtlety end in obfuscation. What are you driving at?"

There wasn't even a shadow of anger in her black eyes. Christ, she was good! Armand thought.

"It occurred to me," Jasmine said, "that you might have considered putting together the funds necessary to compensate those defrauded by Maritime Continental. It would be a very simple matter: a public offering of Société des Bains Mediterranien stock."

Armand's head dropped a notch. "I suppose one could do that."

"I think it's intolerable—even unconscionable—for us to stand by while Alex's reputation is slandered and everything he worked for ruined," Jasmine carried on.

"Noble sentiments," Armand murmured. "Is that what you would recommend, Jasmine, that I take SBM—and with it, the casino—public?"

Jasmine met his gaze. "Yes, it is."

"How many shares do you hold?" Armand demanded abruptly.

"One million."

"And at what level do you think investment bankers such as Lazard or Morgan Stanley would peg a per-share price?"

"Between forty-five and fifty dollars."

"A conservative estimate. I would have thought closer to sixty."

Jasmine shrugged. "It's possible, given the casino's

reputation, current market conditions, the political climate
. . ."

"Answer a question, Jasmine. Answer it to my satisfaction, and I promise to give utmost consideration to what
you've said. *Why* do you need fifty or sixty million dollars?"

Jasmine hesitated. Like a wily lawyer, her cousin never
asked a question to which he did not already have the answer. But if this was the case, why ask at all when the reply
was obvious?

"I need the money to support Louis's candidacy for the
presidency," Jasmine said quietly, then added. "But you
knew that, Armand."

He rose and came around the desk. "Oh, yes, I did. Still I
had to hear you say it. Because for the last year you've been
going around giving people—especially Tufaili and the
other *zuama*—the impression that I'm in favor of Louis becoming president. On that basis you have almost convinced
them to back Louis. But not quite. The elections are three
months off. Tufaili and the others are still sitting on the
fence. And they won't move, no matter how painful their
asses become, until I declare myself."

Jasmine strained to control her temper. She'd had enough
of this miserable chair and Armand's cat-and-mouse games.

"Will you declare for Louis?"

For an instant she was convinced he would laugh in her
face, but his expression chastened her. Like most men who
have the power to grant or deny petitions, Armand Fremont
did not have to resort to belittlement or ridicule. Even so,
her eyelids fluttered, as if to ward off the blow she sensed
was coming.

"No, Jasmine, I won't," he said with quiet finality.

Furious, she threw away the script she'd prepared.

"Why? Why are you doing this? You know there are no
other candidates. You know that the *zuama* bicker endlessly
among themselves for a suitable candidate, nominating relatives who are unacceptable to everyone. You know that
business—yes, that of the casino as well—depends on a

compromise candidate and a smooth transition. So why do you refuse to see what is so clear to everyone else? *Louis is the perfect candidate.* With your support the others will fall into line. No one would dare oppose him!"

"And what would that make Louis if not a dictator?"

"Don't be silly!" Jasmine laughed. "You know Louis hasn't the mettle for that. Besides, there would be people around him—"

A second too late she recognized the trap laid out for her.

"What people around him?" he demanded softly.

"Yourself, of course," she replied, struggling to hold her ground. "The other *zuama*—"

"And you too, no?"

Jasmine felt his eyes probing the very tendrils of her thoughts, waiting to see if her words would quiver with lies.

"Of course I would stand by him. After all, he is my husband."

Armand smiled at the false indignation.

"You would do more than stand by him. Don't you think that the *zuama* understand what kind of man—or half man—Louis is? But their mistake lies in believing that once Louis is elected, they will control him. They underestimate you so badly, Jasmine, that in your position I would be insulted. To tell the truth, you, not Louis, would rule Lebanon. You want the millions to bring yourself, not him, closer to the throne." Armand smiled. "And that is something I would never permit."

She stepped back, the red folds of the dress cascading over bronze thigh. Her eyes sparkled in frenzy that could have been hatred or lust.

"*You* would not *permit*. Really, Armand, how droll! Don't try to downplay your self-interest in front of me. You and the casino have very much at stake here. The wrong man in power can prove harmful, even fatal."

"As would the wrong woman. I am not so much concerned with your greed. That is something I can understand. It is your hunger for power, the satisfaction you drive from controlling others, that I loathe. To be beholden to you or your whims would mean being held for ransom."

Jasmine stepped closer to him, her musk rising in the heat off her body.

"You're right, Armand. I *would* see to it that Louis behaved himself. And I would make absolutely certain that family was rewarded first. You think you know me, but there is so much you've never seen, tasted, experienced. You are a worldly man, but there are a few horizons left to explore. You have only to reach out."

She was standing so close that Armand felt more intimate with her than if she had thrown herself at him.

"Go, Jasmine," he whispered. "And understand one thing. If you and Louis continue your foolishness, I will stop you. Him I shall punish and let go. You I will break!"

Jasmine felt her power recede. She'd come so very close. At one moment she had felt capitulation crackling in his bones. But the moment was gone.

"Not so easily, Armand." She smiled. "Never so easily. And I won't hold you to your answer. I know you will reconsider."

11

Kate slept so deeply that when she awoke she found herself alert and refreshed. It was just after seven o'clock. Armand would be back to pick her up in less than an hour. She rushed into the shower and reentered the bedroom twenty minutes later, wrapping a towel around her wet hair. She bent at the waist and threw her head back, and at that moment saw what was lying on the freshly made bed.

"What is all this?"

A petite, dark-haired woman with a flawless olive complexion and huge caramel eyes smiled back at her.

"Bonjour, mademoiselle," she said. "My name is Marie, and I am your maid. Would you like to try on some of your gowns?"

Kate couldn't believe her eyes. On the bed was an array of evening gowns that could only have come from designers' studios. A dozen pairs of evening shoes were ready for her inspection, and a chest was stacked with frilly undergarments of lace and silk.

"Where did all this come from?" asked Kate.

"Monsieur Fremont ordered it," Marie replied.

Kate ran her fingers along the satin creations. "But how did he know my size?"

She looked around for her pantsuit, but it was gone. Marie gave her a knowing smile.

"I can't accept this."

"Monsieur Fremont will be back shortly," Marie told her. "I promised him you would be ready."

Kate looked around helplessly. "Well, I suppose we don't want to keep Monsieur Fremont waiting, do we?"

Marie beamed her approval.

"You really shouldn't have done that."

"Done what?"

"The clothes . . . everything."

Armand laughed. "But you haven't seen *everything* yet."

As the white Rolls glided along the Corniche, Kate asked, "Who is your driver? I don't think I've ever seen such a big man!"

The chauffeur seemed to take up most of the front seat, the steering wheel all but hidden underneath his massive hands. His bald pate gleamed in the soft interior light, and glancing at the rearview mirror, Kate shivered at the cold black eyes that glittered back at her.

"Salim is a Turk," Armand told her, his voice subdued.

"Where did you meet him?"

"To say I *found* him would be more appropriate. He was thirteen years old at the time and, would you believe, almost as big as he is today. He was working in a carnival, bending steel bars with his teeth, wrestling pythons, doing other things that were far less pleasant than that. All his life he had been treated as a freak, and a freak's work was all he knew."

"Until you came along."

Armand shrugged. "Salim is a very brave, generous man. He would never let any harm come to you, ever."

Kate was expecting Armand to continue, but instead he reached inside his jacket pocket and fished out a long, thin jeweler's case, handing it to Kate.

"Oh no, I can't!"

"Accessories," Armand said.

Kate gasped when she opened the case. Nestled inside was a necklace of diamonds whose double strands came together to encircle an enormous fiery ruby.

Kate shook her head. "I can't accept this. . . ."

"Then consider it a loan for the evening."

Kate stared at the priceless jewelry in her lap. Only as the car drew up to the casino did she quickly pull down the visor and, using its lighted mirror, clip the necklace around her neck.

The exterior of the casino, bathed in red, blue, and white

spotlights, was magnificent enough. But to Kate, struggling with the childhood memories of her only visit here, it seemed that the inside was a regal world beyond compare.

The foyer, its paneled walls hung with priceless tapestries, was brimming with formally attired men and women arriving for an evening's gaiety and, if they were lucky, profit. Their voices and laughter echoed a dozen different languages, from Arabic to Australian English. Doormen and porters in red tunics and fezzes escorted parties into the Oiseau Bleu restaurant or into the gaming salons, or, for those attending the theater, upstairs.

"Good evening, Miss Maser."

Kate glanced up at the tall, rangy man who had suddenly materialized in front of her.

"Kate, may I present David Cabot," Armand said.

"A pleasure to meet you."

"Likewise, Miss Maser. Armand, may I have a word with you? It's London."

Armand excused himself, and Kate turned away as the two men huddled. Then Armand was back beside her.

"Who was that?" asked Kate, certain that David Cabot was an actor.

"My security specialist," Armand replied. "Seems a sharpie may be gracing us with a visit."

"Sharpie?"

"A card sharp. A player who counts down the deck in baccarat—or worse, is in cahoots with one of the dealers who feeds him cards off the bottom."

"Here? In *this* place?"

"Especially in this place," Armand said grimly. "The casino is a magnet for every thief and con man in the world. Don't think you would recognize them, you wouldn't. These bastards act and dress like millionaires. They latch on to an older, wealthy woman for camouflage or use a tarted-up ex-dancer to deflect attention from themselves. If we weren't careful, they would rob us blind."

Chastened by Armand's matter-of-fact explanation, Kate allowed herself to be steered toward the main gambling room, the Grand Salon. On the way she and Armand were stopped a half-dozen times. It seemed that Armand knew everyone, from Arab royalty to European aristocracy to the lowliest pages, and to all he gave equal attention. But maybe a little more to the women, Kate thought. These came at Armand in a never-ending parade, giving Kate a brief nod and once-over, but otherwise directing all their attention—and in some cases, a good measure of exposed bosom—at him. There were dowagers wreathed in black, with faces caked in white powder that set off their rouge and scarlet lips; elegant matrons on the arms of husbands or, as Kate suspected in several cases, gigolos. And then there were beautiful young things; statuesque blue-black Africans, petal-delicate Orientals, none-too-shy Scandinavians, who enjoyed the flirtation and tease. To all Armand was the perfect gentleman, pausing to introduce Kate, then focusing his entire attention on the woman before him, making her feel as if she were the only one in the room.

"You have quite the following," Kate observed, surprised by the irritation in her voice.

"All part of being a host," Armand replied easily.

The main gambling salon was impressive. The ceiling was at least sixty feet high, covered by a rotunda of beautiful polychromed glass. Columns of veined pink marble supported triumphal arches, and a host of crystal chandeliers brought out a rich, reddish hue from the gaming tables below. In spite of the crowds, the room was hushed, thick carpets and wall baffles absorbing sound.

"I don't remember it being anything like this," Kate said at last.

"Wait until you see the Spectacle Hall," Armand told her. "We're opening up a new cabaret tomorrow night."

As she followed Armand around, the excitement in the air began to work its magic. She paused at the roulette table, drawn by the expectant, fearful, sometimes desperate expressions of the players. Their intensity and concentration quickened her pulse; the satisfaction of winning or the resignation of defeat made her heart soar and fall.

"What's in there?" she asked Armand, pointing to the areas cordoned off by velvet ropes and guarded by two gentlemen in black suits.

"Private rooms," he replied. "The play is exclusively baccarat, and the price of admission a hundred thousand dollars."

Armand smiled at Kate's astonishment. "To most of these people that is not a lot of money. Look around you. There's a German publisher from Munich, a multimillionaire. Next to him is the owner of Aeroarmes, purveyor of fine war equipment to the French government. Going into the lavatory is a sober, conservative Swiss banker—I wonder what *his* clients would say if they saw him now. Then you have your sheiks and princes, Indian maharajas, the sultan from Brunei. These people come here for the sport. They don't care what it costs them, as long as they enjoy themselves. If they win, so much the better. But we and they know that they will be back and the house will win the next time."

"So much could be done with the money," Kate said. "It's almost obscene."

"You'd be surprised just what *is* done with it," Armand said lightly.

Before Kate could ask him about this enigmatic reply, Armand turned to speak to a croupier. Kate had noticed him doing this before, stepping up to an employee and whispering a few words. More often than not the response was a nod or shake of the head. Then Armand would move off as though the contact had never been made and slip back into his role of host.

"Armand, I really think we should—"

"Kate, excuse me . . ."

His tone held a warning. Kate looked around, but obviously Armand had noticed something she hadn't. He was leading her toward one of the cashier booths, discreetly positioned in shallow recesses next to the marble columns, when a woman suddenly materialized at his side.

"Monsieur Fremont, thank God!"

Armand glanced over his shoulder. Kate turned and saw he was scrutinizing her. It was as if he were deciding

whether or not to include her in what was about to happen.
Kate looked at the woman. She was young and very lovely,
but in a deeply sad way. Her dress, clinging to a former
beauty, was frayed, her velvet shoes worn down. The fur-
rows and creases of her dark Levantine features reflected a
lifetime of toil. Or was it, Kate thought, something else?
The haunted—and hunted—expression reminded her of illegal Mexican immigrants whom she had represented, the
face of a powerless individual, the face of despair.

"It will be all right," she heard Armand say, so softly that
his lips barely moved. He turned so that the woman was
shielded behind his body and the marble column. "It's all
arranged. I am relieved you made it here safely!"

The woman closed her eyes as though in prayer.

"Bless you, monsieur!" she murmured.

Armand slipped a chit from his pocket. "Take this to the
cashier. He will give you some money. Play table six in the
American Room. Blackjack. The dealer is expecting you. I
guarantee you will have very good luck tonight."

The woman stared at Armand, then, to Kate's amazement, grasped his hand and brought it to her lips.

"Bless you!" she repeated, like a litany.

Kate watched the woman move off to the cashier.
"Armand, what on earth was all that about?"

He smiled tightly. "A favor for an old friend. Kate, I'm
sorry. I must leave you for a moment." He gestured to one
of the security men. "Francois will get you anything you
need. I will be back in a few minutes."

"Is there anything I can assist you with, mademoiselle?"
asked the guard before Kate could catch her breath.

"No, thank you."

Kate found herself walking among the tables, the whir of
the roulette wheel, followed by the rattling ball as it
bounced off the ribs of the wheel, breaking up her thoughts.
What else is going on here? she asked herself. She was so
distracted by Armand's strange behavior that she never saw
Jasmine approaching her.

"Katherine! What a lovely surprise! You came to us after

all." *And how did you manage that, Katherine,* Jasmine wondered, *when the newspapers have labeled you a major suspect in the Maritime Continental affair?*

"Jasmine! Hello."

"Come, you must tell me everything," she said, taking Kate's arm and steering her toward the Grand Salon, the main gaming room. "When did you arrive?"

"Just this afternoon," Kate replied nervously, her gaze daring around the room in the hope of spotting Armand.

"Really! And you've been out shopping already."

Jasmine took a critical measure of Kate's evening gown. It was a Balenciaga creation in the faintest hue of pink, opening like a tulip in the back and suspended from jeweled shoulder straps. The gown was obviously a ready-to-wear, but, Jasmine noted, it molded itself to Kate's figure like a designer original.

"How long do you plan to stay?" Jasmine asked, ignoring Kate's discomfort.

"I really don't know—"

"And that awful situation back in America! The things people are saying about your father. Shameful! Is it true the police thought *you* had something to do with it?"

"I wouldn't have thought you'd have heard about it over here," Kate replied stiffly.

Jasmine retreated a step. "If I offended you, forgive me. It's just that you were the first one I thought of when I heard about Maritime Continental." Jasmine paused. "And Kate, you will learn quickly that there are few secrets in Beirut. The *Middle East Report*, our version of your *Time* magazine, featured the story in its latest issue."

"I'm sorry," Kate apologized. "It's been a nightmare. In fact, that's one of the reasons I'm here. Armand thought it would be best for me to get away for a little while . . . until everything is resolved."

"And it was an excellent idea," Jasmine said firmly. "We are family, Kate. I want you to feel free to call me anytime you wish. Believe me, I can appreciate what you are going through, first having lost your father, now this. I hope you will let me be your friend."

Her nerves settled, Kate felt a rush of warmth for this woman who was reaching out to her. "Thank you, Jasmine. That would mean a great deal to me."

"Then you won't mind if I call and arrange to introduce you to some friends of mine? They are very interesting and amusing people. I know how busy Armand can be, and I will not have you rattling around in that seraglio of his all by yourself!"

Kate laughed. "I'd love to meet them. Thank you." She was about to ask Jasmine to join her and Armand when Jasmine nodded toward the entrance to the Grand Salon.

"Ah, your knight-errant!" She laughed. "Well, I'll leave you to him. Believe me, Armand will help you to straighten everything out. But I expect you to call me tomorrow. We'll go for lunch and have a nice, long chat."

At the cashier's window Jasmine signed a chit for five thousand Lebanese pounds. Then she changed her mind and doubled the amount. She was feeling gay and lucky. Katherine was a beautiful girl, cloying in that innocent, American way. Perhaps, if fate directed, she might entice her to join herself and Louis for some recreation. After all, she'd never had an American girl, and from what Louis had told her, they could be quite splendid.

"Ah, Kate! I'm so sorry to have kept you waiting."

Without breaking step, Armand took Kate's arm and escorted her toward the Oiseau Bleu restaurant.

"Was that Jasmine I saw you chatting with?"

"Yes, she's a wonderful person. She seems willing to go out of her way to help me."

"Really? How very generous of her."

The barb in Armand's words was unmistakable. Kate was surprised, as much by the tone as at whom the sting had been directed. Given everything Armand had said about Lebanese kinship, she hadn't even considered the possibility of differences within the family.

Armand guided Kate to a private dining room, enclosed

on two sides by glass sculpted with intricate frosted designs. As soon as they stepped inside and the glass door was closed, the hum of the restaurant disappeared. Also, while Kate hadn't been able to see into the room, now that she was inside she realized the panels were one-way glass, allowing anyone sitting here to see what was taking place in the restaurant.

"One of my little peccadilloes," Armand remarked, reading her mind. "I like to know what is going on in my humble establishment."

"Uh-huh," Kate replied with a teasing smile.

She slipped onto the velvet banquette and glanced out the window with its panoramic view of the casino gardens, and beyond, the spotlights illuminating the roiling Mediterranean. A sommelier materialized out of nowhere cradling a dusty bottle of red wine and a long dinner candle. He opened the wine and placed the cork in front of Armand.

"We will wait a few minutes for the wine to settle and breathe," Armand said. He grasped Kate's hand. "How are you bearing up?"

"I'm in shock," Kate told him point-blank. "All this—" she looked around the room—"It's like nothing I've ever known."

"You have been through a great deal," Armand said gently. "Give yourself time to put some things into perspective, make your peace."

"There's just one problem. How can I do that when I don't know what happened. Someone or something took my life and turned it inside out. I need to know who and why, Armand."

Kate watched him carefully. His eyes held hers, and she was certain he knew what she was after. He lifted the bottle of wine and moved the candlestick closer to its neck. He dipped the decanter and poured the wine, carefully watching the sediment settle at the base of the bottle. The bouquet of the vintage, held captive for twenty years, exploded over the table.

"Try it."

Kate hesitated, then brought the glass to her lips. The wine was purple nectar, its ambrosia something she had never tasted before.

Armand watched the surprise and pleasure in Kate's face. The legerdemain with the wine had bought him a moment or two, but not more. All his life he had had to make decisions such as the one facing him now, deciding how much people should know, inducing them to act in ways he wished them to act. He had believed that by now the carapace over his spirit was so thick that such deceit could not longer touch him. Why was it different with Kate? Beneath her fingertips his shell felt very fragile.

She needs a truth I cannot give her, not without the risk that she will overreact, say or do something that will ultimately endanger her. Until I have Pierre where I want him, and his accomplice, the truth will have to sleep. . . .

"You could have opened my briefcase on the plane," Armand said. "Why didn't you?"

The directness of the question startled Kate, but she recovered quickly.

"I guess I believe in other people's privacy."

"Even under the circumstances?"

"Maybe especially then." She paused. "And I didn't want to do that to you. I didn't want it to be like that between us." She laughed. "Maybe I'm not as tough as I thought I was."

"Don't underestimate yourself."

Armand stared at the spectrum of colors created by the glass and light. He sipped the wine hoping it would somehow make what he had to say palatable.

"Your father did leave something about Maritime Continental."

Kate jerked back as though touched by flame. "Tell me, Armand. For God's sake tell me!"

He gripped her hand. "It's not much, but it's a start. Alexander had a connection in a London bank who told him that a situation was developing which might, if it got out of control, hurt Maritime Continental."

"What kind of situation?"

"Embezzlement."

Kate shook her head. "So he knew!" she whispered. "All this time he knew something would happen."

"Do not jump to conclusions!" Armand said fiercely. "Alex didn't know how Maritime Continental might be affected. I suspect he was trying to find out more when . . . when he was killed."

"Did he leave a name?"

"Yes. That of his contact in London."

"Did this . . . this contact give my father a name, someone he suspected of embezzlement at Maritime Continental?"

"No, there's nothing in Alex's notes to indicate that," Armand replied, feeling sick with himself.

"We have to talk to this man in London," Kate declared.

Armand held up his hand. "Not so easy. He seems to have disappeared. I am looking into that right now."

"We must find him, Armand! If he knew about the embezzlement, maybe he also knew who at Maritime Continental was involved! Don't you see? This is the kind of information the district attorney can use. It could vindicate me, Emil, the bank!" Kate's eyes were shining with hope. "Let me see my father's notes, Armand. Maybe there's a reference that you overlooked or misunderstood, but something I'd catch."

"Kate, listen to me very carefully and please, please don't take offense. Alex didn't just mention this one name, his source. There was a second man, very powerful, very influential. I am not sure how he fits into all this, but I must proceed with extreme caution."

"Who is he?" Kate demanded, interrupting him. "If he's in New York, then I can help you find him!"

Armand shook his head. "No, he is here, in Beirut. And if he gets wind that I am asking questions, the consequences could be terrible."

Kate reacted as though she'd been slapped. "Are you saying you don't trust me?"

"I am telling you that people's lives are at stake,"

Armand replied. "I am asking, Kate, that you trust me, let me do this my way, the way I know best."

She was tempted to unleash a retort, but she pushed down her anger, forced herself to appear calm.

"What do you think I'd do that would be so terrible?" she asked at last.

"I have no idea. But I think the question is, What could you do in any case?"

"As I said, if I knew exactly what my father had left behind—"

"Kate, with all due respect, you know very little about Maritime Continental's business. And, I would venture to say, next to nothing about the financial circles of London or anywhere else. You don't know which questions to ask or whom to put them to. These are slippery people we are dealing with. If they suspect someone is after them, they will bolt. Or worse, turn on you. I will not permit that to happen."

"Are you in the habit of deciding what's best for everyone?" Kate asked sarcastically.

"Not at all," he replied quietly. "But I do expect someone with your background and intelligence to recognize when you need some advice and be responsible enough to accept it."

Had he said anything but this, had he offered her even a grain of consideration or the flimsiest explanation, maybe Kate would have accepted as much, at least for a time. But Armand's words stung and humiliated. With them he had crossed the boundary of what Kate believed was right and fair.

"Is that your final word on the matter?"

"For the time being it has to be. I hope you understand—"

Kate rose from the table.

"No, I *don't* understand. Frankly, if this is how you do things here, then it's horrible."

Without having intended to, Kate softened her voice.

"You were my father's best friend. You took something that belonged to him, that might help me. I came here because I trusted you, Armand. After all these years, I still remember the first time . . ." Kate's voice faltered. "A friend wouldn't do what you seem to think nothing at all of doing. I don't understand that kind of friendship, Armand. If that's what you call it . . ."

Kate jerked open the glass door and, looking straight ahead walked swiftly out of the restaurant. She had reached the maître d's lectern at the entrance when a powerful hand clamped over her elbow and steered her toward the bar.

"Who the hell are you?" Kate demanded, furious.

Then through her anger she recognized the face.

"So you do remember."

"Yes, Mr. Cabot. I do. Nice seeing you again. Now if you don't mind, I have to go."

"No, what you have to do is listen."

David pressed Kate against the last stool along the bar, which, at the dinner hour, was almost empty.

"Do you know what I do?" David asked her.

"You're some sort of security man."

David shook his head. "Not just some, Miss Maser. One of the best. Ask around if you like."

"Why should I?"

"Because I'm the one who's going to find out who carved the heart out of Maritime Continental."

Kate's eyes widened.

"I don't know what went on back there," David continued, nodding in the direction of the restaurant. "I'll venture a guess and say that Armand wasn't all that forthcoming. Don't be hard on him, Miss Maser. He knows exactly what he's doing, and he has the best resources for the job."

"You mean that Armand told *you* what was in my father's papers?"

"He would have had to, right?"

Kate crimsoned at having made such a gaffe.

"So it seems that everybody except me can know what's going on. Thank you for the insight, Mr. Cabot. Good night!"

"Miss Maser!" Kate looked over her shoulder. "Don't let your ego get in the way. This isn't about people pretending to lead revolutions. Here the game is played for keeps. The whole town is one big ear. Don't go talking out of class."

David felt as though Kate's eyes had pinned him against the padded rail on the bar.

"Thanks for that piece of advice, Mr. Cabot. Why don't we wait and see what you come up with. Maybe you'll change *your* tune!"

12

"Fremont here."

"The London weather stinks," said David Cabot. The undersea cable connection sounded tinnier than usual, indicating to David that the scrambler connection on Armand's phone was working.

"What about our friend at the Regent Bank?"

"It seems that Kenneth Morton, head of the foreign-exchange division, has taken a leave of absence," David replied tersely.

"Paid or otherwise?"

"Otherwise. He claimed a dying father in the south of France."

"Is that the truth?"

"The family has French roots, and the father did retire to Provence. However, Morton is a light traveler. His suitcases are still in the closet of his apartment. Nothing seems to have been taken out of the wardrobe. There were three bottles of milk in front of the door, which means he's either absentminded or left in one hell of a hurry."

"The latter, you think?"

"Yes."

"When will you call again?"

"After Provence."

"David, be careful. If Morton has not been accounted for yet, someone else might be looking. Or waiting to see if a third party is interested."

"I always watch my back, Armand. You know that."

"Humor me and take extra precautions."

"I will. And how is Miss Maser?"

From anyone else Armand would have expected a bantering tone. David's was coldly serious.

"We haven't had much to say to each other since her first

night here."

"I think *you* had better watch out too, Armand. The girl's trouble. Don't let her fool you."

It was a professional's opinion, and Armand recognized it as such. Still, David's tone irritated him.

"I will look after her."

There was a pause on the line.

"When this is all over, the two of you can see what happens," David said gently. "Just keep her out of it for now. Good-bye, Armand."

Slowly Armand replaced the receiver. What the hell had David meant by his last remarks? Why should *anything* happen between him and Kate?

Armand was vexed. David's words had pricked him like a splinter, one he couldn't remove.

Or is it because David sees something, something so transparent that is written across my face for everyone to read but me?

Kate and Jasmine were seated on the terrace of the Phoenicia. Since its owners had been unable to get any beachfront at any price, the hotel had an enormous free-form swimming pool, tiled in three shades of blue. At one end, directly behind the terrace, was a thick glass wall so that patrons of the bar and outside dining area could watch the swimmers' underwater acrobatics. Kate smiled at a trio of muscular young men, their bathing suits little more than thongs, who swam up against the glass and grinned lasciviously.

"You *are* settling in," Jasmine observed.

"What else can I do?"

Jasmine clapped her hands delightedly. "You will be a true Beiruti yet! We are all fatalists."

Kate smiled and sipped the very cold Corton-Charlemagne Jasmine had ordered with their lunch. She hadn't thought that her quarrel with Armand would lead to a wall of silence, but it had. By the time Jasmine had called, asking her to lunch, Kate had been ready to explode.

"If you find me too direct, you must say so," Jasmine said, cupping the waiter's hand as he lit her cigarette. Kate was struck by the sensuality of this simple gesture. "People tell me I am but I don't give a damn. You don't have to tell me anything you don't want to."

"Fine."

"It's no secret that you are carrying a terrible burden," Jasmine continued. "But to tell the truth, the mystery surrounding your circumstances gives you a delicious cachet. Let me assure you, you are the talk of *tout* Beirut!"

Kate squirmed. "I did think people were looking at me when I came in here. I'm not sure I like that."

Jasmine glanced around, her sharp eye taking inventory. "Then again it might also be your outfit."

Kate stared at her blankly. She had chosen a simple white skirt and blue polka-dot silk blouse, appropriate enough, she had thought, for the occasion. Until she'd seen what the other women were wearing, until Jasmine arrived in a jade-green crepe dress with a veil of chiffon over the bodice of paper-fan pleats.

"Your wardrobe is something we can fix very easily," Jasmine said. "The point is that I understand what you're going through. Alexander's death, what happened afterward, well . . . I want you to know that I am here to help you in any way I can. This is not the time to martyr yourself, Katherine. I'm sure Armand is doing wonderful things to end this foolishness. But he is a practical man. He doesn't always know what a woman needs. So whether it's advice or just someone to listen to you, you've only to call. I want to be your friend."

Kate was surprised and moved. She decided to disregard Armand's opinion and trust her own first impression of Jasmine as a decent and generous woman.

"That's very kind of you," Kate said.

When the waiter delivered their lobster salads, Jasmine raised her glass. "*Chin-chin*, my dear. To good fortune!"

Throughout the meal Jasmine kept up a stream of chatter, identifying individuals in the lunch crowd and telling spicy stories about them. She regaled Kate with tales about the various carnival balls that were being planned and insisted that, even if her affairs were settled for the good, she plan to attend the festivities. Kate couldn't find it in herself to say no.

The sunshine and chilled wine began to take effect. The salad was as delicious as the serving was prodigious, and Kate wondered how, as she watched Jasmine devour the last morsel, the woman still maintained her hourglass figure. Jasmine read her mind.

"In Beirut women live outdoors, on the beach and in the water. We love to dance. But oh, the miles we put on when we go shopping!"

After the cappuccinos had been served, Jasmine said, "So tell me, is there any news from New York?"

"Well, I suppose some of it is good," Kate replied. "Do you know Emil Bartoli?"

"I know of him," Jasmine replied. "Certain bankers, who like to call him Bartoli the Borgia, are delighted he's in this mess."

"He's an honest, decent man who's going through hell!" Kate bristled before telling her about her two telephone conversations with Emil. When the New York district attorney's office had learned Kate had fled to Beirut, Bartoli had been rearrested. Only the most persuasive arguments by his lawyers had secured his release, on a staggering bond of five million dollars. Bartoli had no idea who had posted it, and neither, at the time, had Kate. Until, by process of elimination, she arrived at the name of the only man who not only had that much money at his disposal but was willing to pledge it without second thought: Armand. When she had asked Armand about this, he had merely smiled and shrugged.

Kate had been chagrined at being the cause of Emil's further humiliation, but the banker's response had surprised her.

"You did absolutely the right thing," he had told her. "Armand was trying to find out if Alexander left us any clues. You have to look after your own interests. But the two of you share a common goal. Armand is a powerful ally. He has connections all over the world. Work with him, Kate. He's our only chance now." Emil had gone on to say that by fleeing, Kate had cemented the conviction in the court's mind that she was somehow involved in the embezzlement.

"Not that it makes matters any worse," he had finished.

"What do you mean?"

"The federal regulators have decided to wind down the bank's operations in an orderly fashion, then sell off the assets to pay those who lost money. Savage protested, but Washington wouldn't listen."

Kate was stunned. "But that means selling the building!"

"It means more than that, Kate," Emil had concluded sadly. "Maritime Continental will cease to exist."

"They can't do that!"

"Oh, my dear Kate, I'm afraid they can and they will."

"But what will happen to you?"

"I will wait to be vindicated," Emil had answered calmly. "You're the only one who can help me now, Kate. You and Armand."

"I won't let you down!"

"I know you won't. After all, you are your father's daughter."

"My goodness!" Jasmine exclaimed. "Does Armand have any idea what he will do?"

"He has someone called David Cabot looking into things in London."

Kate regretted the words the instant they left her mouth. *The whole town is one big ear. Don't go talking out of class.* The echo of David's voice carried an unmistakable rebuke, but Kate couldn't understand why.

"Who is David Cabot?" she asked hastily, hoping to draw Jasmine's attention away from what she'd let slip. "Armand tells me he runs some sort of security organization."

Jasmine toyed with the links of the gold chain around her neck.

"David . . ." she said, the name lingering in the air. "Oh

yes, he runs Interarmco, one of the best private security firms in the world. But who is he? Let me tell you something, my dear. Everyone wonders about David."

"I don't understand."

"David is a mystery, even in this country, where time inevitably wears down the darkest secrets. You see, one day, twenty years ago, David just appeared in Armand's house. For the longest time no one knew how or why. Then we learned that Armand had made David his ward. High officials were involved, up to and including the British ambassador. The details were almost impossible to come by."

"His ward?" Kate asked incredulously.

"Yes," Jasmine said. "Gradually it came out that David and his parents had been sailing off the Syrian coast and had been attacked by pirates. David was the only survivor. Whether Armand had anything to do with his rescue or whether he had been brought to Armand by someone else isn't know. However it happened, David must have been orphaned by the tragedy.

"After that Armand took charge of David's life, putting him through school and college. There is some talk about David having been involved with law-enforcement agencies before setting up his private security company, Interarmco."

"It's an incredible story," Kate murmured.

Jasmine agreed silently. It would be even more so if she were to tell Kate about Armand's crusade against white slavery and the real circumstances under which he had come across David Cabot.

Jasmine glanced at her watch. "But enough of such morbid stories. Just be careful and don't let David Cabot into your business. I'm not sure that even Armand can control such a man."

Kate's head was still spinning when Jasmine signaled for the check, signed it, and said, "Now we must go out and buy you a few things."

"Jasmine, I really don't think—"

"I won't take no for an answer. Come along."

The two women left the terrace and strode through the

Phoenicia's six-story atrium lobby.

"Has Armand been treating you properly?"

"He's . . . he's very kind."

Jasmine laughed. "My dear, the way you two looked at the casino, I'd say he was being more than kind!"

Kate frowned. Given everything that had happened, she was utterly confused about her feelings for Armand. The rush of girlhood memories that had overwhelmed her, the rising infatuation, had diminished at his lack of trust. She had painful memories of another man who she had allowed into her life . . . and who had betrayed her with a smile and a kiss.

Kate could not deny that something existed between her and Armand, a powerful connection which, because it was still growing and changing, she could not articulate. But whatever it was, wherever it led to, she promised herself not be taken in or swept away. There was too much at stake for her to allow that to happen.

"Are you and Armand good friends?" Kate asked, breaking the silence. "Besides being related, I mean."

"You're asking if we are lovers," Jasmine replied pointedly, laughing at Kate's expression. "Please, it's not that uncommon. But no, we have never been lovers."

"I'm sorry. It's none of my business."

"Don't be silly! I'm not denying that I find Armand very attractive. A woman would have to be blind and dumb not to. But I am married. From what you've seen of Beirut so far, you might think it's Sodom and Gomorrah rolled into one. I don't deny that many women take their pleasures outside the marital bed. I just don't happen to be one of them." Jasmine paused. "And even if I wanted to, I wouldn't choose Armand."

"Why?"

"What was the one thing you noticed about him that night at the casino?"

Kate thought back. "The way he seemed to know everybody."

"And who in particular?"

"The women."

"Voilà! Armand has a duty to play host. And he does so well. Especially with the nubile clientele."

Kate was still mulling that over when they turned down a corridor, as wide as a railroad tunnel, lined with expensive boutiques.

"We can start here," she announced, sweeping into Courreges. The saleswomen flocked around Jasmine like orphan goslings. "This is Katherine Maser, a friend of Monsieur Fremont."

The saleswomen immediately swarmed over Kate. She managed to extricate herself and pulled Jasmine aside.

"I don't have money for this!"

Jasmine pointed to the outfit Kate was wearing. "Where did you get that?"

"Armand told me to go shopping and sign my name. He said it would all be taken care of—and that I could pay him back later."

"Of course it has been arranged. Don't you think *they* know that?"

Kate looked at the eager saleswomen and realized what must have happened. Armand had picked up the phone and arranged credit for her all over the city.

"Jasmine, there's no price tag on this one," Kate said, holding a miniskirt.

"There are no price tags on anything in these stores," Jasmine informed her, delighted. "In fact, the sales receipt you sign will only itemize what you've bought. The prices are added later. Most gracious, don't you think?"

A few days after seeing Kate, Jasmine hosted an intimate dinner party for three. Because the nature of the discussion around the table would be very private, she gave her servants the evening off, choosing to prepare the light meal herself. She loved Arabic food and made a huge tray of *mezze*, an array of Middle Eastern hors d'oeuvres, as well as a dozen *samboussacs*, Levantine meat pastries baked in a feather-light dough.

Although Jasmine maintained a beautiful duplex apartment in the chicest area of the city, know as Ra's Beirut, she loved this, her hillside retreat overlooking Jounyeh, twenty kilometers to the north. Here the Mountain, the Christian stronghold for centuries, dominated the landscape. At the top of its twenty-five-hundred-foot peak was an enormous statue of the Virgin Mary, her arms outstretched toward the town and bay below. Scattered across the hillsides were villas of the rich and famous and, on a coastal strip, the beaches that were their playgrounds. In between was the town itself, filled with theaters, restaurants, and shops that catered to the wealthy. Beyond the floor-to-ceiling glass the Mediterranean was cradling the sun as gently as a mother would her baby.

"You didn't seem to have much of an appetite," Jasmine observed, addressing Pierre. "Has Cleo put you on another diet?"

Both Jasmine and Louis had noticed Pierre's uncharacteristic pallor and that, for the first time anyone could remember, there was space between his collar and neck.

"A touch of the flu, perhaps." As Pierre watched Jasmine serve coffee and liqueurs, he added, "But I don't think you invited me to dinner to ask about my health."

Jasmine ignored the jibe. She and Pierre had always been civil to each other but until recently had had little in common besides blood.

"As it happens, I learned something that concerns the three of us," said Jasmine. "It seems Armand will not, under any circumstances, support Louis's candidacy for president."

Louis paled, his dessert fork clattering onto the china. "What? When did this happen? Who told you?"

All day Louis had been trying to find out why Jasmine had invited Pierre for dinner. But not in his worst fears had he believed that it could be for such a reason as this.

"I spoke with Armand a few days ago, at the casino," Jasmine continued, ignoring her husband's outburst. "Armand will not support you, darling."

"Does Tufaili know?" Louis blurted out.

Jasmine gave him a withering look. "If you say it any louder, he will!" She turned to Pierre. "Sooner or later Armand will declare for *someone*. The question is for whom. The uncertainty isn't good for us, or for you and the Central Bank.

"The bank does not concern itself with politics," Pierre replied in a lofty tone.

"It had better start!" Jasmine snapped. "The governor of the bank serves at the president's pleasure. If Armand supports the wrong man, how long do you think you'll last?"

The thought that his seemingly invulnerable posting could be threatened sickened Pierre. No one could be allowed to replace him, no one! It wasn't only a question of what he was doing there, but if a new man came in, performed a thorough audit . . . Pierre shivered.

"What do you want from me?"

"One of two things," Jasmine replied. "Either convince Armand to stop this nonsense and throw his support behind Louis, or give us the money we need to match the *zuama*'s contribution."

"I can't do either!" Pierre shouted. "Armand doesn't listen to me. You know that. As for money, I don't have any!"

"You're a poor liar, Pierre," Louis laughed. "You buy the earth for your bitch. Surely you have *something* left over."

"My affairs are none of your business! If you need the money so badly, why don't you convince Armand to take SBM public?"

"I tried to," Jasmine said quietly, shocking the two men. "That's exactly what I suggested to him. He rejected the idea completely."

Jasmine let the implication of that sink in.

"The man's mad!" Pierre said, shaking his head.

"Perhaps," she replied. "But his madness can hurt us all. Pierre, I think you should reconsider getting us the money we need. After all, it really isn't so much, given that there would never be any other governors in your lifetime."

Pierre did not reply. He watched the lights in the harbor

and marina come to life.

"I'm afraid I must be going," he said at last. "A previous engagement . . ."

"If you give me a minute, I'll join you," she said. She looked at her husband. "Louis, may I see you for a moment?"

She waited until they were in the privacy of their bedroom, then fiercely gripped his face between her hands.

"I want you to be very calm, Louis. Say nothing, do nothing—"

"It's finished, isn't it?" he said miserably. "Convincing Armand to go public was our last hope."

"No, it wasn't, my pet," she said soothingly. "So much can still happen . . ."

Louis glanced at her fearfully. "What do you mean?"

"Beirut is such a very dangerous place. No man, no matter how careful, is completely safe. A madman, someone with a grudge, can snuff out a life in an instant."

"You can't be serious!"

"And if something like that was to happen, then suspicion would fall on those whose motive was obvious, about whom there have already been whispers. Such as Pierre, keeper of a young, very expensive woman, who was fearful that, because Armand would not support you, his sinecure at the bank would be snatched away from him . . ."

"Jasmine . . ."

"Shh . . . I'm not saying such a thing *will* happen, only that it *can*." She kissed him lightly on the mouth. "I'll be late. Don't bother waiting up for me."

The gods had bestowed upon Louis the rugged, handsome features usually reserved for their own kin. His high cheekbones, strong jaw, and sensuous mouth invariably made women look twice. Once they had, his eyes, moist and enchanting, refused to let them go. Close up, his scent, blended for his exclusive use in Grasse, captivated them. The toss of his head, the slightly hoarse laugh that revealed perfectly white teeth were enough to complete the conquest.

But the gods had not been satisfied with making Louis Jabar beautiful. They had truly indulged him, birthing him into a Lebanese family that was as venal as it was wealthy.

His father had been either a pirate or a trader, depending on whom one asked. The elder Jabar had built up a freighter fleet whose rattletrap vessels plowed across the Mediterranean, ferrying any kind of cargo so long as the price was right. His father's mercantile skills alleviated the necessity of Louis working for a living. Besides, he was the only male among five offspring and as such had unlimited access to the family coffers.

Louis had attended the American University in Beirut and lived in Beirut's posh Manara district, so named after the famous lighthouse landmark. He shot an excellent game of golf at the Beirut Golf and Country Club and had an account at the exclusive Goodies Supermarket. Although he hadn't needed props to maintain a steady flow of bedmates, a wasp-yellow Lamborghini hadn't hurt.

After graduation, Louis—who had spent a great deal of time in the tony cafés of Ra's Beirut discussing events of the day with those who fancied themselves intellectuals— had decided he would go to Paris to pursue a career in journalism. Since every well-bred Lebanese spoke perfect French, language was not a problem. A generous amount of Lebanese pounds, spent buying American journalists drinks, had given him the names of a few people at the *International Herald Tribune* who might be helpful.

Louis fell in love with Paris. He adored its wide boulevards with their array of boutiques and expensive shops and the infinite variety of its excellent restaurants. Above all he worshiped its women. Having installed himself in a grand apartment on the fashionable Right Bank, he explored the city day and night, helped by rich Lebanese expatriates who by now had become more French than the French themselves.

Whatever thoughts he had of becoming a working journalist quickly evaporated. Louis reverted to his old habit of buying drinks, this time at the bar of the Lancaster Hotel, a stone's throw from the *Tribune*, for the newspapermen who had virtually set up office there. Smoky, noisy, and always full of interesting people, the Lancaster became Louis's second home. At the time, Louis thought he could not be happier. But the gods, perhaps tired of their largesse, had other ideas.

In Beirut, Louis had been a regular at tables of the Casino de Paradis. In Paris he became a patron of the casino at Enghien. His game was baccarat, and he was a skillful, daring player, the kind of heavy gambler the casino management loved, because win or lose, he was always a draw. One particular night, however, when Louis was well ahead and thought nothing could stop him, the roof caved in.

She swept into his life on a torrent of red, clothed by Dior, coiffed by Sabrina, scented by Balmain. The first time Louis laid eyes on her standing like the centerpiece of the casino's foyer, he almost lost the hand. The next time he did.

"Have I brought you bad luck, monsieur?" the woman asked. "If so, there must be a way to make it up to you."

Her voice had the smoky quality of ancient whiskey. Her eyes caressed and drew him into her. Quite out of character, Louis was tongue-tied. He was so embarrassed, he lost the following hand as well.

"You are a better player than that," she scolded him gently. "Go on. Keep the shoe. I promise I will change your fortune."

Louis couldn't have cared less if he lost all of the fifty thousand francs in front of him. For the next two hours be played like a man possessed. His opponents came and went, but he remained unassailable. By midnight he had won four times his original stake.

"That's enough," the woman told him. "Now you may take me to supper."

They dined on pressed caviar and champagne, and it wasn't until Louis raised his glass to toast her muse that he realized he didn't even know her name.

"Jasmine Fremont."

"Beirut?"

"But of course."

"My God! Why, this is amazing! How is it we never met?"

She shrugged. "I've been traveling."

"Where?"

"Europe, America," she replied vaguely, then gave him a wicked smile. "You said our meeting was amazing. Finish your champagne, Louis, and I will show you something *truly* amazing."

She would not go with him to his apartment but took him instead to the Ritz and the Fremont apartments on the top floor. Silhouetted against the night pouring in through the French doors, she stripped for him, letting him feast and hunger for her both at the same time. When Louis finally moved toward her, it was she who pounced on him, tearing away his clothes and consuming him with a savagery he had not believed possible. Only much later, whenever Louis recalled that first night, did he understand that Jasmine had raped him.

As though it had been ordained, they became an "item," seen together in the best restaurants, clubs, and cabarets. Jasmine seemed to know anyone worth knowing in Paris, and Louis quickly found himself dining with the city's political and social elite. He also discovered that, in a way he did not quite comprehend, he was molting, discarding an old skin to make way for the new. Suddenly his opinions were being solicited and listened to. Men of enormous political and financial influence invited him to their clubs and homes, sought out his advice on all manners of things having to do with Lebanon. Who was the most reliable banker? Which broker could guarantee entry of shipments? Which waterfront properties were ripe for development?

Louis fielded the questions as best he could. Before long his telephone bills to Beirut exceeded his clothing expenses. He touched on friends and acquaintances he'd forgotten he had, and they in turn were more than eager to help him, knowing that in the Lebanese custom, a small percentage of a successful deal would find its way back to them.

There was only one question that, invariably asked, made Louis uncomfortable. What was it he actually did? What were his own ambitions?

At a dinner party Jasmine interceded.

"Why, Louis has enormous potential to become one of Beirut's leading spokesmen. He is the type of man who can present Lebanon to the world. Surely this is self-evident."

To Louis's utter astonishment, everyone around the table nodded. What was even more amazing was that he, too, believed it. And wondered why, for the life of him, he hadn't seen what now appeared so obvious.

When Louis arrived back in Beirut with Jasmine on his arm, he became convinced that Lebanon, already a mighty bridge between East and West, could become even greater and more influential than it already was—under the leadership of the right man.

Louis had already decided that the fitting way to launch his political career was to marry Jasmine in the most spectacular ceremony Beirut had ever seen. The evening he proposed he was in a panic that she wouldn't accept. When she did, he was ecstatic.

"I only wish I had more of a dowry to bring with me," she murmured wistfully.

Louis scarcely heard her as she explained the setup of the Société des Bains Mediterraniens holding company, which prevented her from selling her shares to anyone other than family, much less on the open market.

"Don't be silly," Louis whispered. "You are *everything* to me. Money"—he waved dismissively—"we can get anywhere. But there is only one you."

It was truly a fairy-tale wedding. Armand presided over the festivities, and while everything was done in the best taste and without regard to cost, Louis believed the casino owner's congratulations and best wishes were more formal than heartfelt. Still, he was shrewd enough to appreciate the value of being related to the Fremonts. In the tribal word of Levantine politics the value of family connections was incalculable, as was the guarantee that help, if asked for, could not be denied. Louis was certain that when he made his political intentions clear, Armand would be there with his support.

Louis had planned to discuss his future with Armand immediately after the wedding. Jasmine dissuaded him.

"It would be better to wait," she counseled him. "He is the kind of man who has to be sure of which way the wind is blowing before committing himself. Go to the others first."

That was not Louis's impression, but he bowed to Jasmine's obvious better understanding and turned his attention to the *zuama*.

Because of his shipping business, Louis's father had been a *zaim*. Since Louis had had no inclination to follow in his footsteps, however, the family business had diminished, and its influence was no longer great enough to allow him to enter the ranks of the *zuama* as an equal.

Jasmine came up with a solution.

"The *zuama* are all equally strong, so no one has a clear advantage. They refuse to choose one man from their ranks to lead them. That's understandable, since that man would obviously favor his family above the others. The fact that you belong to no one is your strength. You could be the natural middleman, arbiter of disputes, the wise judge." Jasmine paused and smiled. "The next president of Lebanon."

Although the presidential elections were two years away, Louis began wooing the *zuama* with Jasmine's expert guidance. The *zuama* received Louis graciously enough but not without suspicion. After wading through the maze of Levantine politeness and double-talk, each *zaim* finally discerned what it was Louis wanted. Families and their advisers were summoned, and there was great debate in the splendid villas that lined Lebanon's sun-drenched coast. It was generally agreed that the idea of Louis Jabar becoming president had merit. The way things stood, each family probably would field a candidate. Each would have limitless resources to draw on—and that meant a bitter public fight, reflecting badly on the *zuama* and, worse, damaging business. The idea of a compromise began to gain favor.

Louis was invited to private banquets where two or three *zuama* urged him to explain his intentions more fully. Louis was quite eloquent. Lebanon's stability and prosperity, he declared, were clearly the result of the labor of men such as those in the *zuama*. In the field of commerce, nothing needed change. But the right man in the presidential palace could, with the help of the enlightened *zuama*, bring even more prosperity to the country through foreign investment.

Of course Louis had the grace not to mention that the *zuama* and their followers, as middlemen, contractors, and suppliers would profit mightily from every dollar, franc, pound, and mark that found its way into Lebanon. He needn't have worried. While listening, the mental abacus of each *zaim* was making calculations furiously.

The *zuama* came around to the idea of supporting an independent for the presidency. One thing lacking, however, and which Louis was to discover only later, was a hook into Louis Jabar, some guarantee that he would not renege on his promises or intentions. This point secretly worried the *zuama*. Jabar was wealthy enough in his own right to launch an election, though not to finance or buy one. The *zuama* were also certain that Armand Fremont, with characteristic silence, had committed his prestige and purse to his cousin's husband. It was a natural enough assumption: in the Levantine world, kin was either supported unanimously or destroyed. Simply by not doing or saying anything, Armand had spoken volumes.

For the *zuama* this became a delicious predicament: if Louis didn't need the money, what else would serve as a handle on the man? The *zuama* searched high and low to solve the riddle, stealthily prying into every corner of Louis's life. Their findings were negligible. Louis neither drank nor gambled to excess. He did not indulge in drugs. He didn't keep mistresses or satisfy himself with little boys. So what *did* Louis do?

The answer, when it came, stunned the *zuama*. It was one

they had never believed possible. But when they were sure, a council of war was held, a decision made, and Nabil Tufaili elected to explain to both Salibis the facts of life.

Louis lit another cigarette and gazed out on the lights sparkling across Beirut harbor. The memory of how Tabbara had made a fool of him still rankled. All that time he had truly believed that Jasmine had everything under control and that Armand Fremont would announce he was backing his candidacy. In fact, it was the only belief Louis had to cling to, because by now the once-generous gods had completely turned their backs on him.

To the outside world Louis had the perfect marriage. His wife was intelligent, but not overly so, gracious, beautiful, and, as far as anyone had been able to determine, loyal. Every man in Beirut hungered for Jasmine. Many hours were whiled away in steam baths and on massage tables debating exactly how varied and exciting Louis's sex life must be. Of course, no one would have had the bad manners to come out and ask Louis. But if they had, his answer would have astounded them. As far as Louis was concerned, he was not a husband but a prisoner.

At first Louis had found Jasmine's sexual demands a challenge. He had been with other women who had thought themselves insatiable and had tamed them all. But not Jasmine. Her demands in and out of bed were legion, her sexual acrobatics passing from pleasure to real pain.

Louis shuddered whenever he pictured their bedroom. It was a dungeon, with sets of handcuffs, leather restraints, collars, a black submission mask, and an array of whips, the most prized of which had been crafted from the hide of a rhinoceros tail. Jasmine was always the dominant partner, taking him whenever and however she pleased. On several occasions Louis had been led into the chamber of horrors only to discover a second woman waiting, a snarling dominatrix who pounced on him, then proceeded to torment him exactly as Jasmine instructed her to.

He despaired because there was absolutely no way he

could extricate himself from the hell of his marriage. Jasmine was his connection to Armand Fremont's money, which in turn was crucial to the *zuama*'s support. He had to admit that he could not *afford* to let her go—even if such a thing were possible. The idea of being Lebanon's next president had grown from a pleasant notion to an addiction.

Resigned to his slavery, he trotted after Jasmine as she flew around the globe to indulge her love of sports and parties. He caught pneumonia in Scotland while she shot grouse, and suffered a mild concussion after one ski run at St. Moritz. When their friends teased him about being accident-prone, Louis just smiled. No one suspected a thing. He thought his life couldn't get worse. Then the *zuama* had called.

The meeting Tufaili had demanded took place at his home, built out of the ruins of a crusader's seraglio.

"The *zuama* were under the impression all was well between you and your kinsman," Tufaili said, the words coming out in a hoarse whisper.

Louis couldn't keep himself from watching Jasmine, who was staring hard at Tufaili.

For a fleeting moment Jasmine was gripped by terror that someway, somehow, Tufaili had learned the one thing she wanted never, ever for another soul to learn. That reference to *kinsman*. She repressed a shudder. There was no way for him to have found out about her parents, was there? Tufaili was so sly, so cunning. Could he have discovered in some way about the mother who had cared for her not at all except as the occasional beating post? Or the father who had cared for her too much . . . and had brought his exquisite tortures into her bed when she'd been little more than a tot? If Tufaili knew—No! She would not let the old bastard intimidate or blackmail her. She mastered her emotions and brought herself to a state where she could purr at the old devil.

"Why, Nabil," she asked, "whatever are you talking about?"

"Let Louis answer!" the *zaim* snapped. "Well?"

"Everything *is* all right!" Louis protested.

"Perhaps. But not well enough."

Louis shook his head. "I don't understand."

This time Tufaili focused his attention on Jasmine. "We believed—because your husband led us to believe—that when the time came, Armand Fremont would support Louis's candidacy, something we made possible."

"Of course he will!" Jasmine exclaimed.

Tufaili wagged a sausagelike finger. "No, not of course. We have learned that Armand Fremont does not think all that highly of your husband. In fact, he is not in the least impressed with his political skill."

Louis was shocked. "This is crazy! How could you possibly know—"

"How is unimportant," Tufaili replied, watching Louis carefully. "The point is we do know. Our sources are beyond reproach."

Louis's head was spinning. A black rage flared in his heart. The humiliations Jasmine had heaped upon him, the secret shame he lived with, the double life he endured, these were all part of the price to realize the dream she had stoked within him. Now it was going to be snatched away.

"I think you are mistaken, Nabil," Jasmine said. "But since you are convinced your information is correct, perhaps you can tell us exactly what it is you want."

"We have already invested a great deal of time and not a little money in Louis," Tufaili replied. "However, if Armand Fremont doesn't change his opinion, or worse, opposes Louis's candidacy, then we all lose heavily." He paused. "And that is unacceptable."

"What would it take to make it acceptable?" Jasmine demanded.

Tufaili smiled benevolently. "Twenty million dollars. Good-faith money or a guarantee bond so that the *zuama* do not end up bearing the entire financial burden of the campaign."

"Impossible!" Louis shot back.

"That's enough!" Jasmine's eyes never left Tufaili.

"Since you presume to know so much already, surely you're aware that we do not have that kind of money."

"Perhaps not. But you are one of the three shareholders in the Casino de Paradis . . ."

"True."

"And think of what those shares would be worth if SBM became a *public* company. Twenty million could be a pittance."

Tufaili leaned forward, his cologne nauseating Louis.

"Dirt cheap considering you would end up with an entire *country*, Jasmine."

Tufaili was right, thought Louis. Twenty million was cheap. The problem was, he might as well have been asking for the moon. On top of that he had given them a deadline to come up with the money, and every day the ticking of the clock became a little louder.

After the confrontation with Tufaili, Louis had been ready to surrender his dreams. Jasmine refused even to consider such a thing. One way or another, she had sworn, the money would be forthcoming, no matter what had to be done to get it.

Even murder?

First, Alexander Maser. Then the scandal at, and collapse of, Maritime Continental . . .

Louis had never associated either tragedy with whatever Jasmine had been plotting.

Now she talks about Armand and how accidents can happen . . .

In spite of the warm evening breeze, Louis shivered. He had never suspected such rage in Jasmine's heart. Now that he had glimpsed it, had been struck by the possibility that somehow Jasmine might have been responsible for what had happened to Maser and his bank, he dared to ask himself whether *anyone* had any control over Jasmine.

13

The thirty-minute drive into Beirut was harrowing for Pierre. He had heard of the discreet inquiries Armand had been making about the debacle at Maritime Continental. Now Alexander's daughter was in Beirut. . . . Why? And what did Jasmine know that she was still keeping to herself? It was all he could do to concentrate on driving through the narrow, winding streets of Ra's Beirut, overflowing at this hour with evening crowds.

"Everything all right at home?" asked Jasmine.

Pierre was startled by the sound of her voice. "Yes, of course."

Jasmine laughed. "Oh, Pierre, you're such a poor liar!"

Pierre gripped the Bentley's steering wheel so tightly that his knuckles turned white. At the last minute he swerved to avoid running down some party-goers coming out of a club.

"Pierre!"

"I'm . . . I'm sorry. Damn people all over the streets."

"I was just teasing you," Jasmine consoled him. "For young girls everything is possible. When they find a man who will provide for their dreams, they think they can dream forever."

"Yes, well, I suppose that's true," Pierre said nervously.

"It's hard to say no to someone you love so much, isn't it? You're always afraid that if you deny them anything, they will leave you."

Pierre managed to avoid crushing the shrubbery bordering the driveway to Jasmine's apartment building. He set the gear in park and slumped against the leather seat. His hands were shaking so badly, he could hardly light his cigarette.

"How did you know, Jasmine? You must tell me! How did you find out about the bank . . . what I was doing?"

"You asked me that before," Jasmine replied in a bored tone. "But my answer is the same: it's none of your business, Pierre."

"Damn you, bitch!"

He swung around, his arm raised, Jasmine never moved, never flinched. He lowered his arm.

"If you had struck me, Pierre, I would have handed you your cock," she said, her voice bone cold. "If you ever raise your hand against to me, I will ruin you!"

"I'm . . . I'm sorry. I don't know what came over me. It's just that—"

"That you feel impotent. And like most men who think they're trapped, you lash out. But not at me, Pierre, *Never* against me. Do you understand?"

"Yes . . . yes, I promise, it will never happen again."

"At least not with me. Now listen carefully because what I have to tell you concerns our good friend Kenneth Morton. It seems that someone has been asking about him in London."

"That's impossible!" Pierre whispered. "Morton has been paid. He's gone to Provence. How could anyone have found out—"

Then Pierre seized the answer to his own question. *"Alexander? Alexander left a message with Morton's name?"*

"For Armand, yes. But it's not Armand who is looking now. It is David Cabot."

The mention of Cabot's name thrust a shaft of fear into Pierre's stomach.

"That bastard! He is a rottweiler. Once he gets his teeth into you, he never lets go!"

"This time he will. I will see to that. But in return I want your best efforts, Pierre, your *best*, in getting Louis the money he needs."

"I promise I will do what I can. But you must understand my position—"

Jasmine reached out and cupped his cheek. Then suddenly she grabbed some flesh between her thumb and forefinger and twisted hard, staring into Pierre's eyes as he screamed.

"But I do, Pierre. I understand perfectly."

Jasmine laughed maliciously as she ambled along the hallway to her apartment. What a perfect old goat Pierre was. How, indeed, had she discovered his embezzlement? The silly fool would never guess the source of her information. She gloated as she recalled that day six months ago.

Cleo had telephoned her half a dozen times before she'd finally returned the call. Ever since Pierre had taken up with Cleo, Jasmine had refused invitations to his table and parties. The more Pierre begged her to include Cleo in her circle, the more studiously she ignored the girl. That was why Jasmine became so puzzled and intrigued that day, finally relented, and called Cleo.

Cleo asked to meet. Jasmine selected a café in the heart of Ra's Beirut. She did not frequent this place, only using it exactly as she was now, to meet people she wouldn't be seen with at the Phoenicia or the Hotel Saint Georges. Jasmine knew the moment Cleo sat down that she had recognized the slight represented by the place chosen for their meeting. The anger and resentment shone on her face.

Cleo ordered coffee from a passing waiter and removed her oversize sunglasses. She stared at Jasmine, who hadn't so much as greeted her.

"You don't like me at all, do you?" she blurted out.

Jasmine inclined her head. "You could have asked me that over the telephone. The answer would have been the same: no, not particularly."

"You think you're better than me."

"Cleo, if this is all you had in mind, you really are wasting my time."

Jasmine was ready to go when Cleo said, "I have something you can use, something valuable to *both* of us."

Jasmine sat back, her eyes taking in the scene around her. The tables next to them were empty, and no one in the café seemed to be paying them any special attention.

"I'm listening."

"But I'm not sure I can trust you."

Jasmine looked at her thoughtfully. The girl was uncertain and defiant, but not frightened. Maybe there was something here after all.

"You need my help," Jasmine said flatly.

"Yes."

"But once you tell me—and if it's something I *can* use—then you have no leverage. In fact I may not need you at all."

"That's right," Cleo replied tightly. "You would be a fool to betray me like that. But you might do it, because that's how you are."

"Such flattery," Jasmine murmured. "Well, it's up to you, Cleo. Neither of us has all day."

Cleo leaned forward. "It's Pierre."

"What about him?"

"You know everything he has been buying for me, whatever I want, really."

Jasmine gave Cleo's outfit a pointed look.

"He's broke," Cleo said, smiling at the surprise in Jasmine's widened eyes. "You didn't know that, did you?"

"You're talking nonsense!" Jasmine snapped. "Pierre has plenty of money."

"No, darling," Cleo purred. "*I* have lots of his money. And he keeps getting more because he has to. Look at me, Jasmine. Think back to everything you know he's bought me, then multiply that by ten. Do you really believe that even Pierre has that much cash from his income and investments? Do you?"

"What are you saying, Cleo?" she asked at last.

"That Pierre is a thief," Cleo replied, a smug twist to her words. "On a grand scale."

"You had better have some proof," Jasmine told her coldly.

Cleo fished in her bag and brought out the copies she had made from pages in the ledger Pierre kept in the safe. A few minutes later Jasmine realized that Pierre was a greater fool than she had ever given him credit for being.

"I assume there's more where this came from," Jasmine said, tapping the pages with her fingernail.

"Much more."

"And just what is it you propose to do with this, Cleo?"

"For the moment, nothing at all. But there may come a day when I feel that Pierre is about to take one risk too many. Or he becomes careless, makes a mistake. Sharing this with you is my insurance."

"Really? How do you know I won't turn around and tell Pierre about your little secret? As smitten as he is, he would still throw you out the door."

"Oh, Jasmine, I don't think you would do that. Because it's your little secret now too. Don't you think I've learned something about you after all this time? You love secrets. You are like a miser with them, always collecting and hoarding, using them only when the moment is perfect, when you get the most out of them.

"No, you won't tell Pierre. You will lock this away in your head and save it until you need it."

Jasmine smiled. "You are playing a very dangerous game with me."

"I'm already in one," Cleo shot back. "That is why I need insurance."

"What exactly do you mean by that?"

"If Pierre falls, I don't want to be next to him. I want enough money to live the way I do for the rest of my life."

"You have plenty as it is!"

"Don't be cheap, Jasmine! It doesn't become you. What I have put in your lap is worth a paltry million dollars."

"And if, as you say, something were to happen to Pierre, why should I pay you anything at all? It would be too late for you to collect."

Cleo laughed. "Leverage, right? Jasmine, if you didn't pay me, I would throw so much shit against your lily-white image, you wouldn't know what was happening. I would testify in a court of law that I, a simple girl, horribly frightened, had discovered the error of my lover's ways and come to you for advice. You, of course, convinced me to stay silent, but just to be sure, I would mention all this in my diary. . . . Are you getting the idea, Jasmine?"

"Quite clearly."

"Then we have a deal?"

Jasmine rose and adjusted her hat. "We have an agreement, Cleo. One million dollars in the bank of your choice if anything should happen to Pierre. Besides that, nothing changes. Do you understand? *Nothing!*"

Cleo dropped some coins into the saucer with the bill in it.

"Keep your airs and pretenses, Jasmine. I don't want them or need them." She looked at the coins. "You know, the one thing that really annoys me about people like you is that you think you never have to pay for anything. Not *this* time. That's why, Jasmine, the coffee is on me."

The memory of Cleo's last words still cut deep, even though by now Jasmine had almost convinced herself that she had gotten her million dollars' worth—if it ever came that she had to pay it.

Of course, Cleo had had no intention of letting her keep the damning photostats of Pierre's transgression, but that didn't matter. Jasmine's memory was almost photographic, as Pierre was to discover a few days later.

Jasmine had waited only long enough to think through the consequences of blackmailing Pierre. As far as she could see there was no way for her to lose. And she was right: the pompous, self-righteous Pierre collapsed as soon as Jasmine began giving him chapter and verse.

Pierre's reaction had given Jasmine an almost sexual satisfaction, a feeling heightened by the fact that she pointedly refused to tell Pierre, in spite of his begging, where she had gotten her information. As she watched him, she saw the faces of suspects leap in front of his terrified eyes. But like most quarry, he was too afraid to recognize the obvious, that what—or who—had brought him to this point was what he most trusted and loved. And so never suspected.

"So what do you want from me?" Pierre had asked when he had recovered his composure.

"At the moment, nothing."

Pierre shook his head violently. "No, Jasmine. You are not like that. You always want *something!*"

"You will know what it is when the time comes," Jasmine had told him. "Until then, your little secret is safe with me."

Just as it is with Cleo. . . .

Whether it was intuition or a twist of fate, Jasmine felt she would not have long to wait. She believed that once a man's luck turns rotten, there is nothing he can do to stop the slide. That afternoon, when Pierre had stormed into her home, weeping and cursing about Alexander Maser's having confronted him with the embezzlement, ranting that Jasmine had betrayed him, Jasmine realized her moment was at hand.

"Then you know what you must do," she had said.

Pierre looked up at her uncomprehendingly.

"What is left?" he demanded miserably.

"I should have thought that was obvious," Jasmine whispered, her eyes boring into his.

Jasmine knew, by his expression of horror, when the implication of her words had registered.

"No! You're insane!"

"It's either that, or you lose everything—your post, your woman, your reputation. You would have nothing, Pierre. Maybe not even the courage to take the last honourable way out."

She leaned toward him, feeling him flinch under her touch.

"I will tell you exactly what to do, whom to call, what to say. These things are not as difficult as you might imagine. And don't worry about remorse, Pierre. When Alexander Maser is gone, you will not shed a tear. You will be too relieved for that."

And he had been relieved, she thought as she entered the apartment, for a while. . . .

Pierre was relieved when he saw there were no lights in his villa. For the first time he didn't even care where Cleo was. He needed to be alone. He deactivated the alarm at the front door and walked straight toward the liquor cabinet in the dining room. He took a bottle of whiskey and a glass and sat in the silent moonlight shimmering across the hills off St. George's Bay.

Pierre gulped down his Scotch and poured out more. He seldom drank liquor, and the single malt, smooth as it was, raced to his head. He prayed it would slow the thoughts whirling in his head like some mad carnival ride, dissolve the fear that burned in the pit of his stomach. Instead the Scotch did exactly the opposite, magnifying the horrors that crawled over him like gremlins. By the time Cleo found him, Pierre, with a drunk's absolute certainty, had decided what it was he had to do.

"Pierre, what happened to you?"

Dressed, just barely, in a Schulmacher black-and-white-check vinyl tube dress, with rhinestone straps and matching earrings, Cleo couldn't believe what she was seeing. She had taken advantage of Pierre's absence to go out to the latest club, the Hippopotamus. For three hours she had danced up a frenzy, changing partners with the music. She had expected Pierre to be asleep when she got home.

"What's gotten into you?" Cleo demanded. "Why have you been drinking?"

Pierre stared at her, his eyes glazed. "For the truth. I drink for the truth."

"Oh, Christ!" Cleo muttered. "Come on, let me get you into bed."

"No! There are things I must tell you. I have no choice anymore. . . ."

The despair in Pierre's voice frightened Cleo. She had never seen him drunk and had no idea what could have happened to reduce him to this state. If there had been warning signs, she'd missed them.

"All right, darling. We'll talk. I'll sit here and we'll talk for as long as you like."

"You know I love you," Pierre blubbered.

"Of course I do."

"And that I will do anything for you."

"Yes."

"But I can't anymore." Tears began dribbling down Pierre's cheeks. "You see, I'm bankrupt. I don't have any money."

Cleo shivered. "Pierre, don't talk nonsense! Of course you have money!"

Pierre shook his head wearily. "Not my money. That's all gone. I use the bank's money."

His words froze Cleo. "What do you mean, darling?" she asked softly.

The confession tumbled out on a river of whiskey. Because Cleo knew about the secret ledgers in Pierre's safe, she had long ago deduced where the money was coming from. But she was astonished at how ingeniously he had gone about his thievery.

"So you see, my love, Alexander somehow found out about me. To this day I don't know how. When he was killed, I truly believed the danger had passed. But it hasn't. Now Armand is asking questions. Maybe because Alexander left something behind that could incriminate me. Whatever it is, Armand will find it. He's a bastard that way. Then he'll break me."

Pierre forced more liquor into himself and coughed.

"I can't stand living like this! Wondering if the next phone call or knock on the door will mean the police. I imagine myself being dragged from my own home in handcuffs. I couldn't endure that, Cleo, I *couldn't*! I must make a clean breast of it, turn myself in while there's still time. The bank will do everything to avoid a scandal. Perhaps I'll be able to pay back what I stole. Yes, of course! The board will agree to that. They'll understand that I'm not really a criminal. . . ."

Cleo drew his head to her bosom. "No, of course you're not, darling. You're a kind, decent, and generous man. But, my love, they will not show you any mercy. No, listen to me, please, for both our sakes."

Cleo was thinking furiously. If Pierre persisted in his demented intentions, everything would be lost. Somehow she had to hold this wreck together, at least for the next few days.

"Pierre, you cannot go to your bank or the police."

Pierre pulled away. "Why?" he implored her.

"Because if you do, you will destroy me as well," Cleo said gravely. "Think, my love. Everything you have done has been for me. Everyone will say that I was the cause. Some will even suggest that I forced you to do these things. Don't you see? I am your accomplice! I will suffer as you will. Can you imagine what will be done to me in prison, darling?"

Pierre shuddered. "But you're innocent. I will make them believe that!"

"They will believe what they want to. I know you understand that. I'm begging you, my love, do not condemn yourself, because if you do . . ."

"I could never let anything happen to you," Pierre whispered hoarsely. "I would die first!"

"No, sweet. You must *live*! We must *both* see this through and triumph! You don't have to go to the authorities—"

"But Armand!"

Cleo cradled his head to her bosom, her cheek against his temple.

"It will all be all right," she crooned. "You'll see, I promise. Now I want you to sleep, just like this, in may arms. It will all be all right. . . ."

Jasmine turned her chair to get out of the sun. She was waiting at the café in Ra's Beirut, and she was annoyed, irritated. She drummed her long, polished nails on the metal table.

Alexander Maser's death had been only the first step, the one she had been looking and waiting for to begin the ruin of the Maritime Continental Bank. In turn, that should have pushed Armand to take the casino public in order to save the reputation of his dear, dead friend. She had been so sure that Armand would answer the call of his conscience and rush in with all the money that was needed. If he had gone public, she would have all the money she needed now to make Louis president of Lebanon. But Armand had fooled her. Perhaps his hide was tougher than she'd thought.

While everything had gone as she'd planned, with exactly the desired result on that cold, lonely road outside Geneva, she still did not have what she wanted . . . needed.

Now Cleo was coming toward her, her face set behind those ridiculous sunglasses.

More trouble . . .

"It's been a long time since you bought me coffee," Jasmine said.

Cleo threw a pack of cigarettes on the table and snapped at a passing waiter. "Vodka—double!"

"And so early in the day," Jasmine murmured.

"I think you'll join me when I tell you about Pierre!" Cleo retorted.

"*Du calme*, my dear," Jasmine said, nodding at the waiter.

Cleo gulped her drink and lighted a cigarette.

"He's falling apart."

"Explain, please."

Cleo recounted Pierre's drunken crisis of conscience and his intention to confess everything.

"Do you think he was serious, given the circumstances?" asked Jasmine.

"Absolutely!"

"Can you control him?"

Cleo bit her lip. Never in her life had she doubted her power over men. But this was different.

"For a while, but not long."

Jasmine was silent for a moment.

"Well then, I think I have to come up with a convincing argument for him *not* to say anything."

"Remember, if something happens, you owe me—"

"Yes, Cleo, I remember!"

Somewhat chastened, Cleo lowered her voice. "Can you do that?" she asked. "Talk some sense into him?"

Jasmine smiled. "Let's just say that I can make him see the errors of his ways."

14

Kate had mixed feelings about seeing Armand that evening. But as she rode to the St. Georges where he'd asked her to meet him, she realized how very much she had missed his company.

Perched on the edge of the same peninsula as the Casino de Paradis, the St. Georges was the unofficial nerve center of Beirut. Every Hollywood star of note had, at one time or another, posed for photographers by the pool. Other celebrities were married in the gardens or conducted affairs in the sumptuous suites, then a few years later hammered out divorce settlements in one of the *cordon bleu* restaurants. Businessmen from every part of the world converged on the Golden Calf lounge to haggle over the price of oil, dispute the quality of pearls, seal deals worth millions with a handshake and champagne toast.

Kate entered the hotel through the Disco Volante bar.

"You look beautiful, Kate. A Lanvin, isn't it?"

Kate smelled him even before she heard his voice. It was the same cologne he'd been wearing on the plane, which had lingered on her skin long after they had arrived.

"Thank you for accepting the invitation," Armand said, holding her gaze.

"You might regret saying that," Kate replied. "I have more questions for you."

"I shall do my best to answer them," Armand said solemnly.

As he escorted her through the lounge, Kate watched Armand being acknowledged by several men. She also noticed that almost everyone was taking a good look at her. To Kate's surprise, Armand steered her past the main dining rooms and into the recesses of the hotel.

"Are we eating in the kitchen?" she asked.

"Not quite."

The room was one of the most elegant she'd ever seen, reminding her of photographs of deluxe ocean liners from the 1930's. The ceiling was two stories high, the intricately carved oak columns and sweeping staircase reflected in a dazzling display of Lalique crystal and glass. The maître d' guided them to a choice banquet from which they could see the entire room. As she passed by the tables, Kate noted that women were conspicuous by their absence. When she mentioned this to Armand, he put a finger to his lips.

"This is deep graveyard. Remember the bar you came through?"

Kate nodded. The tiny Disco Volante had been packed with men whose evening attire was less than fashionable.

"They are journalists," Armand explained. "They monitor the comings and goings of these gentlemen, who are, for the most part, diplomats."

Kate peeked over the top of her menu.

"Certain rules operate here, as in most of Beirut," Armand continued. "The bureaucrats needed a place where they could get together and divide up the world in peace and quiet. The journalists found out and demanded access. Impossible, right? So the hotel came up with a compromise. The journalists would be allowed as far as the bar. From there they could see who came and went but never overhear anything. Now they interpret the meaning of who is dining with whom in the same way the ancients foretold the future by reading chicken entrails—and, I suppose, with about as much success."

"You said 'most' of the people here are in the diplomatic corps. What about the others?"

"They're spies."

"I beg your pardon!"

"Spies. Remember Kim Philby, the highly placed British intelligence officer who was a Russian double agent? He loved this place. In fact, he was such a good customer that the front desk is still holding his mail."

"You're joking!"

"Not at all. Every employee in this hotel is on the payroll of at least two intelligence services. Come down into the kitchens after closing, and you'll hear the waiters trading stories to see who will report what to whom."

"How many of them report to you?" she asked quietly.

The laughter in Armand's eyes flickered and waned.

"Would you like me to order for both of us?" he asked politely. "The *canard a l'orange* is excellent."

After the waiter had gone, Kate excused herself to use the ladies' room. Armand sipped his wine and wondered about her. He could not understand the attraction that drew him to her so strongly. He hadn't seen her since that night at the casino and was surprised that he'd missed her. Kate was a beautiful woman, but no more so than thousands of others in Beirut. He admired her determination and strength, but found it tempered by an abrasive quality that often seeped into her words. Obviously she was still stung by what had happened a few days ago.

So what the hell did he see in her?

He was startled by the question that leapt into his mind. Not once, with any of the women he'd known, had it ever come up. He had always believed that in the long run there could be no permanent place for a woman in his life. Armand, who had worn this understanding like an old, comfortable sweater, suddenly was aware of how sad it was. He loved women, their charm and wiles and wit, the way their throats rippled when they laughed, how they moved in their sleep, the tenderness and generosity they were capable of. But he was all too aware of the cool, slick facade that grew on the hearts and consciences of Beiruti women. He'd seen how the wealth and glamour corrupted, making girls believe that their dreams really did have a price, and that out there were men who could easily meet it. He had witnessed the adultery and perversion, the drugs and degradation. But at the end of it all he had not met one woman to whom he could reveal himself, to whom he could cleave in the night and sleep a trusting sleep.

As he watched Kate coming back, Armand marveled at

the mystery of attraction. *Don't be a fool!* he told himself
angrily.

She was so much younger—and not only in years. And
she was Alex's daughter. But where is the line between an
obligation to a lifelong friend and one's own feelings?

"A penny for your thoughts," Kate said, seeing the preoccupied expression on Armand's face.

He laughed. "I'm afraid you'd be getting change back.
Let's enjoy our meal."

The food was some of the best Kate had ever tasted, and
the duck was, as Armand had promised, unforgettable.
Throughout he provided wry comments on their fellow diners, giving Kate a glimpse into this secret world.

"If I've learned one thing about Beirut, it's that everybody loves to play games," Kate observed.

"The national pastime," Armand agreed. "In Lebanon life
is one big backgammon game, a combination of luck, skill,
and daring."

"Which you seem to pay very well."

"All it takes is practice." Armand changed the subject. "I
have some news for you. Not as much as either of us would
like, but it's a start."

Kate leaned forward eagerly. "About your mysterious
second man?"

Armand shook his head. "The money that has gone missing from Maritime Continental."

Armand explained what he had managed to find out. As
he spoke, Kate became more and more puzzled.

"I don't understand it," she said. "From Rio the funds
went to Panama, then to Geneva. The Swiss police and
banking authorities know that the funds have been embezzled. They *must* have traced the account and whom it belongs to. Why don't they *do* something?"

"Because of Swiss banking-secrecy laws."

"Which stand even if a crime's been committed?"

"There's still Nazi loot under the streets of Zurich. Oh,
there are avenues that, with the proper documentation and
the patience of Job, might lead to a special hearing to deter-

mine whether an account should be opened or not. But they take years to travel, and only one or two out of thousands yield any success."

"So we give up, is that it?"

"I deserve a little more credit than that," Armand chided her. "Contrary to what some think, the Swiss are people who put on their pants one leg at a time."

"You know directors or officials who will help?" Kate asked hopefully.

"There are such people, but that's not who I'm talking about. A bank director who deals directly with clients will never violate their confidence. But the clerks—the detail people, those to whom an account has no face, only a number—will help us. If they can."

Kate's eyes glittered. "So you *do* have someone!"

"I don't want you to get your hopes up," Armand cautioned. "There is a long way to go."

Kate nodded. Patience had never been her strong suit. Her life was being ruled and ruined, yet all she could do was grasp at shadows. But at least there was one thing she could get a straight answer to.

"Armand, I've heard things about David Cabot."

He looked at her sharply. "From whom?"

"Jasmine."

"I see. And what did Jasmine have to say?"

Kate took a deep breath. "She told me David Cabot's family was murdered by pirates while they were on a cruise. David was the lone survivor. After that, you took him in."

Armand selected a cigar from the humidor presented him by the captain, clipped and lighted it.

"It's true. But as always, there is more to the story. I will tell you if you like, on the condition that you never repeat the details to anyone."

"I won't."

Armand nodded. "Very well. You have probably heard tales of a modern-day slave trade in this part of the world. Most of them are true. The routes established centuries ago are still being used, and the victims have not changed either.

They come from across Africa, India, Europe, children, girls
and boys in their teens, young women . . . David almost became one of them."

Armand held nothing back, and the horror of his account
made Kate flinch.

"That was one of the principal reasons your father and I
set up Interarmco," Armand said. "So that we would have a
weapon with which to smash the rings that profited on human bondage and misery. David is the one who wields it."

Armand sat back, his eyes moist, then said, "I don't think
I have ever met a human being who carries as much pain inside himself as David. He is drawn to these stolen, abused
children as a moth to a flame . . . because he almost *became*
one of them.

"There are so many stories I can tell you about him, how
he moved deeper and deeper into the hierarchy of traders,
learning which boats were carrying children, which docks
they would berth at, where they were being held before the
auctions. One by one David went after them. The boats fell
victim to mysterious explosions in the boilers, crippling
them; warehouses erupted in flames; even some of the
traders disappeared, never to be seen again.

"David doesn't know how many children he saved. I
don't think he cares. All he believes is that if he can keep
one child from bondage, it is enough. You see, Kate, even
today there is a part of David that remains that terrified boy
watching his parents murdered, being snatched away and
thrown in with other children. Then realizing what would
happen to them all . . . And that is why he will continue to
do this work to his dying day."

Kate felt a shiver crawl up her spine and let out a deep
breath. She recalled David Cabot's hard eyes, the warning
he had given her the night they'd met, the latent violence
sparking like electricity off his fingertips when he had
touched her.

"So that's why you trust him," she said at last.

"With my life," Armand replied quietly.

"Has he found out anything since we last talked?"

"Nothing yet. But I will be talking to him later this evening."

Kate reached out and touched Armand's sleeve.

"And my father was involved in this."

"Very much so. From the very beginning and without stop, because the slave trade never stops. It is a monster with a thousand heads. Cut off one, and there is still another. A few years ago I thought we had come close to smashing the major rings operating in the Middle East. *And we had!* But in place of five, a new one sprang up. Despite all of David's efforts, we still cannot put a face to the man behind it."

Kate drained the last of her cognac, watching as Armand signed the check. She was stunned by his revelations. They forced her to look not only at the man sitting opposite her and see him in another light, but also back, to her father and the kind of secret life he had led without her ever suspecting its existence.

How much more was there to discover? Kate wondered. Where would it all lead?

As he pulled back Kate's chair, Armand said, "I spoke with Emil earlier. He mentioned that the two of you discussed something that had happened at about the same time the bank came under fire, something to do with one of Maritime Continental's employees?"

It took Kate a minute to recall what Emil had referred to.

"Oh, that. One of the bank's employees was killed in a fire. I thought it was too strange a coincidence. But I looked into it, and there was no connection."

"Why don't you tell me about it?"

She shrugged, then quickly explained about the fire in Greenwich Village that had killed a wire-transfer clerk named Michael Samson, her visit to Prudence Templeton, another Maritime Continental employee who had positively identified the body. "There just wasn't any connection," she concluded.

"By the sound of it there wasn't much to begin with," Armand agreed. "As you say, coincidence."

As they left the restaurant, Armand said, "I hope you are no longer too angry with me, Kate."

Kate was touched. "I'm no good at dealing with secrets."

"With a little luck there won't be any more secrets soon."

Kate thought there might be more truth to Armand's words than he imagined. Everyone told her Beirut was a city whose stock-in-trade was information. This being the case, it was time she started tapping the wells.

That night, as he had told Kate he would, Armand talked to David, who was still in the south of France.

"The locals say Morton is here," David told him, referring to the British banker. "He's an amateur ornithologist. Apparently it's not unusual to hike off into the hills for three or four days. All I can do is wait for him to come back."

"Perhaps not," said Armand.

Quickly he gave David the gist of his conversation with Kate and the strange circumstances surrounding Michael Samson's death.

"I want some background on him," Armand concluded. "Can you do that from where you are?"

"I'm less than an hour from Cannes, where I know a few people who can help me out. Geneva will do the rest."

"It's probably a red herring, David. I don't want you to miss Morton."

"I won't. The local cops don't like him much. Seems he's an arrogant little prick. They'll back me up."

"Watch out for yourself."

Armand imagined the smile behind David's reply. "Luck, Armand."

"Your hunch was right," David told Armand some forty-eight hours later. "There's more—or less, depending on how you look at—to Michael Samson than meets the eye."

He proceeded to explain his findings.

"The trail dead-ends in Malta," Armand said thoughtfully, drinking in everything David had told him.

"That's right. Maritime Continental got its background on

Samson from the Sauer Bank in Zurich. Sauer received theirs from two French banks, one of which was Credit Foncier, Samson's first job. They tell me his French academic and Maltese background records checked out."

"What about the Polytechnique?"

"That's the kicker. They admitted Samson on the strength of his record at the American University of Beirut."

"So . . ." Armand prompted.

"But the AUB archives show that Samson *was* in fact a Maltese citizen."

"How many Maltese have ever studied there?" Armand demanded.

"In the last seventy years, three."

"The son of a bitch is no more Maltese than I am! Nor are we done yet peeling away the layers."

"You think there could be a connection between Samson and what happened at Maritime Continental?"

"The only thing I'd stake money on is that Samson is *not* a Maltese. He created this elaborate, and very successful, cover. Why? The answer may have something to do with Maritime Continental. We'll know more after you deal with Morton and are ready to move."

"Where am I going?" David asked mildly.

"I should have thought that was obvious. Malta."

Alejandro Lopez was not a man who attracted attention. Of medium height, he was wiry almost to the point of being thin, with a smooth, dark complexion that could have marked him as an Arab, Greek, or southern Italian. Women found it difficult to judge his age. There was a crow's nest of creases under his flashing dark eyes, but his full head of black hair and perfect white teeth belonged to a young man. However, all agreed that Alejandro Lopez was a charming gentleman, obviously well-bred and well traveled, and they wondered why he had never been snared in marriage.

By profession Lopez was a wine merchant who owned a flourishing enterprise in the British protectorate of Gibraltar. He was both a familiar and welcome face around the area.

Lopez provided the officers of the British garrison with excellent wines at wholesale prices and even delivered particular vintages for special occasions. His shop and warehouse
provided steady employment for a dozen people, who all
agreed Lopez was a fair and generous boss. His widowed
landlady, aspiring to a second marriage, doted on him and
fantasized about his lean, strong body.

That Lopez spent a great deal of time outside Gibralter
surprised no one. It was considered natural that he should
have to travel far and wide to check vineyards and sample
their offerings. Indeed, Lopez's passport was muddied with
the stamps of a dozen countries around the Mediterranean,
from Portugal to Turkey.

Whenever Lopez was at his office, he spent a great deal
of time on the telephone. Because of the British military
presence, Gibraltar had one of the most efficient communi-
cations systems in Europe. Although a telephone was devil-
ishly hard to come by, given the antiquated Spanish
telecommunications office, Lopez's British friends had seen
to it that he had access to the special lines laid for them.
After all, a reliable telephone was the lifeline of a merchant
doing business across the Mediterranean.

It was also indispensable in the work of an assassin, and
Alejandro Lopez, to those who used such men, was considered one of the finest in the world.

He was in his office going over receipts when his pretty
secretary informed him that there was a caller on the line
asking about a particular champagne vintage. Lopez
thanked her and took the call. Given how brief the conversation was, the secretary guessed that her boss hadn't been
able to fill the order.

That afternoon Lopez took lunch at his usual hour.
Instead of going to one of several restaurants he frequented,
he met a colonel, whom he supplied with Scotland's finest
whiskey, at the officers' club.

Halfway through a light meal of Dover sole, Lopez pretended to remember a call he had to make. His host was gracious enough to let him use the phone in the privacy of the

library. It was from there that he spoke to Beirut.

"This is Charles," Lopez said smoothly, his tone devoid of inflection or accent.

The voice on the other end of the line was cold and remote.

"There is something else to be done."

"Tell me what it is."

The voice gave out the grisly details, concluding "Soon. As soon as you can do it."

Lopez made some swift calculations.

"There will be an extra charge. Twenty percent more."

"The money will be wired to Zurich this afternoon. Second half on your delivery."

"Thank you, Beirut. You will know when I'm done."

When Lopez returned to the dining room, his host asked him, "Good news, I trust?"

He smiled and sighed. "I'm afraid I'll be traveling again."

The bed was a tangle of sheets from which Michael, lying on his side, was watching Jasmine apply her makeup.

"I don't think they'll let you into the Hippopotamus dressed like that," Jasmine said, eyeing Michael's bare torso in her vanity mirror.

"They would if they knew I own fifty percent of the club," he replied lazily.

"Whatever you do, just remain a very silent partner," she advised him.

He stared at her. "It's good to be back, Jasmine. To be with you. To be Michael Saidi again."

During Michael's absence from Beirut, Jasmine had looked after his ever-growing fortune made from the drug trade and white slavery. Tempted though she'd been to appropriate his several million dollars, so desperately needed for her plans for Louis, she had restrained herself. She would have use for Michael for some time yet. . . . And so she had established a dummy corporation to buy small parcels of real estate, interest in night clubs, restaurants, select boutiques, even racehorses. This was the final part of the plan, to be unveiled when Michael Saidi, a self-made businessman, returned from abroad to make his entrance into Beirut society.

Even she had been taken aback at how successfully the Rio plastic surgeon had sculpted Michael's features. She had mounted a picture of Michael as he had looked in New York and had him stand beside it. The resemblance was fleeting. Then she did the same with a photo taken before he had left Beirut. The transition was perfect. No one could say that this older Michael Saidi could not have grown into the kind of man he was today. Yes as far as the world was concerned, Michael Samson was truly dead.

"It's fantastic, isn't it?" Michael remarked lazily, his eyes following Jasmine's fingers as she ran them under her calf and across her thigh, smoothing the stocking. "Armand is turning the Middle East upside down to try to find this 'new slave ring,' yet he doesn't bother to look in his own backyard. He has no idea that I'm the phantom he's chasing . . . God, the look on his face if he ever knew the truth!"

"That may be, but don't gloat or underestimate Armand," Jasmine warned him. "There are many men who did and had to pay the price."

"But you will never let him come *too* close, will you, Jasmine?" Michael said softly, reaching for her leg.

"There's something I want you to do," Jasmine said, brushing away his hand and changing the subject. "Alexander Maser's daughter is here in Beirut."

Michael had already heard this from his contacts at the Beirut Press Agency, but he didn't interrupt Jasmine.

"It seems that she is determined to get to the bottom of what happened at Maritime Continental. It would be prudent for us to know how she's coming along, don't you think?"

"And how would we do that?" asked Michael, already knowing the answer.

"Don't be so coy!" Jasmine said impatiently. "Use your invincible charms."

"Even if it means going to bed with her."

Jasmine's eyes blazed. "She's young, virtually alone in a city she doesn't understand at all, and on top of everything, a bumpkin. I'd like to believe, Michael, that a little kindness and companionship would be enough to endear you to Miss Katherine Maser."

He thoughtfully looked at her. "You're worried about her, aren't you?"

"She's a complication," she snapped. "Just make sure that's all she remains."

"What about Armand?"

Jasmine crossed the room, silk whispering to silk. She was wearing stockings and a garter belt, but no panties, and stood very close to Michael. She looked at him fiercely and gripped the back of his head, drawing him between her legs. "He *has* become a problem," she whispered. "It is really tragic . . ."

The weeks leading up to Beirut's Carnival were some of the busiest, and this year was no exception. The game salons were jammed. At midnight Armand made his customary walk around the casino, a ritual that both players and employees expected of him. In casino jargon, it was called "putting on the face," the chance for anyone to approach Armand directly with comments, questions, or problems.

He started in the main salons, pausing at each table to make eye contact with the croupiers. He whispered a few words of encouragement to the Beiruti "condors," ladies in their advanced years, all rouge and wigs, whose stamina wore down even the most experienced dealers. After six or seven hours of play, the "condors" were just warming up. Armand made one quick swing through the American Room to check out the shipbound tourists who played the slot machines there. He passed into the private rooms and watched the frenetic play of the Hong Kong businessmen. They were like no other players in the world, their emotions flayed raw by the caprice of the cards. They drank and smoked without pause, and in spite of the cool, comfortable temperature, sweat poured off them. They chirped and clicked their teeth, and emitted low growls, as though beseeching the gods to grant them good luck. Armand watched their play for a half hour, during which time the Casino de Paradis added almost a million dollars to its coffers.

Right on schedule, Armand arrived in the kitchens, which were in the middle of the supper rush. Somehow behind the shouting, jostling, and temper tantrums, four hundred magnificent plates would be created and served. The chefs returned his greetings with distracted waves of the hand. Armand didn't take offense. The best chefs were like racehorses, high-strung, with egos as fragile as the Meissen china on which their creations were served. He moved past the kitchen and preparation rooms into the cool darkness of the wine cellar.

The term *cellar* was not entirely appropriate. The Casino de Paradis's wine collection consisted of over a hundred thousand bottles, housed in what could only be described as a cavern. Indeed, Armand Fremont's ancestor had hollowed this vast storeroom out of the bedrock. As a result the temperature and humidity were ideally suited to storing wine. As well as other things.

Armand made certain that he locked every door behind him. Red points of light, indicating primed alarm systems, measured his progress. He walked past bins and shelves containing vintages an oenophile could only dream about, working his way deeper into the cellar until he came to a curved wooden door reinforced with iron bars.

In Lebanon, as in all of the Middle East, the great houses, castles, mosques, and monasteries all had bolt holes so that their occupants could escape in time of attack or siege or secretly carry in reinforcements, food, and ammunition. The casino had two such routes, which connected the hillside bedrock to the coral outcrop and the maze of tunnels, which eventually found their way to the sea. One led directly into the tunnels and was the most dangerous.

If a man did not know exactly which tunnel to take and where to turn, he could be lost indefinitely. The second ran to the hillside itself and a cleverly concealed entrance. Here too there were traps and pitfalls for the careless or unwary who might have stumbled across the tunnel by accident. There was no chance of this happening to the man who had come to meet Armand, since he had spent his entire lifetime in these hills.

"Good evening, Abbot."

"Hello, Armand, my friend."

The two men threw their arms around each other. The abbot, who had taken the name John as a novice, belonged to the Order of the Third Cross. The Greek Orthodox Monastery that he presided over was in the hills between Beirut and Jounyeh. It was unique in the Arab world because not once in its thousand-year history had it been plundered or abandoned.

Armand had been introduced to the abbot by his grandfather. Even then the abbot had been an older man; now he had reached the biblical age of eighty. Yet he still ran the order with unquestioned authority. His brothers were some of the most educated and experienced men in Lebanon, their knowledge ranging from engineering to medicine. Such skills enabled the order to exist independently of the lay world. No visitors were permitted within its gates, and to the outsider it appeared that the order did nothing but cultivate its fields and worship the greater glory of God. Armand had often wondered how the Lord had looked upon this sleight of hand. For all their humility and otherworldliness the monks of the Order of the Third Cross had the most comprehensive and reliable intelligence network in the country. They traveled the length and breadth of Lebanon, among people who either respected or were indifferent to them. They could listen in on conversations in a dozen languages and kept faithful records. In the end this bounty was culled by the abbot who shared it with the only man he knew would never betray the nation for personal gain: Armand Fremont.

Over the years the abbot had provided Armand with invaluable information. Fragments of evidence, gleaned from arcane sources, had been scrutinized and ultimately forged into a weapon, which Armand then wielded in the most delicate fashion. Men who had thought themselves above the law, to whom the practice of corruption was commonplace, who plotted and supported violence against those who would threaten and expose them, it was to them that Armand came, whispering what he knew of their secrets, breaking them with a few words, his threats as lethal as daggers.

Nor had the abbot's cooperation stopped there. The brothers had been instrumental in Armand's never-ending battle against the slave traders. Sometimes an overheard word or careless comment was enough to provide Armand with the clue he needed.

Both Armand and the abbot had carefully observed the rules for these meetings. Most of the time the casiño wine cellar proved to be the best venue. Armand had never set foot in the monastery. It was common knowledge he was an agnostic. But never had the abbot demanded a meeting on such short notice.

"My friend, what urgent matter brings you here?" Armand asked.

The abbot paced around the small table, fingering his heavy silver cross. "Armand, you are aware that most people believe that the opium that goes to America comes from Turkey."

"The majority of it, yes."

"A new source has been born," the abbot said in a low voice. "Here in Lebanon. In the Bekaa Valley."

Armand couldn't believe it. He had never heard anything of the kind. "Do you know *where* in the Bekaa?" he demanded. "Who might be behind it?"

"Not yet. The Bekaa is a den of thieves and murderers. Even for us it is difficult to obtain accurate information. But we will go on trying." The abbot paused. "There has also been a surge of arms shipments into the country. Guns are pouring in from everywhere—Europe, the Soviet Union, even the United States."

He handed Armand a copy of a Lebanese customs report.

"Procured for us by one of the faithful," he said with a sad smile.

Armand scanned the report.

"This says the government manages to intercept less than ten percent of what is getting through," he murmured, looking at the abbot. "Which means there are thousands of weapons out there, in unknown hands. And they are meant to be used!"

"By whom?" the abbot demanded anxiously.

"Anyone who can buy them!" Armand replied. "You know how many sects and splinter groups we have here? Druzes, Shiites, Sunnis, Maronite Christians, Palestinians, Copts. Their differences—and underneath that, their hatred for each other—are never far from the surface. Each group has its backers, with plenty of money. Each realizes that it can't allow the other to arm itself without fear that it will be attacked and destroyed. They're *all* buying, abbot. If this thing doesn't stop, we're going to have private militia in the streets, claiming sections of the city and fighting to defend them."

The abbot looked fearfully at Armand. "It would be civil war. The most cruel and vicious kind, religion against religion, sect against sect . . . But who would want such a thing?" he cried. "It's like starting a fire that can't be put out!"

"Someone does," Armand said in a low voice. "Someone is trying to destroy Lebanon. Someone has realized just how fragile this country is, how little it would take to ignite the hatred. Once the killing starts, the Lebanese code of vengeance would do the rest. The slaughter would go on for years!"

The abbot was silent for a moment, then said, "I fear there is more."

"What is it?" Armand demanded.

"Not what. Who." The sorrow and fear in his friend's eyes twisted Armand's heart.

"Tell me, abbot!"

"One of the brothers in Tangier picked up a rumor about

an assassin. He is known only by a code name: Bacchus. Apparently he lives in Spain, maybe Gibraltar itself. He's reputed to be one of the best in the world."

"I will get you whatever protection you need," Armand said instantly.

The abbot held up his hand. "You don't understand. It's not me we have to worry about. The whispers say the target is you, Armand."

As soon as the abbot was safely away, Armand returned to the casino. He was careful not to hurry, moving through the crowds with his customary grace, stopping to mingle with his guests. When he reached the Crystal, he locked the door behind him and dialed a number in the south of France. David Cabot answered on the first ring.

When Armand told him about the abbot's warning, David said, "So the jackals are venturing forth. . . . We have stirred them up."

"It might still be only a rumor," Armand reminded him.

"Then the abbot wouldn't have raised the alarm," David replied with dead certainty.

"Do you think it is the same bastard who went after Alexander?"

"I'm certain of it."

"Then it follows—"

"That whoever had Alex killed has targeted you now."

Armand closed his eyes. There grew an intensely cold feeling in the center of his back, as though someone had placed an ice cube against his spine, to mark the final destination of the bullet.

"I will be back as soon as I can," David was saying. "Tomorrow night, latest."

"But Morton—"

"I've made arrangements for him to be picked up as soon as he reappears. This thing has gone beyond him, Armand. It's because we've been looking for Morton that you are now in danger." David paused. "I don't want you to be alone. Take some casino security people home with you tonight. I'll have my own people from Geneva in Beirut first thing in the morning."

"David, about Kate . . ."

"She's in no danger. Besides, I don't want to tip our hand. We can't give her bodyguards without letting her know what's going on." David sensed that Armand still had misgivings. "I'll be back tomorrow night," he repeated. "If the situation changes, believe me, I'll see to it that she's covered."

"Thank you, David."

"Get yourself safely through tonight, Armand. By tomorrow I'll have you so well guarded that no one will get within spitting distance of you."

The rooftop restaurant of the Hotel Orient in Tangier had an unobstructed view of the harbor. Surprisingly enough the food was quite good, even though the wine list, Alejandro Lopez decided, left much to be desired.

Nevertheless, his excursion into Tangier had been fruitful. Money had been seeded, and the right people told just enough in order to start the rumor about a killer hired to stalk Armand Fremont. By now, Lopez was certain, Fremont had heard as much as he, Lopez, wanted him to for the time being. Enough to act unwittingly as bait.

15

Jasmine Fremont's annual carnival party, held a week before the parade and festivities, was a "must" for society. In fact, the guest list was often used to determine Beirut's pecking order. Those included were guaranteed to be invited to all the important galas in the coming year. The unfortunates who failed to make the list might as well have hauled out their Vuitton steamer trunks and started packing for Siberia.

Kate arrived just as the evening was in full swing, eleven o'clock, wearing a scarlet crepe smoking jacket, fluid trousers, and voile scarf wrapped into a headband.

"You look too perfect!" Jasmine exclaimed, taking Kate in hand.

Jasmine herself had been dressed by Emmanuelle Khanh, in a revealing knit silk jersey tube. Her jewelry was the latest from Rome, designed by Paco Rabanne. Kate noticed that the minimal look was definitely in. Bared backs, bared midriffs, and transparent material, punctuated by ultrashort, ultrasheer organza dresses with sequined patterns. A harem keeper's dream, she thought.

Jasmine paused along the way to introduce Kate, who was surprised to be greeted like a long-lost relative by people whom she had never met but who seemed to know all about her.

"Where it counts, Beirut is a very small town," Jasmine told her.

Beyond the ballroom was an area screened off by lacquered panels depicting the glorious days of the Persian Empire. The red, black, blue, and gold oils on the screen shimmered in a patina made lustrous by the centuries. Behind the panels was a large square table, shin-high, surrounded by embroidered pillows.

"You remember Louis and Pierre," Jasmine said.

"Yes, of course."

The two men dipped their fingers in a silver bowl and rose to welcome Kate.

"I'm so glad you came after all," Louis said.

"My sentiments exactly," Pierre added. "Please, won't you have something to eat?"

Kate glanced at Jasmine, who said, "I do advise you to have some dinner. The night has just begun."

Slipping off her heels, Kate made herself comfortable on the cushions.

"Whatever it is," she said pointing to the steaming pans on the table, "it smells wonderful."

"The Lebanese call it the Dervish's Rosary," Pierre told her. "Lamb, eggplant, zucchini, tomatoes, and onions, spiced with cinnamon and oregano, all baked in the pan you see, the *siniyyah*. May I serve you a portion?"

The Rosary was even more delicious than Kate had imagined. She quickly got used to sitting on the pillows and eating at the same time. A cold, crisp white wine from Greece was the perfect complement.

"You must forgive us for not having called on you," Louis said, eating baklava with his fingers. "It's been a distressing time for you. We were relieved when Jasmine told us circumstances were looking much more promising."

"They are," Kate told him between bites, wondering exactly how much Jasmine had told them and not wanting to say too much herself.

"Well, now that you've settled in, I hope we'll be seeing more of you," Louis said tactfully.

"And if there's anything I can do to assist you or Armand, please let me know," Pierre added.

As Kate worked her way through the Rosary, a number of men came by to chat briefly with Louis. They were all expensively attired and carried themselves with complete confidence.

Kate had sensed their power. "Who are those men?" she whispered to Pierre when she had the chance.

"Oh . . . well, of course Jasmine wouldn't have told you, not under the circumstances, I mean. You see, Louis is running for the presidency of Lebanon. These men, very rich, very influential, are some of his major supporters. Louis has a strong following throughout the country."

Kate was in awe. When she stole glances at Louis, she discovered she was looking at him in a totally different way. He was no longer a polished, slightly too pretty husband who seemed pale against Jasmine's electric personality. Although the men coming to Louis were all older, they showed him great respect, asking questions and listening to what he had to say without interruption. As for Louis, his features lost their indolence. He looked sharp, alert, and completely in control. Kate was impressed with what she saw and said as much to Pierre.

"Louis would like nothing better than to talk to you," Pierre replied. "Perhaps when your situation is resolved. He is a great admirer of American politics, particularly the late President Kennedy. Who knows? Maybe you can give him some advice—being a lawyer, that is."

Kate laughed. "I think Louis is doing quite well without any help from me."

While Kate was finishing her meal, Pierre talked. But when a beautiful girl came by with a strapping young stud on each arm, Pierre's bonhomie faltered.

"Pierre, it's none of my business," Kate said softly. "But if you have someone to see . . ."

He blushed furiously. "I'm sorry. I should have introduced you. That was Cleo. She and I . . . that is, we . . . the two of us live together."

"I think that's wonderful," Kate said sincerely.

"Yes . . . it can be."

At that moment Kate saw in Pierre's eyes the pain of suspicion, the agony of a betrayal that had not yet come to pass, but which surely would. Kate's heart went out to him. Would she ever forget that morning Ted had come through the door, heavy with the scent of another woman?

"If you will excuse me, Kate," Pierre said, breaking the

awkward silence.

Kate watched him go, hoping very much that Pierre would be luckier than she'd been.

"I must apologize," Louis said, sliding along the pillows next to her. "I've neglected you terribly." Louis looked closely at Kate. "My God, you look as though you've seen a ghost!"

Kate managed a smile. "Just a poltergeist." She quickly changed the subject. "Pierre tells me you're a presidential candidate. That sounds very exciting."

"Hard work is what it is," Louis said modestly. "But yes, I think there's a lot that could be done in Lebanon."

"What exactly do you propose to do if you're elected?"

Louis blinked. "Why, what every president before me has done: make sure nothing changes. The world likes nothing better than stability, Kate. Lebanon prospers because people know it is safe. Our banking-secrecy laws surpass those of Switzerland, our luxuries and amusements rival the best in the world. Millions of visitors come each year, as do businessmen, because we have made Beirut the crossroads between East and West. That is what I must protect and help to prosper." He paused. "But remember we have two million people packed into an area smaller than Switzerland. There are half a dozen nationalities and twice that many religions and sects. There is always the underlying fear that the country could be torn apart by the sum of its differences.

"Let me offer a parable. An old Muslim man, on his deathbed, called for a Maronite priest and insisted on being converted to Christianity. The old man's family was shocked and demanded why he should do such a thing. The Muslim winked and whispered, 'Better one of them to die than one of us.' That is Lebanon in a nutshell, Katherine. We have taken on thousands of years of differences and prejudices. As it stands, each religious group is guaranteed a share of the power. Each knows that its members have someone to appeal to for justice and fair play."

Kate wondered who had written the lines for Louis. She didn't doubt his sincerity and passion, but she did ask herself if Louis was indeed strong enough to hold in check the very forces he had described, forces that could, it seemed, come alive at any moment and overwhelm the sorcerer's apprentice.

"Louis, excuse me, but Jasmine is looking for you."

Kate glanced up at the speaker, drawn by his deep, soft voice. His eyes drank her in unashamedly. As Louis left, the stranger asked her to dance. When they were on the floor and she in his arms, she introduced herself to the compelling man and asked his name.

"Michael. Michael Saidi."

Across the ballroom Jasmine, with Louis beside her, was watching every step that Michael and Kate took.

"Did you tell her?" asked Jasmine, not taking her eyes off the dancers.

"Exactly what we planned."

"And?"

Louis shrugged. "She's an American liberal. She thinks that the Peace Corps can solve the whole world's problems. However, she is bright enough to understand that there are things she doesn't know or appreciate."

Jasmine nodded slowly and watched as the couple whirled by on the dance floor.

"Good. Because she's in the hands of an excellent teacher."

For the first time since that terrible evening in the Berkeley Hills, Kate truly forgot about the upheavals in her life. It was a combination of the setting and occasion and music, but it was also being in the arms of a man who was enjoying her only for herself, who was not in any way connected to the string of tragedies she had fled from.

As they walked off the dance floor, Kate took stock of Michael. He was undeniably handsome, yet his beauty, like his formal attire and cologne, was understated. Six or seven years older than she, he mystified her.

"Who are you, Michael Saidi?" she asked.

He smiled and guided her out on the terrace where there were several other couples.

"Tonight we do not talk about such things," he said. "I am Michael and you are Katherine and that is all we know about each other. We will dance and laugh and be amused by wonderful people. And as we do this, we will get to know each other better than we could any other way."

"What do we do when the night is over?"

"Then we decide what is to become of us."

"As simple as that?"

"Never anything so boring as simple." He paused. "Being an American, how well do you know Beirut?"

"Being an American, not well at all."

"Then we shall change that. Did you bring your car?"

"But we can't go yet!" Kate protested.

"Of course we can. If we want to. Please don't think you'll be offending Jasmine if we leave. This party will still be going on when we come back."

That night Kate felt as though she had been whisked through the very heart of an Arabian fantasy.

The exploration began in Ra's Beirut, an area of old stone houses with walled gardens and tall, elegant apartment blocks, which sprawled around the American University of Beirut. The narrow streets, lighted by ornate, old-fashioned lampposts, ran every which way and were jammed with people. The atmosphere reminded Kate of the Latin Quarter in Paris or New York's Greenwich Village. Except that the pace here was twice as fast, the colors seemed brighter, the variety of everything around her limitless.

Michael took her to a restaurant that could have been found anywhere in the American heartland. There was an old-fashioned soda fountain complete with Formica counter, vinyl swivel stools, and tiny chairs whose wire backs were shaped like hearts. Next to that were refrigerated cabinets filled with pastries including Lebanese delicacies such as *atayef*, a crepe filled with nuts and cinnamon, and the *fleur de Liban*, which resembled a cream-filled napoleon.

The tables were squeezed so close together, they might as well have been communal. Soon Kate was talking to people all around her, including a local celebrity, Joyce Kimball. A tiny, black-haired dynamo of a woman, Kimball was the social columnist for the *Daily Star*.

"We know all about *you*, dear!" she told Kate conspiratorially. "Just between us girls—but on the record, of course—you didn't take that money, did you?"

"For the record, I didn't."

Kimball waved her cigarette holder like a baton.

"I just knew it! All those silly people back home even thinking that you did. They forget to ask themselves the most important question of all."

"Which is?" Kate ventured.

"Why should you, dear? I mean, if your late father, a wonderful man, I'm sure, was in Mott Street—that means broke, dear—all he had to do was ask Armand. Heaven knows, he's almost as rich as the shah of Iran!"

As Joyce Kimball darted toward another target, Michael leaned over and whispered in Kate's ear, "She may seem flighty, but she believes every word she says. Mind you, she prints it, too, so that by tomorrow the rest of Beirut will also believe it, for better or worse."

"Let's hope so," Kate murmured.

Outside once more, Michael checked his watch.

"If we hurry, we can just make it," he said, frowning. "But we will need special transportation to get us out of here. Would you say you're an adventuresome young lady?"

Kate regarded him warily. "Depends on the adventure."

"A ride in a taxi."

Kate was puzzled. "I think I can manage that."

"Excellent!"

Given the congestion in the street, Kate had no idea where the spanking-new Chevrolet could have come from. She hadn't seen Michael lift a finger, yet the car screeched to a stop right in front of them, the rear door flying open. Kate doubted the driver was a day over sixteen. Michael gave directions in rapid-fire Arabic, and before Kate knew it, she was slammed into the soft cushions of the backseat. Then she made the mistake of sitting up and seeing what was going on around her.

The car was weaving through the traffic in a blur. The driver had one finger on the wheel, every few seconds lifting his palm to slam it down on the horn. He used his other hand to emphasize the points he was making in his conversation with Michael, whom he was looking straight in the eye.

"Oh, my God!" Kate cried.

The driver pulled a hard left and barreled down an alley Kate was certain had to be one-way. He got behind a slow-moving Cadillac, leaned out the window, and delivered a stream of curses at the other driver, then spun the wheel and roared past on a blind curve—just as an ancient streetcar lumbered toward him from the opposite direction.

Kate thought it was the last tableau she would ever see. At the very last instant the taxi driver did the only thing possible: spinning the wheel, he hurtled into the driveway of an apartment building, stopping just inches away from a group of old men sitting on the stoop. The driver flashed a smile at Kate.

"We be there quickly. No traffic now."

Without so much as a glance in the rearview mirror, he slammed the car into reverse and roared back into the street. The next time Kate opened her eyes, they were high above the city.

"We'll be in time for the last part of the show," Michael said, sounding very pleased.

Kate got out, one arm on the taxi's roof to steady herself.

"Are you all right?" Michael asked solicitously.

"Fine, fine," she mumbled, wishing the sky would stop spinning.

"This is a very special place for Beirutis," Michael said. "Come, have a look."

The hilltop was cast in a soft bluish glow giving the rocky terrain an otherworldly feeling. He took her hand and

led her up the summit, passing under a magnificent stone
gate that opened up on six tall columns, lonely and defiant
sentinels silhouetted against the night sky.

"All that's left of the Temple of Jupiter," said Michael.
"Once it was the largest temple in the whole of the Roman
Empire."

The silence around them remained unbroken for several
minutes. Then, as they passed through the columns, Kate
heard a plaintive cry, coming from a penumbra below. Set
into the other side of the hill was an amphitheater, its mil-
lennia-old stone seats filled with people. Below, on a stage,
a single woman, a diva. Even from where she stood, Kate
could hear her haunting, melancholy voice perfectly.

"She is Umm Kalthum, the most famous Arab singer of
our times," Michael whispered.

Kate was entranced by her magnificent voice. Then the
song ended. The single spotlight went out, and there was
complete silence and darkness. The entire amphitheater
seemed to be holding its breath. With a flourish the orchestra struck up multicolored lights blazed across the stage, and
the diva was joined by a chorus. She held her arms out to
the audience, clapping her hands, encouraging them to join
her.

"That was wonderful," Kate said as she and Michael
walked back down the hill.

Michael noticed Kate's trepidation as they approached
the taxi.

"Don't worry. I'll tell him we're in no hurry."

Kate did not ask where they were going. She felt perfectly at ease with Michael and was looking forward to being surprised. Their next stop turned out to be the American
University of Beirut, which, taking its cue from the city,
was still open. They walked among the fragrant sycamores
planted a century ago by the university's founder, the
Reverend Daniel Bliss, and stopped off at Uncle Sam's
Snack Shop to listen to students reading poetry and playing
guitar. As they were leaving, they passed under the old
stone archway at the entrance to the campus. Kate looked up

and read the motto inscribed upon it.

May They Have Life and Have It Abundantly.

"That might as well be the creed for all of Lebanon," said Michael. "But then again, you know this. You're a Maser. This is your home."

The comment struck a chord. Kate no longer thought of Beirut as some alien place. She felt comfortable among its people, curious about their customs and habits. The scent of orange and cinnamon and nutmeg were by now familiar; the rapid-fire rattle of Arab and the graceful lilt of French were pleasing to her ear.

They took a seat under a flowering lemon tree in an outdoor café and ordered coffee.

"Michael, I don't want you to be offended," Kate started to say. "I mean, I'm having a wonderful time . . ."

"But?" he encouraged her gently.

"I'm sure you know a lot more about me than I do about you. I feel that's not quite fair."

Michael tossed his head back and laughed. "You'll forgive me if I say how very American you sound."

"I didn't mean to pry," Kate apologized.

"Not at all. In fact, I'm flattered that you ask about me."

Part of Michael's charm lay in his ability to weave words effortlessly, draw his audience into his story. But the true secret of his success was that he couched his lies in the truth. When he told Kate about his father, he did not make him out to be anything more or less than he had been, an old and valued employee of the Casino de Paradis. But he never let his feelings show, the disgust and contempt he had lived with. In the same way, when he spoke about his travels in Europe, places and experiences rolled smoothly off his tongue, yet he never came close to telling her about his job at the Swiss bank. When his narrative reached America, Michael saw, by Kate's shining eyes, that she was completely taken in. His tales of Middle East immigrant life in Brooklyn, how he had started up a modest import-export firm that had prospered, captivated her. Everyone, thought Michael, especially women, loved a rags-to-riches story, with a resolute but modest hero at the heart of it.

"There you have it," Michael said, ending his story as gracefully as an excellent pilot might land a frail glider. "I haven't been back very long, but fortune is still smiling."

"It sounds as if you've done more already than most people even dream of doing," Kate said.

"Not really. Look at yourself. From what I understand, you are a very talented attorney."

"Who knows for how long?" Kate murmured, instantly regretting her words.

Michael covered her hand with his. "Things will work out. You'll see."

Kate thought back to her resolution to get a grip on her situation instead of watching and waiting as Armand played out his mysterious moves.

"Michael, how much do you know about what's been going on at Maritime Continental?" Kate asked at once.

"Just what I saw on television and read in the financial pages," he replied, then added hastily, "That *doesn't* mean I believe everything. The suggestions that you had something to do with any of that are ludicrous."

"How can you be so sure?" Kate asked. "You don't know me at all."

Michael shrugged. "Sometimes one has to go on intuition and faith. I don't think it's naive of me to say you're not that kind of person. That is what I believe."

Michael's sincerity and honesty warmed Kate, driving back the cold admonitions of David Cabot.

"Kate, if there is anything I can do to help you, you have only to ask."

She hesitated, then told Michael the story from her perspective, ending, "You see, the real embezzler is still out there."

"Do the police have any suspects?" Michael asked.

"They're so sure Emil Bartoli and I are the criminals that they are not even looking."

How very reassuring, Michael thought.

"But it seems that a second man is involved," Kate said.

"A *second* man?"

"Someone my father suspected of being a party."

Michael sat back. "There's been nothing in the papers—"

"And there won't be!" Kate said fiercely. "A minute ago you spoke about trust, Michael. Well, I'm trusting you now, to keep everything that we say between ourselves."

"Of course, Kate. That goes without saying. Do you have any idea who this man is?"

Kate shook her head. "Only that he's very powerful and that he is here in Beirut."

Michael let out a low whistle. "I'm beginning to worry about you, Kate. These are dangerous waters."

"Some bastard is ruining my life, Michael. Mine and Emil Bartoli's. He's systematically destroying my father's good name and everything he built. He may be, as you say, dangerous. But I am outraged!"

Michael held up his hands. "Fine. I can understand that. Can I do anything for you?"

Kate thought for a moment. "You were born and raised here, Michael. Not that much could have changed since you've been gone. Besides, you know your way around the city—where people can be found, how to get to them. All very discreetly, of course."

Michael let out a deep breath. "I don't want to exaggerate what I can do, Kate, but I am well acquainted with the right people, and I will help you, any way I can."

Kate felt exhilarated.

Jasmine's party was still going strong at two o'clock in the morning. Kate thanked Michael and stayed only long enough to see Jasmine before pleading a headache and leaving. The spirit of the party had been lost on her. Kate felt she had taken a big step forward: she had made an ally, someone who was ready to help her. Now she had to determine her strategy.

As soon as Kate was out the door, Michael drew Jasmine away into the privacy of her bedroom.

"She knows more than you think!" he spat out, and

proceeded to tell Jasmine everything Kate had shared with him.

Jasmine listened and smoked in silence.

"And you didn't even have to go to bed with her."

"Jasmine, what are you talking about?"

"Don't you see what happened? That little fool doesn't know anything about what is going on. But she *did* tell you how far *Armand* has come in his poking around."

"And who's to say Fremont tells her everything?" Michael challenged her.

"You're right, of course," Jasmine placated him. "But you see, my love, in a little while it won't matter how much Armand knows or suspects. But until then you must be Katherine's *very* best friend."

16

Centuries ago the Phoenicians had made Malta their primary stop along the Mediterranean trade routes. Now a great deal of Middle East influence, in areas ranging from architecture to philosophy, still remained on the island fortress.

The morning following his conversation with Armand, David arrived at Government House in the capital of Valetta. He went directly to see the registrar, who functioned as a kind of chief clerk for the entire Maltese bureaucracy. After the appropriate introductions, he explained to the registrar, a soft-spoken, unassuming man, what he was looking for—and was told politely that such records were completely confidential.

The conversation went on for an hour, David nudging and cajoling, the Maltese standing firm. Finally David announced that he was going to do some shopping, for leather goods for which the Maltese were justly renowned. Specifically, a belt. The registrar offered the names of a few shops he might try.

After lunch David returned to Government House. The Maltese inquired politely if he had been successful in his shopping.

"Yes," David replied. "And because of your assistance I was able to get some very good bargains. To repay your kindness, I beg you to accept this small token."

David placed a long, thin package on the table. The Maltese did not touch it, and for a moment David wondered if he had failed. Then the registrar opened the gift box and took out a black leather belt, which he held between his hands. Without taking his eyes off David, he flipped the belt over, revealing an almost invisible zipper. Holding the belt up with one hand, like a trophy, he pressed the leather between his fingers all along its length. One by one faint, round indentations appeared on the black surface.

The registrar nodded to indicate the folder on his desk.

"You will excuse me while I try this on," he said.

David flipped open the file, his eyes narrowing as he read. Armand had been right. The Michael Samson that Kate had referred to had dug a very deep hole for himself. Very deep indeed. An official document in the file recorded his death at the age of eight.

"What do you think?"

David turned around and looked at the registrar. The belt was very handsome. No one would have suspected there were twenty gold Krugerrands secreted within it.

"It suits you perfectly," David said. "So much so that I have one more you must have."

The registrar nodded happily.

"All right. We're certain that the identity of this eight-year-old boy, Michael Samson, was lifted by someone."

David turned away from the one-way glass overlooking the casino foyer. The flight from Valetta had taken only ninety minutes. An hour after touchdown he was in the casino.

"Yes. Samson's birth certificate was presented in various departments to obtain a Maltese work permit, driver's license, and a passport. You've seen copies of the paperwork."

"He got all that because no one bothered to check the birth certificate against a possible *death* certificate," Armand said sarcastically.

David shrugged. "The Maltese don't watch out for that sort of thing."

"And no one in those various departments remembers a thing."

"Armand, it *has* been seven years," David reminded him. "At best, some clerk probably saw whoever it was for a minute or two across a counter. He wouldn't be able to identify that face by the end of the day."

"No photographs," Armand said. "That bothers me. You apply for a passport, even in Malta, and you have to provide two photographs—one for the passport, one for the permanent records."

"I saw the record. There was a photograph. You can still see the residue of the glue. The Maltese think it fell off and was lost."

"What do you think?"

David was very still. "Someone inside the ministry was paid to steal that photograph."

"Can you find out who?"

"Impossible. I wouldn't know where to begin. It was probably a clerk, but those people are transferred or promoted every couple of years. There's no telling where he could be right now." David paused. "Or even if he's still alive."

"What do you mean?" Armand demanded.

"If I had gone to the trouble—and risk—of getting someone to steal my picture from the passport files, I'd want the thief to deliver it to me. Otherwise there would always be the possibility of blackmail. But now the thief has seen my face—twice, in fact: in the picture and the second time, when he delivers it to me. That leaves me even more vulnerable. The only way I would be perfectly safe is if the thief were to meet with a fatal but not in any way suspicious accident. I'm sure," David finished, "that somewhere in an edition of the Valetta *Globe and Mail* is a story about such an accident. I'm having it checked out now."

Both men understood the implications of David's words. Michael Samson, whoever he was, was far more dangerous than a white-collar embezzler. If he had killed once to protect himself, he would not hesitate to do so again, especially if he was tracked and cornered.

"What is your next move?" Armand asked.

"There isn't one. I'm not going anywhere until I run down the rumor the abbot told us about."

Armand waved his hand impatiently. "I'm not that easy to kill. I have Salim plus the rest of the baby-sitters you've arranged for. No, David. I want you to stay with Samson. Somewhere there has to be a photograph of him, or at the very least, someone who can give us a description. Get your precious computers to start earning their keep."

"You've picked up a scent, haven't you, Armand?" David said softly. "What is it?"

"I am beginning to think that we have two separate threads. The first one is Pierre, which Alexander found for us. But now we have discovered a second, Michael Samson. David, I think that if we pull each thread separately, we will find they are knotted together. . . ."

Not all the passengers of the cruise vessel *Athena* chose to visit the Casino de Paradis. Some boarded the dockside buses waiting to take them for a three-hour tour of the city; others spent the time on their own, walking around the *souqs* that dotted the quays. Only a few elected the option whose price was not included in their tour package: lunch at the Beirut Yacht Club, a three-tier complex built into the hills a hundred yards above the basin and slips, followed by a ride on the funicular to the statue of the Virgin. Alejandro Lopez did not at all mind paying the surcharge.

As Lopez had suspected, the food in the club was mediocre. Clearly neither management nor the chefs gave a damn about the tourist trade. But now he had had a chance to inspect the floor-to-ceiling glass that bordered the dining room and determine its thickness. With this information he could judge which caliber of bullet would best deal with the penetration and deflection when it ripped through the window.

After coffee Lopez rode the funicular, a stopwatch nestled in the palm of his hand. He pressed down on the timer three times going up and, after a walk around the statue, three times going down. Lopez already knew that the funicular's last scheduled run downhill was at midnight, when all the cars were returned to the shed adjacent to the yacht basin. He also knew that on Carnival night there would be no tourists riding the cars, while the Beirutis would be out celebrating elsewhere. His only task would be to slip into the car unseen, which, given the age and indifference of the attendants, wouldn't be difficult.

As for the shot itself, Lopez had no doubts he could make it. True, the funicular would be moving, but the winds were almost nonexistent. The car would not be rocking until it reached the wheels on the next trestle, sixty feet below the point at which Lopez intended to fire.

Gliding past the yacht club, Lopez took one last look at the plate glass and the table where his target would be seated. Sixty yards, the optimum range for his rifle. But Lopez appreciated that his most effective weapon would be surprise. There were many tall buildings fronting the harbor. The police would, naturally enough, assume that the fatal shot had been fired from land. There would be nothing left of the plate glass to give them an indication as to what direction the bullet had *really* come from. Even if they got smart and lucky, Lopez mused, and somehow thought of the funicular, even the most thorough search would never reveal the weapon. The yacht basin, its waters dark and heavy with silt, would swallow up a rifle as though it had never existed.

The air was charged with the spirit of Carnival. As they wended their way down the mountain, Kate saw the streets being transformed. Red, green, and white bunting—the colors of the Lebanese flag—was hung between the tops of lampposts. Cutouts of the country's national symbol, the cedar tree, were pasted in store windows. Street corners were jammed with peddlers, their carts crammed with miniature flags, commemorative T-shirts, and knickknacks of every description. The politicians were also taking full advantage to advertise. Billboards and the sides of buildings were plastered with huge posters of the candidates. Most prominent among them, Kate noticed, was the image of Louis Jabar.

Michael wheeled his little MG sports car off the Grande Corniche and into the center of the city. As she watched the

Carnival finery flash by, Kate wondered where they were going. Michael had called at lunch, asking if she would be free later in the afternoon. There was, he'd said, something he wanted to show her. A surprise.

Michael drove into a large parklike square dominated by a statue of three figures, their arms raised defiantly toward the sky.

"What is this place?"

"It is called Martyrs' Square, in memory of all those who fell in battle for the nation."

The area reminded Kate of Washington Square in New York, a meeting place for Greenwich Village's diverse population. Except here, the traffic was ferocious.

As Michael walked Kate up the street, he was greeted by students whose T-shirts were emblazoned with the logo of the Christian and Arab College. He introduced Kate, but she quickly lost out as the conversation swung from English to French to Arabic. Kate noticed that some of the students were wearing heavy gold crucifixes. She commented on this to one.

"It is a symbol of our commitment," one of them explained. "To ourselves and our Arab brothers. By his donations, Michael Saidi has made it possible for us to begin to make our contribution now, even while we are in school."

"I don't understand. What did he make possible?"

"Many things! Beirut is not all rich people. There are the poor who need food, clothing, and medical attention. Because of Michael we are able to help in many ways."

In a different part of the square, Michael stopped at a Turkish coffee shop where two elderly men were sitting over thimble-size cups, a narghile pipe smoking between them. Kate recognized them as being Druze Muslims by their red fezzes wrapped with a wide white band.

Both men greeted Michael as though he were a long-lost son. They made a place for him and Kate and pressed them to have coffee. Kate accepted the drink but politely shook her head when offered the wooden mouthpiece of the narghile. The conversation, in Arabic, was animated. One

OASIS OF DREAMS 231

of the men patted Michael on the shoulder and disappeared for a few moments. When he returned, he had a dozen children, all well dressed and freshly scrubbed, milling around him. The children were shy at first, but Michael handed out candy and soon they were all over him.

The old man prodded Kate's arm. "Michael's children," he said in broken English. "Good life for them, now."

After they had extricated themselves, Michael said to Kate, "Like any large city, Beirut is a magnet for the poorer parts of the country. More often than not, instead of just the husband or father coming here, the whole family arrives as one. Everything, especially finding a place to live, becomes that much more difficult. Families fall apart, and the children end up in the streets."

"What do these men do?"

"I guess you could call them the neighborhood elders. They help the families if they can."

"Meanwhile who pays for their clothing and food and makes sure they have a place to sleep?" asked Kate, looking pointedly at Michael.

"You've seen a little of what I do with my money," he replied. "Now let me show you how I earn it."

A half hour later Kate found herself walking along the wharfs of the Fifth Basin, the most important docks of Beirut Port. Oil tankers, container ships, merchantmen, and grain vessels were lined up as far as the eye could see, taking on cargo that was moved by giant overhead cranes, huge, ten-wheel forklifts, and armies of stevedores. Here too Michael appeared very much at home. He was met by foremen who led him and Kate to a giant warehouse filled with sacks of wheat and flour.

"Some of this comes from my land in the Bekaa," Michael said proudly, then added with a grin, "Yes, Kate, the man who adores you is a farmer. Don't break his heart and reject him because of his humble origins."

Kate laughed nervously, shocked by his declaration.

"One day I will show you the Bekaa Valley. It has been the breadbasket of Lebanon since before the days of the

Romans. We are so rich here in this little country, Kate, that
we can afford to send food to those who need it. I don't
deny that I profit from this. I would be either a fool or a
very poor businessman not to do so. And while I may not
get my hands dirty in the earth itself, I make sure that its
bounty stretches as far as it can. So there you have it, Kate.
Yesterday you gave me a great gift by showing your trust in
me. Today I wanted you to see that your faith has not been
misplaced. I hope you're not disappointed."

"How could I be?" Kate whispered, looking around her.

Because she was so overwhelmed by what she thought
she was seeing, Kate did not catch Michael's faraway expression. He too was thinking of those clean-cut, pious students from the Christian-Arab College. One of his most
daring and clever coups had been to corrupt those young
men and turn them into heroin dealers. After all, who would
suspect a pusher wearing a gold cross? And the children . . .
even now, the two old Druzes, his middlemen, would be lining them up for inspection by some degenerate Syrian or
Iraqi who needed them young and tight in order to achieve
pleasure.

When he saw how impressed Kate was by everything
around her, he almost laughed. The wheat *was* his, as were
the fields where it had been grown. But the Bekaa gave
forth a much more potent crop than that. Secreted in the
bags of grain, destined not for Africa but New York, was
the highest grade of opium to be found anywhere in the
world.

Michael led her into a small restaurant where, to Kate's
astonishment, pizza dough was being flung high in the air
by grinning Arab boys.

"The best pizza east of Ray's on Seventh Avenue,"
Michael said solemnly. "Some say even better."

Kate laughed. "Impossible!"

She watched Michael disappear into the crowds at the
counter, and a few minutes later he was emerging with two
paper plates bearing steaming, cheesy pizza slices.

"Hello, Kate."

"David!" Startled, she looked up at his cool, impassive gaze. "I didn't expect to see you here. . . ."

"May I sit down?"

Without waiting for an invitation, David did so, turning his attention to Michael as he walked up to the table, pizza in hand.

"You must be Michael Saidi. My name is David Cabot."

Michael slowly put down the plates, wiped his fingers, and offered his hand. "Yes, I know," he said coolly. "Your reputation and that of Interarmco precede you."

"I have heard a few things about you too, Mr. Saidi."

"Good ones, I hope."

David let the comment lie between them.

"You left Lebanon shortly after your father passed away, didn't you."

"There wasn't much to stay for."

"So it would appear. Did quite well for yourself in America."

"You know what they say, Mr. Cabot. America is the land of opportunity."

"And what was it that brought you back, Mr. Saidi?"

"Beirut, Lebanon, these are my homes, Mr. Cabot."

What on earth is going on? Kate asked herself. Then another thought flashed across her mind. How did David know where to find her.

Kate looked past the open doors into the square. There, half-hidden by the crowds, was the white Rolls-Royce. Posted on either side of the car, like piers in an onrushing tide, were two tall, very big men who seemed to be staring directly at her.

They were following her!

Kate rose abruptly, the legs of her chair scraping against the tile.

"Michael, I'm sorry but I have to go. I'll call you later."

"Kate, what's wrong—?"

"I'm sorry!"

Shaking, Kate rushed out of the restaurant into the street.

"What the hell is going on?" Michael demanded.

"Nothing that concerns you, Mr. Saidi," David told him.

When David reached Kate, her anger exploded. "What the hell are you doing here?"

"Not like this, Kate," he said gently, taking her arm. "Not in the street."

She shook him off. "What gave you the right to follow me?"

David opened the rear door of the Rolls. "Please, Kate."

Reluctantly she got into the car, which pulled away as soon as he slipped in beside her.

"Armand told you about a man who had brought your father information that may have been connected to the embezzlement at Maritime Continental," David said.

"Yes, he did but what—"

"The police in Aix-en-Provence found his body this morning. At first it looked like an accident. The man's hobby was ornithology. Climbing up and down those steep hills, across ravines, can be dangerous. But when they examined him, discovered *how* his neck had been broken, there could be only one conclusion: he had been murdered."

Kate sagged back into the leather folds of the seat. Questions raced through her mind, but her shock was such that she could not articulate a single one.

"Armand—" she started to say, then abruptly stopped.

"Armand is out of the country for a little while," David told her. "He will call you if he can. He said that if all went well, he would be back in time for Carnival."

"What am I supposed to do until then?"

"Help me avoid what happened in Aix-en-Provence from happening to you," David replied. "The game is being played in earnest now, Kate. I hope even you can see that."

Emil Bartoli greeted Armand outside the customs and immigration hall at Kennedy Airport.

"It's good to see you again, my friend," he said, relieving Armand of his garment bag.

"And you. Any news?"

"I got hold of Prudence Templeton, as you asked me to,"

Emil said as the limousine headed for Manhattan. "She wasn't at all keen on talking about Michael Samson, but she has agreed to meet us at your hotel this evening after work."

"Do you think she'll tell us anything?"

Emil pursed his lips. "She mentioned to me that Kate had already spoken to her about Samson and that she didn't know what else she could add to that. She sounded frightened—"

"Like someone trying to protect a man?"

"Possibly. Perhaps you could enlighten me about that."

Armand recounted his brief conversation with Kate about Michael Samson, then explained what David Cabot had discovered in Malta.

Emil's expression reflected his surprise and dismay at the details. "My God, what a fool I've been!" he whispered. "All this time I never put the two together—the embezzlement and Samson's death."

"Not Samson," Armand reminded him. "Whomever Prudence Templeton identified, it wasn't he. The man we're after isn't only an embezzler. He's a killer."

Armand checked into the Waldorf, showered, and slept until five o'clock. He donned a fresh suit and went downstairs to the Peacock Alley, the Waldorf's ornate cocktail lounge decorated in an American interior designer's idea of an Iranian royal palace. Emil was already waiting for him in one of the curved banquettes in the back that guaranteed privacy.

"She should be along any moment," Bartoli said, looking across the lounge to the entrance. "Here she is now."

Armand watched a matronly middle-aged woman step through the curtained archway, hesitate. The relief on her plain face was evident when she saw Emil. But just as quickly her smile faded as she noticed Armand.

"Prudence, thank you for coming," Emil said in a courtly fashion. "Permit me to introduce a very good friend of mine from Beirut, Mr. Armand Fremont."

Armand bowed and kissed the back of Prudence's hand.

"It is a pleasure," he said. "Alexander always spoke very

highly of you."

Prudence blushed. "As he did of you," she replied. "I feel I already know you so well."

Prudence settled into the banquette and turned to Emil. "I wasn't aware Mr. Fremont would be joining us," she said pointedly.

"Mr. Fremont has traveled from Beirut because he has come across some very disturbing information about Michael Samson—if in fact that's who he is."

"I . . . I don't understand, Mr. Bartoli. You never mentioned anything about this when you called me."

"That is because I asked him not to," Armand cut in. "Please, Miss Templeton. Hear me out, then help us if you can."

Prudence held her purse in her lap, hands curled tightly around it. "Very well. I'll listen."

Slowly, without leaving out a single detail, Armand recounted what had been discovered about the man who called himself Michael Samson. His heart went out to this poor woman, whose features sagged as she struggled to accept what he was telling her.

"As you can see, Miss Templeton, it is obvious that Michael Samson isn't who he claimed to be. That is why we need your help. The two of you were close for a time, and you positively identified his body. Now we must know anything you can tell us about him—and most important, if you have a picture."

Prudence Templeton's hand shook as she reached for her mineral water.

"I don't know what to say," she murmured. "It all sounds so incredible."

"But it is the truth nonetheless," Emil said. "Please, Prudence, we're counting on you."

"There's so little," she said faintly, beginning to recount her relationship with Michael Samson, the places they had gone, things they had done. She stated emphatically that she had never visited his apartment and that Michael never met any of her few friends.

"He was very shy that way," Prudence finished sadly. "I suppose that's why he never let me take his picture. Not even one of the two of us together."

"But you can give us a description," Armand pressed her. "If you were to sit down with a sketch artist, you would be able to help give a rendering."

"Yes, I suppose I could do that."

"Good. Tomorrow is Saturday. If we could make arrangements for the morning, would that be satisfactory?"

Prudence nodded. Armand reached out to her.

"I understand how you must feel. But you are not the only one who has been duped by this man. And you are *not responsible* for what he did. Perhaps it would be better for you to stay here tonight. That way if you remember something, or if you just want to talk, I will be close by."

"That's very kind of you, Mr. Fremont. But I'd prefer to go home. I'll expect your call in the morning. Now, if you'll excuse me . . ."

Before either man had a chance to protest, Prudence slipped out of the banquette and walked swiftly out of the lounge.

Armand restrained Emil as he made a move to go after her. "Don't."

Emil sat down again. "What if she decides not to help?" he demanded. "Where does that leave us?"

Armand tried to rein in the same fear. "Emil, we have just told her that the man she loved and slept with was a killer. We must give her some time to come to terms with everything. Tomorrow we will try again. Harder, if necessary."

Prudence Templeton walked the fifteen blocks to her small apartment in Murray Hill like a somnambulist. Twice she tried to cross an intersection on a red light and was almost run down. She never heard the insults hurled at her by the drivers.

Once inside, Prudence double-locked her front door, took off her coat, and went into the kitchen to make tea. Cup in hand, she settled herself in her favorite chair and reached for a metal box that had once held expensive English biscuits. Prudence leafed through the memorabilia and plucked out a photograph . . . the one she had surreptitiously taken of Michael one day in Washington Square, the one she had refused to show to Katherine Maser.

Only now, staring down at the photograph, did she allow the tears to come. Prudence had had her suspicions, of course. A thousand times she had asked herself how an embezzler could have found out the codes that were needed to set the machinery of a wire transfer in motion. Not that she didn't know the answer. She did. But she had not wanted to believe it. She smiled faintly. Those Federal Reserve clods, so full of their importance, hadn't found the answer. Even though it was so obvious . . . so very sad and painful.

Prudence looked around the tiny parlor. Which night was it, she wondered? When did Michael come here and whisper endearments in her ear, caress and make love to her while all the while he had been watching and waiting for the opportunity to slip the key to her drawer off its ring, make a duplicate? Because that's the only way he could have seen the taped slip of paper inside the drawer, with the access codes belonging to Alexander Maser and Emil Bartoli.

She shivered, set down her cup, and drew a shawl around her shoulders. To whom had she given herself? Who was that stranger with the silken touch and honeyed words?

She clutched the photograph in her lap. Had a little love been so much to ask for? Had she no right to feel a man's arms around her, be held throughout the cold night when the rain battered the windows?

But the cost . . .

Prudence understood clearly that blame for the calamity that had overtaken Maritime Continental rested squarely on her. Perhaps if she had shown the photograph to Katherine Maser, much of this could have been avoided. Michael Samson, whoever he was, hadn't died in the fire. Oh, God, had he killed the man whose body had been found in the apartment. Michael was alive. Had she given the picture to Miss Maser, he could have been tracked down and caught.

The innocent would have been vindicated, the bank's reputation restored.

Prudence laughed at herself. She could not have done things differently. Michael Samson was real to her. She had felt, tasted, and absorbed him. There had been so little passion or happiness for her that she couldn't bring herself to sully, much less destroy, the memories that still glowed within her.

With the shawl around her shoulders she went over to the gas heater and opened the valve. She returned to her chair and stared at the photograph, remembering. The tea grew cold and bitter. From above came the creaks of floorboards as neighbors settled in for the night. All the while Prudence sat there unmoving. Either by accident or design, she never put a match to the gas. . . .

"There's no answer at her apartment," Armand told Emil over the telephone. He looked at his watch. "It's eight o'clock. Where can she be?"

"If we're lucky, by the time we get there, we'll find out she went out to buy herself a morning pastry," Emil replied. "It will be faster if we meet there."

Twenty minutes later the two men were standing on the town-house stoop. Emil pressed the buzzer to Prudence Templeton's apartment but received no answer.

"The superintendent," he said.

"No, wait."

Armand had noticed a young couple descending the staircase. When the door opened, the two men smiled and slipped inside. A minute later they were on the third floor, a strong odor assailing them.

"Gas!" Emil hissed.

Armand tried the knob to Prudence's door. "Probably has double bolts on it."

Quickly he examined the hinges, which were starting to separate from the frame. He gestured to Emil, who nodded. Armand stepped back, braced himself, and threw his entire body weight against the door. The wood splintered on impact.

The two men covered their mouths and noses with hand-kerchiefs and rushed in. Emil flung open the windows while Armand turned off the gas and came over to where Prudence Templeton was sitting. Her expression was serene, as though she had drifted off to sleep and needed only to be roused. But the bluish tinge to her skin told Armand every-thing he needed to know. He closed her eyes and was about to get out when he noticed the photograph in her lap. He pried it loose from her rigid fingers and made for the hall.

After alerting the superintendent, who immediately called the fire department and began to rouse the other tenants, Armand and Emil retreated outside.

"Why did she do it?" Emil kept asking. "We didn't ac-cuse her of anything—"

"It had nothing to do with us," Armand told him. "Look."

He showed him the photograph of a young man in semiprofile. Emil looked at the picture, then at Armand.

"Samson? Do you know him?"

"I am all but positive," Armand replied. "As soon as I re-turn to Beirut, I *will* be sure!"

As the first police car screeched to a halt at the curb, Armand slipped the photograph into his pocket.

"Can you handle them?" he demanded of Emil.

Emil was taken aback by the concern—perhaps even fear—in Armand's eyes.

"It's Kate, isn't it?"

Armand nodded.

"Go!" Emil said, and turned his back on Armand as if he were a stranger.

Kate closed the last page of the French police report and placed it on the coffee table between her and David Cabot.

"The man you were looking for, the one who tried to help my father, has been murdered," she said flatly. "What does this mean?"

"That the questions we have been asking are making someone desperate," David replied. "And therefore very dangerous."

"But who?"

David had no doubt that Pierre was involved, but surveillance of the banker had revealed nothing so far. Pierre had not deviated one iota from his daily routine. He had not gone out of the country; he had not received any visitors other than foreign bankers whose faces were well-known to David. Yet it was Pierre who stood to benefit the most by the murder of the British bank official, Kenneth Morton. Morton had been the only witness to the fraud Pierre was perpetrating at the Banque de Liban. Without his testimony the case against Pierre would be weakened considerably.

But there is someone else. Pierre's handmaiden. The one who goes where Pierre cannot, makes the connections and arrangements Pierre doesn't dare become involved with. The link to the killer, Bacchus . . .

"David?"

David shook off his reverie. "The Englishman was murdered because someone got wind that we were looking for him, which means that any one of us—you, me, Armand—are potential targets."

"Where is Armand?" Kate demanded. "When is he coming back?"

David calculated the time difference. Armand would have landed in New York a few hours ago. Probably he had already spoken to Bartoli. As soon as Armand had something concrete, he would get in touch. Until then his job was to make sure nothing happened to Kate.

"With whom will you be watching the parade?" he asked.

"I was supposed to see it with Armand," Kate replied. "As well as Jasmine and . . . and Michael Saidi." Kate paused. "David, if you know something you're not telling me—"

"I wish that were the case," David said. "Let's see what happens by tomorrow. Just, please don't do anything without talking to me first!"

Kate shivered.

It was dawn, and David was the only pedestrian on the promenade bordering the Grande Corniche. The occasional delivery truck or empty taxi would pass by, but otherwise the only sound was the crash and hiss of the receding sea.

He was walking the exact route the floats, bands, and entertainers would follow in a few hours. His gaze floated over the units at the very top of the apartment buildings fronting the Corniche, looking for lines of fire and estimating trajectories. His security people had provided him a list of all the tenants and owners. Almost all of them had been there for years and were respectable Beirutis. David hadn't been concerned about them. He'd wanted to know if some relative, a cousin, uncle, or nephew, or any other visitor, had shown up recently. None had.

David reached the reviewing platform where the Fremonts always sat and walked around it slowly. The judges occupied the center row to give them a better view of the floats and bands marching by. Beirut society was clustered behind them, on the higher tiers. He couldn't change that arrangement, but he had had Armand's seat moved from the middle of the platform to the very end, where, if he attended, exposure would be minimal.

There were other measures that would be put in place, some of which Armand would neither notice nor be told of. David calculated that the assassin would try to make his play during the parade. If this was where Bacchus made his attempt, then David wanted not only to thwart it, but to take Bacchus alive. He was as ready for Bacchus as he would ever be. Now all he and Armand needed was a little luck.

17

At exactly nine o'clock in the morning, the nineteenth-century cannon of Beirut's citadel boomed, the parade major gave a shrill blast of his whistle, and Carnival was underway.

There were sixty floats, each painstakingly created during the past year, and representing a particular group of Beirut's diverse population. Between them marched the bands, Nubian singers, Bedouin horsemen, whirling North African dancers with tiny cymbals on their fingers, and white-gloved military parade units. There were jugglers and clowns and fire-eaters, beautiful girls in skimpy swimsuits and men dressed in garish costumes made up of silk, feathers, and leather, topped off by huge, grotesque masks. Thousands of people jammed the Corniche; thousands more were perched precariously on lampposts or crammed onto the balconies of the apartment buildings along the route. Wealthy sailors and yachtsmen entertained guests on their million-dollar vessels that lined the harbor.

But among the revelers were seeded sharp-eyed men who moved smoothly through the jostling crowds. Some were watching the balconies, or the people around them, others stayed very close to the reviewing stand. Walkie-talkies clipped to belts crackled continuously.

High above the Corniche, a lone helicopter crisscrossed the parade route, sometimes swooping down to near rocftop levels, then pulling up and hovering. David held a pair of heavy military-issue binoculars to his eyes. The images from the ground raced back at him with startling clarity. So far he hadn't seen anything too suspicious, nor had his men. David checked his watch. Four hours down, another two to go before the last of the floats had gone by. He adjusted the focus on the binoculars and went back to sweeping the Corniche.

It had been a day Kate knew she would never forget. The floats and parade easily rivaled the Mardi Gras extravaganza of New Orleans, and her place on the reviewing stand, just behind the judges, had given her one of the best seats in the house. Later on they all went to Jasmine's "garden party," held in the private boxes of the Beirut Jockey Club to watch the thoroughbreds race.

"I thought it was one of the best parades in years."

Kate turned at Michael Saidi's words. He slipped into the seat beside her.

"I've never seen anything like it!" she confessed.

Although David Cabot's warning and Armand's absence were always in the back of her mind, Kate *had* enjoyed herself. The overwhelming effect of the extravaganza had simply carried her away.

"No one has seen Armand Fremont all day," Michael remarked. "Traditionally he is one of the parade judges."

"He is still attending to business," she murmured.

They watched as the horses were guided into the starting gate. Then the bell sounded, the barriers snapped open, and the horses thundered out of the gate.

"Well," Michael said at the end of the race, "at least I won a few pounds on the nag." He brandished the lucky ticket.

Jasmine and the others in the box laughed and applauded.

"Kate, you'll forgive me for saying so, but you don't seem to be in the spirit of the occasion," Michael said. "I hope it doesn't have anything to do with our unfortunate encounter with David Cabot."

"No," she replied hastily.

He covered her hand with his. "Please, if you want to talk, I am here for you."

Kate squeezed his hand. "It's nothing, really. David had a message from Armand, that's all. Armand and his little mysteries . . ."

As long as they don't concern me, Michael thought. He was sure that Kate didn't know anything. Still, it would be prudent to stay by her side the rest of the day, just in case. . . .

"But thank you for asking," Kate said suddenly.

"You'll be at the dinner tonight at the yacht club won't you?" Michael asked after the winning jockeys had been presented their trophies.

Out of the corner of her eye, Kate saw David moving toward her. She lifted her chin defiantly, and in a voice loud enough for David to hear said, "Of course I'll be there. We'll sit together."

The dining room of the Beirut Yacht Club was almost empty. At the far end of the room three bartenders were polishing glasses while busboys cut limes into wedges and lemon rind into slivers. The setting sun was bursting through the floor-to-ceiling windows, sparkling off the one hundred tables laden with crystal, china, and crisp, starched napkins. Kate had taken the last chair on the end of the head table, in front of the windows. She was still in the cream pant suit with jade blouse and yellow scarf that she had worn to the jockey club. Kate had returned to Armand's villa when, twenty minutes later, David had reappeared, telling her that Armand's plane was less than a hundred miles from Beirut.

"He wants us to meet him at the club," David had told her, and held up his hand. "Don't ask for details because I don't know any. We're both in the same boat."

Kate watched David pace behind the chairs, a cigarette in his hand. The tension poured off him, robbing the room of its festive atmosphere for Kate.

Suddenly the doors swung open and Armand was in the room, walking quickly and purposefully toward them. He raised his hand in greeting, but his expression remained grim.

He's learned something! Kate thought. She picked up her purse and stood up. Out of the corner of her eye she saw David start to move fast. Then the wall of glass behind her exploded into a million splinters, and David was twisting along the edge of the table, as though spun around by some invisible giant.

The next bullet was silent, passing cleanly through the empty frame. Kate felt its heat sear her cheek and recoiled as David's chest blossomed in blood.

"No!"

Armand was watching the tableau unfold as though in slow motion. In that terrible instant he realized a cruel truth: David, not he, had been the target of the assassin all along. He had become one the moment Armand had sent him after Pierre. All this time David was the one who had been in the cross hairs. . . .

Armand roared out his fury and lunged for David. The bullet never gave him a chance to reach his friend, plunging into his back and sending him crashing onto the terrace. He heard Kate screaming then something like the hand of God propelled him forward again. For an instant Armand clung to the railing—but his momentum was too great. His strength fled from his muscles and he lost his grip, his body crashing onto the hard earth, rolling down the steep slope into the roiling waters below.

One hundred yards away Alejandro Lopez let his rifle sights drift along the target as the gondola slid silently down the mountain. The girl was on her knees, her face white with anguish as she stared into the darkness where the man had fallen. For an instant Lopez's finger curled once more around the trigger. He sighted the middle of the girl's forehead; then, in one swift motion, he snapped on the safety. The targets were dead, he was sure of it, and the girl was not a part of the bargain.

The wail of police and ambulance sirens was lost in the festive din of the city. The blood on Kate's dress had dried, soaking into the fabric, making it stiff against her skin. The yacht club had been sealed off by police, who were lined three deep outside the dining room to hold back the television and newspaper reporters. In front of the doors, beyond which lay the body of David Cabot, stood Salim. He scarcely seemed to be breathing.

Less than an hour had passed since the world had exploded around Kate. She had vivid, disjointed images, seeing David spin around, cry out, and fall, of Armand reaching for him and becoming drenched in blood, of her screaming as she watched Armand career over the railing and plunge into the darkness. She remembered talking to the police in a clipped, wooden monotone, telling them how the room had suddenly been torn apart by flying glass. . . . Kate was determined to hold together so that she could do something to help, all the while fingering the bloody sleeves and cuffs as though they were talismans. David was dead but not Armand. She would not believe that until they showed her the body.

Tentatively Kate edged her way along the deck, her fingers trembling as she touched the railing. Powerful, hand-held lamps lit up the slope as rescue workers, led by firemen, searched for any sign of Armand Fremont. Overhead two helicopters, each with a large spotlight clipped to the belly, circled the cove, the beams dancing off the dark, swirling waters. Farther out were the police patrol boats, moving along the perimeter of the cove, unable to get closer because of the tide and the rocks. Kate had heard someone shouting that Zodiacs were being brought in. These small, fast motorized rubber rafts could navigate the waters of the cove, get in close enough to the shoreline for their divers to search for a body caught between the outcroppings of rocks.

"Kate . . ."

Kate stirred and saw Michael and Pierre standing beside her. She flung herself against Michael, her terror and grief and rage spilling out on her tears.

"I came as quickly as I could. Kate, I don't know what to say. It's all too horrible."

"Kate," Pierre wailed, "the police asked me all kinds of insane questions! Did Armand have enemies? Had he been threatened? Had there been a particularly heavy loser in the casino recently? How could I know any of these things?"

"It wasn't a disgruntled gambler," Kate said softly. "Nor

a madman. Whoever shot Armand and David had thought long and hard about it. They planned everything, Pierre. They knew where they would be and when . . . how they would kill them . . ."

Pierre recoiled. "Kate, what are you saying?"

"That one person didn't do it. Oh, one person pulled the trigger, but he was only the instrument."

"Kate, you're distraught." Pierre said nervously. "This is all nonsense. Conspiracy fantasies—"

Kate's eyes blazed. "Don't you dare believe that! When they find Armand, he'll tell you—"

"Kate, Armand is dead! He was shot in the back. You said so yourself. You *saw* it! Even if he had survived the bullet, the fall, those waters . . . Kate, please don't torture yourself like this!"

Kate covered her face with her hands, sobbing. "God, I don't know what's happening anymore."

Michael put his arm around her shoulders and drew her against him. "Stop it, Pierre," he said. "She is in shock. Don't make it any worse."

He lifted Kate's chin. "I'm going to take you home. There is nothing you can do here. The police will call as soon as they find Armand. Pierre will see to it."

He glanced at Pierre, who nodded.

"I . . . I need a moment alone," Kate whispered.

Reluctantly Michael let her go, watching as she walked over and knelt by David Cabot's body. She drew back the sheet so that she could see his face.

What did you find? she asked silently. *What was it that frightened them so much they had to silence you . . . and Armand? Who is the man in the shadows, the one behind all this? One way or another, David Cabot, I will find out!*

A few feet away Pierre was lighting a cigarette, never taking his eyes off Kate. Then he noticed his fingers were trembling and wondered if they would ever stop, if his heart would stop beating as frantically as it was now.

Pilate, too, washed his hands . . . just when he thought he was a happy man. As Pierre thought he must be. Because the men who might have learned of his secret, who could have threatened him with exposure and disgrace, were gone. The life he had with Cleo was safe. The casino holding company would be taken public and sold. He would be wealthy beyond imagination, able to replace the funds he had stolen, able to give Cleo whatever she wanted for the rest of her life. He would have all this because he had known a kinsman would die, and he had done nothing.

Pierre watched Kate cover David and stand up. She did not turn to Michael but to Salim. "He is gone, and we must go home now, to wait and pray."

The giant Turk trembled as though his massive body were about to break apart. Then his shoulders hunched forward, and Kate took him by the hand, leading him away as she would a child.

The police commissioner personally notified Jasmine of the shootings, apologizing profusely for having to tell her such things over the telephone.

"I felt you should know at once. Within the hour there will be a thousand rumors about what happened. I am sending one of my assistants to be with you. I have instructed my detectives to keep him informed. He will immediately pass on whatever details we have."

Jasmine played her role masterfully, her voice ranging from shock to grief-stricken anger.

"Thank you, commissioner. . . ." She hung up and looked at Louis. "It's done."

Louis's eyes widened, and his face became ashen. Jasmine gripped him by the shoulders.

"This is your moment!" she whispered urgently. "You look perfect, all the grief and confusion in your face. Just don't fall apart on me, Louis. There is more we have to do. Only a little, pet, I promise."

Jasmine disappeared into her bedroom and made one call, to Nabil Tufaili. He and the other *zuama* were there within the hour. Jasmine directed them to the far end of the apartment, well away from the servants, and locked the doors.

She looked directly from one to the next of the twelve men seated before her.

"An enormous tragedy has struck our city and our country," she said. "At the moment the police have few details except that David Cabot is dead and Armand is missing, presumed to have either died of his wounds or drowned. The point, however, is this: an attack on Armand Fremont is an attack on all of us—"

"But *who* attacked him, Jasmine?" Nabil Tufaili asked softly. "Who would want Armand dead?"

"If I knew the answer, I would be talking to the police right now!" she said angrily. "In my opinion, it was the work of some malcontent, or religious fanatic who listens to voices in the wilderness. If something like this can happen to Armand then it can happen to any one of us. Beirut—indeed all of Lebanon—functions because it is clearly understood by *everyone* where authority rests. Or rather where it *should* rest. I believe that this tragedy can be laid at our feet. Yes, all of us here in this room. For months we have been sparring with each other over the right candidate for president. In the meantime we grew complacent. We failed to realize that our discord would spell opportunity for others, the chance to challenge us, test to see exactly how weak we were. This is why Armand died! Because in our squabbling we have let slip the reins of power. And that is what we will take back. Right now!"

"Your proposal, Jasmine?" Nabil Tufaili asked.

"What it has always been—your unconditional support of Louis."

"But what has changed since we last spoke?" Tufaili asked.

"It has been a question of money, hasn't it?" Jasmine replied. "Very well. Now Louis and I have your precious collateral!"

The members of the *zuama* looked at one another.

"The details, Jasmine, if you please."

"Why, I would have thought them to be self-evident: who else can inherit the casino except me and Pierre? And since both of us believe that taking the Société des Bains Mediterranien public is a prudent business decision, the value of our stock in the casino will quintuple. The arithmetic is simple."

Jasmine sat back and regarded the unofficial rulers of Beirut.

"Louis and I would like your answer. Right now."

"Of course, we need to discuss this," Tufaili started to say.

"No more discussions, Nabil. Yes or no."

Tufaili's immediate reaction was that he should leave, but out of the corner of his eyes he saw that the other *zuama* were not moving. The insult Jasmine had flung at them lay at their feet. But that did not change the fear and uncertainty they felt. Whatever opinion they'd had of Armand Fremont, in the end he had been one of them. Now he was dead, and Jasmine Fremont's explanation, so cool and precise, made all the sense in the world to them.

One of the others took the initiative from Tufaili.

"You have the support of the *zuama*."

Carloads of reporters and cameramen blocked the road leading to Armand Fremont's villa.

"Not this! Not now!"

Salim reached across and patted Kate's hand. He extricated himself from behind the wheel of the Rolls-Royce and lumbered in the direction of the reporters scrambling toward the car. Salim blocked their way, talking earnestly to them. Kate saw the journalists shaking their heads furiously. Kate braced herself for the onslaught. Then Salim shrugged and calmly picked up the man closest to him. One minute the reporter was four feet off the ground, arms and legs kicking furiously. The next, he was cartwheeling down the side of the hill while Salim was reaching for his next victim. The press scattered.

"Well, you are certainly in capable hands," said Michael, managing a ghost of a smile. "I know it will be the hardest thing in the world right now, but try to get some rest.

Promise?"

She felt his lips on her forehead. "I will be with the rescue teams. The minute they find anything . . ."

Inside, the house had an eerie quiet to it. Balthazar's grief was etched on his face. He grasped Kate's hand in both of his and brought it to his lips. Behind him stood Marie, her eyes red-rimmed.

"The doctor is on his way," Balthazar said.

Kate realized he was thinking of her and protested.

"Believe me, you will feel better once he is here," Balthazar told her. He gestured toward the window. "That is only the beginning. You will need rest to get through the days ahead."

Balthazar's words took Kate back to the cold days and nights at her father's home on Park Avenue, the sleepless nights spent tossing and turning, the mornings she woke up drenched in sweat. Now she was thousands of miles from home, unsure of what her obligations were or what was expected of her. For that alone she would need strength. To face her grief? She could think of nothing that might help.

Kate stayed under the shower until Marie, concerned, knocked and looked in on her. The doctor had come and gone, as much in shock as everyone else, leaving mumbled instructions and reassurances along with a supply of sleeping pills. Kate sat curled up on the sofa in her room, fingers wrapped around the plastic vial, staring sightlessly at the breaking dawn.

The television was on, its volume just high enough for Kate to hear the French-speaking announcer's mournful tone. The searchers along the slope had found a billfold and key chain that had been positively identified as belonging to Armand Fremont. Also, scraps of cloth had been plucked off the bushes. Clearly he had fallen all the way to the water. So far neither the helicopters nor boats had spotted anything. The divers were searching the area closest to shore but had nothing to report. According to the marine forecaster the tides had been exceptionally strong last night.

Given that Armand Fremont had been shot, had fallen such a great height, the chances that he had survived the current were all but nonexistent.

He's dead, Kate thought dully. *I know it.*

Then, for the first time since the terror had exploded, she began to cry.

On the third day after the shooting the harbor commissioner and the minister of justice arrived at the villa to inform Kate that the search was being called off.

"We have looked everywhere, Mademoiselle Maser," the commissioner explained apologetically. "We even followed the tidal charts all the way up the coast, as far as the grottoes. There was no sign of Monsieur Fremont. We can only presume that his body was carried out to sea."

Kate was silent for a moment, then rose and said, "Thank you for your consideration. You will understand if I wish to be alone now."

She went into the gardens and had no idea how long she had been sitting there when Jasmine came in.

"I wasn't sure if you wanted company," she said. "Just tell me if you do not, and I will go."

Kate spoke as though she never heard her. "I can't believe he's dead, yet somehow I knew that's exactly what they were going to tell me."

"Kate, I can imagine the shock you have suffered—"

"I want to know who killed them, Jasmine!" Kate said harshly. "And why!"

"I want to know that too!" Jasmine replied fiercely. "So does Pierre and Louis and all of Beirut! You cannot imagine the rumors that are sweeping the country. Some are blaming Palestinian radicals, others think it was the work of a religious fanatic, still others dream of dark conspiracies."

"What do *you* think?"

Jasmine twisted a cigarette into her jade holder, the rings on her fingers flashing.

"Armand was a powerful man, more so than you know. I am not talking only about money and property, but secrets.

The secrets of men even more powerful than he. Industrialists, financiers, politicians—they all came to the casino to play, but also to talk, bargain, strike deals. Armand was the honest broker, and the casino was neutral ground. But you remember the fate of the messenger who brought bad news? Well, I think the same thing happened to the broker. An agreement was breached, a promise broken, the blame had to be placed somewhere, and where better than upon the man who brokered the deal in the first place?"

"You're saying we'll *never* know the truth," Kate said flatly.

Jasmine laid a hand on Kate's arm. "Truth is an elusive commodity in the best of times. But whatever it was in this case, it died with Armand. He was not a sentimentalist. He did not keep records or diaries. You know how business is done in the Middle East—with a handshake and the details kept up here." Jasmine tapped her forehead. "Only fools commit secrets to paper."

"I *won't* accept the fact that we can't get at the truth."

"I will not let you punish yourself like this," Jasmine said firmly. "What happened had *nothing* to do with you." She paused. "I do not mean to be cruel, but remember what happened after your President Kennedy was shot. Commissions of inquiry, conspiracy theories, a nation in agony but no closer to the truth for all that. So remember, when the funeral takes place, we bid our farewells."

"The funeral . . . ," Kate murmured. "I never even thought of—"

"I am looking after the arrangements," Jasmine cut in. "If you want to go over them, perhaps write a short eulogy . . ."

"Thank you. I'd like to do that."

Jasmine embraced her. "I will stop by when I can. If you need anything at all or if you just want to talk, call me."

Kate nodded and promised she would. But as she saw Jasmine out, she could think only of her words about President Kennedy. For better or worse people *hadn't* stopped asking questions. The search for the truth continued because that's what was owed the murdered President.

And that's what she owed Armand.

His fingers inched up the smooth face of rock, seeking the tiniest grip. They found a crevice, no more than a hairline fracture, and dug in. Armand waited until the next wave rolled in, used its momentum and poured all his strength into his fingers. He felt himself lifted, and he waited for that agonizing moment when the waters would recede. He had tried this a hundred times before and failed to maintain his grip, had been carried back into the pool formed by the boulders in the grotto. The pain from his wound was excruciating. The shock it caused as well as the frigid waters that robbed his body of precious strength conspired against him. There were, he knew, few chances left. If he could not hold on to the rock, the tide would continue to punish him like a merciless boxer until exhaustion would do its work.

Armand heard the roar of the waters, squeezed his eyes shut, and hung on. He felt as though his arms were being wrenched out of their sockets. The waters inundated him, forcing him to hold his breath until his lungs were aching and blood roared in his head. After what seemed like an eternity, the torrent stopped. Armand gulped down precious air, enough to feed his oxygen-starved blood, and pulled himself forward. Careful not to lose his grip with one hand, he searched with the other for a fissure, found it, and edged forward again, until he lay between two rocks, able to get both arms around one of them.

Armand braced himself as the next wave rolled in, gritting his teeth as his wound was pounded against the outcrop. He did not know how badly injured he was. His entire back felt as it it were on fire, but the first bullet must have missed the lungs; otherwise, he never would have survived this long. But Armand knew where the second bullet had struck him, along the left temple, leaving a gash that, his touch told him, had come within centimeters of being fatal. The salt water had cauterized the wound, stemming the bleeding. But the painful throbbing never stopped. Armand could not recall how many times he had lost consciousness. The fact that he had hung on to the rocks by sheer instinct of preservation was a miracle.

He forced open his salt-encrusted eyelids. He was floating in semidarkness. High above him was the ceiling of the grotto, carved through millennia out of the limestone cliffs. Farther back, where the light petered out and finally disappeared altogether, was a darkness that terrified him. The waters were black and there was no sound, inspiring the imagination to go wild.

Forcing away his dread, he concentrated on the gathering blue of the sea and sky as morning broke over the Mediterranean. In the distance he heard the faint beat of helicopters and the hum of the harbor powerboats searching for him. Fury rose in him because they were looking in the wrong place, because he was helpless to try to reach them. The current had fooled them both. Every sailor in Beirut knew that the cove waters swirl in concentric circles and that once caught, an underpowered vessel or inexperienced sailor was lost. But there were freak occasions when the ocean pulled the water out of the cove, sweeping it down the coast into and through the grottoes that honeycombed the hills north of the city.

One chance in a thousand of that happening, thought Armand. But it had. Just as he had survived not only the bullets but the fall.

The images and emotions were startlingly real, watching David crumple, the rage that had seized him as he tried to reach his friend, then the terrible pain as the shot cut him down, propelling him over the railing. The stones, brush, and earth lacerated him as he fell, unable to grasp at anything on the way down. By some small mercy of God he hadn't broken his neck, but when he plunged into the waters, he was totally helpless, barely able to stay afloat.

To have fought the current would have meant certain death. So he had ridden it, steering as best he could to avoid the reef outcrops until, like a cat tired of its exhausted mouse, it batted him into the grotto.

Armand held his breath again as the current shot over him. He licked his parched lips, spitting out the salt, trying to work up saliva to use as a balm. He felt so tired that he thought he could lie here forever. Yet deep in the pit of his stomach there still burned the white-hot coal of anger.

And Kate, what had happened to her?

The uncertainty of whether Kate too had been a target tormented him. He had no way of even guessing her fate. The assassin might have taken her, too, or perhaps, if there was mercy in the world, the bullets never found her . . . but that meant she was alone with Michael Saidi gliding up next to her like a serpent.

Stop it! To know that—to know anything—you must first survive!

He maneuvered himself so that he was able to pull himself out of the water a few inches. The boats were still out there, as were, he imagined, the men combing the slope and waters. But they would never come this far. Once they could not find him in the cove, they would never believe that he might have ridden the current and survived.

The realization froze Armand's heart. The grotto was immense. Because of the darkness he had no idea how far away he was from the shore. If he tried to swim, he could end up going around in circles until exhaustion pulled him under. But to stay here meant certain death. The wounds had robbed him of almost all his strength. The cold waters would soon do the rest. He had to reach land.

He slipped deeper into the water but found that his fingers would not let go of the rock. The rock had become a salvation neither the mind nor body were willing to lose.

Then if not for yourself, do it for Kate . . . and David. Kate because she may still be alive. David . . . David because he died for you!

Armand closed his eyes and turned away. He waited until the swell rolled in, then plunged into it. His fingers came off the rock like a lover's caress.

The day before the funeral Kate asked to see the senior

detective assigned to Armand's and David's murders, a tall, thin man, with a pockmarked complexion, called Hamse. The first thing she learned was that there had been absolutely no progress in the case.

"I would like to see your reports," she said.

Hamse obliged. He must have known what to expect, because his files soon covered Kate's desk.

"This pile is the religious extremists," Hamse said. "This one, the Palestinians. Here is a list of those who had heavy markers outstanding in the casino. You will note that the federal police in Egypt, Iran, Iraq, and Syria are making inquiries in their respective jurisdictions."

The detective opened another file. "This has to do with the shooting itself. We have determined that the shots were fired from the gondola as it traveled down the mountain, past the yacht club, and toward the basin. The choice of location was brilliant. It all but guaranteed that the killer would get away."

"Why is that, detective?"

"Because there are few men in the world who can shoot so accurately from a moving object at targets that themselves may be moving."

"Are you also saying that you *didn't* think until later in your investigation that the shots could have come from the gondola?"

The detective shifted uncomfortably. "It did not occur to us until much later that such a thing was possible."

"But you just said there are only a few men capable of such shooting. Doesn't that cut down the number of suspects?"

"It would, Mademoiselle Maser," Hamse replied coolly, "if one knew who they were or where to look for them."

"So that leaves us with the other side of the question," Kate said. "Who hired the assassin?"

"Alas, no fewer problems there," Hamse replied, throwing up his hands. "No one would hire such a man directly. The principal and the assassin would never want to see each other. Details would be handled either through trusted third parties or at arm's length—telephone calls, cables, even newspaper advertisements, innocently worded."

"Even if that's the case, you must be able to narrow down the number of principal suspects by motive."

Hamse arched his eyebrows. "Really, mademoiselle? And what motive would that be? Can you assist us in that respect?"

"No, but—"

"In fact, you cannot help us *at all*, can you?" the detective carried on, hammering each word. Hamse gathered up his papers. "I have done you a courtesy, mademoiselle. I will assume that your tone and insinuations are the result of grief. If, later on, you should recall some details that you think will be useful, please call me at once. In the meantime, I extend you my condolences. Good day, mademoiselle."

The cortege consisted of twenty cars, including those of the Lebanese president and his entire cabinet. Behind the cars walked the first rank of mourners, representing the cream of Beirut and international society. Following them were the casino employees and thousands of ordinary citizens who had come to pay their respects.

At Jasmine's insistence Kate rode in the lead car with the family. Ahead of her, gliding side by side, were the hearses, their roofs shorn so that the coffins, each draped with the Lebanese flag, seemed to be carried on a wave of flowers.

In the days leading up to the funeral Kate had met only one person who had come to mourn David, a tall, silent man who had introduced himself as Charles Sweet, David's second in command in Geneva. She had tried to draw him into conversation but had received monosyllables for her efforts.

"We all mourn in our own ways, Miss Maser," the American had told her. "But I promise you one thing: neither I nor anyone else at Interarmco will rest until David and Mr. Fremont's killer has been found and dealt with."

The procession wended its way up into the hills at Jounyeh, and there, overlooking the sea, the two men were laid to rest. As the Maronite cleric spoke the final words, Kate gazed across the sea which seemed so timeless, anony-

mous . . . pitiless. Then she turned to watch the coffin of
Armand Fremont, being lowered into the ground, empty.

When Kate returned to the villa, she found it as empty
and silent as she feared it would be. Sitting in the library,
she thought back to her budding law practice at Berkeley.
Even in the midst of social protest and her stormy relationship with Ted, life had been simple then. Now she did not
recognize herself, didn't know what she wanted or where
she should go.

The thought of going back to New York rankled more
than frightened Kate. To return without being able to vindicate herself or Emil Bartoli was failure. It also meant that
she could expect little mercy from either the district attorney
or the courts. If she surrendered to them, everything was
lost.

Night fell, and she sat on in darkness with her grief and
troubled thoughts. When the door chimes sounded, it was
all she could do to drag herself to the foyer and look
through the judas hole. A sympathetic but unfamiliar face
stared back at her.

"My name is Jean Shihab. I am Monsieur Fremont's attorney."

Kate was suspicious. "You could also be a reporter."

The lawyer flinched. Like all Arab men he was unaccus-
tomed to being challenged by a woman.

"My card," he said, rolling it up and squeezing it through
the lattice grillwork.

"Why are you here?" asked Kate, unfolding the card.

"Please, Mademoiselle Maser—"

"Tell me!"

Shihab glanced over his shoulder conspiratorially.
"Mademoiselle, it is about Fremont," he whispered, "His
will . . ."

She ushered him into the library, where he immediately
unpacked his briefcase and insisted on formally reading the
will to her.

"And regarding the disposition of my holdings in the

*Société des Bains Mediterranien, I hereby pass said shares
to Katherine Maser, to use, hold, or dispose of as she sees
fit,"* he concluded.

Kate waited expectantly, but obviously the attorney was
finished.

"I don't understand," Kate said. "What are these shares?"

"The Société des Bains Mediterranien is the holding com-
pany for the casino," the lawyer said slowly. "Monsieur
Fremont held the bulk of the shares, the minority sharehold-
ers being Jasmine and Pierre Fremont. You, Mademoiselle
Maser, are the new, undisputed owner of the Casino de
Paradis."

"That's impossible!" Kate whispered. "There must be
some mistake."

Jean Shihab shook his head. "No mistake. Monsieur
Fremont had this codicil added ten days ago. I would be less
than candid if I did not say I too was surprised, but such
were his wishes. But I have been Monsieur Fremont's attorney for many years," Shihab said quietly. "In all that time I
have never known him to do something without have a reason—a *good* reason. I wish, mademoiselle, I could tell you
what that is, but I cannot. There were issues on which
Monsieur Fremont did not seek my advice. This was one of
them."

"But what should I do?" Kate demanded.

The attorney hesitated, then at last said, "You should be
very careful, mademoiselle."

PART THREE

*Some men are born into times
they cannot change.*

—Arab proverb

18

Nabil Tufaili's bedroom was completely dark behind wooden shutters. The ten-year-old boy on Tufaili's right whimpered in his sleep. On the left, his twin brother lay curled up, his fist jammed against his teeth. His eyes were wide open, the pupils pinpoints of light, as he stared at nothingness like a catatonic. It was a trick the boy had developed to allow him to step away from the ruin of his body, from the pain shooting through his rectum up into his skull.

The door opened a crack, and a shaft of light made Tufaili stir even before he felt his servant's hand. The servant whispered in his ear, dispelling his master's anger. It was Tufaili's custom to amuse himself with the boys in the late afternoon and sleep until nine o'clock. After that he would wash, scent, and dress himself, and go for dinner at midnight.

Now he slipped into a voluminous, silky paisley robe and swept through the halls of his apartment. The old man, a clerk who had been with Armand Fremont's lawyer for decades, was waiting for him in the study. The clerk had been a prudent investment, Tufaili thought. He had been paying him for several years, ever since it had come to his attention that the clerk had been slighted by the attorney and was seeking vengeance.

Kiss the hand you cannot bite and pray for God to break it.

The old Arab proverb was acted out in thousands of ways every day. If the clerk had brought what Tufaili wanted, then he would play God and break the hand that had committed the injury.

Tufaili accepted the papers, and his heart leapt when he read the cover. Armand Fremont's last will and testament. He licked his thumb and turned the pages, nodding his head as he read the bequests to Jasmine and Pierre Fremont. She and that dullard banker would inherit everything. Tufaili's investment in Louis Jabar, as well as that of the other *zuama*, was safe—No! No!

Tufaili almost tore the page in half. The words concerning the Société des Bains Mediterranien blurred, but they would not change. Neither would the name of Katherine Maser.

Everyone had agreed that Jasmine wore the mantle of bereavement with elegant dignity. Not only did she look stunning in black, but she had kept her demonstration of grief to a few tears. No beating of the breast so typical among Arabs nor any of that maudlin remorse Lebanese Christians were apt to display. By unspoken consent Beirut society accepted the fact that Jasmine was now *the* Fremont to deal with. Equal homage had been paid to Louis, who was already being congratulated on his imminent victory in the presidential elections. No one had missed the implication of Nabil Tufaili's presence nor the fact that he and other *zuama* had monopolized Louis's time. It was very clear how and where the power had shifted and who would soon be in charge.

Given how well and smoothly things were going, Jasmine was taken by complete surprise when Pierre and Nabil Tufaili appeared on her doorstep just as she and Louis had poured themselves a nightcap. She was shocked by Pierre's haggard appearance and the way Tufaili bullied his way through the front door.

"Nabil, how lovely to see you."

Tufaili thrust some papers under Jasmine's nose.

"You didn't know anything about this, is that it?"

"Jasmine, I tried to tell him," Pierre started to plead.

Jasmine rose and stood very close to Tufaili. "Don't you ever behave like that in front of me again!" she whispered. "Louis, get Nabil some champagne. I recall that's his favorite drink."

While Louis got the wine, Jasmine settled herself in the living room. With a wave of her hand she indicated where the others should sit.

"Pierre, are you having a heart attack?"

"Damn you, Jasmine," Pierre whispered. "We should have known something like this could happen. It will ruin us!"

Jasmine looked at Tufaili. "You seem to have managed to put the fear of God into Pierre. How *did* you do that, Nabil?"

By now Tufaili had composed himself. The champagne helped, but not as much as the thought that one day he would pay back this bitch her insult. Choosing how and when would be a labor of love. Tufaili decided to give Jasmine a taste of what was to come and handed the copy of the will to Louis, who read the marked-off paragraphs and slumped back in his chair. "The fool!" he whispered.

Jasmine snatched the papers, read the entire document, parts of it two and three times over. Her low, throaty laugh filled the room.

"How clever Armand must have thought he was!" She looked at the three men. "And this is what frightens you? Can't you see we're dealing with a child here? Nabil, I guarantee that we'll have Kate Maser out of Beirut and the casino sold in a month!"

"You *can't* guarantee that," Tufaili replied bluntly.

"Care to make a small wager? Such as your contribution to Louis's campaign?"

Tufaili was very tempted, wanting to humble and humiliate this woman. But this was not the moment.

"Gently, Nabil," Jasmine warned him, reading his thoughts. "Your contribution and the contributions of the other *zuama* have already been put away in a safe place. Don't think you can threaten me by trying to get them out."

"Just do it!" Nabil Tufaili said hoarsely. "Show me how easily you can steal from Katherine Maser!"

Kate finally managed to fall asleep in the early hours of the morning, images of Armand and his turbulent death churning in her mind. A few hours later she was awakened by a telephone call from Jasmine.

"I had to warn you, Kate. Some of the details about Armand's will have been leaked to the press. Has Jean Shihab been to see you?"

"He . . . he was here last night. Jasmine—"

"Then you know."

"Yes, but—"

"There is no time for explanations," Jasmine interrupted her. "The whole world is about to descend on you. We need to talk, Kate. You, me, Louis, and Pierre."

Kate was relieved. "Where?"

"I am sending a car for you. Will a half hour be enough time for you to get ready?"

Kate had expected to be taken to Jasmine's home up the coast, but instead she was driven into downtown Beirut, to one of the skyscrapers that fronted the Grand Corniche.

"The building is owned by the Banque de Liban," the driver said in reply to her question.

The car swept into an underground garage and stopped in front of an elevator. The driver waited until Kate was inside and the doors were closing before he saluted and disappeared. Kate found herself holding her breath as the express car whisked her to the top floor.

"Kate! My dear, we have been so worried about you."

Kate was warmed by Pierre's greeting. He took her elbow and in a courtly fashion escorted her across an expanse of carpet to a long oval table. Four places were set, each one with a thick white document, pen, pad, crystal water glass, and a small sterling-silver carafe. Jasmine and Louis were at the sideboard, helping themselves to pastries.

"Oh, Kate!"

Jasmine came over and held her at arm's length. "You are bearing up well, considering. Armand is certainly one for surprises, isn't he?"

Kate crimsoned. She felt guilty, like a trespasser who blunders into a party and somehow convinces everyone that she belongs.

As Louis pulled back the chair at the head of the table, Kate protested.

"That is where Armand sat," Louis told her. "As majority shareholder, it is your place now."

Hating every second of what was happening to her, Kate sat down.

Pierre looked around the table and broke the awkward silence.

"We all appreciate how uncomfortable you must feel, Kate," he said. "Frankly, none of us knows what Armand had in mind when he named you as heir, but the fact is he did, and his actions are legally binding."

"That doesn't help me understand what's going on," Kate replied.

"Speaking candidly, we are all at a loss," Louis said. "But the thing to remember is that we cannot shirk the duties Armand left us."

"Do you know anything at all about the Société des Bains Mediterranien?" asked Jasmine.

"Only that it's a holding company for the casino," Kate replied. "Armand also told me that it holds some land and other investments."

"Of minor value compared to the casino," said Jasmine. "Did Armand ever mention our intention to sell the casino?"

Kate was shocked. "No, never!"

Jasmine looked at the others and gave a tiny shrug.

"Well, I'm sure he had his reasons. Nonetheless, that is the case. However, as you know, we are currently a private company. Before any sale is contemplated, we would have to go public."

"Why is that?" asked Kate.

"It's a matter of net worth," Pierre explained. "At the moment the shares are pegged at an artificially low price set many years ago. The value of the casino—both the real estate and its revenues—is far greater now. If the shares were offered to the public, their price would rise a great deal, in part because several potential buyers would bid it up. It stands to reason that we should get the highest price possible."

"Then you've already received some offers?"

"Those were only the opening bids," Pierre told her. "Believe me, the intrinsic worth of the Société's assets is not in question."

Pierre handed Kate a thick leather portfolio.

"This was prepared for us by an independent auditing firm. The pertinent numbers are on the first page."

They may have been pertinent, but they were also staggering to Kate. The auditors had calculated that a publicly traded share of SBM would be worth about fifty-seven dollars. Given the number of shares issued, that brought the figure to just over two hundred million dollars. Of which approximately one hundred and ten million would go to her.

The figures swam before Kate's eyes. All her life she had been around money. Growing up, she had heard the word *millions* bandied about the dinner table. But such money had never been real, never been *hers*.

Kate looked at Jasmine and Louis, then at Pierre. "Why *do* you want to sell?" she asked suddenly. "From what I've seen, the casino is doing very well. And it's been in the family for so long. . . ."

"The world changes, Kate," Louis said. "Armand never married. He did not leave a son to carry on his work. There is no dynasty. On the other hand, you know about my political ambitions, so I won't have the time or the energy to devote to the casino. And Jasmine, well I can't tell you how much I rely on her judgment and support."

"My position as director of the central bank is held for life," Pierre said. "Not only would time be an issue but in my case, as in Louis's, propriety as well. Really, Armand was the only one who could devote himself completely to running the casino. With all due respect, Kate, I don't think those are shoes you could fill, even if you wanted to."

Kate looked around the table. "I want all of you to understand one thing: I find this very embarrassing. I mean, I'm not even family. Armand was my father's friend but our lives, his and mine, became entwined only recently and only because he tried to help me. Now suddenly I've been made his heir, and you're prepared to hand me a check for one hundred and ten million dollars—without so much as saying boo!"

For a moment no one spoke, then Jasmine drew herself up.

"Well, now, I think it is we who should be embarrassed.

Or perhaps even take offense. Why is it so difficult for you to accept what we already have, Kate? That Armand chose *you* as his beneficiary, while leaving us with no more but certainly no less than we had before, was his decision. After all, we are already wealthy. Certainly Armand had every right to do what he did, and we respect that right. Now if you had been some adventuress or had coerced this bequest out of him, then believe me, there *would* be hell to pay. And as for Armand's motive, perhaps it isn't so elliptical. He came to your side because of his friendship with your father and the scandal at Maritime Continental. Don't you think, Kate, that the money from Armand's shares would go a long way toward repaying your father's depositors and re-establishing both his and your reputations?"

Jasmine's words shamed Kate. Here were people who had never done anything but good by her, and she was suspicious of them. Still her every instinct told her that something was not right.

"The will!" she said at once. "There are no references to potential buyers, the state of negotiations, current offers, or even a suggested price. Don't you think that if Armand really wanted to sell, he would have left specific instructions?"

"Kate, really—" Louis started to say.

"No, darling, she has a point," Jasmine broke in. "But there's a simple explanation for that. Armand did not have the time to include these details in his will. Perhaps he was going to put them in another codicil. We'll never know."

"No, that doesn't follow," Kate said slowly. "This *is* a new codicil. If Armand could take the time to draft it, he certainly would have included instructions as to what he wanted done with the casino."

"There's another way to look at it," Pierre suggested. "He made you majority shareholder precisely because you would know how best to honor his intentions."

"Yes, that's possible. . . ."

But what were those intentions? Why didn't Armand state specifically that I was to sell the casino?

Kate took a deep breath. "I haven't had a chance yet to go through Armand's papers. It's likely he left some notes about selling. I think I should look at them first." Kate could tell that no one at the table was happy with that idea.

"If we're less than enthusiastic, Kate, it's because time is a factor," Pierre said. "I'm sure you understand that's a fact of business life." He passed her a letter written on thick handmade paper.

"This is from the personal representative of the sultan of Brunei. The offer is clear: the day we go public, the sultan will offer sixty dollars a share, cash. No question of needing time to arrange financing or to draw up the papers. The latter will be in place, ready for signature, and the money to be wire-transferred into the banks of our choice twenty-four hours later."

"Except that this representative wants our commitment to the sale by the end of business tomorrow," Kate noted. "Or else the offer is withdrawn."

"It costs nothing to say you *want* to sell, Kate." Louis said. "It allows the sultan to go ahead with the paperwork. If, at any time, there is something in the terms that we don't like, we can stop. But this way we are guaranteed at least what I think all of us agree is more than a fair price."

To Kate, the implication was clear. Since she was majority shareholder, the fates of Jasmine, Louis, and Pierre were in her hands. If she hesitated or refused, it could devalue the worth of their holdings by millions.

Kate looked around the table. "Do all of you want to sell on these terms?"

"Yes, we do, Kate," Jasmine replied.

Kate took a deep breath. "I know you want an answer right away, but I'm sorry, I can't give you one. Believe me, I'm aware what's at stake, but I need time to set things right in my own mind. I promise I will call you tomorrow, before noon."

"We understand, Kate," Jasmine assured her. "And we will respect your wishes." She paused. "Just as in the end I am sure you will respect ours."

Dusk was spreading across the ocean, waves of amber lighting the hills of Jounyeh, warming the dead. Kate sat on the stone bench next to Armand Fremont's grave. The wind had already done its work, scattering the flowers that had lain there. Kate touched the marble headstone, so very cold. She didn't think that even the heat of the Middle East sun would ever be able to warm it.

Why did you do it? Why did you leave me with everything? What do you want me to do with it?

And maybe there was no great mystery. Maybe Jasmine had given her the answer. Kate thought back to the accounts that had been wiped out and how easily, with that money, restitution could be made. At the same time Emil Bartoli's name would be cleared, his reputation restored.

And you could go home again. . . . Even the district attorney's office couldn't believe you were guilty if everything was put back the way it was. There would be no stigma, you would have your career back. . . .

Kate thought hard about this. It was true: she *could* return to her old life and pick up its pieces. But was that enough? What about the life she had found here? Could she go back on her silent promise to Armand, to find out who was responsible for his murder and why?

These questions gave rise to still another. Why had Armand left her the casino, saddled her with both obligations and choices? It didn't make any sense. He lived in a world of intrigue. If he had known he might be a target, wouldn't he have made provisions for others to carry on his work? She recalled their conversation that night in the kitchen restaurant of the Saint Georges hotel, Armand's explanations about the casino's connection to Interarmco, its eyes, ears, and lethal hands across the Middle East.

Was there no one else to carry on this work? What about his family? Why wouldn't he have trusted them with the most precious thing in his life?

She ran her fingers over the grave marker again, like a blind woman seeking the answer through braille. It crept upon her as slowly as the receding rays of the sun fell away into the sea.

The casino belonged to Armand, but Interarmco was not only his creation, it was also my father's! And I am the last of the Maser line. . . .

These thoughts propelled her further. She remembered Jasmine's amused observations about Armand's behavior toward Kate, how it was much more than politeness or concern.

He was in love with me. He left me his legacy because he trusted me. And he trusted me because he loved me. . . .

Kate sat trembling under the force of her realization. She knew she was right. Every fiber in her body told her so. But then why hadn't Armand shown his feelings? Why hadn't he ever given her a sign?

Perhaps he did, but she hadn't seen it . . . because she was too blinded by love for him.

Kate looked at the gravestone. *Why hadn't she awakened soon enough to be able to tell him how she felt?*

A cracking sound behind made Kate whirl around, her hands balling into fists. There stood a young priest, with shoulder-length hair and a long, stringy beard. He wore a heavy silver crucifix over his black cassock, and a cap identified him as a brother in the Greek Orthodox Church.

"You are Katherine?" he asked, never taking his eyes off her.

"Yes . . . yes, I am."

"Then you are to come with me."

"Who are you?"

"My name is Brother Gregory. I belong to the Order of the Third Cross."

"What do you want from me?"

"You are to come with me," the monk repeated. "That is all I know. Please, I mean you no harm. My abbot has important things to tell you."

Kate edged away but never turned her back on the monk.

"Look, I don't know who you are or what this is all about . . ." Her words trailed off as, out of the corner of her eye, she saw Salim. The giant Turk nodded in the direction of the monk. Kate never hesitated then to abandon her caution.

"We can take the car—" she started to say.

Gregory smiled gently and pointed to the hay cart by the cemetery gates.

"Prying eyes ignore the humble."

Watching Salim return to the car and drive off in the opposite direction, she felt totally vulnerable. "Where is he going?" she cried.

"He cannot follow." Brother Gregory held out a hooded cloak. "Please, put this on."

"Follow where?" Kate demanded. "I'm not taking a step until you tell me what this is all about."

"I would answer you if I could," he replied. "But I am only your guide. You must have faith, mademoiselle." He gestured at the cloak. "Please, we do not want to tarry."

Reluctantly Kate slipped into the coarsely woven robe and pulled on the hood. *I must be crazy!* Brother Gregory hoisted himself onto the cart and reached to help Kate onto the running board. The monk flicked the whip over the horse's flanks, and the cart lurched forward.

They traveled with only the light of the stars and moon to guide them, along a dusty road that ran like a frayed leather belt along the coast, all but ignored in favor of the modern highway a mile inland. They passed darkened farms, the smell of crops heavy in the night air, and small, brightly lit stores where Kate heard music and laughter. After a few miles they turned toward the hills running along the coast. The road became narrower and finally disappeared altogether, leaving them to bump over a two-wheel path cut into the hills. More than once Kate twisted around to catch a glimpse of the lights of Beirut, now just splinters of diamonds across a black canopy. The farther back the city receded, the greater her misgivings became. Yet every time she thought she was ready to end this mysterious adventure, her curiosity got the better of her.

Or, is it, like the brother said, because I have faith?

The monastery loomed out of darkness without warning.

It was an ancient edifice, built at the time of the Second Crusades, and was one of the few holy places in the Arab world to have never been plundered or deserted. As the cart rattled up to the gates, Kate shivered. This was holy ground, but there was also something else here, something that had nothing to do with sanctity.

Brother Gregory pulled the cord by the door. "Someone else will take you in," he said, taking the reins, "God bless you, Katherine Maser."

Kate watched Gregory lead the horse away and started to call after him when the door opened. An ancient man, his face wrinkled like a baked apple, stood before her, flanked by two younger monks.

"I am the abbot, John. Please follow me."

Without another word the abbot turned and glided across the courtyard, past the low-ceilinged barrack-style buildings where, Kate guessed, the monks slept, and around the back of the monastery. He continued past the vegetable garden and the beehives, skirted a shed that reeked of crushed grapes, and entered a utility shed. Kate glanced up and down the stone walls, hung with gardening tools. Then the abbot gestured at one of his novitiates, who came up to the far wall and, taking a deep breath, put all his weight against it. Stone grated upon stone as the wall swung back, revealing a passageway lit with kerosene lamps. Without a glance at his visitor, the abbot hurried into the tunnel.

Kate followed, then suddenly uttered a high, sharp cry. On either side of the tunnel, resting in vertical sarcophagi carved into the limestone, were the dead. As far as she could see were the bodies of past members of the order, some little more than dusty skeletons draped in clothing reduced to rags, others almost perfectly preserved mummies. The abbot looked over his shoulder.

"There is nothing here that can harm you. Please . . ."

Try as she might, Kate could not take her eyes off the macabre spectacle. She breathed a sigh of relief when they passed out of the chamber, through another hidden door, and proceeded even deeper into the side of the honeycombed mountain. After what seemed an eternity, Kate stumbled into a large room with whitewashed walls and a single window set just below the ceiling. The air was tangy, laden with salt. The area was brightly lit by free-standing lamps, and somewhere in the distance Kate heard the chug of a diesel generator. In one corner she saw a bed, table, and several chairs. As she came closer, Kate's nose curled at the sharp odor of disinfectant and medicines. One of the brothers, who had gone on ahead, was now helping the figure on the bed to sit up.

"No, it can't be!" Kate breathed. "Armand . . . ?"

Kate ran across the slippery floor, sinking to her knees, one hand clutching at Armand's, the other cupping his cheek.

"You're alive . . . ," she whispered.

Armand nodded, smiling faintly. His face was gaunt, the complexion ashen. Kate saw immediately that he had lost a great deal of weight, but in his dark eyes burned the fire she recognized so well.

"It's not possible . . . ."

Armand reached out and ran his fingers through her hair.

"There were moments I thought I would never see you again," he said, his voice rough. "But it was not my time to die."

"Armand, how—"

He shushed her and turned to the abbot.

"Thank you for this service. I will never forget it."

"There is no obligation among friends," the abbot replied. "We shall return when it is time for her to go."

As the monks departed, Kate had a chance to look at Armand's wounds. His waist was heavily bandaged, and as he lay on his side, she saw the patches of blood around his lower back. The dressing wrapped around his forehead was ominous.

"It could have been much worse," Armand said, following her gaze.

"How bad is it?" asked Kate in a low voice.

"The head wound was more blood than anything else. But

the other one . . . well, a few centimeters to the left, and I would have been short one kidney." Armand smiled wanly. "I never would have made it."

"I want to know what happened," Kate said fiercely.

Armand told her everything up to the point where he had decided to leave the safety of the rocks and swim into the grotto. He paused to rest, then continued.

"I had no idea where I was going. It was sheer luck—although the good brothers would argue in favor of divine intervention—that I went in the right direction and reached shore. After that I lost consciousness. The next thing I remember is lying in this bed."

"Who are these brothers?" Kate asked.

"An order almost a thousand years old. Very active politically, although in subtle ways. This entire mountainside is one big ants' colony, tunnels and passages everywhere that each brother knows intimately. They heard about the shooting and the rescue attempts and came down to the grotto to look for me. Very lucky . . ."

"Do you know that everyone thinks you're dead?" Kate said in a low voice.

"Oh, yes." Armand stroked her cheek. "Just as I thought you might be dead too. . . ."

Kate clutched his hand. "They buried your coffin yesterday. It . . . it was awful!"

"I hope people had good things to say about me," Armand replied dryly. Kate saw tears well up in his eyes. "I should have been there . . . for David. He was the finest man I ever knew. He was so good that without realizing it, I killed him."

"What are you talking about?" Kate cried. "An assassin murdered David!"

"Yes, but why was that? Why had David become a target in the first place? Because I made him one."

Armand shifted so that he lay on his back. He looked straight ahead, but all the while he squeezed Kate's hand. Kate could tell, by the different pressure on her fingers, the grief, agony, and anger Armand felt, but which his words, scarcely more than a whisper, failed to convey.

"It is time for you to know everything," Armand said. "There can be no more secrets. I hope you will be able to forgive me, Kate."

"Forgive you? What is there—"

"Hear me out, please. Then give me your answer. You see, it isn't just about David or what happened that night. Everything started with Alexander."

At the mention of her father the color drained from Kate's face.

"To begin with, Alexander did not die in an accident. He was murdered."

Piece by agonizing piece the mosaic came together. As Kate listened, she felt her heart breaking, but she used every ounce of willpower to concentrate on what Armand was telling her, following the twisted skein of events driven by even more mysterious and deadly motives.

"Who is he, Armand?" she asked at last. "Who's the bastard who had my father murdered?"

Armand rolled his head to the side so that he could see her eyes.

"Pierre . . ."

Kate's fury evaporated. She had been expecting a monster, not a mild-mannered banker. "But how can that be?"

Armand explained about Pierre's financial troubles, how desperately he needed the money and the lengths he had gone to obtain it. "Then your father found out about it and threatened to expose him."

"Why?"

"Because he was afraid of the repercussions on me, on our work. . . ."

"There was a man at the funeral," Kate said. "The only one who came to mourn David. His name was Sweet."

"Charles Sweet, David's second-in-command. You will see him again, and he will tell you what you need to know."

"Armand, why did you leave everything to me?" Kate asked urgently. "You must tell me!"

"Help me sit up," Armand said.

Kate slipped her arm around his shoulder and brought him forward. But afterward she did not relinquish her embrace.

It wasn't only her touch that revealed to Armand that something had changed in Kate. He sensed it in her eyes, the tone of her voice, in the air between them. He was responding to it because whatever that unspoken feeling was, he shared it. Armand also understood how dangerous it would be just now to explore it, nurture it. He looked at Kate, praying a half truth would be enough.

"I changed my will because you were the only one I could trust completely. It is no secret that Jasmine and I are not close. Neither she nor Louis have ever had any stake in Interarmco, and to have revealed everything at once, well, it was impossible."

Kate nodded slowly. "Yes, I can see that."

"But let us get back to Pierre," Armand said, relieved that Kate had accepted his explanation. "Have you seen him since my untimely demise?"

Kate told Armand about the meeting she'd had with Pierre, Jasmine, and Louis just this morning. Armand's eyes glittered.

"So I want to sell the casino," he said harshly. "And who brought that up?"

"Pierre."

"Were Jasmine and Louis surprised?"

"No. They agreed with him that it was the best thing to do . . . under the circumstances."

"I'm sure. But under *whose* circumstances? What would Jasmine and Louis gain?"

"A lot of money," Kate said drolly.

"My God! Louis's campaign!" Armand looked at her. "How could I have been so blind?"

"Armand, you're going too fast!"

"Louis is a weakling, Kate. He is as venal as any of the *zuama*. He is because he is their creature, bought and paid for—almost."

Kate was stunned. She had never seen this side of Louis,

had never imagined it could exist.

"I realize it's hard to believe," Armand said, seeing her confusion. "Louis puts on such a splendid face. But believe me, there is no substance to it."

Armand paused. "Just as there is no truth to the claim that I want to—or ever wanted to—sell the casino."

Kate drew back. "You never even considered it?"

"No, Kate. Never."

"Then why did . . . ?"

Armand watched as the truth began to glow like a beacon behind Kate's eyes.

"They were taking advantage of me," she said slowly. "I, who know nothing about the casino, suddenly inherit it all. They are aware that the situation at Maritime Continental will tempt me to sell for enough money to make restitution, clear my name, father's, Emil Bartoli's, and be able to go home and pick up my life and career."

"Was it tempting enough?"

"Almost. I said I needed time to think about the offer from the sultan of Brunei."

"The sultan, no less," Armand murmured. "Pierre *has* been moving quickly."

Kate looked at him. "Pierre was involved in what happened to Maritime Continental wasn't he? He was the mastermind."

"I don't know that," Armand cautioned her. "It seems likely enough, but . . ."

"But what?"

"I see Pierre as a desperate man, on the verge of panic. Could he also have been cunning, methodical, and utterly remorseless? I can't imagine that, Kate."

"The shadow," Kate said slowly. "Pierre's shadow . . ."

"Yes. Someone was using Pierre's circumstances to mask his own actions."

"Who?"

"David died trying to find the answer," Armand replied heavily. "Morton, the British banker who exposed Pierre to your father, was killed because David had come too close to him. Then there was Michael Samson . . ."

The name didn't register immediately, then Kate remembered.

"Samson? The wire-transfer clerk who was killed in the fire in New York. What's he got to do with this?"

Kate was frightened by the terrible sadness in Armand's eyes.

"His name is not Michael Samson," Armand said softly. "It is Michael Saidi."

"No!"

Armand gripped Kate's hand, holding her close.

Piece by piece Armand reconstructed the puzzle that was Michael Saidi. He withheld nothing, not even the suicide of Prudence Templeton and the photograph she had left behind. Armand withdrew it from his pocket.

"That is what I was bringing to show you at the yacht club."

Kate stared at the picture, its edges curled by seawater.

"It is he," she whispered. "Do you think Pierre used Michael to steal from Maritime Continental?" Kate asked, at last.

"It might have happened that way," Armand said. "I cannot see Pierre dirtying his own hands. But we come back to the same question: is Pierre the kind of man who could find and control an accomplice? I don't think so."

Kate seemed not to have heard him. "Then Michael could have had something to do with my father's murder, even indirectly."

Armand caught the dangerous edge to her voice. He knew well the tone of revenge. And vengeance had its place here, but not the way she thought. She did not know how this part of the game had to be played.

"Michael is an embezzler and a killer," Kate said flatly. "God, how I'd love to bring him back to New York to stand trial for the murder of that poor man who died in the fire! Armand . . ."

"Yes, Kate. We must find a way to expose Michael Saidi for what he is. But there is also the matter of Pierre's accomplice. Both he and Pierre must feel safe now, thinking that I am dead. Eventually, of course, I will have to show myself—"

"No, Armand," Kate said, her voice resolute. "I will do what you can't."

"That's impossible! I won't have it—"

"You have no choice! Because you made me your heir, I'm already involved!"

"Damn it, Kate, I can't let you do that! This isn't a game. Pierre and his accomplice have killed three times—four, if you count the attempt on my life. If you get in their way, they will come after you too!"

"They already have," Kate said coldly. "When they murdered my father."

Armand lowered himself back on the bed, breathing hard. "Please, Kate, don't do this. I never meant for you to entangle yourself like this." He stared at her. "This is such an ugly business! You don't know how much I hate this side of Lebanese life, with its countless, endless intrigues that destroy truth and loyalty, even in the family. We have become our own worst enemies, Kate, too greedy, too proud. We think anything is possible and no price is too high. We shall pay dearly for this one day."

"Others will, but not you," Kate said. She leaned very close to him, realizing how quickly his strength was ebbing. "Tell me what to do. Pierre and the others expect me to agree to sell the casino. Maybe by refusing to do that, I can push Pierre into making a mistake, even flush out whoever is working with him. If it happens to be Michael, then . . ."

Armand closed his eyes and lay very still. Kate held her breath, thinking that he was slipping away from her.

"You have to buy us time," Armand said at last. "We need that in order for Pierre's conspirator to expose himself, then we will seize the right moment to reveal Michael Saidi's true face. There is a way this can be done. . . ." Armand fell silent for a moment. "The *only* way." He reached out and cupped her cheek.

19

The cabaret and *salon de spectacle* at the Casino de Paradis closed at three in the morning. The gaming salons and tables were locked one hour later. By six o'clock the cleaning staff had completed their work in the main halls, whose doors would open at eleven.

To Kate, the ornate rooms were somehow more intimate now. She ran her hands over the velvet-soft baize of the baccarat tables and along the columns that soared to the ceiling. She opened one of the roulette tables and spun the ball in its gully, the rattles, as it cracked along the wooden spines of the wheel, sharp as gunshots. In her mind's eye she conjured up the faces of the people she'd seen in these halls. She heard their laughter and whispers, the shouts of joy, the low curse that came too late to ward off bad luck.

She went on like this for hours, moving through ghosts and memories, and it wasn't until she stopped and asked herself why it was all so real that she understood what she'd been searching for. It was not the wood or stone or silk, nor the grandiose architecture or precious ornaments, nor the riches and power and wealth that had permeated the walls like generations of fine old wax, that gave the Casino de Paradis its spirit. Only man had been able to do that. One man, Armand Fremont. She had been roaming the casino to learn even more about the man she had fallen in love with.

She took one last look around her and walked out into the early morning of Beirut. The Algerian street cleaners, stooped over their long-handled straw brooms, glanced up at her, then returned to their work. The morning chill raised goose bumps on Kate's arms. From now on every step she took, every gesture she made, and every word she spoke would be closely scrutinized. She could not afford to show the slightest doubt or hesitation. Her only weapons would be forged from what she knew of her enemy, and she would have to learn much more if she was to triumph.

Kate stepped past Salim into the car. A few minutes later she was on her way to the airport. The first part of the grand design was in motion.

Two hours later the private jet groped its way through clouds and fog to touch down at Geneva's international airport.

Kate held her breath as she approached Swiss customs and immigration, but the examination of her papers was perfunctory, just as Armand had predicted it would be.

"I took the precaution of having a Lebanese passport made for you," Armand had told her. "It is in my wall safe. The combination is . . ."

Charles Sweet, whom Kate had met at the funeral, greeted her at the top of the ramp, an umbrella unfurled to ward off the steady drizzle. In keeping with the terms of a directive David Cabot had left, Sweet had taken command of Interarmco. He had known that, given Armand Fremont's last testament, he would have had to deal with Kate Maser.

"As you must have guessed, Mr. Sweet," Kate said as the car wound its way through Geneva's business district, "Armand left a detailed description of the work Interarmco did on his and my father's behalf," Kate said.

Sweet inclined his head noncommittally.

"I didn't come to meddle or try to change things, if that's what you're worried about," she continued. "I came to learn about what my father was involved in and the responsibilities that were passed on to me by Armand."

Sweet's caution dropped one notch. "Then I will do what I can to help you."

The car drew up before an ordinary-looking commercial building, and Sweet ushered Kate into the lobby.

"Don't be fooled by appearances," he warned, taking her coat. "Anonymity is a prized asset. As for what goes on behind closed doors . . ."

The elevator took them to the fourth floor, where Sweet escorted Kate through the investigations and security areas.

"This was the heart of David's work," he said quietly, pointing at the computers and their attendants in lab coats. "David built up a security data base second to none. Not only do we keep track of the comings and goings of our clients, but their competitors and enemies as well. Most of the time the measures we take are preventive and if we're successful, the client is never aware that her or his enterprise is even in danger."

"Are you successful, Mr. Sweet?"

"Very much so."

Sweet took her to the seventh floor.

"All you see here was set up and paid for by Mr. Fremont and Mr. Maser," he said.

Kate looked across the expanse of desks, filing cabinets, and shelves. The place looked like the editorial room of some major newspaper. Then Sweet began to introduce the people who worked for Interarmco. They represented racial and ethnic groups from forty different countries.

Kate spent hours talking to them. Doctors from Baltimore and Nairobi worked on ways to get medical aid into drought-stricken regions of Africa. Engineers from Amsterdam and Singapore were experimenting with new freshwater systems to be used in the Far East. Black and white South Africans argued about the most effective ways to smuggle books and cassettes into their country so that the hope of freedom would never die. Pilots who had flown the Australian outback plotted routes that would get their cargoes of food and medicines into areas of the world that needed them most.

"I still can't believe it," Kate told Sweet when they had a moment to themselves. "How did my father and Armand manage? How could they keep such a thing hidden?"

"Sometimes the best camouflage is the most obvious," Sweet replied. "Your father's business included a lot of travel. No one thought anything odd about that. The same was true of Mr. Fremont, for whom it was even easier since he had his own place. Your father dealt with corporations and individuals worth hundreds of millions of dollars.

Everyone could understand why these meetings had to be discreet, held in very private or out-of-the-way locations. Mr. Fremont handled it differently. He was a public person and the media loved him. So instead of going out to those he wanted to reach, he simply had them come to the casino. It was the most natural meeting ground in the world. And no one suspected a thing."

"*Why* keep this work secret?" Kate asked. "Obviously it is humanitarian. You'd think that with a little publicity my father and Armand would have attracted other major contributors."

"That's possible," Sweet agreed. "But neither is it unusual for philanthropists to stay out of the limelight. In this case I think they were more effective that way."

"Are you suggesting I leave Interarmco as they had it?"

Sweet nodded and smiled. "I guess I am."

Kate thought it over and said, "I think you're right."

They spent the afternoon going over the details of current projects and ones that were about to be funded.

"Everything looks fine," Kate said. "There's more than enough money at the moment. Once I go over the casino books, I'll have a better idea of how much more can be forwarded."

Charles Sweet rose. "It's been a pleasure, Miss Maser. I am truly sorry we met under such circumstances. However, I look forward to working with you."

Kate shook his hand. "And I with you."

As he saw her out to the car, Sweet asked, "It's none of my business, Miss Maser, but did Mr. Fremont ever mention a *particular* interest he had in Interarmco?"

Kate glanced at the chauffeur, who quietly went back behind the wheel.

"Armand told me about the slave trade," Kate said tightly. "Also about David Cabot. Is there anything more I should know about that, Mr. Sweet?"

"I hope you'll forgive the way I brought up the subject," Sweet apologized, "It's a very sensitive matter. I assume you wish our work in that area to continue."

"Absolutely."

"Then perhaps this will be of interest to you. At the time of his death Mr. Fremont was intent on breaking a ring that had sprung up after so many others had been exposed. This was a very tough nut to crack, and we've been at it for a long time. But now I believe we are getting close. Does the term *The Chosen Place* mean anything to you?"

Kate thought carefully. "No, I'm afraid it doesn't."

Sweet didn't bother to hide his disappointment. "I thought perhaps Mr. Fremont might have mentioned something to you in reference to that, something we could use."

"What is 'The Chosen Place'?" Kate asked.

"We believe it is a transfer point or holding area," Sweet replied. "But we haven't been able to identify the location."

"Please call me as soon as you do," Kate told him. "In the meantime, if I find anything among Armand's papers that might be helpful, I'll let you know immediately."

Sweet opened the car door. "One last question, Miss Maser. Are you going to accept the offer on the casino?"

Kate looked back at him. "You know about that, do you?"

"It's my business to know many things," Sweet told her without a hint of apology.

"In that case, Mr. Sweet, I hope you won't take offense when I tell you that you'll have to wait and see, along with everyone else."

When Kate returned to Beirut and Armand's villa, she found a stack of messages waiting for her. Her eyes narrowed as she went through them. Most were from the same person: Pierre Fremont.

She took a deep breath and conjured up Armand's image, recalled the words he'd spoken to her. His warning tolled in her ears: *"It will be far more difficult than you imagine, Kate. Talking about a murderer is one thing. Looking him in the face is another. Especially when he must never suspect what you already know."*

Kate swore then she could do it. Armand had supported her, but given a warning. She would have to be in control of every moment. Slowly, then, Kate reached for the telephone, dialed Pierre's number, and, when he came on the line, asked him to arrange a board meeting for first thing in the morning.

"I'm sure I can get everyone together," Pierre said. "Kate, we've all been worried about you. I've left messages for you—"

"Pierre, I'm sorry. I found something in the casino books that didn't make sense. That's what I was following up."

"Kate, what are you talking about?"

"Not over the phone," Kate said. "We'll discuss it tomorrow. Eight o'clock in the bank's conference room."

They were all waiting for her when she stepped inside the room. The smiles and warm greetings could not dispel the tension that hung in the air.

"I thought something terrible had happened to you Jasmine said.

Kate took her seat at the head of the table. "Not to me But I've been going over the casino's financial records and have discovered some irregularities."

"Irregularities?" Pierre demanded. "What do you mean?"

"Cash transactions that can't be accounted for."

"How large are these transactions?" Louis asked.

"So far, about two million dollars is missing."

"I can't believe it!" Pierre exclaimed. "The accountants would have spotted something like that. Are you sure Armand didn't leave some memos to explain it?"

"Not one," Kate replied grimly. "I think you can see the problem. Although the transactions were camouflaged, I managed to spot them. If I can do that, then certainly the sultan of Brunei's people will be able to. At best they'll think we're fools. At worst they may feel we're trying to cheat them."

"What do you suggest we do?" asked Jasmine.

"The only thing we can: postpone the sale until I get to the bottom of this."

"No! We have too much at stake!"

Everyone stared at Louis, on his feet, his face mottled with anger.

"A few million gone missing is *nothing* compared to the final figures we're talking about. How can you even consider jeopardizing a deal over so little?"

"I can consider it, Louis, because ultimately it is my decision whether or not there is a sale at all!" Kate told him flatly.

"For heaven's sake, Louis," Jasmine chastised him, "give her a chance to explain. Kate, do you know who might be responsible for this?"

"Not yet," Kate said carefully. "Armand might have been taking the money out for his own purposes. Or else someone in the casino has been stealing."

"Then it's a matter for the police," Pierre declared. "I can assure you the investigation will be discreet."

"There isn't enough evidence yet," Kate countered.

"She is right," Jasmine said. "No matter how quiet the police are, there is always the chance of something getting out. Even a whiff of a scandal could jeopardize our negotiations with the sultan."

"I think Kate should bring us what she has so far," Louis said. "We might be able to help."

"I would prefer to handle this myself," Kate said firmly. "At least for the time being. It is after all my responsibility and—"

"But it affects all of us!" Louis shouted.

Kate rose. "And I will keep that in mind, Louis. Now if you will excuse me, I have a great deal of work to do. The minute I have something, I'll call you."

After Kate had swept out of the room, Pierre turned on Louis.

"Very nicely done! If you hadn't been so stupid, maybe she would have told us something!"

"The hell she would have!" Louis retorted.

"For once, Louis makes sense," Jasmine said thoughtfully, and added, "Unfortunately, there is nothing we can do for the moment." She turned to Pierre. "How is Katherine behaving?"

What little of Pierre's patience was left snapped.

"The hell with you and your riddles, Jasmine! How is she behaving? Like a fool!"

"No," Jasmine replied, drawing out the word. "But now I see why you have so much trouble with women, darling. It's so clear. Our Kate is *protecting* someone, someone she doesn't want to get hurt. . . . Now who could that be?"

Leonard Watkins's only qualification for the post of American ambassador to Beirut had been his prodigious fund-raising ability in his native California on behalf of the President. Watkins thought the efforts had been well worth it. Beirut was his kind of town, wild and woolly, where a man, if he knew the right people, could discover and indulge himself in pleasures that would make even hedonistic Californians blush.

And Jasmine Fremont-Jabar was certainly one of those people to know, thought Watkins. When he'd arrived in Beirut four years ago, she had literally taken him in hand and opened up a world he never believed existed. The best part was that Jasmine was safe. She was filthy rich in her own right, so blackmail was not a threat. She knew Beirut like the back of her hand, whom to trust and whom to avoid. Not once, in any of his adventures, had Watkins felt he was being steered or exploited. He was, however, a politician and knew that sooner or later a favor would be asked. Sitting opposite Jasmine in his office, he sensed the moment had arrived.

Watkins pointed to the champagne chilling in the bucket. "Could I interest you in a bracer?"

"That would be lovely, but no. I don't want to take up too much of your time."

So it's business. . . .

Watkins decided to go on a little fishing expedition.

"Terrible what happened to Armand."

"Awful," Jasmine agreed.

"The police don't seem to be making any headway."

"I don't know much about these things. I suppose it all takes time." Jasmine paused. "Leonard, I've come to you about a very delicate matter. It has to do with Armand's death, although indirectly, I assure you. But circumstances being what they are, I must ask you to hold everything I say in complete confidence. If, after you've heard me out, you feel you cannot assist me, I trust you'll forget the subject entirely."

Watkins rubbed the lowest of his three pink jowls. "Nothing you say will leave this office, Jasmine," he said. "You can take that as gospel. As for helping you out, you know I'll do what I can."

"Thank you, Leonard. I expected no less."

Without mincing words, Jasmine told Watkins about the will Armand Fremont had left behind, giving Kate majority control of SBM and, through it, the casino, she explained the offer that was on the table from the sultan of Brunei.

"There is, however, one small complication. While Kate has agreed, at least in theory, to go ahead with a public offering, she feels some kind of emotional debt to Armand. I'm concerned that this might cause her to have second thoughts."

Watkins was paying very close attention. What he had heard so far could be made very valuable if he found a way to profit from the information. But Watkins considered himself an old Beirut hand by now. This whole culture operated on wheels within wheels. There had to be more.

"Kate left the United States under a cloud. You remember, that nonsense about her having been somehow involved in the Maritime Continental affair? Well, I know she wants to put that behind her once and for all. If the sale goes ahead, she will have more than enough money to make restitution. Those who lost would get all their money back plus interest. Surely a guilty person, beyond the reach of American law, wouldn't consider doing such a thing."

Watkins smiled faintly. "Surely not."

"I think we should encourage her in this direction. For instance, if she were to receive a firm assurance from federal authorities that, upon returning the money, all charges against her and Emil Bartoli would be dropped, I believe that would go a long way toward convincing her to sell."

"I can see where that would be the case," Watkins agreed, but kept his voice noncommittal. He waited for the other shoe to drop.

"Our interest—mine and Louis's—in this matter is obvious," Jasmine said, giving the diplomat what he wanted. "Although Louis has the full backing of the *zuama* for his candidacy, he and I will be able to contribute that much more to his campaign once the sale goes through. Needless to say, the more we can do to assure a victory, the better it would be for everyone."

Leonard Watkins sat back and stared at a photo-portrait of President Johnson. He knew Lyndon well. This was just the sort of horse trading the old Texan would enjoy.

No doubt about it, Louis Jabar was the man Watkins wanted to see in the presidential palace. Unlike most of the rest of the world, which Watkins considered to be made up of ingrates, Lebanon loved Americans. It took U.S. aid money, sure, but it gave good value. American business loved the place, and Louis Jabar had proved himself a man one could do business with. Watkins had sung Louis's praises in Congress, with Aramco, Texaco, Mobil, and DuPont. And as long as everybody was happy, Leonard Watkins could look forward to a long, fruitful, and ultimately prosperous career.

Watkins adopted his best diplomatic manner. "Jasmine, I appreciate both your confidence and the gist of the situation. I think I can see my way clear to suggesting that the Justice Department recommend a full amnesty for Miss Fremont if she makes restitution."

Hell, I can almost guarantee it!

And Watkins could, because Bill Fredricks, the FBI agent attached to the embassy, was an old school buddy of Bobby Kennedy, whose people still ran the Justice Department.

"I knew I could count on you, Leonard," Jasmine said, getting to her feet. "Louis and I will not forget this."

Watkins smiled broadly. He could take that to the bank.

The time had arrived for Kate to make a formal appearance at the casino. Speculation was rampant about the fate of the country's landmark as well as the intentions of its new mistress. Beirutis, indeed most Lebanese, considered the casino *theirs*, and felt they had a right to know what was going on.

Kate recalled how suavely and effortlessly Armand had played host, making each person he spoke with feel special. Kate, on the other hand, wouldn't recognize a soul.

"Give yourself a few hours, and you will have everything you need at your fingertips," Lila Mikdadi assured her.

Lila was a sloe-eyed, olive-skinned beauty of forty. She had been Armand Fremont's executive secretary for over two decades and, as Kate had learned after the funeral, had been carrying the torch for him as long. Yet when told about the will, Lila immediately transferred her allegiance to Kate. "Because," as she had told the younger woman, "I know you will do what Armand would have wished done."

Lila ushered Kate into the study and showed her two cabinets filled with index cards. Each one had an individual's name, his or her addresses, private phone numbers, the pertinent personal details such as current mistresses or lovers, and, in the righthand corner, a passport-size photo.

"Eventually you will have to go through them all," Lila was saying. "But I have a good idea of who's in the city. These will do for now."

While soaking in the bath, Kate studied all two hundred cards Lila had pulled. At the time, she thought the number a little excessive. When she arrived at the casino, Kate whispered a silent thanks to Lila.

There was no avoiding the photographers this time. Anyone coming up the front steps of the casino was fair game. When they saw Kate, the paparazzi pounced.

She reminded herself of the drill Armand had coached her about. She waited in the car until Salim and the other security men had formed a flying wedge. Then she took a deep breath, put on her best smile, and got out. The flash-bulbs stunned her, and the questions, shouted in a dozen languages, were a giant cacophony. Kate waved back but made sure she was right behind Salim. Seconds later she was in the casino.

The staff greeted her as warmly as though they had been with her for years. With Salim at her side, Kate walked into the main salon. The tables were three deep with players, the floor crowded with couples chatting and watching the action. As she stood framed between the elegant mahogany doors with their inlaid cut-glass designs, heads turned in her direction. Kate recognized some of the faces from the file cards. Then the most curious thing happened. As the rounds finished, the tables fell silent, the gamblers and dealers all staring at her. Kate felt a hot flush working its way up her neck, but she stood her ground.

As if on cue the guests parted, making way for an elderly, dignified man wearing an old-style tuxedo. Kate recognized him as the *maître des jeux*, the floor manager who has the absolute last word on what goes on in the salon. Kate remembered Armand introducing her to him, whispering that this man had been with the casino for over fifty years.

The *maître des jeux* walked up to Kate, paused, and bowed from the waist. Then he turned to the crowd and in a strong, clear voice, called out,

"Mesdames, messieurs, I have the honor to introduce Mademoiselle Katherine Maser!"

He faced Kate again and slowly began to clap. Seconds later the ovation was deafening.

Even after the accolades Kate was nervous, because if anyone came to her with any problems, she doubted she could help them. Thankfully everything was under control. The roulette wheels were humming, and the private rooms were filled with players who, that particular night, were losing heavily. The Oiseau Bleu restaurant was packed, and the kitchen was running like a fine Swiss timepiece.

Kate felt a little uncertain about greeting some of the guests—the movie stars whose faces she recognized instantly, the socialite millionaires, and the business magnates whose names were linked to the world's largest corporations. But she quickly discovered that these people sought her out. The topics of conversation seemed innocent enough—fashion, social gossip, current business, and political affairs. Nonetheless, underneath the bonhomie and good cheer, Kate felt she was being watched, her behavior evaluated.

They're looking to see what I'm made of. They're looking for weaknesses . . .

That's when Kate put on her most confident smile, determined to show everyone that it was business as usual at the Casino de Paradis.

Even though she had not left the casino until after two o'clock, Kate was up by seven. Balthazar had prepared a breakfast of fruit, eggs, and American bacon, and it wasn't until she sat down to eat that Kate discovered she was ravenous. Then, when she snapped open the morning edition of the Beirut *Star*, Kate realized that the evening had been more of a success than she had dared to imagine. In her column Joyce Kimball heaped paeans on her, the breathless prose detailing exactly how Kate had been dressed, how her hair had been set, whom she had spoken to and—more important—for how long. The piece ended by proclaiming that in the shadow of tragedy, Beirut still had something to be thankful for: that its pearl, the Casino de Paradis, had passed into such gracious and seemingly capable hands.

Kate was on her second cup of coffee when Balthazar reappeared.

"You have a visitor, mademoiselle. I think you might want to see this one."

"Who is it?"

Balthazar silently handed Kate the card.

Bill Fredricks, the FBI liaison at the embassy, was a Hoover man from the top of his crew cut to his spit-and-polish brogues.

"Good morning, Miss Maser," he said, offering his identification to Kate. "Looks like you're not wasting any time getting acquainted with your new business." He nodded at the newspaper article.

"It's nice to meet you, Mr. Fredricks," Kate said, ignoring his comment. "What brings you here today?"

Fredricks seemed a pleasant enough man, but he had a policeman's hard, constantly roving eyes, drawing in everything, coming to conclusions, making decisions.

"I won't take up much of your time," he said. "This has to do with your status back in the States."

"And just what is my status, Mr. Fredricks?"

Fredricks smiled. "Not so good. At least not right now. But it seems that can change. This came over the telex yesterday. I've talked to my boss in Washington. He assured me it's on the up-and-up. The actual papers are being couriered to the embassy. We'll have them in a few days."

He handed Kate the long message. He watched her read it through, noting her astonishment.

"Is this some kind of trick?" Kate demanded.

"No trick, ma'am," Fredricks said gravely. "Like I said, you'll have the papers as soon as we get them. They'll spell out the details, but you can see the gist of it in what you have there. If you make complete financial restitution, then you and Mr. Bartoli are off the hook. You can go home and get on with your life. It's all there in black-and-white—a full pardon."

Fredricks paused for effect. "Signed by the attorney general himself."

20

"Events are moving more quickly than I had anticipated," Armand said. "Your refusal to sign the papers for the offering has lit a fire under Pierre."

Kate sat on the edge of the bed, looking down at Armand. She had arrived at the monastery while it was still dark. Now the first rays of light peeked through the small window set high in the whitewashed wall.

Kate thought Armand looked better today. She felt more strength in his grip, and his eyes were clearer. Still, she was concerned.

"I don't understand it," Kate confessed. "Fredricks wouldn't tell me why the offer had come through at this particular time. Nor who was behind it. *I* certainly have no influence at the Justice Department."

"But Pierre would, through his contacts at the United States Treasury," Armand told her. "He is trying to push you out, Kate. He sees the opportunity to cover his tracks once and for all and is trying to seize it. How did the others react?"

"Louis was livid. You read him like a book, Armand. He was expecting Jasmine's share to go straight into his political coffers."

"And Jasmine?"

"She stood up for me. She would like the sale to go through, no doubt about that. But she seems willing to support me, at least up to a point."

"That surprises me," Armand murmured. "Jasmine is not one to let gold slip between her fingers."

"I don't know how long I can put them off," Kate said. "The story about something fishy in the casino books worked, but everyone, especially Pierre, will be expecting details, sooner than later."

Armand looked at her keenly. "You are all right, aren't you Kate? I mean, in front of Pierre . . ."

"He doesn't suspect a thing." She gazed into his eyes. "You know what frightened me? Not that I'd give myself away. It was the anger, Armand. I never thought I could hate someone the way I hated Pierre at that moment. Whatever happens, he must pay."

"He will," Armand replied gently. "I promise he will."

They sat in silence for a moment; then Kate said, "When I met Sweet, he told me something peculiar. Have you ever heard the term *The Chosen Place*?"

Armand shifted in bed, and pain shot through his right side, causing him to grimace.

"The Chosen Place . . . No, I don't think so."

"Sweet said it had to do with the slave-trade ring you were searching for. He thought it was important."

Armand tried to think. *The Chosen Place* . . .What could it be? Where? The phrase *did* sound familiar, but he couldn't place it. The drugs had turned his mind to cotton.

"It's probably meaningless," Kate said quickly, anxious because of how pale Armand had become. "A red herring Sweet came across."

Armand was almost ready to agree with her when he started. The Chosen Place! There had been only one— Mouchtara! The ancestral home of Alexander Maser!

"Armand, what's wrong?"

"Nothing," he whispered. "It's the drugs."

As he watched Kate hurry off to fetch the abbot, Armand was thinking furiously. It *had* to be Mouchtara! But was it the headquarters of the ring or a way station? Did they pass children through it or bring the buyers there? And *why* Mouchtara? Because it was abandoned and desolate?

Or was someone laughing at Alexander even as he lay in his grave?

Armand realized he had to find out. He had fought too hard, waited too long to rip the veil off these fiends to give up now. And he would have to do it alone.

Can I? he wondered. *Even if I manage to get on my feet*

and out of here, what would happen if someone recognizes me?

But the risks seemed paltry when weighed against the prize. When Armand saw Kate returning, with two monks following her, he knew how it could be done.

Before boarding the aircraft for her second trip to Geneva, Kate made a phone call she had been putting off.

"Kate! I was becoming frantic! I saw the news from Beirut, about Armand. Are you all right? Of course you are, I saw you on television."

"Emil, I'm so very sorry," Kate said. "I should have called sooner. But I am all right. So much has happened."

"I'm listening, Kate."

Kate described the horror of the assassination, the subsequent investigation, and the final surprise, the contents of Armand Fremont's will making her the beneficiary. Kate could tell Emil had difficulty in digesting all this. She had never known him to be at a loss for words.

"Kate, is there anything I can do to help?" Emil asked at last.

Kate closed her eyes, glad she wasn't talking to him face-to-face. There was so much she couldn't tell Emil, and as far as she was concerned, that was the same thing as lying.

"There's something I need to know," Kate said carefully. "Have you been contacted by anyone from the Justice Department?"

"No."

So they came only to me with their offer. . . .

Kate told Emil about the Justice Department offer presented to her by the embassy.

"I don't know where it came from or why. I don't think it's a hoax."

"It doesn't sound like it," he said slowly. "Kate, I'm at a loss. I never expected anything like this."

"Neither did I."

Emil was disturbed by her tone. "Something's wrong, isn't it? Please, tell me."

She recounted how the other family members wanted to take SBM public, about the buyer who was waiting in the wings, and the enormous amount of money she would receive.

"Emil, that would give us the chance to wipe the slate clean, repay everyone who lost money, and get the bank going again. Most of all we could redeem ourselves."

"I sense a big 'but' somewhere in this."

"To get the money we need, I would have to sell the casino. Emil, I don't know if I can do that. My father and Armand created something unique . . ."

"Kate, I don't understand."

She took a deep breath and told Emil everything she had discovered about Interarmco, how her father and Armand had set it up, what its purpose was, and how it functioned.

"All of that has now passed to me," Kate finished. "You see the problem, don't you Emil? Interarmco's work was meant to be carried on, and that can happen only if the casino continues to exist. On the other hand, if the casino were to be sold, we could use the proceeds to rebuild Maritime Continental. It's a chance you've earned a hundred times over."

The line was silent, and for a moment Kate thought they'd been cut off. When she heard Emil's voice again, she was struck by his calm and reason.

"If I knew nothing about your father's work, perhaps I would feel you *should* sell," he said. "But that is not the situation. You are right: we cannot permit his work to fail. It would be the worst kind of betrayal of everything your father and Armand stood and worked for. That, maybe more than the casino itself, is your legacy, Kate. You must be true to it."

Kate's eyes filled with tears.

"I swear I'll find another way to help you, Emil," she promised.

"I know you will. And I don't want you worrying about me. With all due respect to American bankers, we Venetians can still teach them a trick or two."

Kate laughed.

"Godspeed, Kate. Please look after yourself. Beirut seems to be a dangerous place these days. Call me so I won't worry."

"I promise, Emil. Bless you."

Kate was deeply saddened when the connection was broken. She had lied to a man who trusted her and whom she held dear. She was convinced that in the end she would vindicate Emil Bartoli. But to be able to look him in the eye again wouldn't be easy for a long time to come.

"Miss Maser, I didn't expect to see you again so soon," Charles Sweet said. The new director of Interarmco settled himself in the aircraft seat opposite Kate.

"Thank you for coming out to meet me."

Sweet shrugged. "I'm intrigued."

"I need your help," Kate went on, explaining what it was she was looking for.

Sweet let out a low whistle. "That's a tall order. I could probably do it, but it would take time."

"Which I don't have!" Kate said urgently. "Armand told me that David Cabot had especially good relations with the French police. Surely there is someone who would be willing to help if it meant helping David."

Sweet's eyes darkened. "Are you telling me that the information you want has to do with why David was killed—and by whom?"

"I know you're turning over heaven and earth to find the assassin. Believe me, I want him as badly as you do. So I'm asking you to trust me."

"On one condition," Sweet said tersely. "That you share whatever you find."

"If it's directly related to David's killer."

"Agreed."

"I'll call you back in Beirut."

"You'll have to move faster than that," Kate told him. "I'm going directly to Paris."

Charles Sweet studied her for a moment. "You were

pretty damn sure I'd help you, weren't you?"

"We both want the same thing," Kate said. *"That's* what I was sure of."

Kate arrived in Paris in time to see the sunset work its magic on the spires of Notre Dame Cathedral. A limousine whisked her away to the Ritz Hotel, where, after a bath and a change of clothes, she had an aperitif at the bar. Later Kate enjoyed a delicious meal at the Tour d'Argent and, before returning to the hotel, took a walk along the Seine.

Waiting for her in her room was a message from Charles Sweet. Kate read it, smiled, and turned out the lights. The next morning she went to the club her father had belonged to and asked whether he had left anything behind. The manager was sympathetic and assured her that had that been the case, the club would have shipped the personal effects to New York. Kate accepted his offer of coffee, asked a few more casual questions, thanked the manager, and left.

Her next stop was the city's central police prefecture on Isle de la Cité, where she met a tubby, chain-smoking, obviously nervous Inspector Denis Caron. The policeman hustled her into his office, closed the door, and drew the blinds.

"I have talked to Monsieur Sweet," he blurted out. "You are asking questions about Monsieur Cabot's death."

"No," Kate replied calmly. "About his murder. And that of Armand Fremont."

The Frenchman threw up his hands. "But that happened in Beirut, mademoiselle! What makes you think I can be of any assistance?"

"You can be. I need telephone records, especially those for long-distance calls. The number is—"

"No, mademoiselle, no! Absolutely not! I cannot obtain lists of telephone calls without a warrant from a *judge d'instruction*. To do that I need a reason."

"I just gave you one," Kate remarked.

"You gave me a fantasy! You have no proof that a French citizen was involved with Beirut!"

"I didn't say it was a *French* citizen."

Caron blustered. "Citizen, resident, visitor—it doesn't matter! It simply cannot be done."

Kate decided to bluff. "As I recall, David Cabot had done the impossible for you."

The inspector wavered. "I am deeply sorry about what happened to David," he said at last, lighting a fresh cigarette even though he had one in the ashtray. "But I beg you to understand that the last time I helped David there were . . . consequences. Political figures were involved. After they fell, were convicted of their crimes, it became known that I had been a key factor in their demise."

Caron inhaled deeply. "I should have been a hero, mademoiselle. Instead the opposite happened. The powers that be no longer trust me. They cannot remove me, but they can and have seen to it that my career ends at this rank. I can never hope to advance. So you will forgive me if this time I choose to put my family and my pension first."

"I understand, Inspector," Kate said. "I hope I did not add to your troubles."

"No, mademoiselle. You have only reminded me of them."

As he did every Thursday, Inspector Denis Caron left the central *prefecture* at three o'clock. Fifteen minutes later he was leaning up against the zinc counter of a bar frequented by the station police. Over the years Caron had spent many pleasant hours here, trading shoptalk with his colleagues. Now he drank alone. A pariah who came to his old haunt in the middle of the afternoon when no one else would be there.

The owner-bartender was a generous soul who took time out to listen to Caron's ramblings. A former policeman himself, he was the model of discretion. Had he wanted to, he could have profited handsomely from the gossip he'd heard in his shop. Since there was no one else to serve, the bartender pulled up a stool and half listened to Caron's monologue about the killing of a wealthy Lebanese casino owner and his security man. As Caron droned on, the bartender's attention faded.

But the attention of the Moroccan cleaner who was sweeping the floor in front of the bar did not fade. Although he never let on, he understood French perfectly. He had been working here for almost two years, silent and invisible. No one paid any attention to him, but the cleaner didn't miss a word that was said. Some days he learned nothing; others were a gold mine. The Moroccan bowed his head over the broom handle. As he listened, his heart beat faster. He too had heard about the murders in Beirut. Rumors about the assassin's identity were rampant, and now some woman—an American!—was asking questions.

The Moroccan wet his lips and shuffled along. He wondered how high a price he dared fix for these nuggets.

As Kate's plane from Paris was touching down in Beirut, Jasmine's private line was ringing at her home high in the Jounyeh Hills. When she recognized the caller's voice, her throat went dry.

"Katherine Maser is asking questions," he said, and detailed what Kate had tried to learn in Paris.

"She was at the club where Alexander Maser was a member," the caller continued. "She was at the prefecture on Isle de la Cité. She must be stopped. Either you look after it, or I will!"

Jasmine was stunned by his words.

"I don't want her hurt!" she said quickly. "I need her—"

"That is none of my concern!" the caller told her harshly. "See to it she stops poking her nose where it doesn't belong. I will know if she doesn't. I am listening and watching."

Jasmine shivered. It took her a few seconds to realize the message was complete and she was listening to the dial tone.

From the airport Kate went directly to the casino and her meeting with Anatole Benedetti. Benedetti was a Sicilian, a short, stocky man with eyes as black as those of the Palermo wolf. His trademark was a white dinner jacket with a fresh rosebud in the lapel.

"Benedetti has been with me for years," Armand had told Kate. "As a general manager he has no equal on either shore of the Mediterranean. The staff is loyal to him, and he is loyal to me. Benedetti will stand by you, but he disdains weakness. Learn from him, but never let him—or anyone else—forget who is really in charge."

Although Benedetti greeted her respectfully, Kate sensed his reserve. Kate had asked Benedetti to chair this first meeting, which included the heads of the four casino departments: gaming, financial, catering, and security. The chief of each division read a brief report detailing the previous day's activities. Since there were no immediate problems to resolve, the talk turned to how best to capitalize on what was shaping up to be a record-breaking summer.

At the head of the table Kate listened and watched carefully. She made her own notes, even though Lila was sitting to her left, keeping an accurate transcript. After everyone had had their say, Kate spoke up.

"What about the Asians?"

The division heads looked at her and frowned, obviously at a loss to understand what she was getting at. Benedetti sat back in his chair and regarded Kate with a shrewd smile.

"What did you have in mind, Miss Maser?"

Kate took a deep breath. "It seems to me that we have been concentrating solely on the European and North American markets."

The head of gaming interrupted. "We have to. That is where our competition—Enghien, Baden-Baden, and so on—focus their attention."

"I understand that," Kate argued. "And I'm not suggesting these markets should be ignored. I am talking about developing a whole *new* set of clients."

"Such as?" the chief of financial asked.

"The Asians."

Kate went on to explain that gambling was not a pastime but a passion in places such as Hong Kong, Tokyo, Singapore, and Manila.

"There is an incredible amount of wealth locked away in

that part of the world," she continued. "For the most part these people don't venture out. Why should they? Hong Kong provides everything they need—not only the gambling parlors, but the hotels, restaurants, and distractions. Maybe that's why no one else has thought of approaching them, because it seems like a closed market."

She looked around the table. "Maybe that's why we *should*."

The men around the table exchanged pointed glances. The Asian propensity for gambling was legendary, and as they pondered Kate's words, each was thinking the same thing: the idea was feasible. A concentrated effort to bring the gold and dollars of Hong Kong to Beirut *might* work. If it did, it would pay off in a staggering way. Why hadn't anyone thought of this before?

Anatole Benedetti voiced the common question. "Miss Maser, what made you think of this possibility?"

"I lived on the West Coast of the United States, Mr. Benedetti," Kate told him. "The Asian community is a vital force in places like San Francisco. More, the Asians deal primarily in portable wealth—gold, diamonds, platinum. If we can get them to come to the Casino de Paradis, they will bring their collateral in their suitcases."

The expressions of the men around the table were impassive, and for a moment Kate wondered if she had made any impression at all.

"Miss Maser," Benedetti said. "As I am sure you know, all of us have heard the rumors that there is a buyer for the casino. Permit me to ask you directly, do you intend to sell?"

Kate looked straight back at him. "Yes, there is a buyer. I had been led to believe that Armand Fremont was considering selling. However, I have found no instructions among his papers to that effect. So as far as I'm concerned, gentlemen, the Casino de Paradis is *not* for sale!"

Benedetti rose and pulled back Kate's chair, offering his hand.

"It will be a pleasure for us to work with you, mademoiselle," he said, looking at the others. "As for your Asian idea, we think it has great possibilities. I suggest that we give it serious consideration and make it a priority topic on the next agenda."

When Lila Mikdadi tapped on the door two hours later, Kate was still hard at work.

"You have a visitor," she announced, giving Kate a pointed look.

Kate looked up, puzzled, "Who is it?"

Lila stepped aside and Michael Saidi entered.

"Michael!"

"Hello, Kate." He looked back to make sure the door was closed, then said lightly, "I thought you might have been avoiding me."

Kate did not move from behind the desk, grateful for this obstacle between them. Anger poured through her as she watched Michael approach, his body moving so gracefully, his smile beguiling.

You're a killer! A thief and a murderer!

Kate longed to scream these words at him. Her fingers curled around a heavy paperweight and she could see herself picking it up, rushing at Michael.

"Kate, are you all right? You look terribly pale."

"I'm sorry, Michael. I've been so busy."

Michael looked around the office. "I can imagine. There's talk that the casino is up for sale."

"Someone is interested in buying," Kate corrected him. "That's not the same thing."

"Then I take it you're not interested in selling."

She shook her head.

"Kate, you seem uncomfortable," Michael said gently. "I didn't mean to upset you."

She sat down, trying desperately to calm herself.

"I am so worried about you, Kate," Michael walked over to her. "There is so much for us to explore and learn. Please, don't cut yourself off from me like this," he whispered, his lips sliding along her ear.

Kate felt his hand slide along the sides of her body until

they reached her hips. He lifted her out of the chair, then cupped her buttocks and pulled her toward him, hard. Without warning, his lips crushed her own.

Instinctively Kate struggled, but as Michael's grip tightened, she let herself go limp. The trick worked. Nothing would turn off a man like Michael more than a woman who'd become a rag doll.

"Kate, I'm sorry. I was carried away." Michael stepped back and laughed. "It's the effect you have on me."

"Later, Michael," Kate said faintly. "There will be time then . . ."

"Oh, yes," Michael replied. "No matter what happens, I'm not letting you become a recluse."

As soon as the door closed behind Michael, Kate staggered into the bathroom. The cold water roared out of the faucet, soaking the front of her dress. She didn't care. She plunged her face into the water, rubbing her skin hard to rid herself of his touch. Then suddenly she was crying hysterically, thinking of Armand lying on that narrow bed, helpless. At that instant she wanted desperately to be with him, to hold and comfort him, and she asked herself how long she could go on without him.

Michael poured himself a short whiskey from the liquor trolley in Jasmine's living room.

"Is it another man?" Jasmine demanded.

Michael snorted. "Impossible! Who else could she have met?"

"Then why turn away from you?" Jasmine mused. "Before, she was ready to pour her heart out to you. Now she pushes you away as though she doesn't need to confide in you—or anyone . . . as though she has found someone else."

"Perhaps there is more to Katherine Maser than we gave her credit for?"

Jasmine thought back to the soft, evil words she'd listened to only hours before. Kate had brought those about too.

"Someone is looking out for her," she said. "Someone who is giving her advice. I thought that might have been the case. I should have looked into it. Now you must do it."

"It won't be easy," Michael warned her. "If there is someone else, she will not open up to me."

"You're resourceful!" Jasmine snapped. "Find another way. Have some of your people follow her."

Michael nodded. "That can be arranged."

Jasmine's eyes glittered. "But we can do more! It is time that Miss Maser's gilded cage was rattled a little bit."

Then she told him what she had in mind.

21

When Balthazar informed Kate that Inspector Hamse was waiting to see her in the library, she rushed to him, fearful there might be fresh bad news.

She flung open the doors. "Inspector, is anything wrong?"

"Perhaps, Miss Maser. We will determine that at police headquarters, if you don't mind."

Kate was shocked. "But why?"

"So that you can tell me a few more things about Armand Fremont's murder," he responded softly.

"I've already told you everything I know."

"Ah, Miss Maser. You did in fact tell me a great deal, that is true," Hamse agreed politely. "But that was before I knew that you could have a motive for wanting Fremont dead."

"Motive?"

"Your inheritance, Miss Maser." He chuckled. "All those tens of millions of dollars you will be getting if you sell the casino."

The last person Kate expected or wanted to see on the steps of the Beirut Central Police Station was Joyce Kimball, the gossip columnist. Kate averted her eyes, hoping she could slip by, but the tiny black-haired woman darted toward her like a crow to a shiny penny. "Kate, you *must* tell me!" Kimball said breathlessly. "Is it true what they're saying, that you're being questioned about Armand's murder?"

"First of all, Joyce, I don't know who 'they' are," Kate said angrily. "Second, I have the feeling that you know more about what's going on than I do. By the way, how *did* you know where to find me?"

"Oh, I have my ways, darling." Kimball tittered, struggling to keep up as Kate swiftly took the steps and went into the station.

"And one of those ways would be Inspector Hamse, would it?"

"Sweetie, you know I can't reveal my sources."

"Then don't expect a damn thing from me either!"

Kate slammed the door in Kimball's face. She whirled around to confront Hamse.

"If you have questions to ask me, you could have called, and I would have been glad to help you. Why do it like this?"

"This is an official investigation, Miss Maser," Hamse said in a bland tone. "Not a social call."

"I didn't think you wanted a circus either!"

"This way, please, Miss Maser."

But someone did. It was as though this had all been carefully arranged. . . . All right, Mr. Hamse. You have your fun now. When we're done, I'll get the answers I want!

Kate expected Hamse to be rude, bullying, loud. It was on the tip of her tongue to tell him she wanted a lawyer present. Instead, the inspector appeared completely indifferent. He placed a tape recorder in front of Kate and took out some papers stapled together. In a bored tone he began to ask his questions.

Kate forced down her anger and concentrated on Hamse, alert for any attempt to trick her. She expected the first few questions to be perfunctory—name, age, current residence, and so on. But soon Kate thought that everything sounded vaguely familiar. She was trying to understand why when suddenly it became very clear: every question was the same, word for word, as the ones put to her by police officers on the day Armand and David had been shot!

Kate snatched the papers from Hamse's fingers, scanning the questions and answers. It *was* the transcript of her previous interrogation! Hamse hadn't bothered to add or change a single word.

"You bastard!" Kate whispered. "What the hell are you up to?"

Hamse reached out and tugged the transcript out of her hand. He smiled pleasantly and opened the door.

"Thank you for your cooperation, Miss Maser," he said in

a loud voice. "You're free to go . . . for the moment. But please don't try to leave Beirut."

The reporters crammed outside the door scribbled down every word, and the photographers caught Kate's expression of anguish and surprise.

After a few days of hounding, the press melted away from Kate. Weary of hiding and being chased, she didn't even ask herself what had made the reporters and photographers disappear like morning dew. She certainly didn't connect it to the call and visit from Bill Fredricks. The FBI agent attached to the embassy met Kate at the casino. He handed her a large, sealed envelope, along with a release.

"I'll wait in case you have any questions," Fredricks said.

Kate read through the document. It was couched in the obligatory legalese, but the gist of it was plain enough. If Katherine Maser personally made financial restitution to the individuals and organizations listed below, the actions taken against Maritime Continental Bank would cease. Its charter would be reinstated. On the last page was the distinctive signature of the attorney-general.

Kate let out a deep breath. These thousand or so words meant she could go home again, clear her name and Emil Bartoli's. It could be a new beginning.

Except that nothing could begin until she finished here. Nothing.

"It doesn't say anywhere that Emil and I are completely exonerated from any guilt or malfeasance in regard to what happened," said Kate. "Or that there will be a public apology from the government."

Fredricks shifted uncomfortably in his seat. "Ah, yes. Well, you're right there."

"In fact, Mr. Fredricks, the impact of the amnesty is all but voided without such a clause. For me or Mr. Bartoli to have any credibility in the business community, it has to be stated in black-and-white that we had absolutely no knowledge of, nor anything to do with, what happened at Maritime Continental."

"Miss Maser, let me clarify one thing," Fredricks said bluntly. "This offer is nonnegotiable. That's the word from Washington, and it's final. I'm not going to try to con you by saying you're getting everything. But it's a hell of a lot more than you have now. Or are likely ever to see again. You and Bartoli can work on your images later. In the meantime, take half the loaf."

Kate pushed the document away. Bill Fredricks took his cue and rose.

"Do you have any idea what you're going to do, Miss Maser?"

Kate stared back at him. "Mr. Fredricks, you'll know as soon as I do."

"The offer won't change, Miss Maser," Fredricks warned her.

"I'm sure it won't," Kate said.

A half hour later Fredricks was in the ambassador's office. As soon as he finished his report, Leonard Watkins was on the phone with Jasmine.

So she really had no intention of letting them sell, thought Jasmine. The conclusion surprised her. She had thought the public humiliation, followed by what should have been an irresistible offer, would have been enough to topple Kate's reserve. Now it was up to Michael.

Sitting on the terrace of the Phoenicia Hotel, Jasmine watched the bronzed young men gliding by behind the thick glass of the pool. If she felt any temptation or lust, neither her expressionless face nor her eyes, hidden behind gargantuan sunglasses, betrayed it. Across the table Pierre nervously stirred his iced tea, the tall spoon rattling against the glass.

"Pierre, do stop that. It's getting on my nerves."

He mopped his face with a handkerchief. He felt distinctly uncomfortable at places like this. The architecture was gauche, all concrete and right angles, and the noise reminded him of a school playground at recess.

"How could she not have accepted the attorney general's

offer?" he asked for the tenth time.

Jasmine didn't bother to reply. Pierre's litany had become excruciatingly boring.

"You said she would, Jasmine. You told me there wouldn't be any more problems."

Pierre was caught between the twin vises of anger and fear. After Jasmine had laid the groundwork with the American ambassador, he had begun his lobbying in Washington and New York. The Banque de Liban was a respected player on Wall Street and had many favors outstanding from Fortune Five Hundred chief executives. These men were more than happy to make phone calls to Washington, where, between their influence and Pierre's personal friendship with senators on the finance committee, discreet pressure had been brought to bear on the attorney general's office. The attorney general himself was of the opinion that the Maritime Continental affair was nothing more than a wart on an elephant's ass and was quite willing to gain a few markers of his own in return for structuring the amnesty offer. All told, Pierre had been convinced that under the circumstances Kate *couldn't* say no.

"She's not going to take SBM public, is she, Jasmine?" Pierre blurted out.

"I think she can be persuaded," Jasmine murmured. "Katherine doesn't yet know just how hard this world can be."

"What are you talking about?"

Jasmine turned to face him, her wide-brim hat effectively shielding her face.

"What's gotten into you, Pierre?" she demanded softly. "You're acting like a scalded cat."

"I wasn't thinking so much of myself as of Louis and what needs to be done for him."

And about the audit at the bank. It was only weeks away, and Pierre knew there was no way he'd survive it unless he was able to move quickly. It wasn't only a matter of replacing the money. Records had to be altered, computer programs aligned, the paperwork carefully reviewed so that absolutely no clue was left behind. Pierre had dealt with the auditors before. They were sharp, keen-eyed men who worked for a prestigious, international consulting firm, chosen precisely because it had no connection whatsoever with the Lebanese government. Such men could neither be bought nor influenced. And they missed nothing.

"What are you going to do?" asked Pierre.

"You can be sure, Pierre, that Katherine *will* see the wisdom of taking SBM public," Jasmine said. "We *will* get our money."

Less than a mile from the Phoenicia, in a futuristic villa designed by the Israeli architect, Moshe Safdie, Louis Jabar was sitting in the middle of a circular room facing ten men. He felt very much like a butterfly about to be mounted behind glass by lepidopterists. Nabil Tufaili surveyed the trays of hors d'oeuvres and tea laid out for his guests and shooed away his houseboys.

"We've all had quite enough of this nonsense," Tufaili told Louis as the other *zuama* helped themselves to *tabbouleh* and *kibbe qurass*. "Your clumsy attempt to persuade Katherine Maser to go back home has failed. She's no closer to agreeing to take SBM public than she was when this whole affair started. Our patience is wearing thin."

"What happened had nothing to do with me!" Louis replied hotly. "It was Jasmine's idea."

Louis caught the glints of amusement and contempt in the other men's eyes. He was about to explain, but Tufaili cut him off.

"We love you like a son, Louis," the *zaim* said. "But you have not treated us with the respect and deference a son must show. We have indulged you and invested heavily in you, but you remain tied to the apron strings of a woman—" Tufaili held up his hand, stifling Louis's protest.

"Sometimes it is much wiser to listen. We have watched Jasmine orchestrate your campaign, and until now we have considered her an asset. But no more. She is obsessed with Katherine Maser, obsessed because she is desperate. She covets the money the sale of the shares will bring. She hungers for the power she will have at her fingertips, power over you, Louis. And through you, over us. She has no wish to contribute to your success. She wants it for herself."

Louis's mouth was dry. "You're wrong," he managed to say.

"No, we are not," Tufaili said with cold finality. "It pains me you should say such a thing even when you know it to be untrue."

Tufaili glanced at the men around him. If a signal passed between them, Louis missed it.

"We have decided to set a new condition for our support of your candidacy. You must sever your ties with Jasmine!"

Louis could not believe what he was hearing. "But she's my wife!"

"No!" Tufaili thundered. "You are *her* wife. You were always weak, Louis. We knew that. But we believed that if we showed you our support, you would know to whom your allegiance must be given."

"I have proved my loyalty to you!" cried Louis. "I have done everything you have asked of me."

"You will do one more thing," Tufaili said. "You must *demonstrate* your loyalty to us. Otherwise, Louis, I swear, we shall make a beggar out of you!"

"How! How can I show you what you want?"

Tufaili folded his hands across his kettledrum belly.

"The Fremonts seem to be having their share of bad luck lately. I fear that it hasn't yet run its course, especially if Jasmine happens to be at a certain place, at a certain time."

The personal representative of the sultan of Brunei was a tiny man with smooth, shiny skin that reminded Jasmine of saltwater taffy. He was perfect in every way, from the sheen on his handtooled English shoes to the thick, slicked-back helmet of hair. Sharif Uday was also the only person in front of whom Jasmine felt uneasy, even afraid.

"I would be less than candid if I told you I was pleased with developments, Mrs. Jabar. We expected you to be much further along by now. The fact that we have not been notified by Miss Maser of her intention to sell distresses His Excellency. It is not a question of the legal and other fees we are absorbing. These are a trifle. It is a matter of honor. This delay is an affront to His Excellency."

Jasmine heard every word, but her attention was on Uday himself. Not only was he lost in the cavernous space of the Phoenicia's presidential suite, but the chair in which he sat was too big for him. Jasmine watched Uday cross his legs without his feet ever touching the carpet. Jasmine collected her thoughts and quashed her anger at Uday's reference to her married status. No one had dared to refer to her as Mrs. Jabar in years.

"As you undoubtedly know, Miss Maser has had certain personal difficulties lately—"

Uday held up his hand. "Please, I am aware of this farcical attempt by the police to link her to Armand Fremont's murder. If one were superstitious, one might say Miss Maser is hexed."

"Given what's happened, it has been difficult to guide Katherine in the right direction," Jasmine said carefully. "She understands that from a business point of view, going public is the best thing. But she is young, inexperienced in financial matters. Sometimes she thinks with her heart instead of her mind."

Sharif Uday tittered. "Ah, my dear Mrs. Jabar. But that is why you are there, to persuade her, to act as the wise counsel."

"Which is exactly what I am doing."

Uday caught the note of impatience in her voice.

"But not well enough," he replied, his whisper more terrible and final than if he had thundered forth his judgment. "And if you cannot remedy this, then regretfully I will have to advise His Excellency to terminate these negotiations forthwith."

Uday's unblinking stare left Jasmine with no doubts that he would do just that.

"If I am to accomplish what we all want, I must have a free hand."

"That has always been understood."

"In which case some of the things that may happen in the near future will seem, . . . shall I say contradictory?"

"We do not concern ourselves with methods, Mrs. Jabar. Only results count. Besides, since you have so much at stake here, I trust you to choose the appropriate action."

Sharif Uday cocked his head like a praying mantis.

"Besides, I confess I am intrigued by your intentions. I trust I will recognize your 'free hand,' as you put it?"

"Absolutely. You won't be able to mistake it for anything else."

"I still believe you are wrong to do this," the abbot repeated as he watched Armand Fremont don the robes of the cloister. The pain, even for so small a task, was evident.

"There is no other way," Armand replied, tying the cord around his waist in a double loop. "I must know what this 'Chosen Place' is."

"But it may not be what you think," the abbot protested.

"Sweet did not pluck the words out of the blue," Armand said impatiently. "If that is where the slave-trade group is headquartered, or if they are using it as a transit point—"

"Then what will you do?" the abbot asked pointedly.

"Return and get help."

The abbot shook his head. "At least take two of my brothers with you. You are still weak, Armand. If something should happen, there will be no one to help you. Please!"

Armand laid a hand on the abbot's shoulder.

"I am touched by your concern. But I cannot allow anyone to be endangered by what I do."

"In that case, the brothers will stay close by," the abbot replied stubbornly. "There is a small church near The Chosen Place. They shall pay a visit to the priest there."

Armand followed the abbot out of the bowels of the monastery, emerging to gaze upon a sky littered with stars and a huge orange moon hanging in the west. He came over to the dilapidated truck that the order used to ferry its grapes and vegetables to market. The two monks who would serve as escorts were waiting.

"Godspeed, my friend," the abbot said, embracing Armand.

"Remember," Armand told him, "not a word to Kate. Unless I do not return. Then tell her everything. My not coming back will be proof enough that I was right."

"I pray it will not come to that."

Armand settled himself in the flatbed on a mattress of straw, wrapping the coarse blanket around him. The truck lurched forward, and he winced, the jolts shooting pain along his spine. It would be easier, Armand thought, once they were on the highway.

When the truck finally reached the smooth macadam, Armand settled down on his back, looking at the stars. The Chosen Place . . . he knew in his gut there could be only one.

He had not visited Mouchtara for years. After his father's death Alexander had maintained the property. But like any grand home, the cost of doing so had proven prohibitive. The family retainers had been pensioned off, the flocks and herds divided among the farmers, the fields allowed to lay fallow.

"It is part of a past that has no meaning for the present or future," Alexander had told him. "Some things are best left behind."

Perhaps that was true. But it might also be that for other men Mouchtara had become very useful, its isolation and abandonment exactly what they were seeking. The Chosen Place . . .

Somewhere along the road between Beirut and Sidon, Armand fell into a dreamless sleep. When he awoke, he discovered that they were well into the mountains, already past Joun and Deir Moukalle, the truck moving cautiously along the pitch-black twisting road. Armand bit off a chunk of bread and softened it with water from a canteen. He ate the cheese and raisins the brothers had packed for him.

Two hours later they turned north, passing Bori, and later, Amateur. The sky was still dark, but Armand could feel the night lifting. The air grew cooler as they climbed higher into the hills. Then, without warning, they were at the edge of the Barouk River.

Armand slipped out of the flatbed and checked the contents of his knapsack. He had binoculars, a compass, water, and a bundle of religious leaflets—the abbot's touch. If someone challenged him, the pamphlets might make them think he was a proseletyzer. Armand hoped the beard he had grown had changed his appearance enough so that he would go unrecognized.

He came around the front of the truck. One of the monks stopped him and handed him a heavy object wrapped in burlap. Armand felt the outline of a gun.

"The abbot suggested you carry it," one of the monks said calmly. "There are dangerous animals in these woods."

Armand tucked the gun into the pocket of his robe, thanked the two monks, and set off down the incline. He knew the Barouk from childhood days and forded the river where it ran only knee-deep. When he reached the other side, he looked back; the monks and the truck had disappeared.

He proceeded along the road, little more than a cart path, that led from the river to the Mouchtara. There was always the risk that if The Chosen Place was in fact occupied—by the kinds of people he suspected were there—then a patrol might intercept him. But going this way made for better time and was not as difficult as the trails in the woods. Armand knew he had to reach his vantage point before the sun came up. He also had to conserve as much of his strength as possible. After an hour he left the cart path, disappearing into an all-but-invisible trail, which, if memory served, swung around the property and ended thirty or forty yards from the main house. He smelled the smoke from a campsite or fireplace even before he cleared the last of the woods. He climbed a small knoll, disappearing into the copse of willows that grew on it.

He collapsed in the tall grass, his heart pounding. He lay there, sweat pouring off him, until the pain from his wounds was reduced to a dull ache. Then he opened the knapsack, withdrew the binoculars, and inched forward.

Mouchtara!

The pitiful edifice that he looked upon broke his heart. The entire left wing of the once-palatial residence had crumpled, leaving a gaping hole. The center portion remained as he remembered it, except that the twin towers were missing their turrets. But there were lights on inside, and several trucks in what used to be an immaculate courtyard. As the sky lightened, the shadows became men.

Armand counted six, all with rifles slung over their shoulders and one carrying a rolled-up whip. In the gathering dawn he heard orders being shouted, received by surly replies, and smelled the odors of cooking. He took another sip of water, pulled the cowl of his robe farther over his head, and waited.

The first child was no more than seven or eight, a pale, thin boy with skinned knees and elbows. He was dragged out of the house and hoisted into the back of the truck. The others followed rapidly—four boys and six girls. The girls were older, thirteen to eighteen, their expressions conveying silent horror and helplessness. Armand bit his lip, drawing blood. Unconsciously his right hand had slipped down, curled around the gun.

Madness! He wouldn't get within ten feet of them without being shot.

He trained his field glasses on the men as they walked to and from the main house. Not one face was familiar, but he committed each one to memory. The reckoning would come, he thought, watching them board the truck.

As the last man came out and jumped into the driver's seat, Armand lowered his glasses. Then he heard a shout. Another man was walking out of the house, shouting and waving. Instantly two of the guards scrambled to his side, their heads bobbing as they listened to their orders.

Armand pressed the rubber guards of the binoculars against his eyes. It had to be someone important, someone who was in control of these cutthroats. But the face was obscured by the two henchmen. He swore, willing them to move. When they did, Armand sucked in a deep breath.

Standing in the courtyard was the new master of Mouchtara: Michael Saidi.

22

As the summer season unfurled itself over Lebanon, Beirut gossip predicted it would be one of the busiest and most profitable in years. A record number of cruise ships were scheduled into port, hotels reported full houses until September, and the airlines indifferently overbooked their seats by twenty percent. It seemed that the whole world had decided to come to Beirut, and those who sought to put their finger on the reason for it looked to one person: Kate Maser. If publicity, even the worst kind, was a godsend, then her notoriety was the loom that spun newspaper stories into silver and gold.

The design and manufacture of playing cards was one of the most carefully guarded secrets in the casino world. In Europe one company, innocuously called Bellam Novelties, had a virtual monopoly to supply the European gaming houses. It had also been the purveyor of cards, chips, and other paraphernalia to the Casino de Paradis ever since Aristide Fremont had opened its doors.

Located in London's Southwark district, Bellam Novelties was housed in an old factory on the Thames. In appearance it was no different from the hundreds of other dilapidated brick-and-stone edifices fronting the river. The inside, however, was a different story. It had been gutted to the timbers, the centuries-old brick sandblasted and reinforced. The windows were all wired to a central alarm and every door reinforced with steel sheets. The company had its own security personnel who patrolled the grounds from dusk to dawn, and every employee, down to the floor sweepers, was carefully vetted.

Bellam Novelties' business demanded scrupulous security. For over a hundred years it had been producing playing cards destined for the great gambling palaces of Europe, eventually reaching the fingers of kings and courtesans. At first glance they appeared plain enough: shiny white background with large numbers and symbols or brilliantly colored depictions of the face cards. The secret to the company's success and reputation was on the back of the cards. The design was cast in pale blue ink, but even this gentle hue immediately confused the human eye. There were whorls and swirls and loops, all tumbling against each other in an apparently haphazard fashion. The eye could discern no pattern and so didn't give the backing a second glance. Which was precisely the intention. In fact, the design on the backing had been created by the same engravers who, at the Bank of England, designed the British paper currency. The plates used to print the cards were guarded every bit as carefully as those in the vaults of Threadneedle Street. But there was a difference. If a scratch or nick occurred in a currency plate, the mistake would be spotted when the bills were printed. That batch would immediately be destroyed. Or, if for some reason the error slipped by, the bills would become a collector's item and were quickly removed from circulation. A flaw in the plate used for playing cards could be disastrous. Like other card manufacturers, Bellam Novelties had their "readers," experts who examined fresh cards with the care of jewelers scrutinizing diamonds. If they spotted the tiniest flaw, the entire shipment, except a small number of the cards needed for testing and evidence, was destroyed. The internal investigation would be merciless, with only one question to answer: had this been an honest mistake, or had the engraver deliberately marked the plate so that in turn, certain cards could be "read" by an accomplice who knew what to look for?

There was only one way the system could be beaten—if an engraver and a reader worked together. In the hundred and seventeen years of its existence Bellam Novelties had guarded against just that kind of collusion. If scrutinized the backgrounds of these two types of workers twice as carefully. Internal security watched the men at work and paid informers to spy on them when they left the factory. The engravers and "readers" were aware of this and made their lives easier by not fraternizing. The security people were aware that their subjects knew they were being watched. It became a gentleman's game in which both sides understood the rules, accepted the conditions, and went about their business without so much as a word. But there was another part to this game, and it had to do with who could outwait whom. As almost always happens, the watchers dropped their guard first.

Henry Doust was seventy-six years old, with wisps of gray hair over a liver-spotted scalp and a bowed back from years of being hunched over the engraving table. His two sons had been killed at Dunkirk a quarter century before, and his wife, who had never gotten over her loss, was confined to an asylum in Lanchashire. Every month the company automatically sent half of Doust's paycheck to the hospital. The man needed little to get by, and the rest was enough.

The truth was Doust *wanted* more. He had worked for Bellam Novelties all his adult life. In the engraving fraternity he was a legend. To his employer he was a model worker, careful, reliable, steady of hand and eye. Everyone admired him because of how he handled the tragedies life had heaped upon him. Not a soul suspected that Henry Doust, who had seen the Reaper at the foot of his bed more than once, feared one thing more than even death itself: the fact that when he was gone, no one in all the world would remember him for more than five minutes. Doust craved a portion of fame. He had decided to leave his mark on the world in the way he knew best.

Peter Allen was in the throes of midlife crisis. He had married above his station to a woman whose people had land in Kent and who never lost the chance to let him know about it. After fifteen years Allen had reached the top of his ladder. He was a senior "reader" who would rise no higher. But that was not true of his dreams, which dwelt on board a sixty-foot yacht somewhere in the turquoise waters of the Aegean, crewed by bronzed young women who catered to his every whim. Every time he conjured up this image, Allen imagined the expression on his wife's horsey face when she would realize that he was gone forever. It was the only thing that kept him from killing her.

Whether it was chance or the inevitable meeting of two kindred spirits, Henry Doust and Peter Allen came to know each other's dreams. Like the most subtle game of chess, the opening moves were deathly silent. Advances were carefully thought out, the words chosen with great care. Even when they were sure of each other, when they accepted the justice of what each wanted, the two men never uttered the words *theft* or *robbery*. They agreed that there was only one way for Doust to get his immortality, Allen his freedom.

But their secret dreams might never have come to pass had it not been for a third person, the missing cipher, which, when in place, made the equation work. To this day neither Doust nor Allen had any idea how this woman had managed to look into their hearts and see the secrets hidden there. But she had, and both had gazed upon her in awe, convinced that whatever powers she had, she held their destinies in her hand.

As always Peter Allen took his two-week vacation at the end of June. His wife was already in the country and was expecting him on the eight o'clock train from London. She was kept waiting because by then her husband was clearing customs in Beirut.

A month earlier Allen had emptied the account he'd opened for himself without his wife's knowledge and into which he had managed to deposit over a thousand pounds. In addition to the airline ticket and hotel reservations, the money had bought Allen two suits, one of them a black tie, from Savile Row's finest tailor. When he stepped through the doors of the Hotel Saint Georges, Allen felt he truly belonged in this world of unabashed opulence. The admiring glances he drew from women confirmed his belief.

At eleven o'clock that evening Allen left his suite and was driven by the hotel's limousine to the casino. Looking every inch a rich, indolent British expatriate, he went directly to the baccarat tables and watched the play for a few minutes. Allen was careful not to look at the cards too long at any one time. As a new face, he would draw the most attention. He watched the others at the tables as if evaluating their play. Not that it would matter.

Ten minutes later Allen spotted what he had been waiting for. The card that came out of the shoe appeared, for all intents and purposes, like any other. Except that Allen knew what to look for. In the top left-hand corner, if the eye could follow the whorls and swirls, was a perfect capital *D*, the kind drawn by monks to set off the first letter of the first word in an illuminated manuscript.

Allen sat down and took out his thick billfold. He handed the dealer a wad of twenty-pound notes. With icy calm and dead certainty he began to play.

By the casino's standards the winnings were not that large, half a million dollars. But because Allen was an unknown, either as a regular player or a "sharpie," the *maître des jeux* alerted Kate and Anatole Benedetti. Within minutes a hidden camera snapped Allen's picture. Two hours later that image was being transmitted to Interpol in Paris. At the same time discreet questions were being asked at the Hotel Saint Georges. Certain numbers of its staff were approached and asked to keep an eye on Mr. Peter Allen of London.

The next morning, when she arrived at her office, Kate had the London and Paris police reports. Peter Allen was not wanted on any charge anywhere. In fact, he had no police record at all. Kate took a look at the tally sheet of the previous evening's winners and losers. Two other players had scored, though not as much as Allen. There were also some heavy losers. All told, it had been a normal evening with the casino coming out far ahead. Kate dropped the report into her drawer. Just to be sure tonight, she herself would be on the lookout for the Englishman.

Allen arrived punctually at eleven o'clock. He was politely greeted by the other players, all of whom had been there the previous night. This did not surprise Allen. Most gamblers are notoriously superstitious. Watching a man win a half million dollars in three hours made them want to be close. Luck had a way of rubbing off.

They were all disappointed. Forty hands later the Englishman had given back almost half of his previous night's winnings. Behind their impassive expressions the dealer and the *maître des jeux* relaxed. The odds were going against the player as they inevitably had to. It was quite likely that not only would the casino recoup all of its half million, but also substantially lighten the player's wallet.

It didn't happen. Down to a hundred thousand in black-and-gold thousand-dollar chips, the Englishman raised the stakes and won. Within the hour he had made up all his lost ground and was ahead by fifty thousand. As other players dropped away, only two were left to challenge him, a Kuwaiti prince and an Egyptian. The Kuwaiti indicated that he wanted to raise the stakes. The other two players were consulted and agreed. The *maître des jeux* glanced at Kate, who nodded. Three hands later the Englishman was ahead by almost a million, and the Egyptian had dropped out.

The Kuwaiti, Hijal ibn Talal, snapped his fingers, and his retainer opened a briefcase full of large-denomination American currency. "One hand, one million dollars," he whispered.

Kate did not take her eyes off the Englishman. She could feel it in her bones that Peter Allen was cheating. But how? The *maître des jeux* was waiting. Kate looked at Benedetti, then nodded.

The cards were snapped out of the shoe, two for each player, face down. Allen turned up the corners just enough to see his hand. The next card to be dealt was in the shoe, its bland design innocuous to everyone except Allen. He saw the *D* and the symbol at the tail, which told him the card was a four. Allen couldn't have asked for better. He was holding a jack and the five of clubs. A four gave him a natural nine, the same as twenty-one in blackjack.

Allen said, *"Carte."*

Hijal declined. The dealer flipped over the Kuwaiti's cards to reveal a king and an eight. The Kuwaiti flashed Allen ten thousand dollars of gold-and-platinum dental work.

"Neuf à la banque!"

The table exploded as the other players began jabbering in four different languages. Benedetti shifted his eyes, and smoothly and silently the casino security people moved in to make sure than no one made any moves, either to the winner or the money. The briefcase was taken from the hands of the Kuwaiti's factotum.

"I would like that, thank you," Allen said, pointing to the case.

"Will you be cashing out, sir?" Benedetti asked politely.

"Yes, I think I will."

"Then I suggest we take everything to the vault."

Without waiting for Allen's reply, Benedetti indicated that the Englishman's chips should be gathered up and counted. He already had one hand on Allen's elbow and was steering him toward the all but invisible door next to the cashier's wickets. Kate followed them into an office that was bare except for a desk and two chairs.

"May I offer you champagne, Mr. Allen?" she asked.

"No, you may not. But I would like an explanation—and my winnings."

Kate was watching for the smallest sign of fear, but Allen's face never lost its composure. He appeared relaxed and totally in control.

That meant he had the luck of the devil or was as dirty as sin, Kate thought.

"It's our policy to convert such amounts into a cashier's check," Kate said, playing for time. "Is that acceptable?"

"It's also your policy, Miss Maser, to wire-transfer winnings to the bank of my choice anywhere in the world. Which is exactly what I'd like you to do."

Kate smiled. The son of a bitch was a thief and telling her as much to her face!

"Would you mind waiting here for one moment, Mr. Allen?"

"I'm tiring of this, Miss Maser," he warned. "At the moment I still feel as though I am being treated as a guest. But if something should happen to change that, I assure you, the consequences for you and your establishment will be grave."

Kate looked him in the eyes. "I think we understand each other."

Peter Allen smiled and looked away. In his mind's eye he saw the sparkling waters of the Mediterranean surrounding a beautiful, unspoiled island with houses of whitewashed walls, blue shutters, and red-tile roofs. At the foot of one such house a sixty-foot motor sailor bobbed next to a dock, and on the teak deck stood a laughing young woman, holding out her brown arms to him.

Kate and Benedetti went back to the private room, now closed and roped off. The *maître des jeux* and the dealer were waiting.

"Take it apart," Benedetti said harshly, pointing to the table. "And the shoe as well. Get Shulmann down here from Jounyeh. I want every card in the deck under a microscope!"

In his villa in the Jounyeh Hills, Professor Aaron Shulmann was blissfully unaware that he was about to become the center of the drama being played out at the Casino de Paradis. In another life Shulmann had been a master forger whose only mistake had been giving in to his vanity. He had tried to do what every paper expert in the world considered an impossibility: forge the American Express traveler's check.

Perhaps Shulmann had foreseen the future, because he had made Beirut the center of his operation. And in Beirut, even after one has been arrested, tried, and sentenced to three hundred years in prison, a deal could be struck. Armand Fremont had gotten Shulmann out of jail, in itself no small feat. In return Shulmann vowed to devote his considerable talent toward making sure that suspicious paper of any kind—bank notes, bearer bonds, securities—never caused the casino to lose one cent of revenue. Over ten years the professor had earned back his "consultancy" fee a hundred times over.

But Shulmann, like so many elderly men, loved the company of young women. He could afford the best and indulged himself whenever the urge arose. Tonight he wasn't even looking, but she was so delectable, he could not resist. Now, six hours later, Aaron Shulmann lay alone on his bed, naked and snoring as loudly as he had been when the girl, the job she had been paid to do finished, had slipped from beneath the sheets and into the night. The room reeked of cigarettes, spent sweat, and champagne. The man with the legendary unerring eyes was blind drunk.

"It appears we may have a problem," Kate said.

"Not the least of which is that you have kept me waiting in this cell for over an hour," Peter Allen replied.

He said this without rancor, in a matter-of-fact tone which implied that he was, without a doubt, right.

"What is the nature of your problem, Miss Maser?"

"There may have been certain irregularities at the table this evening."

"Really? Would they have anything to do with my winning?"

"They might."

Peter Allen rose. "The next thing you're going to tell me is that the casino has the right to withhold winnings for twenty-four hours while it conducts its investigation. Am I right?"

"You know the rules," Kate observed. "Tell me, Mr. Allen, where else have you played?"

Allen ignored her. "Unless you have other questions for me, or are suggesting that I was in any way involved in these 'irregularities,' I strongly suggest you let me return to my hotel. I shall be by at exactly eleven o'clock tomorrow evening. I will expect you to show me a wire-transfer receipt with the name Royal Bank of Athens on it. The amount shall be two point one million United States dollars.

The account is 8074. If, for whatever reason, you do *not provide* me with this satisfaction, my solicitor, whom I will contact, will be in touch with you."

Peter Allen reached for the door, then looked back and flashed a smile. "All in all, Miss Maser, it was truly a pleasure."

Twenty-four hours later Peter Allen once again appeared at the Casino de Paradis. He was immediately escorted to Kate's office. He examined the wire-transfer receipt while Kate stared at him, remaining silent.

"Good as gold," Allen pronounced.

"Travel safely," Anatole Benedetti said softly. When Allen looked at him, the Sicilian's eyes pinned him to the wall. "And don't ever come back."

Peter Allen's rented limousine took him directly to Beirut Airport, where a chartered jet was fueled and ready to fly him to Athens. Only when he could see the jewellike lights of Beirut beneath him did Allen start to shake. It took half a bottle of whiskey to begin calming his nerves.

He checked into the Athens Hilton and slept until noon, rented a car, completed his business at the Royal Bank of Athens, and did some shopping. Outfitted in jaunty nautical garb, he instructed the driver to take him to the port of Piraeus.

Allen tipped the driver handsomely and walked along the pier to slip eighteen. As promised, the yacht broker was waiting for him, all smiles. Obviously the transfer from the Athens bank had gone through. Allen looked past the broker to the magnificent motorsailor riding in the water. The broker was babbling about papers that needed to be signed, but Allen didn't hear a word. It was all coming true, just the way it had been planned. "I have to make a phone call," he told the broker. "I'm afraid it's long-distance."

The broker assured him he would be happy to oblige. Allen smiled and took another look at the boat. He wished Henry was here to see it.

For the last three days Henry Doust had gone about his business as usual. He was alert for any changes around him, a new face, people watching him, or someone asking questions about Peter Allen. None of that happened. Each evening Doust watched the BBC world report and exhaled a sigh of relief when there was no story out of Beirut. Then he went on with his preparations.

On the same morning that Peter Allen arrived in Athens, Henry Doust removed his life's savings from his bank and sent a check to the asylum in Lancashire. He had been assured by its director that the amount would be more than sufficient to cover the care his wife needed for the rest of her life. That done, Doust went downstairs to where his neighbors, a nice but struggling couple with a baby, were living in a tiny apartment. He explained that he was retiring to the country and was offering to sublet them his four-room flat. Embarrassed by the young mother's tears, he handed them a copy of the agreement and the keys, and fled.

When he left Bellam Novelties that afternoon, Henry Doust took two things with him. The most valuable was his set of engraver's tools, which he had used for over forty years. He knew that they wouldn't let him keep it, but he liked to think that once everything was finished, the set, along with the deck of playing cards, would be displayed in the proper museum.

Allen's call came at about the time Doust thought it would. With eyes closed and a contented smile on his lips, he listened as Allen related his adventure. When Allen asked Henry to join him, Doust was not surprised.

"I don't believe that would work, Peter. But it's a lovely thought, and I thank you for it. Godspeed, my friend."

Dressed in his best suit, Doust took a taxi. His first stop was Fleet Street the hub of British journalism and home to the biggest and splashiest of the tabloids, *News of the World* He asked the taxi driver to wait while he went inside and handed the porter a large manila envelope with instructions that it be delivered to the editor in chief. Now his and Allen s deal with the woman was fully executed.

Twenty minutes later the taxi stopped again. This time Doust got out, tipped the driver generously, and proceeded up the steps. As he grasped the door handle, he paused to slow the beating of his heart. When he opened that door, he would be leaving the world he knew forever. And he would never be able to go back.

But at least they will know I was there.

Henry Doust walked up to the young man behind the circular desk in the lobby.

"Welcome to Scotland Yard, sir," the officer said politely. "How may I assist you?"

Doust smiled shyly. "I believe it is I who can assist you." He laid his billfold-size case of tools on the desk. On top of that he placed a deck of playing cards. "The head of your forgery department will be very interested in these."

Even as Henry Doust was being interrogated by Scotland Yard detectives, the *News of the World* presses were rolling. The first copies, destined for the continent, were rushed to the airport. Because the *News* was so popular in Beirut, and given the nature of the story, the executives decided to double the consignment. As a result, fifteen thousand issues were airfreighted out of Gatwick Airport and appeared in Beirut kiosks just as people were winding up their day and wondering what the evening would bring.

Kate pushed away a copy of the *News* and sat up in her chair.

"Anatole, what on earth happened?"

Benedetti, who had been watching the people milling below in the casino foyer, turned around.

"We were snookered."

"What do you mean?" Kate demanded.

"I mean that Henry Doust and his accomplice, Peter Allen, took us for a little ride."

"I'd call two-million-dollars-plus more than a *little* ride!" Kate snapped.

"That's not all it's going to be," Benedetti warned her.

"What do you mean?"

"We know the cards were marked. Shulmann is certain of it, and his opinion has been backed up by two other experts. The saving grace is that the tainted cards came out of a batch that was used only at that particular table."

"Doesn't that seem strange to you?"

"Not at all. When the cards come in, we divide the shipment among the tables. When a table needs a fresh supply, the dealer takes it out of the stock reserved only for that table. Neither Doust nor Allen could have known which table would eventually get the marked deck. Allen was prepared to play at each one, for the minimum stakes, until he spotted a tainted card. He just got lucky on his first try."

"Which means that all the losers at his table that night have a claim against us," Kate murmured. "They'll say it was a rigged game and demand their money back. Meanwhile the winners will have slunk off into the night."

Benedetti caught the bitterness and defiance in Kate's voice and ventured a guess as to where it was leading.

"We have to make good the losses," he said quietly. "Right now we're facing a public-relations disaster. The best damage control for us is to give the losers, especially high rollers like the Kuwaiti and the Egyptian, their money back. They are angry enough as it is. Worse, they feel they have been publicly humiliated."

"Why don't you arrange for me to meet with both as soon as possible?" Kate said.

Benedetti hesitated. "You may wish to reconsider," he said. "Both men are Muslims. They don't have a high opinion of women to begin with. Right now they are focusing their blame on *you*, because you are the one ultimately responsible. I am not saying they wouldn't accept your apology. It just might carry more weight if it came from me."

Kate knew Benedetti was right. Muslim men disdained dealings with women. She saw evidence of that every day.

"I have to issue some kind of statement," Kate said, changing the subject. "Lila says the phones haven't stopped ringing. What do we know so far—and that we're absolutely sure of?"

Benedetti took a deep breath. "We have been in constant touch with Bellam Novelties in London. They and Scotland Yard are working this thing on their end. But there doesn't seem to be any more to it than what Doust has already laid out for them."

"And for *News of the World*."

"Yes, that too. The big question is whether or not Peter Allen was in fact Doust's accomplice. Doust insists that he masterminded this whole thing himself and that Allen just happened to be the one who cashed in."

"Isn't he overlooking the coincidence that both he and Allen worked at the same place?"

"Not really. What he is doing—and Allen as well—is laughing at all of us. Allen has made no secret of his movements. I had him trailed to Athens and Piraeus. I can tell you exactly what he packed on that boat of his and where he was headed. He can be picked up at any time. The only problem is that we don't have any evidence against him—or it's circumstantial at best. Just because he worked at Bellam Novelties doesn't *prove* that he and Doust were in cahoots. Nor has he behaved like a felon. Allen has been a very cool customer."

"What about his wife?"

Benedetti gave her his best Gallic shrug. "She is beside herself. Apparently he kept her waiting at the train station half the night. Do not ask what *that's* all about. The long and the short of it is, she is a witch. If I had been in Allen's shoes, I too would have run for the hills. In any case, we can rule her out as accomplice."

Kate rose and walked to her desk, her fingers toying with the links of her bracelet.

"I can understand Doust's need to show off what he could do in front of the world. He had nothing. These head-lines"—she gestured at the stack of newspapers—"are his legacy. That's why he confessed and will tell us everything we want to know except the most important thing."

"Which is?"

Kate held up her hand. "Then there's Peter Allen, the front man. According to you, he has the best possible motive a man who's about to commit a crime can ask for: a dragon for a wife. So both motives are logical. We can understand and accept them."

"But?"

Kate ignored Benedetti's skeptical expression and pressed on.

"They could have chosen any casino in Europe. They chose this one. Why?"

"Doust said they drew straws—literally. You got the short one."

Kate shook her head. "I don't buy that. But there's another question: why do they decide to do this now?"

"According to Doust, it took them this long to organize their plan," Benedetti replied.

"Again, that doesn't wash. Doust has been alone for years. Allen has been in a miserable marriage for almost as long."

"You're looking for the ghost in the machine," Benedetti said softly.

Kate braced herself with both arms and leaned forward on her desk.

"I'm saying that Doust and Allen had the expertise, wherewithal, and motives to do what they did. *But someone else pointed them in our direction.* Damn it, Anatole, there are too many coincidences! A mystery player almost breaks the casino bank. Just when we need him most, Shulmann is found drunk. He can't even describe the girl he'd picked up, and your attempts to find her lead nowhere. She's disappeared. Shulmann cost us invaluable time. If he had been sober, he could have told us right away that the cards had been marked. You could have alerted Bellam Novelties, and Doust would have been picked up before he had time to deliver his package to the *News*. That alone would have stopped this thing cold. But someone wanted the *News* to have the story."

Benedetti stared at her for a long time, then went over to

the phone.

"Whom are you calling?"

"Scotland Yard. I will ask the British to let me 'assist in their inquiries' as they put it. If I can get five minutes alone with Doust, if I shake him hard enough, he will let something drop."

Although Benedetti had tried to soothe Hijal ibn Talal's ruffled feathers, nothing came of it. The letter of apology, and the opened line of credit equaling the amount that had been lost that ill-fated evening, went unacknowledged. Kate would have let the Kuwaiti sulk except for one thing: all of the casino tables were doing terribly, with revenues having dropped seventy percent. Kate's intuition told her that gamblers, a superstitious, high-strung breed, were waiting for some kind of signal before they would plunge back in. She had done all she could, giving extensive newspaper and television interviews. Time and again she reiterated the facts of her case, weaving her arguments as though she were addressing a jury. Except that this jury didn't care about *her* arguments. She wasn't one of them, a player.

Kate switched tack. She found the best, most expensive jeweler in Beirut and commissioned him to create a masterpiece in twenty-four hours. Ordinarily this would have been an impossibility, but when he heard what Kate wanted, the jeweler gave her a crafty look and said that, yes, since he had a model to work from, he could create the piece in the time required. Naturally there would be an outrageous surcharge.

The next day Kate sent Hijal ibn Talal a handwritten invitation to meet her at the casino, at the same table where he had been the loser. Kate was counting on two things: that the man would be intrigued enough by her boldness to come, and that he would gossip about the invitation so that by the evening everyone in Beirut would know about it. She was right on both counts.

At five minutes to eleven Kate left the Crystal and made her way through the foyer. The crowds were much larger tonight, and the signals the dealers sent her indicated that business was picking up. The baccarat salons remained empty, but in passing, Kate had noticed and recognized at least a dozen high rollers talking quietly in small groups. One of the guards unclipped the velvet barrier roping off the table, and Kate went around it to where the dealer usually stood. One minute after eleven she was still waiting.

Kate was gathering up her evening bag when the glass double doors to the salon opened and Hijal entered in a swirl of white robes and soft clicking of worry beads. The glittering black eyes betrayed nothing.

"I am honored you have chosen to accept my invitation, Your Excellency," Kate said.

Hijal did not move. His entourage, which had crowded in behind him, held its collective breath. Without dropping her gaze, Kate lifted the lid on the wooden box set on the baize in front of her. She reached inside with both hands and withdrew the gift.

The audible gasp from Hijal's retainers could be heard into the next room. Shimmering against the deep green of the table cover was a large casino chip about the size of a three-by-five file card. It had been crafted from one piece of solid gold and had the figure $1,000,000 engraved across the center. The borders were an intricate scrollwork studded with tiny diamonds, rubies, and emeralds, the favored gems of the Middle East.

"This is legal tender, your excellency," Kate said. "And has nothing to do with the arrangements that, as you know, have already been made for you. It is my gift to you, a small token of regret for what happened."

The Kuwaiti's eyes shifted from the chip to Kate, then back again. Suddenly he walked over and picked it up, hefting it in his hand.

"And if I were to gamble with this and lose it?"

"Then you would lose it, Excellency. I ask only that you remember there is no other in the world like it."

"Another could be made easily enough."

"True. But whether one or a thousand, they would all be

copies."

Hijal smiled faintly. "Then I shall give you a chance to redeem it. You and I shall play one hand. The stakes are this." He pointed to the chip.

"I'm afraid house rules do not permit me to wager, Your Excellency."

"Really? But it is *your* house, is it not?"

The barb was as cruel as it was intentional. Kate flushed but reined in her anger.

"It is simply a matter of house policy," she repeated.

"I see," Hijal said thoughtfully. "In that case, allow me to propose a compromise. One of my people"—he indicated his factotum—"will play for you. After all, it doesn't matter to whom the cards are dealt, does it? Unless, of course, you have objections to this too."

The intention was clear. The Kuwaiti was challenging her domain, questioning her right to her territory.

"Very well, Your Excellency. One hand."

Hijal quickly placed three decks of cards, wrapped in cellophane and sealed, on the table.

"With these cards, if you don't mind. Unless you think they are marked."

"Whatever pleases you," Kate said tightly. "After all, Your Excellency is an honorable man."

Hijal's eyes flared for an instant. Even to raise the subject of honor before an Arab was a dangerous thing.

The *maître des jeux* himself put the cards through the automatic shuffle machine, then stacked them in the shoe. He looked at Hijal and his assistant, both of whom indicated they were ready. Hijal turned up the corners of his cards and shook his head. He would not be taking another card. The factotum raised his cards just enough so that Kate could see them. A king and a six. Since the face card was zero, Kate's total was six, too far from the magic number, nine, to stand, but high enough so that if she drew anything above three, she would bust and lose. Kate, whose gaming experience was limited to a little blackjack in Vegas, tried her best to keep the confusion from her eyes. But Hijal was smiling broadly. Obviously a professional had spotted the floundering amateur. Kate knew it was now or never.

"If I were you," she said casually, addressing the factotum, "I would take another card."

The *maître des jeux* slid the card out of the shoe and flipped it with the spatula. It was a three. He flipped over Kate's other cards, and the hush in the room shattered. He did the same with the Kuwaiti's hand to reveal an eight.

"I salute you, Miss Maser," Hijal said. "You played very well."

"You mean, for an amateur I was very lucky."

The Kuwaiti laughed. "That too. Now I believe this is yours."

With great ceremony he handed Kate the gold chip. Kate would not accept it.

"No, your excellency. I ask that you keep it. It is really a gift now, with no value other than that which you and I place on it. For my part, that is quite substantial."

Hijal inclined his head. "You are a subtle woman, Miss Maser. I think the Lebanese in you is starting to show. That is good. As for your gift, I do accept it, and as you say, its value is substantial."

Hijal snapped his fingers, and an attache case snapped open, filled with neatly stacked bundles of cash.

"Now, if you don't mind, I would like to win back some of the money I lost."

Anatole Benedetti returned from London the next day.

"Congratulations on your play with Hijal," he told Kate. "You certainly made an impression."

"How did you hear about that?"

"It was the buzz in all of the London gambling clubs. I think we will be getting those players back."

"Let's hope so," Kate said. "How did it go for you?"

"Not as well, I'm afraid. Scotland Yard let me in to see Doust, but I could not get word one out of him."

"Was he afraid that something might happen to him if he talked?"

"It did not seem that way," Benedetti said slowly. "In fact, Doust has nothing to be scared of. He is going to jail for a very long time. I suppose if someone wanted to, they could arrange to have him killed on the inside. But that is not what held him back. Henry Doust is one of those old-fashioned people who, once he strikes a bargain, holds up his end of it."

"Then we have to go after Allen," Kate said.

"That might not be so easy."

Kate looked at him sharply. "Why? I thought you were keeping tabs on him."

"The last word the Greek maritime patrol received from Allen was that he was headed for Istanbul," Benedetti replied. "That was four days ago. He should have reached the Turkish coast forty-eight hours later. Instead a sixty-foot motorsailor has been found drifting in Turkish waters without a soul on board. The vessel has been vandalized, and the authorities presume that pirates, who roam the waters between Alexandria and Istanbul, had fallen upon this easy prey, killed the owner and passengers, then proceeded to loot the boat. It had to have happened quickly, because no distress signal had been logged. . . ."

"We must flush out Pierre now!" Kate was saying. "Before he's responsible for more killing."

Armand saw the anger flashing in Kate's eyes. He sat up in bed, wincing from the pain, a constant reminder of his condition. Thinking back, Armand considered himself blessed that he had been able to make it back to where the two monks were waiting for him. He didn't know where he had found the strength.

Armand had been furious—and afraid—when the abbot told him about the attempts to intimidate Kate. The police harassment coupled with the amnesty offer from the embassy was repugnant to him. The attempt to discredit the casino and Kate had shaken him to the core. He was proud of the way Kate, with her quick reactions and presence of mind, had averted a disaster.

"Kate, come here, please."

She immediately sensed a new tenor in Armand's voice, one she had never heard before, and which, for a reason she couldn't define, worried her. She sat down beside him, waiting.

"Something happened that made me leave the monastery."

Armand recounted how Sweet's comment to Kate had triggered a clue he had followed up on. He told her about the journey to Mouchtara and what he had seen there, including the person of Michael Saidi. Kate was horrified.

"Saidi is much more dangerous than we ever suspected," Armand said.

Kate's eyes blazed. "Then we have to find a way to stop him!"

Armand shook his head. "If we can. Kate, I want you to understand one thing. The rot, the plotting, has gone beyond my means to stop it. There was a time, not long ago, when I believed that it was possible to see Lebanon through this horrible time. I was wrong. Perhaps too vain as well. I cannot roll back the clock or remake events that have gone before. The Arabs have coined a fitting proverb for such circumstances: 'Some men are born into times they cannot change.' I never thought I would be one of them."

The finality and despair of Armand's words made Kate shiver. "Does that mean you're giving up?" she asked in a low voice.

"No. Those who have done evil, who have contributed to our wretchedness, must be stopped. But in order for that to happen, I must let go of the past."

For a moment the meaning of Armand's words escaped Kate. Then she understood. "Armand, no!"

He reached out to her and said, "Kate, remember we talked about this. We agreed that if matters forced us to do this, then we would."

Kate bit her lip. "Damn it!" she whispered. "It shouldn't have come to this!"

"But it has. And there is nothing we can do about it."

Kate brushed away a tear. "Very well, Armand, but I'm

not going to let Pierre walk scot-free."

"How do you propose to fight him?" Armand asked quietly.

"Face-to-face. I think that Pierre is more afraid of the person behind him than he will ever be of us. So I have to choose the moment, sit him down, and say to his face that he is a killer."

Armand could imagine the scene, how powerful Kate's outrage would be. How would Pierre answer it? Would he laugh, be indignant, wilt and confess? It was so dangerous . . . but perhaps the only way.

"Please, Armand. Don't stop me. What you're intent on doing will *help* me. Together we *will* flush out not only Pierre but his accomplice as well." Kate paused. "You said you wanted the guilty punished. Don't be willing to sacrifice everything unless you're sure about that."

For the hundredth time Armand asked himself if he was doing the right thing. He had not told Kate that he had his suspicions about the identity of Pierre's accomplice. But only the highest stakes would expose that individual.

"All right," Armand said at last, with a tenderness that overwhelmed Kate. "Take off Pierre's mask. But please, don't make me regret this."

She touched his cheek. "There can never be anything to regret."

As he watched her pick up her things to leave, Armand felt torn. So much had already happened to them. Now even greater dangers lay ahead. What if he never saw her again? How would he live with himself?

"Kate," Armand called out hoarsely.

Perhaps it was the way the light fell on her face, or the intense, knowing look in her eyes, but at that moment Armand's confusion about his feelings for Kate soared away, like a soul released from a dying body. The words he had waited so long to say at last came over his lips.

"I love you, Kate."

She came to him then, molding her body to his, her kisses raining over his face. Then all at once she was laughing, tears streaming down her cheeks.

"I thought I'd *never* hear you say that!"

"I've been a fool," Armand said. "No one has ever touched me the way you have, so suddenly, so completely. I was afraid, suspicious . . ."

"Not anymore, darling. Not ever again."

They held each other for a long time, lips and fingertips exploring.

"I had better go." Kate murmured.

"Promise me you will be careful," Armand pleaded, "and whatever you do, stay well away from Michael Saidi."

"Michael's time will come," Kate said softly. "He will not outrun his destiny."

23

Pierre Fremont was seated at his Louis XIV desk, studying the latest figures of the national budget. His office at the bank was his haven, an eighteenth-century stage complete with tapestries, fine oriental rugs, ornate gilt-edged mirrors, and a domed ceiling with gold-leaf detail. When the double doors banged open, slamming against the walls, Pierre's hands involuntarily flew forward, knocking a sterling-silver inkwell onto an irreplaceable Aubusson.

Kate marched into the room, followed by an apoplectic secretary.

"I want to see you tonight, Pierre. At the Oiseau Bleu, in Armand's private dining room. Nine o'clock. Please don't be late."

"Kate! What is it? What's going on?" Pierre called after her.

Kate whirled around. "You'll find out tonight." She paused and added, "But I suspect you already have a good idea!"

That same evening Cleo left the villa she shared with Pierre and drove down the mountains to Ra's Beirut. Although traffic was heavy, Cleo piloted the Maserati like a madwoman, careening around hairpin turns and passing on blind corners. Horns and curses followed her headlong flight.

"*Ma'alesh*," Cleo kept whispering to herself. "*It doesn't matter!*"

The moment she had dreaded, which she had half convinced herself would never come, was at last upon her. Her home and its priceless possessions had proved to be the mirage she had always suspected they were. Pierre had once told her, "We Beirutis can never conquer. But by the same token, we can never *protect* anything either. We survive because we will *do* anything. If one thing doesn't work out, another will. We don't fuss. We have a drink and wait and see. Remember, Cleo, *ma'alesh* . . ."

She spun the wheel, and the sports car rocketed toward Martyrs' Square, all brightly lit up as though for a parade. Cleo juggled the Maserati into a parking space and ran across the square, into a small café that was half-empty, where Jasmine sat smoking, her jade cigarette holder balanced like a mace between her fingers.

"The bitch knows!" Cleo spat out, breathing hard. "Pierre is sure of it!"

"I assume you are referring to Kate," Jasmine replied. "What does she know?"

Cleo's eyes blazed. "About Pierre's thievery at the bank! What else?"

Jasmine studied her impassively. "Pierre is certain of this?"

"He came home a wreck! Apparently Kate stormed into his office and ordered—*ordered*—him to be at the Oiseau Bleu tonight. She said he knew very well what it was all about."

"So Pierre jumped to conclusions," Jasmine murmured.

"Pierre can jump any damn way he wants to. *I'm jumping out!* I want my money, Jasmine."

"Don't you think you're overreacting?"

Cleo laughed harshly. "Don't start with that. I told you, I would not let Pierre drag me down with him."

Jasmine considered, then said, "Very well. You want to leave. I won't stop you. Check with the Sauer Bank in Zurich at noon tomorrow. I'm sure you will find everything in order. But I want you to do me a favor."

Shaking her head furiously, Cleo said "No favors! In fact, I can guess what you want!"

"Only that you go to dinner with Pierre. I will make it worth your while," Jasmine added. "One hundred thousand dollars."

Cleo stopped short. "What can be worth that kind of

money to you?" she asked suspiciously.

"I should think that would have been obvious," Jasmine replied. "I want to know *exactly* what goes on between Pierre and Kate."

"You mean you don't trust him."

"I mean that sometimes Pierre has a selective memory when he's telling me things."

"In a way, I admire you, Jasmine. Pierre is going to be ruined, but you will still find a way to profit."

"Do we have a deal?" Jasmine demanded.

Cleo gathered up her purse. "Tell your bank in Zurich to make sure the extra money is there."

"Just out of curiosity, what *are* you going to do?" asked Jasmine.

Cleo smiled back. "You'll always be able to find me through the international gossip columns, darling."

Kate was deliberately late for dinner with Pierre. It was all part of the plan, as much as the security men who had been seeded around the dining room close to Armand's private cubicle. What Kate hadn't anticipated was Cleo's gliding in alongside Pierre. A complication, but a minor one.

Kate had had champagne sent in and gave Pierre enough time to have several glasses. She did not expect him to be drunk, but even the slightest advantage would be useful if not crucial. Then Kate made her entrance.

The champagne had gone untouched, and the water glass to Pierre's right was empty. He and Cleo sat side by side, not saying a word.

"Good evening," Kate said.

Pierre looked up at her, his eyes glazed, his expression vacuous.

"Kate."

Cleo nodded but did not say a word.

"I was not expecting to see you, Cleo," Kate said. "Under the circumstances."

"I don't know what these circumstances are," Pierre said abruptly. "You barge into my office and behave like a lunatic. I do you the courtesy of presenting myself, as you asked. As far as Cleo is concerned, there are absolutely no secrets between us. If you insist that she leave, then I will go with her."

Kate watched Cleo smile slyly over the rim of her glass.

"Very well, Pierre. If that is the way you wish to do it."

She noticed his fingers picking at the corners of his napkin.

"You have every reason to be worried, Pierre," Kate said, trying to keep the tremors from her voice. "You are a thief who has looted his own country's central bank."

Pierre continued to toy with his napkin, his eyes downcast.

"And you are a murderer too. You met my father in Paris and he threatened to expose you. So you decided to kill him. You had a second meeting, and that's when you had his car tampered with, knowing that it would only be a matter of time before he would die.

"But that wasn't enough for you, was it? You had to determine *how* my father had known, *who* had told him. That led you to Kenneth Morton in London, whom you murdered in Provence."

"You're insane!" Pierre shouted. "This is all fantasy!"

"You bastard!" Kate whispered. "Look at me and tell me I'm lying! Go ahead, look! You can't, can you? That's because you know you're guilty! And I'm going to prove it!"

Pierre laughed, an ugly, braying sound. "If you had proof, you would have had me arrested by now. Or at least tried to."

"I can still do that, Pierre. And I will unless you give me the name of your accomplice."

"So now it is a conspiracy!" Pierre barked. "Do you really think anyone will believe you, Kate?"

Kate pushed a letter toward him.

"Tomorrow copies will be hand delivered to the prime minister's office and the press, including the major American and European newspapers. I give you twenty-four hours, Pierre, before you're forced into accepting an audit. After that comes the rest. Believe me, I can link you to my father's murder, and I will. So give me the name of your accomplice who made the arrangements, hired the killer. Unless, of course, *you* did all that."

Pierre had sagged back in his seat and was staring over her shoulder. Kate turned around and saw three men materialize by the maître d', who was shaking his head. To Kate the situation was obvious. The men wanted a table but had no reservations. Then without warning the maître d' was suddenly propelled backward, as though he'd been kicked in the chest. The dessert trolley tripped him up, spinning him around and revealing a dark red blotch on his white tuxedo shirt. Dying swiftly, the maître d' tumbled into a banquette and the arms of a woman who reared back in horror.

Automatic weapons appeared in the hands of the three men, and machine-gun fire raked the security men who sprang into action. Within seconds the diners were on the floor or cowering under tables. The intruders ran swiftly to the private dining room.

Arms reached for Kate and yanked her to her feet. A cold muzzle was jammed against the side of her neck.

"Don't hurt anyone else—"

Her words were cut off as one of the gunmen wrenched Cleo from Pierre's arms, dragging her around the banquette.

"No!"

Pierre didn't have a chance. The gunman hit him across the face with the back of his hand, and he dropped to his knees. More screams erupted as a hail of bullets cut down two of the security guards who had crashed through the restaurant doors. Kate staggered back as the gunman released her. Two of them were holding Cleo, her arms locked behind her back, pushing her toward the kitchen doors. The third gunman emptied his clip into the restaurant, an obvious warning to the brave or foolhardy.

Her head pounding with the screams and moans, Kate crawled over to Pierre, who was on his knees. He looked around wildly for Cleo, and when he saw the swinging doors, tried to scramble to his feet.

"No, Pierre!" Kate cried. "You won't get her back that

way. They'll kill her if you try."

Pierre stared at the doors through which Cleo had disappeared; then all at once the fight went out of him. When he turned to her, Kate thought she had never seen a more desolate and hopeless expression.

"Why?" Pierre whispered, weaving from side to side. "Why did they take her?"

Pierre groaned and opened his eyes, squinting against the glare of light bouncing off the white-enameled bed frame. At first he was disoriented, then realized he was in the hospital. Seconds later the terror came rushing back, and he tossed weakly from side to side as though trying to fight off invisible attackers.

He wanted to flee back into the dark arms of the narcotic that had put him to sleep. His head was pounding from the gunfire, and Cleo's face, so terrified, swam like a mirage before his eyes. Just as quickly there followed bitter shame because he had done nothing to help her, let her be stolen from him without raising a hand.

"Pierre . . ."

Pierre turned and saw Kate standing over the bed.

"Please, Miss Maser. A few minutes. No more."

Pierre heard the doctor's words and cried out weakly when the physician left the room. Kate reached out and took hold of his arm.

"We will get her back," repeated Kate.

"Where is she?" Pierre gasped.

"We don't know yet. The police are combing the city. They have a good description of the man."

"There were three of them."

"Two didn't make it." Kate leaned forward. "You have to tell me why Cleo was taken."

Pierre trembled. Why was it Cleo, not Kate, who had been abducted? Jasmine had sworn nothing would happen to Cleo.

"Pierre, you must talk to me," Kate urged him. "Don't you see? You've been betrayed. I was the real target, wasn't I?"

"No," Pierre whispered.

"There's no point in lying anymore!" Kate cried. "Or protecting anyone. I was the intended victim. That's what you were told, believed all along. Whoever is working with you, Pierre, doesn't trust you any longer."

"I don't know anything."

Pierre's cries brought the doctors, who insisted that Kate leave.

"You don't have to do this because you are afraid of me," Kate said. "You *know* whom you should be terrified of now."

The minute Kate stepped outside the hospital, her nemesis, Inspector Hamse, returned with a vengeance, subjecting her to hours of questioning about what had happened at the casino.

"These things do not happen by chance, Miss Maser," he said. "Two people are dead, one has been kidnapped, and others hurt. This took place on your premises, and all you can say is you don't have any idea why? You insult my intelligence, mademoiselle!"

"It seems I've said little enough in order to do that!" Kate replied. "There haven't been any threats against me or the casino. As far as I can tell, nobody holds a grudge against any of my employees. Your own investigation should tell you that much. So I ask you, Inspector, since you claim to know Beirut so well, what the hell do *you* think happened?"

Hamse crimsoned under the sting of her words.

"Gunmen firing automatic weapons at innocent people in a public place is not the natural order of things in my city, Miss Maser. But then again, so many things have taken place since you arrived, yes? Perhaps your problems followed you here from America!"

"I've told you everything I can," Kate retorted. "Why don't you tell me what you're doing to find Cleo?"

Hamse looked thoughtfully at her. "Nothing less than we are capable of, Miss Maser. You have my word on that."

"I'm not the one who needs your promise, Inspector.

Cleo does."

Kate had the Casino cashiers set aside a reserve of a million dollars in cash. She wanted to be ready to act as soon as the kidnappers set the terms of Cleo's release. She had just completed the arrangements when the last person in the world she expected to hear from, Nabil Tufaili, called her.

"I must see you, Miss Maser," the *zaim* said. "It is of the utmost urgency."

"Mr. Tufaili, I'm sure you can understand that this isn't the best time—"

"Miss Maser, I am quite aware of your recent difficulties. That is precisely why we must meet. In fact, I insist on it. Ten o'clock tonight, at my offices in the Arab-American Bank on the Corniche. My man will show you up. And come alone, please. I think that when you hear what we have to tell you, you will be glad there was no one else."

Intrigued by Tufaili's mysterious summons, Kate arrived at the waterfront high rise at precisely ten o'clock. Tufaili was as good as his word: a silent man in a black suit ushered her into the elevator and, once she was inside, pressed and locked the top button. The elevator rose swiftly, its doors opening directly onto an opulent suite filled with Scandinavian-designed rosewood furniture and primitive art from Africa and Asia. The common theme, Kate quickly discovered was priapism.

In the center of the room, on a semicircle of sofas and easy chairs, were ten men, including Nabil Tufaili. Kate recognized many of their faces from newspaper and magazine articles. She knew their names and recalled what Armand had told her about each one of them. They were the *zuama*.

"Thank you for being punctual, Miss Maser," Tufaili said without preamble. He indicated a single chair set in front of the group. "May I offer you tea?"

Kate settled herself and fixed her eyes on Tufaili. "No, thank you."

"Very well. I trust we can dispense with the introductions? You know who we are."

"Oh, yes, Mr. Tufaili."

"Then allow me to tell you the reason we asked you to join us. Miss Maser, if there is one thing Beirutis detest above all others, it is disorder. Our land thrives because we are men of our word, the honest brokers, if you will."

Kate raised an eyebrow, but if Tufaili noticed, he chose to ignore it.

"I deeply regret telling you that your activities in Beirut, the traumatic events and tragedies that have centered around you, have gravely threatened the equilibrium that is so precious to us. I am certain you did not intend for this to happen, but nonetheless it has. I sympathize with your loss and the burden that you bear. But no matter how great it is, we cannot sit idly by while you inflict chaos upon us."

Kate had used all her energy to rein in her temper, but she had to say something now, even though she knew Tufaili would consider it the ultimate rudeness to be interrupted by a woman.

"I take it you have some advice for me, Mr. Tufaili?"

"Indeed I do. It has come to our attention that certain interests have offered very generous terms if you were to take SBM public and sell the shares."

"And how do you know this isn't just another rumor, Mr. Tufaili?" Kate asked sharply.

"Because you do not deny it. Even if you had, it wouldn't matter. Our sources may not be quite as thorough as we would like, but the information they provide is always reliable.

"But as I was saying, we feel that this offer opens several doors. By accepting it, you would become a very wealthy woman, much more so than you are now. I am remembering your recent history, Miss Maser. Think of all the wonderful causes you could support when you return to America.

"Which brings me to my second point. This is the perfect opportunity for you to leave Beirut. Believe me, Miss Maser, there isn't anything here for you now, now will there ever be. But by leaving under these circumstances, you save face. No one can say you were beaten or that you ran. On the contrary, Beirutis will understand perfectly that you took the only reasonable way out."

"What about my conscience? Will that tell me I was being reasonable?"

"I am not your spiritual adviser, Miss Maser. But—and this brings me to my third point—your departure would find great favor among us. Personally we have no quarrel with you. But neither will we allow you to upset the balance we must maintain here. You are a *strega*, Miss Maser. A witch, a bearer of ill fortune. I'm afraid that neither we nor Beirut can afford you. And we will use all our powers of persuasion to convince you of that."

"Am I to take that as a threat?"

"But of course. That's exactly what it is."

Kate rose. Her voice was cold and level.

"You are a contemptible man, Mr. Tufaili. As are all of you. A young woman is abducted at gun point from the casino, two of my staff are shot, hundreds of innocent bystanders are terrified, but instead of extending your hand to me, you issue threats. That tells me everything I need to know about you gentlemen, your values and sense of morality. I have nothing to discuss with you!"

"Miss Maser!" Tufaili called to her. "We have overlooked your insults because of your ignorance of our customs. But it is clear to us that besides being a very dangerous woman, you are also a stupid one. Please, do not underestimate us. You may have inherited a casino, but you are no Armand Fremont. We can break you with a snap of our fingers. Within days, if we so desire, your employees will leave, and no one, no matter how much you offer to pay, will take their places. Your credit line at the bank will be scrutinized, and auditors will pore over your financial records like termites. Word will spread among the so-called 'jet set' that you are a pariah, and your tables will be empty.

"Believe me, Miss Maser. We can accomplish all this and much more. Weigh your decision in light of that very carefully. Because in the end no one will show you any pity. You will be quite alone. And when we throw you out of our

country, you will return to America and the welcome arms
of a federal prison.

"You rejected one deal, Miss Maser. Don't make the
same mistake twice."

"Thank you, Nabil. I'm sure that she took to heart what
you had to say."

Jasmine hung up the phone and turned to Louis.

"It went as we planned."

"You're insane!" Louis whispered. "First Cleo is kidnapped. We never agreed to that, Jasmine! You said no one
was going to get hurt. That's what you promised! Now you
involve Tufaili. Sharif Uday is bound to get wind of this,
and when he does, he'll tell the sultan to pull out of the deal.
Everything you're doing only destroys the casino that much
more!"

"Don't be an ass!" Jasmine retorted. "As long as Kate is
in control and refuses to sell, we have nothing!"

Louis swung away, drawing deeply on his cigarette. In
the reflection of the floor-to-ceiling window he watched
Jasmine walk out of the room.

Tufaili was right, he thought. She has become too dangerous, uncontrollable.

And at that moment, when he pictured his wife dead,
Louis savored the thought of freedom for the first time.

One of the greatest Crusader castles in Lebanon had been
built in 1099, on a promontory cut in the Mountain overlooking Saint George's Bay. The Lebanese themselves
avoided the castle, believing it to be haunted. Cleo knew
this and had given up any hope of being rescued.

The chamber had walls of cut stone and a floor of
pounded earth. The only light and heat came from kerosene
lamps and a coarse horse-hair blanket. The bed was a thin,
dirty mattress, and a bucket served as the toilet.

Cleo could not tell whether it was day or night. The remains of her evening gown lay in tatters over her bruised
body. Her bare feet bled from deep cuts, and her face was

grimy from the dirt and smoke. Sitting there, one might
have thought she was a statue . . . until one looked into
those wide, shining eyes staring out at some invisible point,
eyes that were blinded by horror, full of the red, dancing
pinpoints of slowly gathering madness.

Cleo could not remember how many times she had been
raped. There had been only two of them, but they were
goats, and now she could feel nothing below the waist.

She still had no idea why they had taken her, and now it
didn't matter. Because whether it was for ransom or for
sport, what had been done to her could never be cleansed
away. Cleo, the child of the streets who had forgotten to
mistrust good fortune, now understood that neither wealth
nor power—those things she had believed would always
protect her—were omnipotent. Men came and took what
they wanted. When they were done and tired of her, they
would go, leaving her to crawl, like some stricken animal,
into its lair. There was nothing more they could do to her.

Cleo had no idea of how wrong she was.

The door to the chamber opened, and two men stepped
inside. Cleo smelled something she had almost forgotten:
the bracing, sensual scent of masculine cologne. Hope
stirred like a current rising from the ocean depths.

This second man remained in the shadows where Cleo
could not see his face. One of the men who had raped her
came up and shoved her so that she was facing the wall. He
sat very close to her, his breath foul in her face.

"Tell me, Cleo, all about your keeper, Pierre," the voice
behind her said.

Confused, Cleo did not know how to answer.

"Pierre has secrets. I want you to tell me what they are."

Then Cleo understood. Pierre had only one secret. It was
terrible, and if revealed, it would destroy him. But it was
not a thing worth dying for. She would leave him, of course,
because he would be ruined. But she would have her beauty
and her youth. She would survive and find someone else to
belong to.

Haltingly at first, because she hadn't uttered a word in

days, Cleo told her anonymous inquisitor all about Pierre's embezzlement of funds from the Banque de Liban. With every word she felt the current of hope becoming stronger, surging upward to carry her away.

"Is that all?" the man asked her.

"I swear that is his only secret."

The man sighed. "If you only knew how frightened he is for you. He will do anything to get you back. It is quite pathetic, really. But we should not disappoint him, should we? We should send you back to him."

Cleo closed her eyes. "Yes."

"Are you going to stay with him, Cleo, after he's ruined? Tell the truth now!"

Cleo did not hesitate. This man held her life in his hands. "No."

"Oh, Cleo, that is so disappointing. But so predictable. I think Pierre deserves better than that, don't you? After all, what else will he have left besides you?"

"Then I will stay! If that's what you want me to do. I swear!"

"I wish I could believe that, Cleo," the inquisitor said softly. "But I must be sure of that. There's only one way to be sure."

The inquisitor signaled, and the razor in his servant's hand began its work.

24

Louis Jabar's religious inclinations rested entirely on the Maronite community's political clout. For that reason he had struck on the idea of addressing the community leaders in their place of worship, St. Sophia's Cathedral. Now, as he waded into the crowds lining the church steps, Louis wondered if God would ever forgive him for what was about to happen.

The fact that a political rally was taking place on consecrated ground did not raise any eyebrows among Beirutis. What did was that Nabil Tufaili and a number of other powerful Arabs were attending. Religious objects such as crucifixes and icons were anathema to Muslims. The fact that Tufaili and the others were present gave everyone an idea of the force uniting behind Louis Jabar.

Inside, Louis escorted Jasmine and his retinue of advisers to the right-hand pews. Then he moved across the aisle and paid his respects to Tufaili. As the crowd settled, Louis mounted the circular staircase to the pulpit directly in front of the left-hand side pews. His expression was confident, his smile, dazzling. Without uttering a word, he had the audience in his hand.

Louis turned and focused his gaze on Jasmine. She had never looked more beautiful, reminding him of that night so long ago when he had first seen her in the casino at Enghien. Perhaps because he knew he was looking at her for the last time, Louis threw her a kiss, pressing two fingers against his lips and flinging out his arm.

For old time's sake, the kind I'll never have to endure again. You were a beautiful bitch, Jasmine, beautiful, mad and deadly.

As he arranged his notes on the lectern, Louis glanced at his watch. Less than five minutes.

Jasmine only pretended to listen to Louis's words. Since she had written the speech, she watched the audience's reaction. There was no question of Louis's skill as an orator. He had a magnetism that was irresistible. He was like a rare urn or vessel, beautiful but utterly useless unless filled. As Louis's address became more and more passionate, Jasmine thought how well she had filled this empty, pretty man.

Later Jasmine would remember the moment perfectly. Louis had one hand out to the audience, the fingers of the other gripping the lectern. His head was thrust forward, his eyes blazed with righteous conviction. Then the bomb, hidden in the eaves, exploded, and it seemed as though the very wrath of God had been unleashed on all below.

The death toll, when it was finally tallied, was fifty-seven. Everyone agreed it was a miracle more people hadn't died. Some, including Louis Jabar, Nabil Tufaili, and the "fixers" in that first pew, were killed instantly. Others took longer, choking and bleeding to death as they lay crushed under the debris. When the first photographs of the carnage appeared, people gasped at how the cathedral had been cleaved in two, as though by some divine sword. Those who had been sitting on the right-hand side uttered silent prayers of thanks.

The tragedy in Beirut made headlines around the world, and a single photograph symbolized the horror: the widow of the president to be, Jasmine Fremont-Jabar, lifting her dead husband's body from the rubble, her head thrown back, her face twisted in grief.

The police investigation was swift and decisive. Rumors about a ruptured gas main were immediately quashed. Inspector Hamse solemnly pronounced that this was a case of political murder. The bomb had been placed directly above the pulpit. The only target could have been Louis Jabar. Hamse assured the international press that the perpetrators would be tracked down and punished.

But that was only the beginning. Infuriated by the savage murder of their leader, Maronite youths went on a rampage in the Arab quarters, smashing windows, looting, dragging out shopkeepers and beating them. The Muslims responded in kind, and soon the telltale popping of automatic weapons was heard all over the city. With most of the *zuama* dead, there was no authority to reestablish order. Prodded by the National Assembly, the outgoing president declared a state of emergency and flooded the streets with brigades from the national police force, whose commanders promptly ordered a curfew.

Kate was told of the tragedy only minutes after it had happened, but she couldn't get in to see Jasmine at the hospital until very late that night. When she finally came face-to-face with her, Jasmine turned her away.

"You could have helped us, Kate," she said. "You should have stood behind the family and publicly supported Louis. My God, what has happened to our house! First Armand, then Cleo taken, now Louis murdered. Please, Kate, don't say a word to me. If only you had followed our advice, co-operated with us by agreeing to get rid of that damn casino! Instead Armand's enemies became your enemies, and in the end it is we, not you, who pay!"

Kate struggled to say something, not in her defense but a word or two of comfort. But Jasmine's lost, embittered expression told her she had come too late, with far too little.

In spite of the curfew, violence raged across Beirut for the next few days until the combatants had exhausted themselves or been arrested and shipped off to jail by the police. The summer that had blossomed with such promise wilted and began to die.

Kate closed the Casino de Paradis completely. Business at the gaming tables had trickled to nothing, and the Oiseau Bleu had been shut off for repairs. Across the city the story was the same. Restaurants, night clubs, cabarets canceled shows and laid off staff. Along the waterfront and in the *souqs* merchants sat outside facing empty sidewalks, their store windows plastered with signs offering huge discounts. The few adventurous bargain hunters shopped with a vengeance.

It seemed to Kate that the city, even the entire country, was holding its collective breath. What frightened everyone, but what no one dared to mention, was that with Louis dead, Beirut was adrift, fearful of what might happen next. The traditional authority, the *zuama*, to whom ordinary people could turn for help and justice, had been crushed under the same rubble.

Most Beirutis forgot all about Cleo's abduction. But not Kate. She waited hour to hour, day to day, for any scrap of news. She had tried calling Pierre, but he was neither at the bank nor at home. When Kate went to his villa, she couldn't get past the front gates. Jasmine was no help. She was in mourning, preoccupied with the funeral arrangements for her husband. Rumor had it that the interment was being postponed because the government feared a public funeral would rekindle the violence.

But Kate didn't give up. She called Inspector Hamse every day, demanding to know the progress on Cleo's case. She sent telegrams to Pierre's home and bribed the manager of his club to call her if he showed up. But it seemed that Pierre had dropped off the face of the earth until one evening, as Kate was picking at her dinner, Balthazar rushed into the room.

"It's Monsieur Fremont!" he gasped. "He's here—"

Haggard and wild-eyed, Pierre pushed his way past Balthazar.

"Did you hear?" he demanded.

"Hear what? Pierre, what's happened?"

"Less than an hour ago I received a telephone call from a man who claims to have Cleo. He said he was going to release her, bring her here . . ."

Pierre looked around wildly as though expecting Cleo to materialize at any second.

"I don't know anything about this. Tell me exactly what's happened."

Pierre drained a large brandy and recounted the brief conversation.

"I didn't recognize the voice. All he said was Cleo would

be freed, and that I should wait for her here."

"I don't understand," Kate said. "No one called *me*."

"They must have!" he insisted. "Maybe one of the servants answered—"

"I've been here all day. I'm telling you I never got such a message."

"They will release Cleo," Pierre carried on with the desperate conviction of a man straining to hold on to what he believes is a miracle.

"Have you contacted the police?"

"No!" he shouted. "He said he would kill her if he saw police."

The telephone rang. Pierre's eyes shifted to Kate, who hesitated, then picked up the receiver.

"Look in the road outside your house."

The voice was so cold, Kate thought it came from a tomb. Instantly the connection was broken. Kate took a deep breath.

"He said outside, in the road," she whispered, her voice shaking.

Before anyone could stop him, Pierre ran from the room.

"Pierre!" Kate shouted. "It could be a trap!"

She raced after him, sprinting down the driveway. Beyond the wrought-iron gates, set against the bone-white moonlight, she saw a lone figure standing in the middle of the road. Together with Pierre, Kate pushed the gates apart and stumbled onto the blacktop. What they saw froze their hearts. The figure was Cleo, standing stock-still, her arms outstretched, in her hands a large boudoir-style mirror.

"Cleo . . . ," Pierre whispered.

He managed to take two steps before Cleo whipped her head around. Beside her Kate heard Pierre as he retched and staggered back. Kate couldn't take her eyes off Cleo's face . . . or what was left of it. Two long scars ran from below each eye, over the cheekbones and by the sides of the mouth to the jaw. A host of smaller cuts, crusted with blood, crisscrossed her nose and forehead. The savage mutilation was so precise that Kate knew instinctively that no amount of plastic surgery would ever restore the beauty the knife had carved away.

"They gave me a mirror so·that I could see myself," Cleo whispered hoarsely. "I told them everything, but still they destroyed me. Pierre, please, help me, forgive me."

Cleo stepped forward, her movements as rigid as a zombie's, her arms beseeching Pierre to take her. He shrank back from her.

She froze. Her ruined lips trembled, and a terrible scream pierced the air, riding on the winds that course around the mountain. It was a lament that shook Kate to the core, leaving her sickened by the evil and ugliness that was emerging from behind the perfect facade of Beirut.

Michael padded around the bed on which Jasmine was stretched out, luxuriously naked. He sat down on the divan opposite her and lit a cigarette. She rolled over on her side. Her voice was low, the words trembling on her lips.

"We finally have everything we wanted. Louis is dead, the *zuama* with him. The city is in chaos, and soon you will be president of Lebanon."

Jasmine trailed a red fingernail along Michael's toes. "And you and I will be together."

Yes, Michael thought. That was part of the bargain, and one he intended to keep, because Jasmine was nothing if not lethal. She had suspected months ago that Tufaili would find her influence over Louis intolerable. So she had devised a plan that would eliminate both him and Louis. The first would take care of the threat to her, the latter, of a man she despised, yet who would become a national icon, and whose mystique and respect would inevitably pass to his widow . . . who could then choose to legitimize the candidate who stepped forward to take her husband's place.

Yet, Michael reflected, she could not have done it without me.

Jasmine had devised the perfect plan, but she did not have the means to know exactly when to strike. Ironically it was Nabil Tufaili's passion for young boys that solved the problem. Michael had gone to his two old men in Martyrs' Square who bought and sold children. He told them to find two very special young boys, the kind Tufaili would not be able to resist. After the boys had been brought to Beirut, they were cleaned, fed, clothed, and told what was expected of them. Special instructions were also drilled into them until they could recite them in their sleep. They were promised that after this they would be sent to the homes of old men, whose appetites for sex had waned, and where they would be companions and helpers instead of bedroom ornaments.

Michael's boys became his eyes and ears in Tufaili's villa. Since Tufaili did not recognize their existence outside the bedroom, he took no special precautions in their presence. His voice carried when he held discussions with the other *zuama*, and even though he was blissfully unaware of it, he talked in his sleep. Over time Michael learned all the details of Tufaili's ultimatum to Louis, how Jasmine was going to die, where, and when.

The trickiest part had come at the end. Michael and Jasmine couldn't act until the bomb had actually been placed in the cathedral of Saint Sophia. The killer working for Tufaili had waited until the day before Louis's appearance to finish his work. Michael had his own experts waiting, two Palestinians who were graduates of the North Korean school of terrorism. He managed to get them inside the cathedral a scant six hours before the rally. The Palestinians had had just enough time to neutralize the bomb meant to kill Jasmine and to substitute their own explosive device, powerful enough to destroy anything within a forty-foot radius, but not so potent as to bring down the entire church.

The Palestinians, Michael thought, had done an excellent job. He'd keep them in mind for anything else that came along . . . as it undoubtedly would.

"What are we going to do about Kate? I suppose the easiest thing would be to revoke her papers and throw her out of the country."

Jasmine slid one hand up his leg. "The easiest, yes. But

certainly not the most profitable."

"What do you mean?"

"Don't you think Kate would leap at the chance to help a distraught widow, not to mention a friend, if at the same time she thought she was contributing to the greater good of Lebanon?"

Michael's eyes widened. "You don't mean . . . ?"

"Oh, yes, I do," Jasmine whispered. "Once we tell her that *you* are running for the presidency, she will realize that she must sell the casino to pay for your election. From her point of view, what is there to think about? She satisfies her naivete by helping to put the 'right man,' as it were, in the presidential palace. Afterward there's plenty of money left over to clean up the Maritime Continental mess."

"So much money," Michael said softly. "It seems a shame—"

"I should have said, Kate *thinks* there is money left over," Jasmine corrected herself. "I will see to it that Sharif Uday does not give her all of it at once, just enough for what you need. The rest, according to contract, will come after the election."

"The results of which Kate may not live to see? But then who will get her estate?"

"Pierre and I are the only other shareholders, except that we all know what a bad boy Pierre has been. I don't think he'll have any use for his share, do you?"

Michael smiled, but his skin was crawling. In the beginning Alexander had created a problem. Then Armand, with his control over the casino and vast influence in Beirut, had been the problem. Jasmine had known then that if she intended to maneuver Michael into the presidential chair, Armand would have to be dealt with.

And so he had been.

Then there had been David Cabot . . . the business with the cards at the casino that she'd worked through an unsuspecting Shulmann . . . then Cleo . . . Louis and Tufaili.

Michael crushed out his cigarette and leaned back as Jasmine entwined herself around him.

"It will be so simple," she said in a low, throaty voice. "No one cares about Kate Maser. When she dies, the waters will simply close over her."

The funeral of Louis Jabar and the *zuama* resembled a military procession. Police lined the entire route, and truckloads of soldiers were stationed at strategic points around the city. The entire city held its breath, waiting to see where violence would erupt. But it seemed that the warring parties, on this day at least, had put aside their differences in honor of the dead.

Kate stood close to Jasmine at the grave, watching as government ministers, members of the diplomatic corps, and representatives of international companies filed past to express their condolences. Afterward Jasmine stepped up to Kate and whispered, "We must talk. It's very important."

Kate thought Jasmine wore her bereavement with dignity and grace. The cool reserve that surrounded her was gone, replaced by a sad, inner reflection. For a split second, when she saw Jasmine in the privacy of her home, Kate felt awkward. Then the two women embraced each other fiercely.

"I'm so sorry about the other day," Jasmine said. "I behaved like a complete bitch. What happened to Louis was not your fault."

"Do the police have any idea who did it?"

Jasmine shrugged. "They suspect the Palestinians. They're the troublemakers of the neighborhood, with their crazy politics and blind hatred. How can you deal with a people so violent, who blame their troubles on everyone but themselves?"

"I guess if you don't have anything to begin with, you have nothing to lose."

"Ah, Kate, Beirut is a terrible riddle. I keep asking myself who would want to have killed Louis. What purpose could his death have served? The terrible thing is, I have no answer. Louis was not a brilliant man. But he *loved* this country, he knew what it needed. Kate I realize this is a horrible time for you too," Jasmine continued. "If the situation were any different, I wouldn't even raise the subject. But this city—the whole country—is on the brink of catastrophe. What happened to Louis is a warning to all of us. A minute ago I said that he was a man who loved his country and knew what it needed. Well, I know another man who feels the same way. I think he is the one who should run for the presidency in Louis's place." She paused. "Michael Saidi."

Kate paled. A thief and a killer like Michael at the head of a government . . .

Jasmine smiled. "I thought you'd be surprised."

"I didn't think Michael had any political ambitions," Kate managed to say, searching for a way to tell Jasmine the truth.

"He never did. But the country cries out for a strong, decent man. A patriot."

Kate almost choked. She had to stop Jasmine now!

"Remember what you learned at school, Kate," Jasmine went on. "Nature abhors a vacuum. If we do not choose a replacement for Louis, one of the *zuama*'s families will. Is that what you want for Lebanon?"

"No, of course not."

Kate was on the verge of revealing Michael's secret past, but couldn't get the words out. "Why are you telling me this?" she asked at once.

"Because I need your support. There is almost nothing left in Louis's coffers, and rest assured, the *zuama*'s families will not stay idle. Michael will have his share of challengers. I am certain he can beat them, but only if we give him what he needs."

"That would mean going ahead with the sale of the casino," Kate said. "There's no other way to get the money."

"In the end that is your decision, Kate," Jasmine told her. "It always has been. But it's not about money anymore. Lebanon is part of who you are. I will do what I can for Michael. The rest is up to you. But please, don't leave it too late. Because others won't."

At that instant Kate knew exactly what she had to do. The

idea was fraught with danger. Everything would depend on
split-second timing. There would be no second chance. And
she began explaining to Jasmine what it was she had in
mind.

The next day Jasmine Fremont-Jabar called on the senior
editors of Beirut's newspapers asking them to meet her at
the Hotel Saint Georges. Intrigued, they all attended.

"The horror must end," the widow said, her words ringing over her listeners. "It has been paid for with blood and
life itself. I say—all of Lebanon says—it is enough."

Warming to her theme, Jasmine outlined the need for an
exceptional figure to take command of the country's future.
Then from behind the curtain stepped Michael Saidi. First
there was only silence. Then Jasmine took his hand in hers,
and together they raised them high in the air.

"Ladies and gentlemen," she said, her voice breaking
with emotion. "I give you the next president of the Republic
of Lebanon!"

Then, like a master magician tantalizing his audience,
Jasmine swept Michael offstage, saying that a full press
conference would take place the next day.

Pierre smiled vacuously as he watched Michael Saidi don
the mantle of presidential candidate. He was a ghost of his
former self, having lost a great deal of weight. Food, once
his consuming passion, now nauseated him. His skin hung
in folds along his neck, and his eyes, red-rimmed in dark
hollows, shone with dull, constant pain. But now, at least,
he understood Jasmine's grand design and how great a fool
he had been, how deftly Jasmine had played him. Ever since
that dreadful moment in front of Kate's house, Pierre's
world had shrunk to the confines of the hospital. He lived
and slept in a room adjacent to Cleo's and went home only
to bathe and change his clothes. No amount of persuasion
could move him, not even the sober reports of the plastic
surgeons, specialists flown in from the United States, who
told him that nothing in the world of medicine would ever

give Cleo back her perfect face. With a great deal of surgery and time, the scars would be reduced, but they would never fade nor be erased.

Pierre spent most nights watching Cleo sleep. He ran his fingers along the down on her forearms to reassure her she was not alone and touched the stiff fabric of the restraints around her hands. On her second day in the hospital Cleo had smashed a water glass. Pierre had barely caught her hand in time before she could plunge a sliver into her wrist.

During most of the day Pierre sat by Cleo's side. The doctors did not want her to speak, to avoid moving the muscles under her facial skin, and kept her under heavy sedation. But Pierre spoke to her anyway, convinced that she could hear him. By now the horror of her face no longer repelled him. He had stared at it for so long that he'd memorized the tiniest nick and furrow. He thought she was still so very beautiful that when he told her he loved her, the words, for the first time, did not come from fear that she would leave him, but out of perfect love.

As the days passed, Pierre had realized that Cleo was now his forever. The torment he had endured since the day he met her, that she would one day walk from his life, had disappeared. The world was so cruel and fickle, much like Cleo herself. It worshipped beauty and youth, but shunned those very gods and goddesses when fate struck them down. No, the world would no longer reach to embrace her. Instead it would shun her, force her to move through it behind a veil for the rest of her life.

And that's why she will belong to me forever, Pierre thought dreamily. *I am the only one who will continue to love her as I always have. I will never leave her, and she can never leave me. Her power over me is no more.*

Now he knew who was responsible. At first Pierre had wanted nothing but the most horrible death for Jasmine. But even in the midst of his pain he understood why such a hideous act had been carried out. Jasmine had never trusted him. Jasmine, the survivor, never left anything to chance, especially not the fact that somehow Katherine Maser might pry out of Pierre the truth about what had happened to her father. So she had taken Cleo and tortured her and afterward knew all that Cleo did . . . how close he really was to breaking.

In the end there had never been any choice at all, Pierre thought sadly. Cleo's beauty had to be sacrificed so that he, Pierre, would realize that those with the power to mutilate also had the power to take Cleo away forever.

Oh, yes, the secrets were all safe in the hands of those who treasured and understood them, but paid for, as they always were, by those who had been tempted by, but knew nothing of, their power. But they wouldn't touch Cleo anymore. She was now wedded to him for eternity.

At the monastery of the Order of the Third Cross, Armand Fremont and the abbot John were huddled together in the abbot's quarters. Yesterday Armand had been thunderstruck as he listened to Jasmine's speech broadcast over the radio. He was even more overwhelmed when Kate had been spirited into the monastery that same night and told him what she intended to do.

"Madness!" Armand thundered. "I will not let you take such risks!"

"We have no choice!" Kate replied vehemently. "There will never be another opportunity like this one."

They had argued for hours, but Armand had failed to come up with a better alternative. In the end he had capitulated. With the abbot playing devil's advocate, they had worked out the details.

"My love, be very, very careful," Armand had pleaded as Kate was about to leave.

"You know I will," she replied, kissing him deeply. "Because wherever I go, you are with me."

Armand shook off his reverie and turned his attention to the abbot.

"There can be no doubt," the abbot said, his voice ringing with conviction. "Michael Saidi is the man at the center of the opium traffic in the Bekaa Valley."

He gestured at the two monks who were standing beside him. "Listen to what they have to say."

The first monk spoke of farmers he had met during his sojourn in the Bekaa, how late in the evening, after the meal and many glasses of arak, they told him about the sticky flower, the poisonous resin it secreted, how much they had been paid and who the paymaster was.

The second brother, who ministered to the seamen and stevedores along the docks, told of large quantities of weapons that were off-loaded day and night from freighters sailing under a dozen different flags. He spoke about the vast sums of money which changed hands, and which, according to the stevedores, ended up in the pocket of a shadowy young man, a merciless killer, whose name could only be whispered.

"How could something like this have been going on without my knowing about it?" Armand asked wonderingly.

He was beyond revulsion and anger. His heart was filled with remorse.

"The man responsible has the slyness of a serpent," the abbot replied. "He controls his vanity and pride, working in the shadows and the gutter until—"

"Until he is strong enough to come out!" Armand whispered. "When he can make himself legitimate, step into the chaos he is responsible for, use what he has built to coerce, silence, or destroy whoever opposes him . . ."

"Oh, my God!"

The revelation blinded Armand.

"*Jasmine . . .*"

Yes, it had to be she! All this time he had been convinced that it was *a man* who was the master puppeteer, working the shadows. Not once had he considered it might be a woman.

Jasmine . . . who had used, then destroyed, her consort, Louis; who had had her opponents, the *zuama*, slaughtered; who had then crippled her accomplice, Pierre. All this so that she could make a place for her chosen one, Michael Saidi, grooming him for the day when he could step into the light.

Slowly Armand turned to the abbot, his eyes reflecting his fear.

"Kate . . . ," he whispered. "Kate is alone with her."

Armand heard the monastery bells toll midnight. The press conference was scheduled for eight o'clock in the morning. It was too late to warn Kate. Armand had no way of knowing how close Jasmine was staying to Kate. More than likely the two of them were still working on the details of the announcement. If a brother was sent to Kate and was seen by Jasmine . . .

"It is in God's hand now," the abbot said quietly, reading Armand's thoughts. "All we have now is faith."

25

Beirut's National Press Club was an impressive empire-style building located in the heart of the city.

"It's the favorite watering hole for every reporter stationed in the Middle East," Jasmine had told Kate. "Your idea of using it was brilliant! After the taste I gave them at the Saint Georges, we'll be guaranteed international coverage."

Kate silently agreed, but for reasons Jasmine knew nothing of. She hadn't told Jasmine about Michael, nor what she had in mind to do. Kate felt bad about this, but the high stakes she was playing called for extreme caution. She knew Jasmine would be devastated, but Kate hoped that later on, after she had explained everything, Jasmine would understand.

As for the choice of the press club, Kate considered that it met her requirements perfectly. Its location, across the street from the presidential palace, was, she thought, an ironic touch.

By seven o'clock the main hall, with its hundred chairs and a large podium, was packed with reporters, camera and sound men. A few minutes before the conference was to begin, Kate had a slide projector set up on a desk next to the podium. When Jasmine asked her about that, Kate had replied, "A surprise."

Punctually at eight o'clock Michael Saidi, wearing a hand-tailored blue suit with a red-and-white tie, stepped up to the podium. A hush settled over the crowd as he began to speak.

"My friends," Michael said, "I stand before you today because our land is on the verge of chaos. Internal strife threatens to pit brother against brother. Such a thing must not be allowed to happen. In recent days Lebanon has lost many good and just men. Some, like our beloved Louis Jabar, can never be replaced. Nonetheless, their work must continue. To this end I humbly put forward my candidacy for the presidency of our great nation!"

Pandemonium erupted as reporters began shouting questions. Michael played the crowd masterfully, waiting for the hubbub to die down, then began taking questions from the most influential reporters first.

Kate watched the charade continue for a half hour. Michael raised his arms for silence.

"I would now like to introduce you to the two people who have been instrumental in convincing me to take this step, and without whose support none of this would have been possible."

Michael gestured toward the front row. Jasmine rose first and came up to the podium. Kate waited, then, her heart pounding, followed. She stood beside Jasmine, doing her best to smile, as she listened to Jasmine explaining why she had endorsed Michael Saidi. When her turn came, Kate leaned toward the microphone and said, "Sometimes, as we all know, a picture is worth a thousand words."

Kate ignored the puzzled looks from her audience and brushed past Michael as she stepped over the the slide projector. She pressed a button, and a giant photograph of Michael appeared on the wall.

"This is the man we know as Michael Saidi," she said, her voice ringing over the crowd.

Kate touched another button, and a second photograph appeared, an enhancement of the one Prudence Templeton had surreptitiously taken of her lover in Washington Square so long ago.

"And this is Michael Samson, embezzler and murderer! They are, ladies and gentlemen, one and the same man!"

For a moment there was complete silence. Kate watched a hundred pairs of eyes scrutinize the two photographs. Then some of the reporters began looking at Michael.

"This is crazy!"

Kate whirled to look at Michael. His face was drained of color, and he was trying desperately to regain his composure.

"No!" Kate said into the microphone. "This is the truth!"

Michael tried to address the audience. "Clearly there is a misunderstanding here—"

"No, there is not!"

Heads swiveled toward the speaker at the back of the room. The reporters gasped as Armand Fremont, escorted by Salim, made his way down the aisle, moving slowly, and obviously in great pain, his eyes fixed on the podium.

"It can't be you!" Michael screamed. "You're dead!"

"As you had planned me to be? As you can see, I am not so easy to kill."

Armand continued speaking as he moved inexorably toward Michael.

"Tell me," Armand demanded. "Why did you steal from the Maritime Continental Bank, use Prudence Templeton the way you did?"

Michael leaned forward on the lectern, his voice defiant. "I don't know what you're talking about! You're insane!"

"It was all part of a grand design, wasn't it? A scheme concocted by you—" He paused. "And your accomplice!"

Armand's arm flashed out, finger pointing at Jasmine. Standing next to her, Kate was shocked. Then she saw the mocking smile on Jasmine's lips.

"My father . . . ," Kate whispered. "*You* were the one Pierre ran to when my father threatened to expose him! You made sure he would have a fatal accident . . . and then you had the British banker killed when David Cabot was getting too close to him. *You* were the shadow Armand was convinced was behind Pierre, except that it never occurred to Armand that the shadow might be a woman."

Kate was so intent on Jasmine that she failed to see Michael edge toward the back of the stage.

"There is more," Armand was saying, looking around at the journalists who were scribbling furiously.

"The motive for Michael Saidi's thievery was not only money—money that has been used to expand his drug and slave-trading empire—"

This revelation sent up a cry from the press corps.

"He and Jasmine undoubtedly thought that if they caused chaos at Maritime Continental, I would come to its rescue. The only way I could possibly raise enough money to do so would be by selling the casino. And who would benefit from that? Pierre Fremont, *an embezzler in his own right!?*"

The reporters were hanging on every word.

"But I had dismissed him as the accomplice. So that left *only* Jasmine."

Jasmine threw her head back and laughed. "This is sheer fantasy. You have no proof! You cannot touch me."

"Michael!" Armand roared.

Kate whirled around in time to see Michael bolt through the stage curtains.

"The police are everywhere!" Armand shouted. "You can't escape."

At that instant there came a sharp explosion, unmistakably a gunshot.

In Beirut, mourning takes many forms, but it is never allowed to interfere with business. The families and close friends of the murdered *zuama* did not miss one second of the spectacle being played out at the National Press Club. Within the hour, meetings that were to last most of the day were under way. Whether revelations about Michael Saidi were true or not, the point was he was finished politically. And Jasmine Fremont along with him. Her widow's cloak was threadbare. The vacuum had reappeared, and this time one of their own had to fill it. Over sweet tea, Chivas Regal, and cigarettes, a consensus was formed, a figurehead agreed upon.

The new generation of *zuama* breathed a sigh of relief. They would reclaim their country. The anarchy would be dealt with, and as soon as the candidate announced himself, calm would prevail. Everything would change, and nothing would change . . . and that was as it should be.

"How the devil could he have gotten away?" Armand stormed.

The hapless chief of Beirut's police force fidgeted. He had no idea what to say to a man who had been presumed dead and buried, yet who, hours earlier, had materialized at his front door. The story Fremont had had to tell was no less incredible, but since the police chief knew very well how things worked in Beirut, he had paid very close attention and acted exactly as Fremont had instructed him.

If he could return from the dead, what else could he do? The chief had wondered, surreptitiously making the sign that warded off the evil eye.

"I followed your suggestions implicitly," the official said. "All the exits were sealed. No one had anticipated that Monsieur Saidi would be armed."

"Or that your men couldn't shoot straight!" Armand retorted.

Armand sank into the soft folds of the leather sofa in the press club's executive office. The right side of his body felt as though it were on fire. His skin was clammy to the touch, and his head was pounding.

"Enough!" Kate said sharply. "We wish to be alone."

The police officials hesitated, then filed out. Kate came to Armand and handed him a glass of ice water.

"They'll find him," she said reassuringly. "His picture is all over the television. He can't get away."

"He can and he will! Don't underestimate this man."

"If only Jasmine would tell us something!" Kate said, frustrated.

"She won't say a word."

Jasmine had been taken away by the police but had refused to speak. She knew damn well, Kate thought, that it was Armand's word against hers. The accusations may have cast a long shadow, but Armand had no proof to buttress them. The police would be able to hold her only as long as it took her lawyer to appear and demand that she be either charged or released.

"There's only one other person who might know where Michael has disappeared to," Kate said slowly.

When she spoke the name, Armand nodded. "It's possible."

"It's our only hope," Kate told him.

"There is something we have to do first," Armand said.

By the sad look in his eyes Kate divined exactly what that was.

"Must you, Armand? After everything that's happened, do you still have to go through with this?"

"*Especially* because of everything." Armand looked at her tenderly. "It's over, Kate. Nothing we can do will ever bring it back."

"This is highly irregular, Monsieur Fremont," Sharif Uday was saying, his tiny black eyes fixed on Kate and Armand in an unblinking stare.

"Not if you wish to purchase the Casino de Paradis," Armand replied.

Although it was almost noon, the representative of the sultan of Brunei was wrapped in a voluminous silk dressing gown that covered even his feet. Ringed behind him were the London lawyers who had been waiting in the wings to broker the sale of the Casino de Paradis.

"And what of Mrs. Fremont-Jabar?" Uday inquired.

"Under the circumstances her presence is not required," Armand said flatly.

Uday was not so sure, but the point was moot. He had been trying to get hold of Jasmine for hours. He had learned the police had released her, but there was no answer at either of her residences.

"Perhaps we *should* wait," Uday suggested. "After all—"

"And perhaps your principal is not seriously interested in acquiring the casino," Armand said. "The paperwork is in order. Your people are here. We can finish this quickly, if that's what you want."

Uday's intelligent eyes probed the man who had returned from the dead. The moment Uday had seen Armand Fremont alive, he had been convinced the sale would never go through. In one stroke Fremont had made himself a legend. He could either take power in Beirut himself or play the role of kingmaker. Yet here he was abdicating.

The circumstances made Uday uneasy, and he had expressed his reservations to the sultan. But the reply was unequivocal: conclude the deal as quickly as possible if there was still the opportunity to do so.

"Very well, Monsieur Fremont," Uday said, pushing forward a stack of bound documents.

Forty minutes later Armand was handed the last file and signed on the last page.

"SBM is now a public company," he said.

The sultan's representative affixed his signature to another document.

"His Excellency agrees to purchase all outstanding shares for sixty dollars per share. The money is to be transferred immediately."

For the next half hour Armand and Sharif Uday, guided by the lawyers, wended their way through the last thickets of paperwork. One of the attorneys placed a phone before Armand.

"Hello, Emil."

Over the speaker phone Emil's voice sounded calm, as though it were perfectly normal to converse long-distance with the dead. "The money has been wire-transferred and is in your account."

"Thank you. You know what to do. I will talk to you shortly."

Armand rose. He and Uday shook hands across the table.

"Any regrets, Monsieur Fremont?" Uday asked casually.

"None that I can't live with."

"Hello, Pierre. May I come in?"

Pierre blinked rapidly. He was standing in the doorway of his home, dressed as though he were ready to leave for the office in a three-piece suit, starched white shirt with a pale yellow tie, and polished wing tips. He looked past Kate at Armand. Neither surprise nor recognition registered in his glazed eyes. Pierre smiled vacuously.

"Yes . . . Yes, of course."

The elegant home smelled musty, the drawn shutters

leaving it in folds of darkness. The stillness made Kate shiver.

"Can I look in on Cleo?" asked Kate.

Pierre hesitated, then led her to the bedroom door. This room was dappled with afternoon sunlight. The French doors were open to the garden, and there were flowers everywhere. Cleo was sleeping, her ruined face stark against the white linen pillow. Armand paled and turned away.

"How could you have let them do this, Pierre?" he whispered. "Michael and Jasmine would have destroyed Lebanon as surely as they destroyed Cleo."

Pierre reached past Kate and gently drew the door closed. He shuffled back into the darkness, toward a chair surrounded by a litter of newspapers, magazines, and food wrappers.

They passed an end table where the telephone receiver lay off the hook, emitting a soft whir. Kate moved to replace it.

"No!" Pierre said sharply. "The newspapers have been calling incessantly. I'm afraid they will wake Cleo."

Pierre sat down in a high-back leather chair, facing Armand and Kate as though he were holding court.

"So you found Michael out," he murmured. "I saw it all on the television, you know. You were always so clever, Armand. But you will never get him."

"We will, if you help us," Kate said.

For a long time Pierre remained silent, staring away into space. Occasionally his eyelids would flutter, or a nervous tic would dance at the side of his mouth.

"It all began with your father," he said at last. "If it hadn't been for him, then maybe none of this would have happened."

Kate closed her eyes. "My father . . ."

"Or maybe it was love," Pierre continued, as though he hadn't heard her. "Yes, I think it was that, something that your father couldn't fathom. You see, no one in the world really understood what Cleo means to me. They looked at me and thought, 'Ah, there's no fool like an old fool.' But I did what I had to do to keep Cleo happy. If everyone had just left us alone, we would have been fine."

Pierre's voice trailed off, and for a few minutes he sat with his head angled like a bird's, as still as a catatonic. Then suddenly he asked. "Do you understand, Kate, that I had no choice? Alexander was going to take everything away from me. I couldn't let him do that. So I went to Jasmine, who promised me everything would be all right. She contacted the wine merchant, arranged for everything."

Kate remembered what Armand had said about the assassin who had killed David and had come within a hair's breadth of killing him. The abbot had called him Bacchus. *The wine merchant!*

"Pierre," Kate said weighing her words as carefully as if she were stepping around quicksand. "Did you ask Bacchus to help you with Armand too?"

"Oh no!" Pierre protested. "That was Jasmine's idea. You see, she had far greater ambitions to fulfill . . ."

Kate's heart beat painfully against her chest as she spoke. "Do you know where Jasmine has her special place, somewhere she and Michael would go and no one in the world could find them?"

Pierre smiled dreamily. "I am particularly fond of a line in the Book of Proverbs: *There is a generation whose teeth are as swords* . . . But they do not see themselves as this. They believe they are the reincarnated nobles of the cedar, the kings and queens of Tyre to whom Solomon sent emissaries to buy cedar for his temple in Jerusalem."

It was hopeless, Kate thought. Pierre kept sliding between fantasy and reality, like a circus clown on a seesaw. She felt a tug on her sleeve, caught Armand's warning look, and realized he had picked up on something she'd missed.

"I must look in on Cleo," Pierre was saying. "I have to take care of her now. I have always taken care of her, you know."

He was puzzled by the silence, and even when he looked around, it took him a moment to realize he was alone.

Pierre went and sat in the chair beside Cleo's bed. She

was still sleeping, and he hummed softly to her, as a father
would a lullaby. His fingertips drifted over the stitches on
her face, nerve ends screaming when they met the harsh,
tough skin.

Pierre's eyes lost their tenderness and concern. Never taking his eyes off Cleo, he reached for the phone and dialed
the international operator. A few minutes later he was
speaking to Gibraltar, asking about a very rare, very expensive vintage of champagne.

As soon as they were outside, Kate saw that something
was terribly wrong. Armand clutched his right side, grunt-
ing in pain. Kate draped one of his arms around her shoulder and guided him to the car. Salim jumped out and helped
her settle Armand in the backseat. Kate ripped off his jacket
and drew back at the sight of the blood-soaked shirt.

"The stitches over the wound have torn," she said frantically. "We have to get him to a hospital."

Salim jumped behind the wheel as Kate did her best to
stem the bleeding and make Armand as comfortable as possible.

"You'll be all right, darling," Kate whispered over and
over again.

Armand gritted his teeth as the heavy car careened
around the corners.

"You must tell the police," he gasped. "Michael . . .
Michael is at Mouchtara!"

Kate looked at him, puzzled. "But how . . . ?"

Then she knew. It was Pierre's reference to the cedars.
That was the clue Armand had seized.

Kate cradled Armand's head in her lap trying to soothe
him. All the while her thoughts were racing. The police?
No, they had had their chance and bungled it! She couldn't
trust them to go after Michael. He was far too clever. But if
nothing were done, he would disappear—and come back
one day to murder and wreak havoc again!

Kate swore to herself that would not happen.

As soon as they arrived at the hospital, Salim ran inside

to get the emergency team. Within minutes the car was surrounded by doctors and nurses who were lifting Armand onto a gurney.

"He has lost a lot of blood and gone into shock," one of the physicians said.

"But he'll be all right!"

The doctor glanced at Kate over his shoulder. "You got him here in time," he assured her.

Kate started to follow them inside, then stopped. *You swore you wouldn't let Michael get away!* Praying that Armand would forgive her, Kate ran back to the car.

"You must take me to the airport!"

Salim hesitated, looking intently at Kate. "It is for him that you do this?" Salim asked at last.

"For all of us."

Salim nodded and started the car. As soon as they cleared the hospital gates, Kate reached for the radio-telephone and called Armand's pilot, telling him to have the helicopter ready for take off.

She sat back, trembling, and caught a glimpse of Salim's eyes in the rearview mirror, studying her intently. When they reached the airport, drawing up next to the waiting helicopter, Salim turned back to her.

"You will need this."

He took out his revolver and silently stuffed it into Kate's bag.

Mouchtara . . . The Chosen Place.

The helicopter was already high in the early evening sky, winging its way back toward Tyre. Kate shivered, as much from the stillness around her as from the cold wind that blew off the Shouf Mountains. She did all she could to push her fear away, but the fact remained she was here, alone . . .

There were no lights in the windows or doors, and the effect, as Kate moved closer, was one of utter desolation. In the central courtyard the fountains were overgrown with weeds, the gaily colored mosaics cracked beyond recognition. Lions rampant and stallions rearing lay broken beside pedestals. Vines and ivy had overtaken the walls, burrowing into the mortar and splitting it along erratic cracks.

Kate came up to the heavy front door and pushed it open. The horseshoe staircase was still there, but the marble steps were shattered, some gone completely. Dust, leaves, debris littered the stone floor from which weeds now sprouted. Kate looked up and saw a great horned owl gazing down upon her with benign indifference.

She understood now why her father had almost never spoken of Mouchtara. It belonged to a different time, a dead time. In her mind's eye she saw how it might once have been. But certain things are not destined to survive. Mouchtara was one such place.

Kate moved silently through the rooms. There were signs that someone had been here. Empty tins of food, bottles, and scraps lay strewn across the floors. And clothing . . . Kate leaned over and picked up a threadbare sweater that might have belonged to a ten-year-old.

As she stepped into the walled garden, all roots and vines, she heard a voice call out softly.

"So you found me, clever Kate."

Kate whirled around to see Michael, still wearing the suit he'd had on at the press conference. The only difference was the gun in his hand.

"No, it *wasn't* you, Kate," Michael said thoughtfully. "Armand ran me down, didn't he? By the way, what happened to him? I didn't see him getting out of the helicopter."

Kate's mouth was dry, but she forced the words out. "Armand is in the hospital. His wounds ruptured."

"So you came here all by yourself."

"Just me, Michael."

"In that case you're either very brave or very foolish. Even with that pistol in you bag."

Michael laughed. "That's all right. Leave it where it is. You couldn't get it out in time anyway."

Michael came closer but stopped beyond arm's reach.

"We could have been wonderful together, Kate," he said

softly. "Did you ever think of that?"

"No, never."

"Then tell me, why *did* you come?"

Kate looked at him steadily. "I had to see you one last time. I wanted to ask you why you did so much harm to people whose lives never touched yours."

"Because that is the way of the world, Kate," Michael replied. "We are all predators or prey. I was not born to be the latter. Tell me, did you think that by coming here alone you might get me to surrender?"

"No, I never thought that. I told you why I'm here. Just to look."

"And the gun?"

"To protect myself, if I had to."

Michael stared at her intently, then began to pace.

"No, if you were coming to kill me, you wouldn't have been so obvious. And if you are waiting for help, you must know I'll be gone long before it arrives."

Michael shot her a dazzling smile. "You must be wondering what I'm doing here." He pointed to a pair of suitcases next to the gaping hole where French doors once stood. "This is my bank of last resort, as it were. Over the years I've hidden away a fortune in this place. I'm sure your father would find this amusing if he were here. A fortune in gold coins, Kate. The world's most negotiable currency. Not only will it keep me alive, but it will also preserve everything I have built. You think your little charade at the press club ruined me? No, Kate. That was only a minor setback. The drugs, the children—and now weapons—these will all continue to flow through my hands."

Michael smiled again.

"But even if you managed to take me in, what could you prove against me? Prudence Templeton is dead. She was the only possible witness, but even so much of her testimony would have been hearsay and speculation. As for Beiruiti courts, they couldn't touch me. There is nothing at all to tie me into illegal activities."

"Except Jasmine's word," Kate reminded him.

Michael snorted and turned away for a second. "That's ridiculous! Jasmine wouldn't dare speak against me. She's in it up to her ears—"

Michael whirled around just as Kate was drawing out the gun.

"Oh Kate, Kate," he said softly. "You thought I turned my back on you. How sad. I was only testing you, and you failed. Now put the gun back into the bag and the bag on the floor."

Kate met his gaze head on. "No, Michael. This is where it stops. I may not be able to squeeze the trigger before you fire. But on the other hand—"

Michael's eyes flickered between Kate's face and the pistol in her hand, held barrel down.

"It wouldn't even be close," he whispered, and cocked the hammer.

The roar of gunfire shattered the stillness. Kate felt herself falling, not knowing whether the bullet had hit her or if she had thrown herself to the ground on sheer instinct. When she raised her head, she saw Michael lying in front of her, his chest a bloody mess.

"Killing you is something neither one of us would have been able to explain. Given what happened at the press conference, we would have been prime suspects too. I really couldn't have that."

Kate staggered to her feet to face Jasmine.

"But how did you get here?"

Jasmine lowered the shotgun a fraction and laughed.

"There were only so many places Michael could have run to. He couldn't go to any of his bolt holes in Beirut, nor would he leave the country penniless. That left Mouchtara, although I confess I had no idea he'd squirreled away so much here."

Jasmine paused. "I also guessed that if either you or Armand had figured out where Michael had gone, one or both of you would come here. And that if he saw you, Michael would kill you. . . ."

Jasmine looked thoughtfully at Kate. "You brought a gun.

Would you have used it?"

Kate did not hesitate. "If I'd had the chance."

Jasmine shrugged. "It's over Kate. For you and Armand. I heard about the sale of the casino to Uday. It seems I have a fair bit of money coming to me from my shares. I trust Armand will be a gentleman about that. The two of you should get on with your lives. Be happy together. It is a far better fate that most of us who stay behind will ever know."

Jasmine motioned with the shotgun, and Kate stepped back, inadvertently touching Michael's body. She started, turned, and looked down. When she raised her head, Jasmine, along with Michael's booty, had vanished.

EPILOGUE

Unlike their glamorous cousins in Monte Carlo and St. Tropez, the people of Villefranche on the French Mediterranean seacoast jealously guarded their privacy and clung stubbornly to the old ways. The village remained exactly as it had for centuries, with one cobblestone lane that wound its way along the docks and past ancient buildings whose renovated apartments took up entire floors. On the ground levels were the butcher, baker, and a newsstand where Kate picked up her papers every morning. It was exactly two hundred and forty-one steps, most of them uphill, to the rented villa nestled in hills overlooking the sea.

Kate arranged the papers on the patio table where she and Armand took their breakfast. The international and overseas editions were a day old, but that didn't matter. The news they followed did not change very much.

Kate padded into the bedroom, where Armand lay in a tangle of sheets. She stopped short when she saw the scars on his body. They still had the power to anger her. Sometimes she would rationalize and say that this was a small price to pay for his life. But the scars reminded her of so many other things, things she hated and which still trapped her in nightmares. She knew that the scars would not heal and the nightmares not subside until she and Armand had truly put Beirut behind them.

Kate brushed back Armand's hair, closing her eyes as his warmth enveloped her. Sometimes she was frightened of this love she had for him, because it was so complete and she could not imagine her life without it. But perhaps that was what made it so rich, why every minute they were entwined seemed like an eternity.

Kate slipped her hand across his chest, fingers trailing along his hip and into his groin. Armand groaned and rolled over, his arms reaching for her even before his eyes were open.

"No," Kate whispered, straddling him. "Let me do everything . . ."

They had breakfast late that morning and, not wanting to cloud their contentment, did not glance at the newspapers until much later.

"The fighting is getting worse," Kate said, then read aloud, "Government militia has cordoned off the Belt of Misery, but the Palestinians are taking the fight to other parts of the city. Jabal is hanging on to control by his fingertips."

"Not for long," Armand commented.

In the wake of the mysterious shooting of Michael Saidi and the disappearance of Jasmine Fremont, Amil Baruk, son of a slain Christian *zaim*, had become president of Lebanon. But the loose coalition of families and "fixers," which had agreed on his being the figurehead, splintered and disintegrated under the weight of suspicion, real or imagined slights, and ever-present greed. Soon Beirut and all of Lebanon were rocked by sectarian violence that pitted Maronite Christian against Sunni against Shiite.

A week before Baruk's inauguration, Kate and Armand quietly had left Beirut. Inspector Hamse was convinced that Kate knew something about Michael Saidi's death, but the murder weapon was never found, and he had nothing to back up his suspicions.

Armand had also used this time to bring Charles Sweet to Beirut and explain to him about the pipeline of human traffic that ran through Mouchtara. This, coupled with the information provided by the monks of the Order of the Third Cross, gave Interarmco vital information about the ring. Sweet promised it would cease to exist before too long.

When at last the time had come for them to go, Kate had turned to Armand and said, "You could have it all back, you know. The casino, your home, everything that is dear to you."

"The casino could exist only as long as the oasis existed," Armand had replied. "Now the desert winds are blowing, the sands shift, and soon the oasis will be only a mirage. The Beirut I knew is no more. Many do not see this, do not want to believe it, but it is true. There was nothing you or I could have done to stop that."

Armand had put his arms around her and drawn her close. "Besides, I already have what is most dear to me. With the money from the sale, you and Bartoli can put Maritime Continental back in order. Interarmco's work will continue. After that, who knows . . ."

The memory of that moment made Kate smile. She reached across the table and took Armand's hand.

"I think we should carry on the tradition," she said.

"Which one?" he asked, puzzled.

"Casinos."

Armand raised his eyebrows. "Not too many of them for sale," he said dubiously.

Kate grinned. "Who said we can't build our own? I hear the east coast of Australia, around Brisbane, is paradise. And the government is always looking for investors."

Excitement gleamed in Armand's eyes, and they talked about the idea. When they rose to walk into Villefranche, Kate took one last glance at the newspapers.

"I still don't understand about Jasmine," she said somberly. "Why was she at Mouchtara? She *couldn't* have known that I, that anyone, was coming there."

Armand shook his head. "That was never an issue. Jasmine had her own agenda. After Michael bolted from the press conference, she realized he had become another liability—like Louis, Nabil Tufaili, and all the others. She couldn't trust him *not* to talk if things became unpleasant. So . . ."

They walked in silence for a time; then Kate said, "But isn't it strange how there hasn't been a word about Jasmine? It's as though she's disappeared off the face of the earth."

"Not Jasmine," Armand replied. "She's a survivor. One day you'll be walking down a street in Athens or Singapore, and there she'll be."

There were still a lot of boats in the Beirut Yacht Club
harbor, but the knowledgeable eye could tell that most of
the important vessels had gone, and for the first time in
decades slips were actually available for rent or sale.

Reclining on the upper-deck lounge, Jasmine wondered
idly if she should buy some berths as an investment.
Anchored in the middle of the harbor, the ninety-foot
cruiser, belonging to her Brazilian racing boat sponsor,
rolled lightly in the outgoing tide, lulling her into sleepy re-
pose.

Soon, she reckoned, it would be time to start over, as
soon as that upstart president, Baruk, realized how things
really worked in Beirut. Michael might be gone, but she still
had her network and connections. Baruk might be the president, but if he wanted to keep his office, there would be
some hard horse-trading in the days ahead.

Jasmine sighed, rolled over, and waved to her masseur.
As his practiced fingers kneaded her muscles, her eye
caught a lovely three-masted schooner pulling out to sea.
She tried to place the vessel but couldn't. She was still
thinking about it a moment later. . . .

A hundred yards away the hired pilot steered the
schooner past the channel buoys. Although his primary expertise lay elsewhere, Bacchus was a good enough sailor to
have taken the place of the real pilot, who was lying uncon-
scious in the back of a van parked on the docks.

He cleared the last buoy and handed the helm to the skip-
per. In a few minutes the launch would come to pick him
up. Bacchus walked to the stern and looked at the man and
woman sitting on the deck, staring back at the harbor. He
had broken a cardinal rule: never come near a client. But
under the circumstances his curiosity had gotten the better
of him.

After glancing at his watch, he slipped a tiny transmitter
from his pocket. He counted off eight seconds and pressed

the red button.

"*Via con Dios.*"

The blue and white cruiser erupted in a wall of flame. The man stood up and peered intently out over the water as if he had to see the wreckage sink for himself. The woman beside him flinched but didn't stir. Bacchus was intrigued by her. The whole time he was on the boat he had never heard her say a word. Nor had he seen her face, hidden behind a white veil fixed to her sun hat. Then the wind came up and lifted the veil. Bacchus drew a sharp breath when he saw the scars crisscrossing the woman's face. She must have felt his gaze, because she turned to him and met his eyes. A tiny smile crept across her lips, lighting the face, exotic, mysterious, utterly ruined, like the city behind them.

THIS FAR FROM PARADISE

by Philip Shelby

Amidst the beauty of her Caribbean island home, Rebecca McHenry's young life seems charmed. Then, in a single day of unimaginable treachery and deceit, she is stripped of her dreams and her birthright.

Determined to regain control of her life, Rebecca realizes that money and power are the only weapons that she can use to fight the enemies who wish to destroy her. Yet throughout her struggles and triumphs, Rebecca's burning belief in love and paradise stays alive.

"A rich blend of exotic destinations, the world of high finance, hostile corporate takeovers, adventures and romance."

—Quill and Quire

"Fast-paced, compellingly plotted . . . popular fiction at its best."

—The Hamilton Spectator

DREAMWEAVERS

by Philip Shelby

The Dream Begins
The year is 1907. When Rose Jefferson inherits her father's corporation, she also inherits a world full of treachery and manipulation. Deceived by a cruel husband, Rose must battle the forces inside and out to maintain control of Global Express and bring her dream invention to reality: the creation of the first credit card.

Blind Ambition
Rose's determination will cost her more than money, for as world war breaks out she begins her own battle with her weak-minded brother, Franklin, and her embittered son, Steven, and eventually with Franklin's beautiful wife, Michelle, a threat to Rose's dream. But Michelle has her own dreams in the form of her daughter: Cassandra.

Deadly Vengeance
Cassandra Jefferson—born of love, educated by tragedy and deprived of more than just her inheritance. She will use Rose's vision against Rose's own son to attempt the destruction of the destroyer—but in the process, will she shatter her own dreams?